KINGDOMS OF SHADOW AND ASH

HR MOORE

W0009666

Published by Harriet Moore
Copyright © 2022 HR Moore

IBSN: 978-1-7397219-3-0

Titles by HR Moore:

The Relic Trilogy:
Queen of Empire
Temple of Sand
Court of Crystal

In the Gleaming Light

The Ancient Souls Series:
Nation of the Sun
Nation of the Sword
Nation of the Stars

Shadow and Ash:
Kingdoms of Shadow and Ash
Dragons of Asred

Stories set in the Shadow and Ash world:
The Water Rider and the High Born Fae
House of Storms and Secrets

http://www.hrmoore.com

MAP

For an online version, go to:
www.hrmoore.com/knownworld

Chapter One

FYIA CREPT AROUND THE circular battlement, her heart thundering in her chest, her back pressed against the cold, hard stone. The big, full moon cast eerie shadows, and every flicker sent adrenaline through her veins.

King Perdes lay in wait, but he didn't know from which side she would approach, and Fyia wanted to keep it that way.

I am not a warrior. I am not a warrior. I am not a warrior. She silently chanted the words like a prayer; a reminder she had to be smart. She was swift, and she was nimble, and she was stealthy.

It had taken many years, but she had already knocked four arrogant, selfish kings off their perches, starting with her own father, and this final one would be no different.

She inched further around the battlement, looking down at her black pants and tunic one last time, making sure nothing would reflect the moonbeams. She'd smeared her face and hands with mud, her hat pulled low on her brow, hiding the shock of white that punctuated her long brown hair.

I am not a warrior.

She took one torturous sidestep at a time, placing each foot with extreme care. Three steps and she would be in sight.

Fyia summoned her power, a wild pull of magic, and called to her Cruaxee. An eagle—her eagle—cried out in the distance. Perdes inhaled sharply and shuffled his feet. She let silence fall until it yawned menacingly into the night.

'No. Stay back,' said Perdes, his voice directed to the other side of the battlements. No surprise, given the two wolves she'd sent to stare him down.

I am not a warrior. But …

She ran on light feet, making no sound, then leapt, her wolves snarling, keeping Perdes engaged. She sank her dagger into his back once, twice, then pulled it out, whirling away as he tried to face her. He looked surprised as he collapsed to the floor.

'Filthy cheat,' he spluttered, wheezing through the blood.

Fyia leaned against the battlements, her wolves coming to her side. She wiped and sheathed her dagger. 'Well, here's the thing, Perdes … I wouldn't have won if I'd challenged you to a fair fight.'

'Women have no honor.'

'You want those to be your last words?'

'My army will defeat you.'

'Last I checked, your commanders had surrendered, and were drinking with my generals in my war tent.'

'My people will never follow you,' he choked, blood leaking from his mouth. 'They follow warriors, kings, not *little women*.'

Fyia laughed, even though her stomach dropped at the truth in his words. 'You're right, I'm no warrior. I am not tall and broad and formidable to look at. But turns out I can stick a dagger in a man's back just fine. Not to mention, I have a few assets you do not ...'

'*Witch* ...' He made a disgusting gurgling noise, and then his eyes fluttered closed.

'Careful, if the Fae'ch hear you, they'll curse your afterlife ... they would never class *me* among their ranks.'

'You are nothing next to me ...' He dragged in a breath. 'I am a king!'

'And yet, I have my army, yours too, my magic, and, oh yes, I have a brain—something you lack ... something all of you lacked. You got fat and lazy, and I conquered five kingdoms. I believe I'm the only leader alive who can lay claim to that.'

It would not be an easy road, bringing her kingdoms together, but she had already come so far, even though the world had laughed and sneered and waved her off as an *inconsequential female.* She'd demanded their respect at the point of her army's sword, but garnering the respect of her people ... that was a less simple task, and just one of the many reasons why she *would* find the dragons.

He grunted, but no words followed.

Fyia crouched by his side and watched as he took his last labored breath, then reached down and removed his crown. She'd put it with the others ... she'd cast it into the fiery pits of Hell.

Fyia walked out under the portcullis, then across the bridge over the castle's moat, her wolves flanking her. She'd removed her hat, and her hair flowed freely down her back, Perdes' crown perched atop her head.

Her generals waited, a sea of lower-ranking commanders behind them. She emerged like an angel of death, a witch, someone to be feared, her beasts snarling at her side.

Sensis Deimos, the leader of Fyia's victorious army, stepped forward, throwing herself to her knees before her Queen. The others did the same, no one daring to look up. They barely dared to breathe.

'Rise, Sensis,' said Fyia. Sensis was tall and powerfully built, with long, plaited auburn hair and pale green eyes. 'Do something with this, until we can rid ourselves of the gaudy thing.' She threw Perdes' crown, and Sensis caught it with ease.

'Of course, Your Majesty,' said Sensis, bowing her head.

Fyia offered Sensis her forearm, and her general clasped it, her grip brutal. Fyia pulled Sensis in until their bodies collided, Fyia's head reaching just above her friend's shoulder, and Sensis slapped her on the back.

'You can get a five-pointed crown now,' Sensis said, her voice pitched low so none of the others could hear. 'Maybe with a gem from each kingdom … it would set off your pretty blue witch eyes.'

'Piss off,' said Fyia. 'Actually, don't … do something useful and get a celebration going.'

'It is my greatest honor to serve you in any way you desire,' she said. She stepped back and bowed low.

'Don't make me punch you in the face.'

'If you're going to threaten violence, at least make it realistic.' Fyia's wolves growled. 'See, now I'm scared.'

'Good. I'm …' Fyia trailed off, her gaze finding the woods beyond her general's shoulder.

'Go,' said Sensis. 'I'll hold down the fort until you return.' Sensis flashed Fyia a conspiratorial smile, then surveyed the curious commanders. They were still on their knees, most chancing glances at their Queen. 'King Perdes is dead,' she said, in a voice that carried … a voice used to being obeyed. 'Long live Fyia Orlightus, Queen of the Five Kingdoms of the East.'

Fyia acknowledged the cheers of her army, a thrill travelling up her spine at what she'd accomplished. What they'd all accomplished.

Fyia took off into the woods, her army still chanting her name, Sensis issuing orders, quieting them down.

Fyia's shoeless feet ate up the ground, each pace renewing her connection with the forest. She drew on the power it offered, letting it fill her, pushing out the terror that lingered from the battlements. Her wolves chased her, pushing her faster, others joining them, snarling as they ran. Fyia pumped her arms, sprinting, flying, letting the forest show her the way.

She broke through the tree line, heading for the sheer drop over a cliff not fifty paces away. The wolves fell back, snarling as she ran for the edge, their discomfort peppering the bond between them. Fyia didn't falter, didn't miss a step as she threw herself into the void, her arms outstretched.

The wolves howled, and Fyia gasped, relishing the rush of wind that bit her skin.

She fell and fell and laughed, knowing it would kill her. At this speed, if she hit the river, the impact would be fatal, but the rush … the rush chased all the things she needed it to away. It left freedom … euphoria.

An eagle screamed below, and Fyia closed her eyes, connecting with her Cruaxee, watching through the eagle's eyes as the enormous bird swooped under her, caught her, slowed her fall, then reversed it.

The pump of the eagle's wings made Fyia's stomach drop, and she laughed again. They climbed, and she shivered with anticipation, excitement flooding her when she felt the downward tip, the beginning of a dive. Only when they were hurtling towards the ground once more did it finally begin to sink in: she was Queen of the Five Kingdoms.

She'd done it; what everyone had said she could never do … that she *should* not do … that the magic would not tolerate. They'd been wrong; the magic had wanted her to win, had aided her at every turn. Of course it had. She had a Cruaxee, was magic-touched, and fire-touched—even if only a little. She had more magic than most could ever dream of.

Maybe her people would refuse to follow her, or rail against the changes she would make, or think her quest for dragons evidence of lunacy.

But those were not problems for this day, for finally, it was done; she'd slain the old Kings, defied all the odds, and united the kingdoms. She ruled them all, nothing left to stand between her and her dragons. For she knew they were out there, regardless what others thought, and she would find them, no matter what it took.

Adigos stalked through the camp, past fire after fire, group after group of drunken soldiers. They didn't care who'd won the war, not really. They only cared it was over, that they could go back to their children, wives, and lovers. They drank, not because Fyia had united their five bickering kingdoms, but because they hoped to never dig latrines again. To never march day and night to outsmart their enemy. To never face another battlefield, nor lose friends to an enemy blade. They rejoiced, for they would eat slops no more—at least if their purses could afford it.

They were drunk and spirited, and it was contagious.

Adigos walked and walked, careful to keep to the shadows. He passed brawls, card games, bodies passed out on the floor, bodies writhing against each other, all manner of sounds escaping into the night. He was jealous of their carefree existence, if only for this one night. He'd had that once, and he wanted it again.

He finally reached the barn near the castle's walls. The invading forces had commandeered it for their officers' mess, and the sounds of a party blared from inside. But outside, the mood was tense.

The Queen's bodyguard stood watch, guarding a twenty-pace perimeter around the building, and those at the campfires were subdued, brooding, the air heavy with some unspoken threat.

Adigos paused at a fire close to the perimeter where an old man warmed himself. The man watched the barn intently, not seeming to notice Adigos.

'May I sit?' Adigos asked.

The man's head turned, his features cast in shadow. 'If you must.'

'Not celebrating?' said Adigos, lowering himself onto a tree stump. This far south, it was warm most of the year, but the nights were cool, and Adigos held out his hands to the fire, the familiar habit comforting.

'What is there to celebrate? My King is dead, and now we have a *witch* queen.' He practically spat the words.

'You liked King Perdes?' asked Adigos, picking up a stick and poking at the embers.

'Served him my whole life.'

'Was he a good king?'

'Was to me.'

'To his people? Did they love him?'

'You're not from these lands?' said the man. He scrutinized Adigos anew.

'No,' said Adigos, 'and I've been away awhile. Did they? Love him? They loved the King in my lands before she …'

The man nodded his wizened features, as though Adigos had just fallen into place in his mind. 'I can't say they all did, but I did, and I'm not alone.' His words were menacing and full of promise. Not everyone would make things easy on the new Queen, then.

The man turned back to the barn, and Adigos followed his gaze. A flicker of movement in the trees caught Adigos' attention. He watched carefully as a shadow crept from trunk to trunk, and a slow, victorious smile spread across his lips.

'Have a good evening,' said Adigos, getting to his feet. The man made a non-committal noise, and Adigos melted into the woods, trailing the shadow he'd come to see.

Adigos crept through the woods, staying downwind, placing his feet with the utmost care, so as not to snap a twig or stumble on a root. The moon shone brightly, the trees sparse, allowing him to see a way ahead, and he finally spotted her, leaning against a tree. She observed the back entrance to the barn, and his pulse quickened. She was out here all alone, and she hadn't sensed him …

Adigos unsheathed his dagger and moved forward, praying she would stay put, that she was too preoccupied to feel his approach. He used the cover of the shadows, the sounds of the hooting owls and rattle of the snakes, the wind creaking the branches and rustling the leaves.

She shifted, pushing away from the tree as though finally deciding to go inside, but Adigos was so close he could almost touch her, and he would not let her get away. He lunged, grabbing her waist with one hand, holding his dagger to her throat with the other, relishing the power he held in his hands.

'It's not safe out in the woods alone,' Adigos growled into her ear.

'I'm never alone …' The woman tipped back her head and walked her fingers up his arm. She found his head, which still hovered near her ear, and grabbed a handful of his hair. She tugged, just hard enough to make him part his lips. She did it again, and he had to fight the urge to groan. 'Took you long enough,' said his Queen.

He ran his nose down her neck. 'You knew I was here?'

'My wolves picked up your scent days ago. Why did you wait so long?'

'After what happened last time, I thought it better to … gather intelligence.'

'Wise choice.'

Adigos brushed his lips against her neck. She shivered, then pushed his dagger arm away. She faced him, his arm still on her waist, and he pulled her towards him, lowering his head.

She shoved him away. 'Debrief me after the feast.'

He could do nothing but watch as she made her way towards the barn, two of her wolves appearing out of the darkness to walk at her side. Adigos took a deep breath, clearing his lungs of her intoxicating scent, then trailed in her wake.

The barn—which Sensis had done a passable job of turning into a feasting hall—went silent when Fyia entered. All except Rouel—a member of her personal guard who could have made a lucrative living as a minstrel—who was in the middle of a particularly catchy refrain. He sketched a bow that had his hand skimming the floor, staying down until he finished the song. Fyia shot him an arch look as she walked to the makeshift dais and throne.

She sat, and her wolves lay at her feet. 'Continue,' she said, gesturing to Rouel to get on with it. Music flared from his lute, and the party resumed. She ignored the incessant looks in her direction, most furtive, but plenty blatant.

Sensis, and Edu Ceres, the head of her personal guard, approached the dais. They made a show of bowing low before Fyia beckoned them forward, so they could take their places behind her, one on each side. They looked remarkably similar to one another, the same height, broad shoulders, straight noses, and fair skin, although Edu's muscles seemed somehow less impressive, and he had a shock of white hair, tied back in a bun.

'Fun party,' said Fyia, sardonically. She hated these things, but knew them to be a necessary evil. It was better for her subjects to see who she really was than create a persona of their own, and she enjoyed watching her wolves fan the flames of the fear her reputation had already kindled. 'Anyone I should worry about?'

'No,' said Sensis, at the same time as Edu said, 'Yes.'

Sensis rolled her eyes. 'You take things too seriously, my friend.'

'That's my job,' said Edu. 'I have one person to keep alive. If you lose a few on the battlefield, that's war. If I lose Fyia ...'

'It's called taking calculated risks to ensure victory, and we're here, so I'd say it paid off,' said Sensis. 'It's no different with the safety of our Queen ... maybe you should try it sometime and let her enjoy herself.'

'The day I start taking notes from you is the day we should cast our eyes to the line of succession ...'

'There's a line of succession?' said Sensis.

Fyia could hear the smile on Sensis' lips, and was sure Edu would be fighting one of his own. There was no line of succession—as her critics kept reminding her—but that was a problem for another day.

'Are you two done?' said Fyia.

'For now,' said Sensis.

'What concerns you, Edu?'

'The big one over there,' said Edu.

Fyia found the very large, very attractive man gesticulating in their general direction.

'Who is he?' said Fyia.

Sensis laughed. 'He's King Perdes' distant cousin. The rest of his family fled when they realized they'd lost.'

'He's taking a ... different approach,' said Edu.

'Which is?' asked Fyia.

'You'll see,' said Sensis, doing a poor job of hiding her amusement.

'Oh, Mother ...' said Fyia. She fought to keep her expression neutral as the man began moving towards the dais.

'Don't pray to her,' said Sensis. 'She can't help you.'

'Then who would you suggest?'

'The Warrior,' said Edu, 'to help you fight him off.'

'The Whore,' said Sensis. 'Might give you some tips.'

'Helpful,' said Fyia.

'The Friend,' said Rouel, who had perched his slight frame on the edge of the dais, 'to tell you nothing about that man looks problematic at all.'

'Or ... oh, my ...' said Sensis. 'Maybe you should seek help from a jealous almost-former-lover ...'

Adigos had just slipped in through the door.

'Wait, they never did it?' said Edu, looking to Sensis for confirmation.

'I don't think they ever did ... wait, did you?' said Sensis.

'Could we deal with one problem at a time?' said Fyia. She eyed Perdes' cousin, who was getting dangerously close, and seemed a little unsteady on his feet.

'Is Adigos still a problem?' said Sensis. 'Have you been holding out on me?'

'I feel a song coming on ...' said Rouel.

One of Fyia's wolves growled, and they all fell silent. The growling, they had learned the hard way, wasn't just for show.

'My Queen,' said Perdes' cousin, bowing low.

'Yes?' she said, fixing her face into a bored mask.

He looked up from his bow, unsure of what to do. 'May I ... approach?'

'No,' said Fyia.

'May I ... um ... stand?'

'If you must.'

He hesitated for a moment before raising himself to his full height. 'Your Majesty, I am Lord Max Perdes, cousin of the former King Perdes. May I be the first to declare fealty to you, and to request your hand in marriage?'

Fyia cocked a mocking eyebrow, but he continued, seeming not to have noticed. 'I have extensive lands, lucrative trading connections in the west, and ...' he leaned in conspiratorially, '... I'm working on a trade agreement with the kingdom in the north ... with the Black Hoods.'

It was all Fyia could do not to laugh out loud. The Black Hoods traded with nobody, save for the Fae'ch, who were just as secretive.

'I appreciate your offer, my lord, and am glad of your fealty, but I decline the proposal of marriage. Enjoy the celebration.'

He furrowed his brow then took a step forward, apparently not used to rejection. His good looks and connections meant he'd probably never heard the word *no*, his life no-doubt full of fawning sycophants.

Everything in the room went still, all eyes on the man approaching their Queen without leave. Edu and Sensis stepped forward, but Fyia sent them an almost imperceptible head shake; she wanted to see what this fool would do. He stopped in front of the wolves, who had lifted their heads, yellow eyes fixed on the threat.

'That's it?' he said. 'You won't even let me court you? Our match would be advantageous to all five of your kingdoms ...'

Fyia looked at him, but said not a word, her face giving nothing away.

He frowned, waiting for her to say something, then fidgeted, his gaze flitting as uncertainty crept in.

Fyia tilted her head to the side and watched him closely. He bowed, finally realizing his mistake, and Fyia waved her hand, shooing him away. He went without protest, and the room breathed a collective sigh of relief.

By the time the party died down, Fyia had received three marriage proposals. The one from Max Perdes, of the Sky Kingdom, one from a merchant from the Kingdom of the Moon, and one from a former Princess of the Kingdom of Sea Serpents. Nobody from her homeland—the Starlight Kingdom—would be so stupid as to propose marriage, leaving only the Kingdom of Plenty unrepresented. Maybe they were more sensible, or less drunk, or maybe they'd lost courage after the first three rejections. Either way, she was happy when the night drew to a close.

'Kick them out,' Fyia said to Edu when she could take no more. Edu summoned Fyia's personal guard, who saw to it that every last person found the door, leaving only Edu, Sensis, and Adigos, who'd been skulking at the back all night.

'Adi!' said Sensis, approaching Adigos with her arms wide open. She embraced him. 'Long time.'

'I went as fast as I could.' His eyes flicked to Fyia as she lowered herself beside the fire pit.

'Gods, it feels good to lie down,' she said. She rolled onto her back, one of her wolves nuzzling her arm.

'It feels good the war is over,' said Sensis.

'Don't get too comfortable,' said Fyia. 'We're leaving tomorrow.'

'We are?' said Sensis.

'Well, not you. You'll need to stay, and … you know … lead the army, but the rest of us.'

'Where are we going?' said Edu.

'To the ford town in Plenty—Selise. I intend to build a new palace there.'

'Why there?' asked Adigos.

'It's a central spot between all five kingdoms ... or at least as central as it's possible to be. It's prosperous, easy to access, and good for trade. I've sent Essa an eagle; she'll meet us there.'

'To design the palace?' said Sensis.

Fyia nodded. 'She won't be happy I'm dragging her away from her workshop, but she's the only one I trust.'

The following morning, Fyia, Edu, and Adigos mounted their horses. Fyia was restless and couldn't wait to get going. She had few friends in the Sky Kingdom—something she would have to rectify.

Eagles circled overhead, screaming as they swooped, chafing against the Cruaxee bond.

'They want to go home?' asked Adigos, manoeuvring his skittish mare next to Fyia's stallion.

'Their work is done, and they long to be free.' She closed her eyes, reaching for the magic binding them to her. She tugged on the strings, then let them go, feeling the eagles slide from her control. She opened her eyes as they cried out in farewell, flying north, back to the mountains they called home.

'We wouldn't have won without them,' said Edu, shielding his eyes against the rising sun.

'We owe them a great debt,' agreed Fyia. She shook off the sadness that washed over her. Her eagles urged her to go with them; they would miss her, as she would miss them. If only she could ...

Two of her wolves stepped out of the woods, sensing her agitation.

'Will you let them go too?' asked Adigos.

'I've released the whole pack,' said Fyia. 'These two want to stay.' She urged her mount to a walk, heading for the trees.

'Surely you'll name them now?' said Adigos, falling in beside her.

'They're wild animals, not pets,' said Fyia.

'Well, if you won't, I will.'

Fyia rolled her eyes.

'The bigger one, let's call her …'

'Fluffy,' said Edu, smirking at Fyia's pained expression. 'What? She's very fluffy.'

'Keep up,' said Fyia, squeezing her legs. Her horse leapt into the air, and Fyia felt every excited bunch of his muscles, no saddle beneath her. He jumped again, then took off at a gallop, hurtling through the trees. Her wolves yipped with glee, racing alongside, Fyia's hair and cloak streaming out behind her.

Adigos' mare was fast, and he caught Fyia, whooping with excitement as he came level, narrowly avoiding a branch. They ran for another league before reining in their horses, walking to let Fyia's guard catch up.

'Gods, it's good to have some fun,' said Fyia.

'That it is,' said Adigos.

A twig snapped close to their left, and Adigos screamed, 'Down!' as an arrow passed a whisper from his ear.

'*Warrior*,' said Fyia, whirling back the way they'd come.

Adigos tried to follow, but his mount reared and bucked, an arrow buried in her rump. Adigos cried out, and Fyia reigned in her stallion as he was thrown from the saddle. He landed hard, letting out a grunt, his horse racing away.

Fyia was at Adigos' side in three ticks, but men and women approached from all directions. Her wolves snarled, then attacked, the sound of ripping flesh filling Fyia's ears as she tried to make sense of it all.

'Go!' cried Adigos. He winced as he rolled to his feet, drawing his sword. 'Run! I'll hold them off.'

But before she could, she fell, registering an impact against her shoulder. She hit the ground and it hurt everywhere. Her horse—not a part of her Cruaxee—fled, and then she was being yanked to her feet, pulled up by Adigos.

'Do you have a weapon?' he hissed, as the ring of armed men and women moved in.

Fyia counted twelve. Twelve—armed to the hilt—against two and her wolves. Fyia drew her dagger. 'This is all I have,' she said in a low voice.

'*By the Whore*,' said Adigos, assessing the threat. Fyia watched as his mind worked out their odds, calculating, then realizing their chances weren't good.

Silence settled as their attackers moved forward on soundless feet, step by step, never taking their eyes from Fyia.

A grunt of pain broke the silence, then a thud, the unexpected sounds distracting them all. Adigos and her wolves didn't miss a beat, lunging forward, taking the fight to their attackers.

I am not a warrior ...

'Behind that tree!' shouted Adigos, skewering the woman charging him.

Fyia moved, but was yanked back by her hair. She staggered back a pace, then whirled, surprising her attacker by grabbing his arm. He loosened his grip, and she spun herself around ... *but I can stab a man in the back just fine.*

The man went down just as a weight hit Fyia between the shoulders, throwing her forward, pinning her in place. Fists showered punch after punch on Fyia's head, neck, back. Fyia went limp, and the

21

onslaught ceased. Her attacker's weight shifted forward, and Fyia grabbed her, rolling them over. She didn't hesitate for a tick before snatching up her dagger and sticking it in the woman's flesh. A woman who could not have been much older than Fyia's twenty-eight years.

The remaining attackers ran—only two still alive—and Fyia blinked as she took in the scene. Her bodyguards stood over the fallen, checking to make sure they were dead, blood and gore everywhere, littering the forest floor.

Edu and Adigos rushed to Fyia, dropping to their knees on either side of where she knelt. 'Are you hurt?' asked Adigos, his hands and eyes searching her for damage.

'I ...'

'There's blood coming from your shoulder. Get the healer!' Edu shouted at a guard.

'I can't see any other blood,' said Adigos.

'I'm fine,' said Fyia, pushing them off. 'Help me up.'

A horse with a fearsome woman atop screeched to a halt nearby. Sensis. She barked orders about perimeters, scouts, and only the Gods knew what else.

Fyia shot a look at Edu. 'We're in trouble now,' she said.

'What happened?' demanded Sensis. She slid off her horse and threw her reins to a soldier.

'We were attacked,' said Fyia.

Adigos rolled one of the dead onto his back. 'I spoke to this one last night,' he said. 'He told me Perdes was good to him.'

'Let's hope that's all this is,' said Sensis. 'We need to move, and I'm coming with you.'

Fyia's head went fuzzy, and she retched.

'*Mother* ...' said Adigos.

'Where's the healer?' Edu snapped.

'Get a carriage,' Sensis barked.

Fyia sank to the ground and let them fuss; it made little sense to argue when they were right.

Chapter Two

FYIA WOKE TO FIND herself in a plush carriage, her head in Adigos' lap, his hand stroking her hair. She tried to sit, but a blinding pain gripped her brain, so she gave up.

'What happened?' she asked, swotting away his hand. 'Is my horse okay?'

'The healer gave you something to knock you out. He said he told you to rest, and that you were being difficult. Your horse is fine. Mine is too, thank the Gods.'

'And? Do I have any lasting injuries?'

'You took an arrow to the shoulder, but it was only a flesh wound. The healer's more worried about pressure in your head, given the pounding it took. He instructed us to monitor you closely.'

'I'm fine. Help me up.'

Adigos slipped his hands under her and eased her up next to him. Her head pounded like it was under attack from ten thousand nails, but she forced herself to ignore the agony.

'Here,' said Adigos. He handed her a bundle of herbs. 'The healer said to chew these; it'll help with the pain.'

Fyia took them and looked out of the window as she bit down on the bitter green leaves. She could feel her wolves, glad they were safe, but scowled when she saw an entire squadron of soldiers escorting them. 'So much for travelling in secrecy,' she said.

'Sensis took over … you know how she is.'

She did know. Sensis was the best general the world had ever seen. She was ruthless, made hard decisions with empathy and conviction, never took chances she didn't have to, and inspired awe in those under her command, in everyone, really. Without Sensis, Fyia wouldn't be Queen of more than a single kingdom.

'Fyia, I'm …'

'Debrief me,' she said, cutting him off. Fyia wasn't in the mood to discuss how he'd betrayed her.

'I just …'

'Debrief me or leave. I have no wish to hear more of your apologies.'

He looked into her eyes, and she found a softness there she hadn't seen before. 'I missed you, and I'm glad to be back by your side.'

'It might not be for long if you make me ask a third time.'

Adigos held Fyia's gaze for a beat, then looked down at his hands. 'It's not what you want to hear.'

Fyia frowned. 'Did you even make it to the Fae'ch?'

'Please … give me some credit. I made it, they let me in, they even threw a party in my honor.'

'Insufferable hedonists.'

'That they are,' said Adigos, flashing a roguish smile.

'I don't need details of your debauchery.'

'Why?'

Her features set like stone. 'What did they say?'

'They said, if you want to know about their dragon egg, you should ask them yourself.'

'Did you snoop around?'

'I didn't get a chance. They watched me every tick I was there, which was all of a day before they kicked me out.'

'That's it?'

'I didn't see your brother, if that's what you mean.'

'Did you ask for him?'

'Should I have?'

'He was your best friend ...'

'He abandoned you.'

Fyia turned her gaze out of the window once more. 'He did what he needed to do.'

'You forgive him?'

'There's nothing to forgive.'

'Do you forgive me?' His words were a plea.

She closed her eyes, refusing to look at him. 'What you did will cast doubt on my legitimacy forever. It will add fuel to the arguments of my enemies ...'

'Fyia, I ...'

'You're sorry ... you regret it. You've said all the things you're supposed to say. But you defied a direct order. You made a kill that should have been mine.'

'You said yourself, you're not a warrior ...'

Fyia saw red, turning so fast she had to brace herself against the pain in her head. 'I'm Queen; I've never shied away from any part of that, including killing the men in my way.'

'I was trying to help.'

'You were trying to make a name for yourself ... to prove yourself the great warrior you think you are. You wanted glory, songs, women to fall at your feet ...' Even though they did that already. 'When I need help, I ask for it. You betrayed me, and I would've been within my rights to execute you.'

'But you didn't, because you knew sending me away would hurt me more. And it did hurt, every moment.'

'Because you longed to be in the middle of the action … to be a part of the stories.'

'Because I longed to be with you.'

The blood drained from her brain as she looked into his eyes, flicking from one to the other, trying to see into his soul. He seemed to believe his words, but did he mean them? Would he make the right choice next time, or was his ego too strong to overrule …?

Her head hurt.

'I've learned my lesson,' he said quietly. 'I will never disobey you again.'

'I can never trust you again …' She wobbled, and had to grab his leg so as not to fall to the floor, the edges of her vision going black.

He took hold of her shoulders. 'You can,' he said, 'and I'll prove it, but right now you have to rest. You can't go into the Vipers' Nest like this.'

He was right, and better to sleep on Adigos than risk falling on the floor at every lurch of the carriage. She lifted her legs onto the cushioned red velvet bench, then rested her head in the crook of his shoulder. He dropped a muscular arm around her, and she nestled in, wrapping both of her arms around his much larger one. They'd travelled like this on countless occasions, and the familiarity was comforting. He was warm, and strong, and smelt faintly of leather, and not two turns of the carriage wheels later, she was asleep.

Fyia's carriage pulled up outside a colossal stone building. Copper runners zigzagged across the front, from the top, where a dragon clock ticked, all the way to the bottom, where the runners dipped into the small channel of water that circled the building.

Few dragon clocks existed, and the ones that did were spread across Fyia's kingdoms. The mechanisms were much like any other, but the numbers—one to twelve—started and finished either side of a dragon head, which sat where the number twelve would in any other clock.

They had once been used for more than just telling the time, or so said the legends, but for what, no one knew, at least in Fyia's five kingdoms. Magic had long been outlawed, and the fae and witches had fled, the old kings killing the magical for sport whenever the opportunity arose. It was one of the many things Fyia would change ...

Fyia stepped down from the carriage, and a deep rumbling ground through the air. She looked up to see a metal ball drop out of the clock. The sound of metal on metal reverberated across the open piazza as the ball rolled down the copper runners. Fyia watched as it travelled down the left side of the building, then dipped into the water with barely a splash.

'Auspicious,' said a tall old woman, who was walking—spine ramrod straight—down the steps towards them.

'Stop,' said Fyia, starting up the stairs. 'We'll come to you.'

'I'm as fit as a fiddle, Your Majesty.'

'Even so ...' Fyia climbed the endless stairs Sensis had lined with guards. The old woman sank into a deep bow when Fyia reached her.

'Spider,' said Fyia, 'it is good to see you.'

'And you, Your Majesty. If you'll come this way, the Extended Council has assembled.'

'The Viper's Nest,' said Sensis.

'That name is typically reserved for the Small Council,' said the Spider, with a stern look.

'Can't imagine it's much different,' said Sensis.

The building was ornately decorated, with mosaiced floors, patterned ceilings, and glassless windows. The city had been built long ago, when the lands had been warmer, when a frost this far south was virtually unheard of. Now, although not yet cold, the leaves only just beginning to turn, they still had need of their cloaks. Come the winter, the place would feel no warmth for three long cycles of the moon.

The Spider led them up a set of stairs, then along a wide corridor, where mechanical artwork lined the walls, making whirling, clicking noises as it moved. Fyia couldn't say she was a fan, not when she compared the artwork here to the wild paintings of her mountainous homeland.

'They're amazing, aren't they?' said Adigos, admiring a piece that depicted the movements of the sun.

'Hmm,' said Fyia, throwing him a questioning look. 'Not exactly what I was thinking …'

'Brace yourselves,' said the Spider. She paused before a set of huge metal doors covered with cogs of various sizes.

Fyia nodded, a seriousness descending over the group as they positioned themselves. The Spider pressed a hidden button, and a loud clanking filled the air, the cogs spinning as they swung inwards, revealing the council chamber beyond.

The chamber was vast, stretching all the way up to the clock tower above, some of the clock's internal mechanism visible. Towering columns ran down either side, and rows of stained-glass windows admitted muted light. Under the columns, lesser diplomats and courtiers lined the walls, and at the far end stood a long table, packed with expectant faces all craning for a look at their Queen.

Fyia held her head high, looking every inch the conqueror as she entered the chamber. Music began, floating across the air from somewhere at the back, and Fyia had to suppress a laugh at the shocked faces all around; evidently Rouel had snuck in ahead of them.

Fyia's wolves led the way, prowling towards the table, with Sensis and Edu—large and formidable—flanking her. Fyia surveyed the faces as she walked purposefully to the elaborate chair at the head of the table. Sensis and the Spider took the chairs to either side of Fyia, Edu and Adigos standing guard behind, her wolves sitting at her feet.

Fyia nodded to the Spider, who said, 'Your Majesty, with your leave, I bring this meeting to order. The members of your council would swear fealty.'

Fyia nodded. Her wardens—one for each of the five kingdoms—stood, bowed, and declared their loyalty, and then the rest of Fyia's Extended Council followed suit. Nobody missed the mocking edge from Lord Eratus Venir, the newly appointed warden of her most recently conquered kingdom. That he'd made it to her new capital before Fyia was impressive; he must have ridden hard from the Sky Kingdom.

'The next order of business,' said the Spider, 'is from Lady Lyr Patrice, the Warden of your homeland, the Starlight Kingdom.'

Lady Lyr stood, inclined her head to Fyia, then addressed the table. 'My lords and ladies, I petition the council for an increase in soldiers at the border between the Starlight Kingdom and the dark lands beyond.'

Fyia bristled. 'Those lands have names. The Land of the Fae'ch, and the Kingdom of the Black Hoods,' she said, looking Lady Lyr directly in the eye.

'Of course, Your Majesty,' said Lyr, clenching her teeth.

'What purpose would troops serve?' asked Sensis. As High Commander of Fyia's armies, her troops would be the ones to answer any such call.

'To protect against raiders,' said Lyr, 'and as a show of strength ... so they don't get any ideas.'

'So *who* doesn't get any ideas?' said Sensis, not bothering to hide her frustration.

'The Fae'ch, and the Black Hoods.'

'What ideas might they get?' asked Sensis.

'Ones about invading our lands ...'

'Has either given any indication they are considering an invasion? Have there been raids?' said Sensis.

'There have been rumors. We must be proactive ... not give them an opening.'

'Why would they want an opening?' said Sensis.

'I don't presume to understand the motivations of those ... people.'

Fyia clenched her fists under the table, reminding herself to be civil. The people of her homeland split into two broad camps: bigots and scaremongers who had an over-inflated sense of their own self-worth ... people like Lady Lyr, or Fyia's parents, and the progressives, like Fyia. Much as Fyia hated Lady Lyr and everything she stood for, the other bigots confided in her, so she had a use.

'Your request is denied,' said Fyia. 'You have no evidence of hostility, and no good will come from provoking our neighbors.'

'But ... Your Majesty ... the people of the Starlight Kingdom will not be pleased.'

'Do you mean to say ensuring harmony in the kingdom of my birth is outside your capabilities?' said Fyia.

Lady Lyr seethed, unable—or maybe unwilling—to hide her anger. 'I will, of course, do what I can …'

Fyia looked back to the Spider, ending Lyr's time. 'Lady Nara Orchus, of the Kingdom of Sea Serpents, and Lord Fredrik Feake, of the Kingdom of Plenty, would like to make a joint petition,' said the Spider.

Fyia turned her attention to the two figures rising from their seats.

'Your Majesty,' said Lady Nara, whom Fyia had always liked, 'Lord Fredrik and I are concerned about our trade prospects with the lands across the Kraken Sea.'

Fyia's kingdoms exported much to those lands, and the Kingdom of Sea Serpents shipped the goods to all the far-flung regions of the known world. Fyia inclined her head.

'We are concerned with the … ah … tense relations between Your Majesty and the Emperor across the sea,' said Fredrik. 'We fear trade will be adversely affected.'

He looked expectantly at Fyia, who said nothing. Instead, she held Fredrik's gaze until he continued. 'We would respectfully suggest Your Majesty explores a … uh … marriage contract with the Emperor, to secure peace and favorable trade agreements for the good of all five kingdoms.'

Fyia's gaze flicked between Nara and Fredrik. Maybe she wasn't as fond of Lady Nara as she'd originally thought …

'I will say this once, and once only,' said Fyia. Her tone caused the room to go still, and nervous tension permeated the air. 'I will never marry the Emperor, or anyone like him. I have not toiled for so long, risked so much, lost so many, only to give my kingdoms to a greedy, self-serving man. Especially a man with a reputation for brutality, who is harboring both my treasonous parents and many of the pitiful royals who fled my kingdoms at the first sign of their defeat.

'Trade is important—crucial—and will continue as it always has, whether or not I marry a foreign leader. They need our goods as much as we need theirs.'

'But, Your Majesty ...' said Fredrik.

Fyia waved her hand, halting his words. 'Fear not, Lord Fredrik, for I have work for you. I plan to make Selise the heart of my combined kingdoms. I intend to build a palace, which will act not only as my home, but more importantly, will become a center of trade for the world.

'We shall invite merchants to our lands. We will wow them with the treatment usually reserved for dignitaries, and then we shall make deals to secure good relations for generations to come.'

'I can only applaud such a vision,' said Fredrik.

'But to achieve our full potential, we must change the way things work,' said Fyia. The air went still once more, and Fredrik's face drained of all color. 'We will make the markets fair and accessible to all.'

Fredrik's mouth pinched. He and his peers had long run the markets like their personal playgrounds, demanding exorbitant taxes and giving prime spots to their friends.

'And all workers will be paid fairly across the Five Kingdoms.'

'Well ... I ... I'm not sure what you mean?' said Fredrik.

'Which part is unclear?'

'Workers are already paid.'

'You do not think everyone deserves *fair* payment for their work?'

'We should consult with the merchants, Your Majesty. These things are delicate ... should not be rushed ... especially if such action could hamper commerce.' Fredrik looked delighted with his argument, obviously thinking he'd found an excellent button to push.

'It is very simple,' said Fyia, her tone brooking no argument. 'As of the first day of the next cycle of the moon, any person wishing to operate in any market in any of my five kingdoms must pay all workers fairly— men and women. If they do not, they will be fined, and shall not be allowed to trade. I trust the two of you,' she indicated to Lord Fredrik and Lady Nara, 'can work out the finer details and enforce the new rules.'

Fyia nodded to the Spider, who moved onto the next item on her list, even though Fredrik and Nara still stood. 'Lord Sollow Antice, of the Kingdom of the Moon,' said the Spider. Fredrik and Nara finally returned to their seats.

'Your Majesty,' said Lord Antice, standing and bowing deeply.

Fyia gripped the arms of her chair. Gods give her strength ...

'We request you visit the Moon Kingdom,' said Antice. 'We should like to bestow on you an honorary degree from the university, and build a statue in your likeness to be placed proudly in the main atrium. It will replace the statue of the former King of Moon that stands today.'

Lord Sollow Antice had previously been Prince Sollow Antice, firstborn son of that very king. There was no love lost between the father and son, but that didn't explain his current motivation. He was too sweet by half ...

'Thank you, my lord.'

'There is but one other thing,' said Antice. Fyia nodded, unsurprised. 'I presume you need the services of the Guild of Architects to design your new palace? I would be delighted to summon our most accomplished members …'

Fyia sat back in her chair. 'Remind me, Lord Antice, how many women are in that guild?'

Antice faltered, and Fyia didn't miss the flash of irritation in his eyes; not so sweet after all.

'The Guild of Architects does not admit women, Your Majesty.'

'How about your esteemed military academy? Or the healers' college?'

'As Your Majesty is aware, those institutions are only for men.'

Fyia gave him a long, hard look. 'Not any longer.'

Antice paled. 'You can't mean …'

'I assure you, I can. Sensis will deal with the military academy. The Spider will compile a list of leaders for the healers' college and guilds. And my dear friend Essa Thebe—our most brilliant inventor—whom I have already asked to architect my new palace, will make a short list of candidates for Chancellor of the University.'

'Your Majesty!' said Antice, his fists balled at his sides. 'I must strongly advise against this. The people of Moon will consider it an attack on their way of life. It would not be an exaggeration to say we will see blood in the streets …'

'You mean from the stampede of women rushing to register for an education that should have been available to them since birth?'

'No, Your Majesty, from the people who will lose their livelihoods. We will simply have too many workers … it will throw off the balance.'

'Then admit fewer men,' said Fyia, 'although I very much doubt your words are true. Are we done?' Fyia looked at the Spider.

'One more petition, from Lord Eratus Venir, of the Sky Kingdom,' said the Spider.

Fyia's stomach dropped. *Wonderful.* She turned her eyes to the gnarled old man making a show of struggling to his feet. It was a façade; if he were truly so fragile, he'd never have made it here before her.

Lord Venir said nothing for a few moments, letting a vicious silence rip across the room that sank its claws into everyone present. As a representative of the most recently vanquished kingdom, he was somewhat of an unknown entity, and that made people nervous.

'Your Majesty,' he said eventually, with a deep bow, 'I have but one question.' He paused a beat, trying to intimidate her, but Fyia refused to be bullied. She looked at him with boredom in her eyes. 'Where are the dragons?'

A collective gasp went through the room. They'd all been thinking it, but apparently only Venir had the balls to ask out loud. Fyia respected him for that.

'They have not yet returned,' said Fyia, 'unless anyone present is harboring a dragon?'

Silence.

'Do you believe, Your Majesty,' Venir continued, 'the legend is false? That uniting the Five Kingdoms will not, in fact, bring back those beasts? Or maybe—and I say this with the greatest of respect—you are not the one destined for that path?'

Fyia's wolves snarled, and she felt Adigos and Edu tense behind her.

'Did you expect them to puff into being overnight?' asked Fyia, her tone mocking. 'Five eggs are all we have left, and the *Kings* outlawed magic.'

'They did no such thing,' said Venir.

'Yes, they did,' said Fyia, 'for everyone but a handful of men behind the walls of a secret guild. They chased away the Fae'ch—the custodians of magic, and Cruaxee, and fire-touch—even the priestesses of the Sea Serpent are forbidden to practice. As of this moment, I decree that magic is legal, and may be practiced by anyone who wishes. The knowledge held in the guilds and university will be freely shared.'

Antice and Venir spluttered unintelligible exclamations, but fell silent when Fyia turned fierce eyes upon them.

'The priestesses of the Sea Serpent will be delighted,' said Lady Nara. 'I shall send word to them immediately.' Fyia nodded in acknowledgement.

'It will be good for trade,' said Lord Fredrik, 'but will wipe out the existing black market. We'll have to watch for unrest on that front.'

'The Spider will see to that,' said Fyia.

Lady Lyr had gone pale. 'You're going to encourage those … *people* to come back into our lands? This is the opposite of my request. The Starlight Kingdom will not stand for it.'

'You forget yourself, Lady Lyr. The Starlight Kingdom is *my* homeland. My people will welcome this news.'

'What of the dragons?' Venir asked again. 'What if they do not return?' Antice nodded in agreement, and he and Venir shared a meaningful look.

'They will,' said Fyia, her voice unwavering. *They had to.*

Chapter Three

THE SPIDER SHOWED FYIA and her entourage to an enormous townhouse after the meeting—Fyia's official residence in Selise until her new palace was ready. It had rooms enough to accommodate them all, as well as space for banquets and balls, and a garden that butted up against the river Sage, half a league before it merged with the river Empirisis. Empirisis flowed all the way from the Blue Mountains in the east, where it formed the border between Moon and Plenty, across Plenty's vast countryside, then through the Kingdom of Sea Serpents to the sea.

Fyia paced back and forth in front of the hearth in the large sitting room. The Spider sat on an uncomfortable-looking sofa, Adigos leaned against the frame of a floor-to-ceiling window, and Sensis lounged on a chaise longue, eating chocolate-coated strawberries.

'Gods, I'd forgotten how good these things are,' said Sensis, popping a strawberry into her mouth.

Fyia rolled her eyes, and the Spider tutted at the decadent display. Chocolate had become scarce since their lands had cooled, and eye-wateringly expensive.

'What will you do?' asked Sensis.

'The only thing I can do,' said Fyia. 'I know the location of only two eggs.'

'Fae'ch and Black Hoods?' said Sensis.

Fyia nodded. 'So off to the Fae'ch mountains I shall go.'

It wasn't an idea she relished, but she had no choice, and she longed to see her brother—an added bonus. Certainly the Fae'ch were the better of the two options, because with the Black Hoods, no one knew what was legend and what was true.

'You're running away?' said the Spider, with a cruel smile.

'I know that's how some will see it, but … convince them otherwise,' said Fyia.

'That's not my job,' said the Spider, 'and leading your council as your stand-in does not play to my skills.'

'Then who?' said Adigos. 'Sensis?'

Sensis laughed. 'The Queen's sending me to Moon to deal with the military academy, remember? And it's not a job for me either; military command and political councils are different beasts to tame.'

'I have to find the dragon eggs,' said Fyia. 'If I can't do that, it's only a matter of time before we have another war on our hands.'

'You're the legitimate ruler of the Five Kingdoms, even without dragons,' said Adigos.

'I know,' said Fyia, hotly, 'but not everyone sees it that way, especially given *your* actions during the war.'

'You know I'm sorry,' he said, his features betraying his guilt.

'You riled a few people up at the council meeting earlier, too,' Sensis said to Fyia.

'Rightly so,' said Adigos.

'It was stupid,' said the Spider, placing her hands calmly in her lap. 'You should have got them on side, and said you would consider marriage options. Only when they owed you something should you have introduced your ideas for the markets and guilds ... slowly ... step by step.'

'I will neither pander nor play politics,' said Fyia. 'If I start that way, I set the tone for my entire reign. But you're right, I need someone to keep them in line while I'm away.'

'There is only one person,' said Sensis, with a chuckle.

'You can't be serious ...' said the Spider.

'She's right,' said Fyia. 'No one else is both capable and trustworthy.'

'She's a hedonist,' scoffed the Spider.

'Who?' said Adigos.

Fyia inhaled deeply, then held her breath. 'My aunt.' And convincing her would be a challenge.

It took a day's hard riding to reach the Temple of the Goddess. They tracked the river Sage and its adjacent canal upstream into the heart of the Kingdom of Plenty, but it was a beautiful autumnal day. Fyia smiled as she watched farmers working in the fields of the lowlands, tending to sheep and cows, or cutting late hay.

The Kingdom of Plenty provided much of the meat consumed within the Five Kingdoms, and it was good to see life continuing as normal, despite the war she'd brought to their doorstep. Plenty was the second kingdom she'd conquered, so they'd had time to adjust, and they were generally a good-natured, easy-going people. Unless she messed with the bloodlines of a prized variety of sheep, there wasn't much that would truly upset them.

The Temple of the Goddess was an imposing marble building that sat atop a square pyramid, with steps on all four sides. At the top, a terrace wrapped around, where the devouts of the temple regularly laid booby traps to prevent unwelcome visitors from making it inside.

Fyia paused at the bottom and looked up the steep stairs. A man wearing nothing but a loin cloth watched them, leaning against a pillar.

'I'll wait for you here,' said Edu, looking nervous. It was the first time Fyia had seen any hint of fear in his eyes.

She smiled, but didn't openly mock him in front of the guards. 'Everyone will stay here aside from me.'

'You're not going in there alone,' said Adigos. He flicked his pale blue eyes past Fyia to the devout at the top of the steps.

'You *want* to go inside?' said Fyia.

'It's too dangerous for you to go alone. What if someone attacks you?'

'The risk is minimal,' said Edu, 'but Adigos is right; we can't be too careful.'

Fyia chuckled, turning to walk up the steps, Adigos hot on her heels. 'Don't speak unless they ask you a direct question,' she said. 'Don't stare, keep track of your possessions at all times, and for Gods' sake, don't let them corner you.'

'You make it sound as though we're going into hostile territory. How bad can a bunch of old women be?'

'Oh, you sweet summer child.'

The man at the top bowed to Fyia and ignored Adigos—the shrine's devouts did not take kindly to other men.

Fyia stifled a laugh at Adigos' frown. *Just you wait* …

The devout led them through an atrium filled with light, channels of steaming water crisscrossing the floor. The temple sat atop a hot spring, hot water piped through every inch, so it was always at a temperature that allowed for barely any clothes.

They passed several naked devouts as they walked, Adigos stepping up beside Fyia, glaring at them all. Moans and gasps drifted out from the many alcoves, and Adigos' head whipped around, sending Fyia a look of disbelief. 'Don't they have rooms?'

'It's not a brothel,' said Fyia. 'You can wait outside if it's too much for your sensibilities. Really, you act as though you were born in Moon …'

'You know very well *this* is my homeland,' said Adigos, 'but not everyone in Plenty is quite so … liberal.'

'Maybe they should be.'

He looked aghast. 'They're not like this in your home kingdom …'

'Some of them are,' she said with a wink.

Adigos stuttered, searching for a response, but they reached a wooden section of wall, and the devout pulled a lever.

'Brace yourself,' Fyia whispered.

The wall tipped forwards, supported on either side by chains. It fell to the floor, where it formed a bridge across a particularly wide channel of water, and on the other side …

'*Sacred Warrior*,' muttered Adigos. He pulled Fyia back as she made to step onto the bridge. 'You cannot be serious.' His face was inches from hers, his features almost pleading.

'Don't show weakness,' said Fyia, 'or you're done for.' She pulled out of his grasp and headed into the melee, the only word she could think to describe the debauched scene.

In the center of the space, three middle-aged women lounged on low couches, entirely naked. Each woman had three or four male attendants—all naked too—and were engaged in all manner of activities. One had a devout feeding her peeled grapes while her finger and toenails were painted, another received a massage, a man on each limb, and the third—her aunt—had one man's head between her breasts, and another kissing his way up her thigh.

'Starfall!' said Fyia, her voice an excited greeting.

Her aunt looked around, her features lighting up when she saw her niece. 'Fyia, darling, what a lovely surprise! Join in, by all means. And who is this delicious piece of man flesh?' she asked, eyeing Adigos. 'You should rid him of his clothes … awfully hot in here.'

Adigos flinched.

'Oh … you didn't bring a prude?'

'Leave if you're uncomfortable, Adigos,' said Fyia softly, sinking onto the couch next to her aunt. She beckoned one of the men to her side. Adigos went rigid as Fyia instructed the man to kiss her neck, then tipped her head back and let out a sigh. She hummed in appreciation as another gave her a foot rub.

Fyia watched Adigos as he watched her. She didn't miss the flaming fire of desire in his eyes. He'd always wanted her, since they'd first met, when she'd been sixteen and him twenty, her brother's best friend. She'd almost given in, just once, before he'd betrayed her for the first time. In another life, they would have been married … a life where her brother hadn't become Fae'ch …

Starfall clapped her hands, and the devouts got to their feet, then left the room. 'For Gods' sake, sit, Adigos. Don't think I don't remember you from your youth. You can't be shocked … not really … given what I recall of your exploits.'

'I'm not shocked,' he said. He sat next to the woman with drying nails. She leaned towards him, and he backed away, trying and failing to put distance between them.

'He smells nice,' she said.

Fyia stifled a smile. It was true; he did.

'So, Niece, what is it you want from me this time? I helped rid you of your parents, and I have my just reward,' she said, motioning around her, 'yet here you are again.'

'I have five kingdoms,' said Fyia.

'But no dragons,' said the woman who'd been having a massage, a glint in her eye.

'Or eggs?' said Starfall.

'You should find those,' said the woman next to Adigos. 'Not something to leave up to chance. May I …?' she said to Adigos, hovering a hand over his upper thigh.

'No,' said Adigos.

'Oh, good. I like them feisty.'

Adigos pursed his lips, small lines appearing on his brow. She wouldn't touch him without consent, but that wouldn't stop her from teasing him.

'But you can't leave your kingdoms shepherd-less,' said the first woman.

'You'll need someone you can trust …' said the second, mischievously.

'A safe and proven pair of hands,' agreed the first.

Starfall looked keenly at Fyia. 'So? How are you going to convince me when I have everything I need right here?'

'You expect me to believe that?' said Fyia. 'Look at the three of you, baiting me; you haven't had this much fun in years. I can practically see the cogs in your formidable minds spinning and whirling, calculating what you should demand of me.'

'We're *all* in on this?' said the first, as though the suggestion were ridiculous, but her keen eyes betrayed her interest. 'You only need one of us to lead in your absence … and you have the Spider. What purpose would we serve?'

'New positions are becoming available,' said Fyia.

'New positions?' said the second woman, leaning forward. 'Where?'

'Moon,' said Fyia.

'Moon,' repeated the woman, obviously weighing up the pros and cons.

'It's a shame we have such a wonderful life here,' said Starfall, with a shrug.

'You're a terrible liar,' said Fyia. 'Name your price.'

So they did. It was eye-watering: riches and accolades and property rights. They would most likely use none of it, the pleasure of the negotiation their true reward. It mattered not, for they were worth every copper, so after putting up a half-hearted fight, Fyia gave them all they asked.

'They stole my favorite dagger,' said Adigos. He complained to the Spider as they sat in the sitting room of Fyia's temporary residence.

'I told you to keep track of your possessions,' said Fyia, with a smirk.

'When will they arrive?' asked the Spider.

'Tomorrow. They're having a farewell party tonight.'

'I dread to think what that entails,' said Adigos.

'I bet they loved him,' said the Spider, sending Fyia a wide-eyed look.

'Like a cat loves a mouse,' said Fyia.

The Spider chuckled. 'I'll make preparations. Good night.'

The door clicked shut, and silence settled over the room. 'What did Starfall mean, about helping to get rid of your parents?' asked Adigos.

He moved to sit next to Fyia on a formal sofa, his bulk taking up most of the space. Warmth radiated off him, and she resisted the urge to reach up and play with his wavy blond hair. She craved the simple intimacy with a force that surprised her.

Fyia gave him a searching look. 'You know what happened.'

'I know you staged a coup, and had your parents bundled off across the Kraken Sea, but I didn't know Starfall helped.'

'You were with my brother, so I guess that makes sense, and few know what really happened.' Fyia could trust almost no one—she'd learned that the hard way—but there was no harm in telling Adigos now. 'After I refused my parents' edict to marry the Emperor across the Kraken Sea, I ran away. That meant, when I decided to overthrow them, I needed help from inside the castle.

'Starfall lived there, and invited my parents to her rooms one night for dinner. Her personal guards bound and gagged them, then carried them out through the secret passages. I went in the same way with my force, and took the castle without spilling a single drop of blood.'

'Why did she help you?'

'There was no love lost between her and my parents. My father was her younger brother, and Starfall was supposed to rule. My father pretended he had no interest in the throne, then organized a coup of his own, forcing a vote of no confidence in Starfall before she ever ascended the throne. She never saw it coming … that's what eats her up the most.'

'Didn't she want to rule herself once your parents were out of the way?'

'No. She'd never wanted it all that much anyway. She wanted freedom more … and revenge.'

'And hedonism,' said Adigos, raising an eyebrow.

'Nothing wrong with that,' said Fyia, a challenge in her eyes.

Adigos held her gaze, and the air went taut. A smile played across Fyia's lips; it had been a while since she'd enjoyed herself with a man, and Adigos had a lot to offer. She let her eyes roam across his broad chest, down his torso, across the bare, muscular forearm that rested across his thigh. She flicked her gaze back to his face: angular jaw, high cheekbones, light blue eyes, and her lips parted involuntarily.

He leaned in, invading her space, his eyes searching hers. His lips were achingly close, but he was hesitant. After everything that had happened, it wasn't surprising, but she didn't want him to hesitate. She wanted him to kiss her, take her, to have one place and time where her power and position didn't matter … to have an equal.

She lifted her fingers to his face, eyes on his lips, so close she could smell the whiskey on his breath. She shouldn't do it, not with him, not after everything, but she so wanted to … needed to. She skimmed her fingers over the prickle of his stubble, then ran her thumb across his lips. He parted them, gently biting the pad of her thumb before licking the skin with the tip of his tongue.

She closed her eyes against the sensation, desire pooling everywhere. She scraped her nails through his hair, and he sighed, leaning in so their cheeks touched. She rested against him, then exhaled sharply as he tugged her earlobe with his teeth. He lifted his fingers to her neck, caressing her with featherlight touches, then moved his lips, brushing them across the sensitive skin behind her ear. She tipped her head back, giving him all the access he wanted, her hand fisted in his hair.

The door clunked open just as Adigos finally got around to kissing her properly, sucking at her neck. He froze, and she let out a hiss of disappointment, her wolves growling as they approached.

'Your wolves were trying to get in,' said a light, female voice, '… oh, sorry, I can come back … wait, is that … Adigos? Okay, no, I'm staying.'

Adigos kissed Fyia's cheek, then pulled away, standing. 'Impeccable timing as always, Essa,' he said.

'It's so nice to see you too,' said Essa, cocking an eyebrow.

'I would hug you, but …'

'… Gods no,' said Essa, shuddering and circling a hand in the general direction of his nether regions.

'See you tomorrow,' said Adigos, sending Fyia a smoldering look.

Fyia lifted her head in acknowledgement.

'Your Majesty,' said Essa, bowing low. She was short, with dirty blond hair and a round, full face to match her curvy figure. Her grey eyes were sharp as knives, the juxtaposition striking. 'I would say I'm sorry, but I think I just saved you from yourself.'

'It's been a long time,' said Fyia, disappointment coursing through her.

'Since you saw me? Or since you indulged in carnal delights?'

'Both, but longer for the delights.'

'You can't be short on suitors?'

'I've had proposals, if they count, but no-one so bold as to propose anything less permanent, and I've been with the army; Sensis would string me up by my hair if I fooled around with her soldiers.'

'The trials and tribulations of being Queen.'

'Indeed,' said Fyia. She patted the space next to her on the sofa, and Essa sat. 'What about you?'

'Suitors?' said Essa.

'Or carnal delights?' said Fyia, with a grin.

'No,' said Essa. She shook her head, turning introspective.

'I'm sorry,' said Fyia. She put her hand on Essa's arm. 'It will ease in time.'

Essa gave a tight smile.

'My brother has a lot to answer for,' said Fyia. She leaned back against the sofa, raising her eyes to the intricate pattern winding its way across the ceiling.

'If he'd taken up his rightful position, you wouldn't be Queen,' said Essa.

'No, you would.'

'Of only a single kingdom, and I would've made a terrible queen … I'm happy in my workshop.'

'Are you?'

'You know I am. Inventing is my only true love.' A shadow passed behind Essa's eyes; her only true love, aside from Fyia's brother … 'I hear I'm to appoint a new Chancellor of the University?' she said, visibly forcing herself out of her reverie.

Fyia nodded. 'Apparently, I'm better at making enemies than enticing lovers to my bed.'

'The men of Moon may hate you for a while, but just think of all the women who can finally get an education ... and you can't make a clock without breaking an egg.'

'Do you really think they made the clocks with dragon eggs?'

Essa shrugged. 'That's how the saying goes.'

Fyia entered Essa's hastily assembled workshop at the top of the tallest tower in Selise. The sun was peaking over the horizon, rays of golden light punctuating the space. Four assistants bustled about, one measuring out brightly colored liquids, one hovering next to a bubbling pot, one taking a reading from a large solar simulation that hung from the ceiling, and one looking at the sky through a telescope. Essa was at a workbench, her face shielded with metal as she worked with a flame.

Essa didn't look up, so Fyia leaned against a bench and watched the activity. She could see the dragon clock through the window, a metal ball appearing at the top just as a ray of light illuminated the dragon's head. Such a mystery, how they worked, what they did ... She'd often wondered why the old Kings hadn't torn them down, against magic as they were.

Essa pulled off her shield and placed it on the bench. 'The Emperor across the Kraken Sea has created flying machines,' she said, leaving whatever she'd been working on to cool.

'What? How?'

'I don't know the details, or if it's really true, but we should send spies to gather intelligence.'

'Done,' said Fyia, 'but how do you know?'

'A trader,' said Essa. 'He supplies several inventors in the Kraken Empire. I've packed a few things for your trip.' Essa picked up a bag and handed it over. 'It's all the usual stuff; water purification, medicines, navigation devices, and a dagger that will stay sharp … I found a new way to edge the metal, and added a special coating …'

'Thank you.'

'And please will you deliver this to your brother?' She held out a small, perfectly round, perfectly smooth metal ball. It was almost gold, but with hints of other colors—pinks and blues and greens—just below the surface, catching the light.

'Essa …'

'Don't judge me. Just take it, please.' Essa didn't meet her eyes.

'Okay,' said Fyia. The ball was small enough to fit in her palm, yet surprisingly weighty. 'Should I tell him anything when I give it to him?'

'No, thank you.'

Fyia didn't pry. They'd been friends for a long time, but Essa was a private person, and Fyia respected her privacy.

'Starfall will work with you on the stuff in Moon,' said Fyia, 'and Sensis will be there to ensure compliance.'

Essa nodded. 'We leave today. What about the plans for the palace? Who needs to see them?'

'Nobody. I trust your judgement, and you know what I want. The Spider or Starfall will help if you need anything.'

Essa nodded, then bowed. 'Safe travels, my Queen.'

Fyia pulled Essa into an embrace. 'You too.'

Fyia entered the council chamber, the members of her Small Council already waiting. Whereas the Extended Council included the wardens from each kingdom, as well as other key figures, the Small Council was less concerned with representation and more concerned with action. Every member of the Small Council played a crucial role, and Fyia expected them to be loyal to her first, and to their home kingdom or other interests second.

Along with Starfall, Sensis, and the Spider, who handled general leadership, the military, and intelligence respectively, she'd made two new appointments: Lady Nara Orchus of the Kingdom of Sea Serpents, to handle trade, and Lord Eratus Venir of the Kingdom of Sky, ostensibly to handle the kingdoms' finances, but also because Fyia wanted to keep an eye on him.

'You may by wondering why my aunt, Lady Starfall Orlightus, has joined us today,' said Fyia. The looks on Nara and Venir's faces said they knew exactly why Starfall was in attendance, but Fyia continued anyway. 'As you know, I am heading north, to the lands of the Fae'ch.'

'In search of dragons,' said Venir.

Fyia frowned, but he didn't even have the good grace to look abashed. 'While I am away,' she continued, 'Starfall will be my deputy. She has absolute authority in all things.'

'You're not worried she might betray you, as she did your parents?' asked Venir.

Fyia ignored him. 'While I am away, Sensis will travel to Moon, to reorganize the military academy. Nara will oversee the reformation of the markets, the Spider will appoint new academic and guild leaders, and Venir, you will ensure our coffers remain full upon my return.'

'Your Majesty,' they said together, accepting their tasks.

'Will you select a husband while you travel?' asked Lady Nara.

'You've given up on my marrying the Emperor so soon?' Fyia sniped.

Nara's cheeks colored. 'That was Fredrik's idea, not mine. I only wish you to marry *someone* … there are no dragons, so … and alliances would make us stronger … enhance trade …'

Venir interrupted Nara's stumbling words. 'Given the way King Milo was slain, not to mention the way you won your own home kingdom, you can't blame us for having questions.'

Adigos shifted almost imperceptibly behind Fyia. 'I can and will blame you for your questions,' said Fyia. 'I conquered all five kingdoms, and punished the men who snatched King Milo's kill from my hand.' Nara and Venir's eyes flicked to Adigos, Nara's eyebrows shooting up before she remembered to get them under control.

Fyia's wolves growled, and everyone at the table stiffened, even Starfall.

'Next time you question my right to rule, my Cruaxee will give you a permanent reminder of how badly you are mistaken.'

The air vacated the room, and a dark, foreboding silence settled. Nara and Venir averted their eyes.

'Venir, I am in need of a spy in the Kraken Empire. We've heard word they've invented flying machines.' A collective gasp filled the air. 'You will travel there, under the guise of a trade mission, and find out what you can.'

Venir flinched. 'But, Your Majesty, I have much to attend here … my lands …'

'Do not seek out my parents. If they try to contact you, ignore their request.'

53

Venir paled. 'But they're in the Emperor's palace … I may be unable to avoid them.'

'Then keep conversation to a minimum, or feed them lies … whichever you prefer. Act in accordance with the spirit of what I ask, and remember, the Spider's web is wide.'

Venir looked at her for a long moment, apparently speechless. 'Your Majesty,' he finally managed, bowing his head.

Fyia stood, and all at the table did so too. 'Starfall will take the meeting from here,' she said, nodding to her aunt. Starfall smiled, itching to get going.

'May the Gods protect you on your journey,' said Nara. 'I will pray to the Warrior to keep you safe from the Black Hoods.'

Fyia inwardly rolled her eyes; why was everyone so scared of the Black Hoods? 'I rather thought you might pray to the Whore, or I suppose the Goddess … anything to marry me off.'

'Your Majesty, I …'

'Hold your tongue, girl,' said Starfall. 'She's using you for sport.'

Fyia smirked as she left. 'May the Gods protect you all,' she called back over her shoulder. *For I fear you need it more than I.*

Chapter Four

FYIA WATCHED FROM THE walls as Sensis rode out of the city, heading for Moon, the others safely tucked inside their carriages. They hadn't been apart in years—not since the beginning of the war—and Fyia relied on Sensis in a way she didn't on the others. She had no choice; no one else could reform the military academy, but an ache filled Fyia's chest as her friend's form shrank into the distance.

'You know they had a point yesterday,' said the Spider, emerging from the shadows. She pushed back her hood as she stepped up beside Fyia.

'I would hope so,' said Fyia. 'Otherwise, why do I pay them such exorbitant sums?'

'You need to marry eventually,' she said, ignoring Fyia's weak attempt at deflection. 'Unless you plan to leave instability in your wake ...'

'You'd marry me off to some foreign ruler? Like a brood mare?'

'Considering the dissent you face, it would be a wise path, although marrying from within your own kingdoms has advantages also.'

'Maybe I should fuck one man from each kingdom, get myself with child, and call it a babe of all the lands …'

'That would certainly be novel,' said the Spider, with not even the barest hint of emotion.

'I will consider marriage when I deem it necessary, or—Gods forbid—when I find a man I actually desire.'

Silence settled for a beat.

'I hear Adigos will join your party when you travel north?'

Fyia spun to face the Spider. 'Are you lecturing me about my choice of travelling companions?'

'Every choice you make is analyzed and stored away for future use. Not everyone in your lands has accepted you as Queen … they will use any small thing to undermine you. Adigos' past actions already lead to questions regarding your legitimacy. If you will not send him away, I advise discretion, that is all.'

'I am a paragon of discretion, am I not?'

The Spider coughed. 'I am but your adviser, Your Majesty. Safe travels.'

Fyia's party left Selise not two turns of the clock after Sensis. It would take five days of hard riding to reach the Fae'ch Mountains, and after the first day, no one was looking forward to the next four. It had turned unseasonably cold, the wind driving rain into their faces, and it would only get worse the further north they travelled.

They pulled off the busy trade road that ran north from Selise, across the Kingdom of Plenty, and dismounted in a clearing above a stream. They quickly set up camp, throwing up their small travelling tents and starting a fire.

Fyia's wolves hunted, then two of her guards set about skinning and gutting the rabbits and putting them on spits.

Fyia, Adigos, and Edu washed in the freezing stream water, ate their fill, then sat around a fire. 'Thank the Gods it's stopped raining,' said Adigos, putting his gloves by the fire to dry. The guards had their own fire a stone's throw away, and Rouel entertained them all with his lute, his fingers flying over the strings as though they had a mind of their own.

> *There once was a Kingdom of Dragons,*
> *But the King, he fell off the wagon.*
> *He drank so much, most times in his cups,*
> *The dragons fled from the King.*

> *Five eggs they left in the kingdoms,*
> *With legend that they would return,*
> *When the Five Great Kingdoms saw peace once again,*
> *And the clocks tolled the time of the birds.*
> *And the clocks tolled the time of the birds.*

Adigos rolled his eyes as Rouel strolled over, ever the performer, working his crowd. 'Those songs should be banned,' said Adigos, throwing a stick into the flames, 'and you should stick to guarding.'

'Why?' asked Rouel, still playing the tune.

'They're bullshit, and people think they're real.'

'You don't think there were dragons?' asked Rouel.

'Of course there were dragons, but who can say if they'll ever return?'

'They will,' said Fyia, anger flaring in her veins.

'Why would they?' said Adigos.

'I can feel it,' said Fyia. She instantly wished she hadn't, hating the pitiful way Adigos looked at her.

Rouel leaned in, obviously sensing new fodder for a song. 'What do you mean, you can feel it?' he asked.

Fyia focused on the crackling embers, letting silence stretch out into the night.

Edu shooed Rouel away, then followed him. 'I'm going to bed. I'm on watch in three turns.'

'Night,' said Adigos.

'You don't believe the dragons will return?' asked Fyia, when Edu had gone.

'I didn't say that,' said Adigos. 'I don't have great faith though, given how little magic we have left.'

'I have plenty of magic.'

'You and your brother both, but is that enough?'

Fyia turned sharp eyes on him, dread clawing at her guts.

'Don't worry, he never said anything, but he seemed … I don't know … at peace maybe, when I left him with the Fae'ch. They wouldn't let him live there if he wasn't magical, and of course there's the matter of his face …'

'I won't discuss my brother.'

'I know,' he said, 'and I truly believe if anyone can bring back the dragons, it's you. I just … don't know if I believe it's possible.'

She met his gaze, and her instinct to fight melted in the face of the sincerity she found there.

She shook her head and looked back at the fire. He snagged her hand. 'You're extraordinary either way, Fyia. You've already done the impossible. You will reform our lands—of that I have no doubt—with or without the dragons. You don't need them to become a legend, you've already done enough … already have the eyes of the world upon you, songs sung about your exploits …'

She leaned back, resting her head against his shoulder. 'I want more than that.' He wrapped his cloak around her, shielding her from the cold. 'I don't care about being a legend. I care about my people. Our lands are cooling …'

'I love that about you,' he said, kissing the top of her head. 'That you care. That that's what drives you.'

She put a hand on his hard chest and snuggled into his warmth, almost purring.

'I love you, Fyia,' he murmured into her hair. 'Since I first met you.'

'Don't,' she said, bunching her hand in the fabric of his tunic, 'we're not doing that.'

'Fyia …'

She lifted her head to look at him. 'I want you in my bed, I won't deny that. I want … comfort, but I can't forget what you did.'

He closed his eyes and exhaled loudly. 'Will you ever forgive me for killing King Milo?'

'That's not what I meant …'

'Then, what?'

Her words had confused him … of course they had. 'You betrayed me long before Milo.' Fyia shook her head against the memory of his first betrayal.

'What are you talking about?' His eyes bored into hers.

'Did you know we were almost engaged?'

Adigos frowned, then shook his head slowly.

She couldn't suck in enough air, but she pressed on, needing to finally tell him. 'I convinced my parents to agree to the match. You weren't from the most advantageous family, but I sold them on your potential, and, of course, your relationship with my brother helped.'

Adigos was still as a statue, his muscles rigid under her hand, his eyes glued to hers.

'You'd said all the right things: you loved me, would only ever want me, that I was *special*.'

'All true.'

'Stop it,' she said, snatching her hand away and rearing back. 'Show me some respect.'

'I …'

'I saw you one night on the stairs, pushing a maid into an alcove.'

Adigos shook his head, an incredulous look on his face. 'I was young and foolish; sex occupied at least half of my waking thoughts. It was … only sex.'

'Of course. You would never stoop so low as to *marry* a maid.'

'Fyia …'

'I told my parents I'd changed my mind. It was another item to add to the long list of my imperfections … another reason for them to remove me from the line of succession. If I couldn't handle my personal affairs, then what hope did I have of managing a whole kingdom? People would dupe me with regularity.'

'I'm … Fyia … I'm sorry.'

'Don't be. I should thank you. You taught me not to trust the words from people's mouths. If you hadn't, I probably wouldn't be Queen.'

'My words were true. I do love you. You are special.'

'But not the whole truth.'

'I've never wanted anyone like I want you,' said Adigos, his hand cupping her face.

She hated herself, but it was nice to be touched, so she leaned in. 'And you can have me, for sex. What fraction of your waking thoughts does that occupy now?'

He let out a noise of exasperation, removed his hand, and moved as though to get up. She felt the loss of him … didn't want him to leave, so pulled him back and straddled him. She wove her hands into his hair, tugging gently so his head tipped back, forcing his eyes to meet hers. 'Do you want me?' she asked, feeling the evidence in his breeches that he did.

He closed his eyes and inhaled deeply. When he met her gaze once more, his eyes showed conviction, and he slid his hands to her behind, then squeezed. 'There's nothing in this world I want more.'

She smiled and lowered her lips to his, explosions firing in her brain at the contact, blocking out anything but the feel of him against her.

She'd been starved of this for so long ... too long, and her body rejoiced. Her lips parted, a soft moan escaping as his tongue probed into her mouth. His hand roamed across her hip, into the dip of her waist, then skirted the swell of her breast. She shivered, tipping her hips, moving against him.

'If you're going to take this any further, please spare your guards and do it somewhere more private,' said Edu, in his most disapproving tone. They broke apart and looked up at him. 'Rouel came to get me, because you are late for watch duty, Adigos.'

Fyia turned back to Adigos, kissed him one last time, then stood. Her breathing was ragged as she walked to her tent, but she kept her eyes trained forwards.

The rest of the journey to the Fae'ch mountains was hard, the wild, high country of the Starlight Kingdom cold and unforgiving, and the group was sullen and subdued.

Edu conspired against Fyia and Adigos, giving Adigos watch duties designed to keep them apart, and requesting meetings with Fyia when Adigos was free. Adigos slipped into Fyia's tent each night when his watch was over, but Fyia was always asleep, exhausted from the day's hard riding. They would sleep tangled under the furs, but every morning, Adigos would wake to find himself alone, Fyia already running with her wolves.

'I'm confident we'll make it to the entrance of the mountain today,' said Edu.

Adigos tracked Fyia as she joined the morning briefing, his chest tightening at the sight of her wild hair and rosy cheeks after her run. She didn't go far—it was too cold for that—but she needed to blow out the cobwebs each morning … she'd always been that way.

'We'll arrive before the sun goes down,' said Edu, 'but the climb into the mountains is perilous.'

The lands of the Fae'ch were a vast ridge of mountains that separated Fyia's home kingdom—the Kingdom of Starlight—from the Kingdom of the Black Hoods in the north. The going was treacherous, steep and frozen, and if the Fae'ch were in the mood for games, it would be booby trapped with magic.

'Keep your wits about you,' said Edu. 'The Fae'ch probably don't want to harm us, but they might decide to play a bit; let's not make it easy for them.'

'And my wolves will not be with us,' said Fyia, stroking their heads. 'The Fae'ch won't permit them inside; they'll wait here in the woods for our return.'

They mounted, and Adigos trailed behind Fyia as Edu had instructed … such a killjoy. He had to settle for watching Fyia's swaying back as Rouel rode beside her, subtly trying to break Fyia's silence on her and Adigos' romantic entanglement.

Edu sent Rouel warning looks, but it didn't do much to deter him. Adigos was happy for Rouel to continue; he was keen to know her thoughts on their relationship as well. If only Edu would cut him some slack, he would ask her himself, and do other things …

'Get down!' shouted a guard from the front, at the same time as a shout came from behind. Adigos' horse went up on her hind legs at the first clash of steel. She pawed at the air, then went over, throwing him to the ground. He narrowly missed being squashed, then rolled to his feet, frantically trying to avoid the stamping hooves of the other horses.

He drew his sword as he sought Fyia, glad to see a defensive circle around her. By the time he reached her, there was little for him to do; her bodyguards had dispatched the threat with brutal efficiency. Five men and three women lay dead on the ground, a single man left alive, now on his knees, a knife to his throat.

There was a reason Fyia had won five kingdoms, and this was it. She'd insisted on ceaseless training, and had put Sensis and Edu in charge of delivering it. The result was that her army was an unrivaled force, and only the best of the best made it into Fyia's personal bodyguard.

Fyia dismounted, standing in front of the man on his knees. 'What do you want?' she said, quietly.

'You, dead.' He spat at her feet.

'Why?'

'You're not our rightful ruler. You killed your parents with witchcraft. We don't want nothing to do with your kind.'

'I didn't, actually,' said Fyia. 'They're alive and well, living in the Emperor's court across the Kraken Sea. Nor did I use magic to achieve it.'

'You killed the Kings with witchcraft,' he hissed.

'For those, I did use magic, but I'm no witch.'

'You're *unnatural*.'

'Who sent you?' asked Fyia, whirling away.

'We don't take orders from no-one.'

'Accept the old Kings?' she said, leaning back against a rock.

'They ruled by right.'

Fyia nodded to the man whose knife was at the captive's throat. Red blood oozed from the wound he inflicted, and the captive fell to the ground.

'Hide the bodies. I don't care if the animals eat them, but I don't want a spectacle.'

Adigos watched every move she made, and Gods, she was magnificent. She did what was needed without hesitation or apology. She was eerily calm ... always. In control, unphased. Some called her cold, calculating, aloof, but she had to be ... anyone in her position did. When kings acted this way, they were applauded.

Adigos retrieved his horse, dismayed to find her lame. The Fae'ch could heal her, but there was no way he could ride.

'You'll have to walk,' said Edu, seeing his predicament.

Adigos' jaw dropped open. He hadn't thought Edu was angry about him and Fyia, at least, not angry enough to make him *walk*. Or was Edu just angry at himself for the near miss, needing someone to take it out on?

Fyia rolled her eyes. 'He can ride with me,' she said. She moved her mount up next to Adigos, and offered him her arm.

'You don't have a saddle,' said Adigos. Fyia raised an eyebrow, ready to turn away. 'Which is absolutely fine,' he added hastily. He grabbed her arm and swung up behind her, her stallion prancing as his weight landed. He gripped Fyia's waist.

'The climb is steep. If you fall off, don't expect sympathy from me,' said Edu. He motioned to a guard at the back of the group to lead Adigos' lame horse.

'And if you do fall, don't take her with you, or we'll be having words.'

Adigos nodded, and as soon as Edu turned away, pulled Fyia flush against him. 'I've been imagining you in my arms all day,' he murmured.

She said nothing, but leaned her head against him, then urged her stallion on.

Chapter Five

THE CLIMB WAS STEEP, but they'd selected horses for this purpose, and they handled it with ease. Fyia luxuriated in the feel of Adigos' muscled chest against her back, the flex of his arms as he held her, the press of his thighs against hers. He was concentrating hard on staying upright, so had taken only the smallest of liberties; a stroke here, a squeeze there, a brush of his lips on her nape.

Fyia was used to riding this way. She had an affinity with animals—even those not in her Cruaxee— that allowed her to sense their emotions. She gave Adigos the occasional caress, but was careful not to distract him. Aside from the possibility of him getting hurt, and pulling her off too, she didn't want to risk delay.

They reached the mouth of the tunnel into the mountains as the sun dipped towards the horizon. The approach was a vast channel carved out of the rock, each side lined with circular cogs of various sizes. A portcullis blocked the entrance, but instead of metal bars, the structure was all whirling cogs, weights, and vials of suspended liquid. The barrier rose as they neared, every part of it seeming to come alive as needle-like points lifted free from the ground, steam rising from the holes that housed them.

Fyia had never seen this place for herself. She had to force her features into a calm mask, desperately wanting to gawk at everything.

A stooping man stepped under the portcullis, bowing low as he stopped before Fyia's horse. 'Welcome, Your Majesty.'

'Thank you,' said Fyia. She swung her leg over the front and slid to the ground, then took the man's hand in both of hers. 'What is your name?'

He looked into her eyes for a beat, seeming to search her soul. 'I have many names.'

She smiled. Of course he did. 'What should we call you?'

'Your errand boy, I suppose.'

'Is that what you would like us to call you?'

'I'd like for you to leave this place and never return, but what I would like doesn't matter, so why bother asking?'

With that, he turned and walked back under the gate, beckoning for them to follow. 'Your guards and horses will be taken care of here,' said the old man, pointing to the right, where three Fae'ch awaited them.

Edu nodded to the guards, who peeled off, only Adigos, Edu, and Fyia entering the mountain proper through a gaping black hole in the rock. By the time Fyia realized Rouel had tagged along—the only guard cocky enough to try his luck—they were all too preoccupied to send him back.

Fyia's skin bristled, her senses telling her both to run, and that she'd been nowhere safer. All around them, thick forest appeared. The sound of running water filled the air, and birdsong, and laughter. Fairies flitted across the path ahead, their wings lit as though they were fireflies, sprinkling dust behind them as they flew.

'Are you seeing this?' Fyia whispered to Rouel.

'If by *this* you mean an enchanted forest and literal fucking fairies, then yes.'

Okay, good.

'Was it like this last time?' she asked Adigos, who'd come up close behind her.

'No. It was nothing but a stone tunnel when I was here before.'

'So this is an illusion?' Fyia asked.

'What is an illusion anyway?' said the old man. 'I can touch, and smell, and taste this forest. If I eat the berries, they will kill me. Is that not real enough for you?'

'I …' Fyia couldn't think of words to respond, then remembered she didn't answer to this man.

They approached a large weeping willow that bowed over the edge of a lake, a small boat peeking out from under it.

'The lake was here before,' said Adigos. 'It's full of magical creatures. One nearly pulled me under when I got too close.'

'Gods,' said Rouel, stepping away from the edge.

They all eyed the water nervously as a sea of swirling lights came to life beneath the surface.

'What is that?' said Fyia, awed by the spectacle.

'The children of the lake,' said the old man. 'Seems as though they like you. Come, we should not keep Axus waiting.'

'Axus, not Isa?' said Fyia.

The old man laughed. 'Isa does not deign to speak with the likes of you.'

Fyia's blood burned hot, but she heard the Spider in her ear saying, *play the game.* She gave a curt nod and followed the man, wondering what would happen if she pushed him into the lake. The surface of the water rippled sharply, suddenly punctured by … well … what punctured it, Fyia couldn't really say, but water droplets showered them.

'Gods,' said the old man, 'they haven't done that in … since … well, I … come along.'

The forest fell away as they continued. They stepped out onto a rope bridge suspended across a chasm, which wobbled and groaned dangerously as they crossed.

'This here last time?' asked Fyia.

'No,' said Adigos, 'although I'm not sure I came down this tunnel.'

Fyia wondered how many tunnels the mountain hid in its depths, where they all led, how many secret doors let Fae'ch or Black Hood spies into her kingdom …

They left the bridge behind and walked through an archway to where a series of large stones lay in an almost circular pattern on the floor. Smaller stones sat within the crooked circle, most with a shiny pebble on top, the pebbles a seemingly random array or colors. Lines of metal wire connected everything together, and Fyia moved towards the structure, her mind trying to make sense of it, but nothing seemed to fit.

'What is this?' she asked, admitting defeat.

The old man gave her an indecipherable look. 'This way,' he said, then led them through another arch. They found themselves in a chamber with a domed roof full of stars, mats laid out on the floor beneath.

'Sit,' said the old man. He disappeared behind a wide pillar of stone, a younger man appearing from its other side the same moment.

'Welcome, Fyia Orlightus. Fire-touched, magic-touched, Cruaxee, and Queen of the Five Eastern

Kingdoms,' he said, with a half bow. 'You honor us with your visit.'

To the Fae'ch, her magical abilities were of far greater import than anything she'd done to make herself Queen.

'Thank you,' she said, inclining her head. 'Axus, I assume?'

'Correct.'

'Isa's consort?' she said, probing for conformation of the rumor. The man was tall but reedy, with sandy colored hair, brown eyes, and pointed ears that marked him as fae.

The Fae'ch counted a plethora of magical creatures among their members, from the tiny, mean-spirited fairies, who traded magic dust for ear bones, to the regal winged fae, whose magic was largely unknown, to pixies and sprites and witches and dryads, and every other kind of magical being, who between them boasted all manner of magical faculties.

When the Five Kingdoms had outlawed magic, the magical had fled here, the only place they could find to call home … the only place they could make into a fortress and defend.

Some of the magic-folk had tried to fight back, but magic had weakened after the dragons disappeared, and their power hadn't been enough.

Axus appraised her for a long while. 'Isa's deputy … among other things,' he said. His lips twitched into a smile. 'Sit, please.'

Axus and Fyia sat facing each other over an empty fire pit, which roared to life as soon as they settled on the ground. Edu, Adigos, and Rouel sat behind Fyia on the second row of mats.

Axus looked expectant, waiting for her to begin. Unlike most courts, the Fae'ch dispensed with pleasantries. No one would enquire about their journey, nor offer refreshments, unless they asked for them. No one would show them to their sleeping quarters, indeed, sleeping quarters would not be prepared until they requested them.

'You know why I am here?' Fyia asked, looking Axus in the eye and refusing to look away, holding his gaze in a way that many would find uncomfortable. Axus didn't seem to notice, his fluctuating eye color the only reaction she could discern, and she had no way to decipher what that meant.

'You seek the dragon egg,' he said, tilting his head to the side, but still not looking away.

'I do,' she confirmed. 'Will you show it to me?'

'No, but I can assure you, it has not hatched.' His voice was suddenly ethereal, and Fyia became uneasy, the hairs on her arms standing on end.

'You've seen it yourself?' she asked, forcing her disquiet away.

'No one may enter the chamber, but we would know if it had hatched.'

'How?'

'Magic.'

Fyia paused a beat, reeling the conversation back in before it ran away from her. 'Magic is tricksy, and can be fooled.'

'You question Isa's power?' said Axus, his tone sharp.

'Of course not … but, has she seen the egg since I united the Five Kingdoms?'

'No one may enter the chamber, even Isa.'

'You're lying,' said Fyia, knowing it to the very core of her being. Something in the magic she kept tramped down within her sensed his deception.

He laughed. 'Your skills are quite good, considering your lack of training.'

'I wanted nothing more than to be trained as a child. Alas, my family does not appreciate magic the way I do.'

'I am aware.'

'I'm not leaving the mountain until I see the dragon egg.' The words were harsher than she'd intended, but discussion of Fyia's magic irked her—magic she so desperately wanted to use, but did not know how. That the fae before her knew more about her own skills than she did ... she put the thoughts from her mind; she wasn't here to discuss magic.

'Will you conquer our lands if we refuse?' said Axus. 'The way you took everyone else's?'

'I only took from those who refused to work with me.'

'And if we refuse to work with you?'

'The Fae'ch do not oppress their own people, at least, from the little I know of you.'

'No. Your people are the specialists there.' His tone was bitter. The fae lived to a great age ... maybe Axus had experienced the violence of the Kings firsthand.

'Not *my* people,' said Fyia. 'I welcome magic in my lands. I wish to bring it back into the open.'

'But there are those who wish to overthrow you, who do not believe you rule by right, who hate magic, who are fearful.'

'Which is why I must see the dragon egg,' said Fyia. 'With a dragon, I can improve things for everyone. Those with magic are already free to live anywhere in my kingdoms, and with a dragon, I can protect them ... protect everyone who needs it.'

Axus let silence fall. It stretched until the men behind Fyia twitched with discomfort, but she wouldn't give Axus the satisfaction of watching her fidget ... she would sit here all night, still as a statue, if that's what it took.

'I'll make you a deal,' said Axus, his lips twitching once more. 'We will throw a party in your honor. If you are still awake and in attendance at dawn, I will show you the egg.'

Fyia knew the deal to be fraught with danger. The Fae'ch had countless ways to put her to sleep: by drugging her food or wine, using the smoke from burning herbs, casting spells, putting her under a thrall. Most of it she could probably resist, and her own magic would help keep her safe, but she would have to avoid … well … everything.

'Deal,' she said.

A predatory smile crept across Axus' face. 'Good. The bells will lead the way.'

Fyia nodded. 'Then I wish to rest before the party begins.'

Tinkling bells tolled through the bedroom Fyia had requested, waking her from a deep sleep. She had washed and eaten, then slept, needing all the respite she could get after the long journey if she were to stand any chance of staying awake until dawn.

The tinkling became insistent, and Fyia stood. She pulled on a clean tunic and close-fitting pants, the only kind of clothes she'd packed for the journey. She dragged a brush through her hair, tied it in a knot at the base of her skull, then headed out.

The living room was empty, doors to Adigos and Edu's sleeping chambers wide open, no sign of them anywhere … the Fae'ch tricks had apparently started already.

She left their quarters and followed the bells through twisting passages lit by sparkling fairy lights and scented with jasmine. After many twists and turns, the bells stopped abruptly in front of a seemingly innocuous part of the wall, in a tall bit of tunnel. Fyia looked around, trying to work out what she should do next, when steam rose from the floor by her feet. She jumped back as a section of solid rock slid to the side, only the smallest of scraping noises accompanying the movement.

Fyia stared at the vast stone cavern now before her, filled with dancing Fae'ch, banquet tables, and musicians. She couldn't hear the music, nor see any food, and the space was brightly lit, the attendants wearing ordinary clothes like hers.

The hole she looked through was halfway up the wall, with a good view of everything below, a platform and stairs leading down to the party only a step away.

She let her eyes roam across the strange scene, taking in the cogs set into the walls at seemingly random intervals, and the particularly large dragon clock perched above a set of ornate doors at the far end of the hall.

As she watched, the doors swung open, and three figures clad in black cloaks entered, their hoods up. Black Hoods? Fyia gasped and stepped forward, determined to find out what they were doing here, but, as she crossed the threshold, everything changed.

A ripple of magic flowed across Fyia's skin, and the stone wall snapped closed behind her. Suddenly, everyone wore black cloaks, with their hoods up so she couldn't see anyone's face. The room had gone dark, lit only by flickering candlelight, enchanting music floating up to where she stood. Her clothes under her cloak were little more than scraps of cloth hiding her most intimate parts, her feet bare. Her hand went to her hair, feeling elaborate braids pinned up on her head.

The hall had transformed into an enchanted forest, filled with lush greens and delicate white and pink flowers. A blanket of mossy grass covered the floor, gnarled and twisted trees here and there, revelers chasing each other around them, or canoodling in their wide branches. Butterflies and fireflies flitted about, along with fairies sprinkling dust on those below.

Fyia moved tentatively down the steps, scanning for the group of Black Hoods, trying to remember details that might help her single them out. They'd been tall, and purposeful, and moving as a pack, but it was useless; the light was too dim to make out any details, and everyone looked the same.

Fyia descended the remaining stairs, dizzy on magic, the smell of frankincense filling her nose. She wanted to dance, sing, laugh … but she couldn't wear herself out so early in the evening. The magic would keep her high for a while, and then her body would tire from the onslaught and crash. She should find a secluded vantage point and watch … conserve her energy.

She headed for the nearest tree, only a handful of paces away, when a tall fae man approached, offering her a goblet of wine. 'Your Majesty,' he said, in a rich, deep voice that made her shiver.

'No, thank you,' she replied. He nodded and stepped away.

She'd barely made it a pace further when a second figure approached. 'Your Majesty,' said a high-pitched female voice, 'please accept a honeyed fig … my gift to you.'

Fyia shook her head. 'I thank you for the gift, but I am not hungry.'

'Not for food, at least,' said the woman, in a singsong voice. 'Smart of you to eat before the party.' She clicked her fingers and disappeared.

After three further attempts to lure her, Fyia finally made it to the tree and leaned back against the trunk. Feet appeared in her eyeline. She looked up just in time to see a man jump down and land lithely. He claimed the remaining section of trunk, nudging her over a little to make room for his wide shoulders. By the time he'd made himself sufficiently comfortable, the whole side of his body pressed against hers.

She turned her head to look at him, finding his eyes already seeking hers. They were brown, and deep, and clever. His head was shaved, or at least, it looked that way from what she could see, her fingers itching to reach out and touch it. She clenched her fingers into fists, fighting the sensation—probably a side effect of all the magic, or maybe the Fae'ch were purposefully scrambling her emotions.

He reached down and took her hand, her breath catching at the unexpected contact. 'We should dance,' he said, in an unfamiliar accent, then tugged her away from the tree, towards an open area where others frolicked to the music.

She opened her mouth to protest, telling her limbs not to comply, but her feet seemed to move of their own accord … and it was a party after all.

The man slid a hand to the small of her back, and she placed her free hand on his shoulder, then looked up into his eyes. His features were mischievous as he whirled them across the moss-covered ground, bits of plant sliding between Fyia's toes. His sure movements convinced her to trust him, so she didn't fight his lead … she even let herself enjoy it.

They danced at a furious pace for … she had no idea how long, but when the music mellowed, and he slowed them, she was breathless, a beaming smile across her face.

'You're not what I expected,' he said, with an enticing smile.

She cocked an eyebrow. Of course he knew who she was; everyone in this room probably did. Maybe she was the only one who saw the cloaks. Maybe everyone else was watching her dance in the clothes she'd donned in her room. The man spun her under his arm, and she laughed.

'Who are you?' she asked.

He only smiled and spun her again.

'You know who I am, so it's only fair.'

He pulled her close. 'My name does not matter.'

'You're Fae'ch?'

'No.'

She faltered. 'You're a Black Hood?'

He looked away. 'Why would you assume that?'

'You are,' she said, the thrill of it overwhelming her senses, excitement stealing her breath. 'I have so many questions.'

The music slowed further, and he pulled her flush against him. 'What do you want to know?' he asked quietly, his lips beside her ear.

She closed her eyes, giddy, almost drunk … all the things he could tell her. If only she could clear her mind … think. Her thoughts zeroed in on the feel of his breath on her skin, his smell … what was that amazing scent? It was like …

'Fyia?' The word was a low growl, and when she met his gaze, his eyes were smokey.

They stopped dancing. 'Do you have a dragon egg?' she said, her voice barely more than a whisper.

An almost severe intensity entered his gaze. 'Do you?' he said.

'I asked you first.'

He put a hand on her cheek, then pressed his forehead to hers. She sensed the wild … frozen lands,

77

towering trees, the scent of pine, the sound of running water close by. It was tranquil, but brutal, a harsh place where only the strong could survive.

A strange sensation pinged against her mind, and she panicked, pulling away sharply, breaking the contact. 'What did you do?' she asked, hating the edge of hysteria in her tone.

She didn't know who this man was … What was he doing? What was *she* doing? Why had she let him get so close? Her wolves howled, and nearby eagles cried in her mind.

The man winced. 'Gods,' he said, staggering back a pace.

A figure dancing next to them turned, catching his arm. 'Cal?' said a woman's voice. 'Cal, are you okay?'

'I'm fine,' he said, pushing the woman away. 'We should go.'

'Wait,' said Fyia. She grabbed the man—Cal—by the arm, but when their skin made contact, an animal's roar filled her mind, so loud, so angry, she released him. She grasped her head with her hands, and eventually it ebbed, but when she looked up, Cal and the woman were gone. *Gods damn it.* Her one chance to speak with a Black Hood, and it was over before it began, and … what had he done to her?

This was why the Kings had outlawed magic from the Five Kingdoms. Why they'd taken such drastic action to rid their lands of the magical. Cal had successfully reminded her magic was dangerous; those who had no power of their own at the mercy of the magical.

Fyia had magic, and still she'd been vulnerable, with no education other than what she'd been able to teach herself. And what she'd taught herself was how to suppress her magic, so it didn't break free and cause mischief, or hurt someone.

There seemed to be no lasting effects, but still, she'd been stupid; she'd let him get close enough to harm her, when she didn't even know who he was. She'd trusted him, had let him press his forehead to hers ... but then, maybe he'd used magic to achieve that too.

Fyia spent the rest of the party hiding in a tree. Not the most noble approach, but one that was sure to result in a favorable outcome. It also provided a good vantage point, not that anything of note happened, only Fae'ch revelry that became increasingly amorous as the night went on.

Fyia ran over the encounter with the Black Hood again and again. What had he done to her? Why had she heard her Cruaxee? Why had she heard a strange animal roar in her mind?

She would tell Edu what happened, and he would give her *that* look ... he would be insufferable. She knew she'd been stupid, but the Black Hood had been so compelling, so intriguing, so very much in possession of bottomless brown eyes ... he'd taken control, despite knowing who she was ... a welcome change, a relief even.

By morning, Fyia was irritable. She breathed a long sigh of relief when the illusion shattered, the hall returning to a cavernous stone space, music ceasing, food disappearing, her own clothes returning.

The magic floated her to the floor, where she landed on her feet. Most of the Fae'ch disappeared in a puff, leaving only a few slumbering revelers, including Edu and Rouel, who were asleep under a table.

Adigos strode towards where she stood, worry written in every movement. He grasped her arms and looked her over. 'Are you alright?' he said, running his hands this way and that, checking for any sign of injury.

'I'm fine,' she said, batting him away, 'and glad to say, awake. I'm impressed you lasted the night.'

'Hey,' he said, pulling her into a rough embrace, wrapping an arm around her head, 'I spent the night searching for you, and fending off a never-ending stream of extremely enticing Fae'ch.'

'You didn't sample any delights at all?'

'I learnt my lesson last time. It all seems wondrous on the surface, but underneath, they're monsters ... and anyway, I only have eyes for one woman,' he said, looking down at her.

She lifted her hands to his waist and met his hopeful eyes. 'I told you, Adigos, whatever happens between us can only be physical. You can fuck whoever you please.'

'I know,' he said, stroking her hair, 'because you don't think you can trust me ... but I'm going to win back your trust.'

She shook her head in exasperation, and he took hold of her face. 'You'll see,' he whispered. He ran his hands down her arms, stepping back as footsteps approached.

'Edu,' said Fyia. 'Fun night?'

Edu's cheeks flushed. 'I'm sorry ... I couldn't find you.'

Fyia waved a hand. 'We'll assume they hid me with magic.'

Fyia filled them in about the Black Hoods, and Edu's look of admonishment was moderate compared to what she'd been expecting. Probably embarrassed he'd been unable to find her ...

'I wonder why they were here,' said Edu.

'Maybe they come a lot,' said Adigos. 'Or maybe for a trade meeting, or simply because they were passing by ...'

'Or they got wind of us being here, and came to see Fyia in the flesh,' suggested Edu.

'I trust you had an enjoyable night?' said Axus, his footsteps so silent they hadn't heard his approach.

Fyia nodded in a non-committal way. 'We'd love breakfast, if that's on offer?' she said.

'Ah, yes,' said Axus, with knowing eyes, 'you must be hungry. Right this way.'

Axus led them through a door under a big metal cog, into a small ante-chamber packed with tables full of Fae'ch noisily gossiping over breakfast. The room went silent as they entered, the hairs on the back of Fyia's neck standing on end. Axus led them to a table towards the back, a lone figure already seated there.

The figure turned and stood, his eyes meeting Fyia's. She hesitated for only a split tick before rushing forward, throwing her arms wide. 'Veau! Brother! It's so good to see you.'

'It's good to see you too,' he said, pulling back to bow, 'Your Majesty.'

He looked well, his usually thin frame having filled out a little, the river of golden scales across his face seeming to shimmer, giving him a luster he'd never had before. His light hair was glossy, his grey eyes shone, and he looked happier than she'd ever seen him.

He stiffened as he lifted his gaze to the others. 'Adigos, Edu.' He clasped each of their forearms, then nodded to Rouel. 'I hear you are partly to thank for my sister's victory.'

'Well, maybe not Adigos,' said Edu, with a wink.

'It was all Sensis,' countered Adigos.

'I won't argue with you there,' said Edu. 'That woman is a marvel.'

Veau waved his hand, indicating they should sit, and a mouthwatering array of bizarrely mismatched dishes materialized: deviled eggs, honeyed cardamon swirls, rose water rice pudding, cheese on toast with anchovies, and a whole host of other random yet tempting delights. 'Please, eat.'

Surprisingly, Axus left them, and the room's other occupants returned to their own affairs, only the odd surreptitious eye flicking their way.

Fyia pulled the small metal ball from the inner pocket of her tunic and pressed it into her brother's hand under the table. 'Essa wanted me to give you this,' she said, leaning in so no one else could hear. 'I don't know what it is, but I'm guessing you do?'

Veau nodded, squeezing her hand, the ball already gone. 'Thank you,' he said. 'Now, tell me why you're here. You've got five kingdoms to run, with goodness knows how many people plotting to kill you …'

'You know why I'm here.'

'The return of the dragons is a myth,' said Veau, 'nothing more.'

'How can you think that?' she said, rearing back from her brother.

'Do you think every fairy tale is true?' he asked. 'Will the sea serpents return to wreck the ships of the damned, and the rivers turn to flame? Will the sky turn grey when the clocks turn black, and the fish throw themselves on the land? Will the north turn green as the ash rains down, when the dragons cast their shadows?'

'Maybe not all of it …' said Fyia, defensively. 'Not every song verse speaks the truth.'

Rouel coughed.

'Then why are you so certain the dragons will return?' said Veau, his features set in a smug arrangement designed to enrage her.

'Because I can feel them,' she hissed. Her brother was the only being capable of bringing out her inner child with quite such aplomb.

'What do you mean?' he said, his features losing their teasing edge.

Fyia knew Veau was open to most things, including the return of the dragons. He was pushing her buttons on purpose, because that's what brothers did, and she was reacting like a dream because she was tired and cranky, and preoccupied by thoughts of men with shaved heads.

But Veau had always fixated on her magic, magic that, like his, no one in their old lives had understood. If she could feel the dragons, her magic was surely at play, and that had piqued his interest.

'When I sleep, I feel their scales under my fingers. Sometimes they're angry, and I have to flee their fire, sometimes sad, seeking comfort. They don't feel like normal dreams.'

'It never happens when you're awake?'

'Sometimes, when I daydream.'

'Is it like with your Cruaxee?'

'No. I can control my Cruaxee. I can't control the dragons. The one time I tried, they nearly roasted me alive.'

'In your dream.'

'Yes, but it's visceral.' She dropped her voice, so only Veau could hear. 'I once woke after getting too close to the flames in my dream to find my skin red and blistered.'

'I've heard of dream walking,' said Veau, 'but never like that … never in a way that could hurt.'

Fyia shrugged and reached for a cardamon swirl. 'Maybe seeing the dragon egg will help.'

'They're going to show you?'

'Axus said they would if I could stay awake through last night's party.'

Veau stared at her a moment, then grabbed a swirl of his own.

They ate, Fyia mostly silent as Adigos quizzed Veau about his life with the Fae'ch. Veau was tight-lipped, saying only that he was learning a lot, his magic had calmed, and he was glad he'd found his true place in the world.

Fyia was dying to ask him about Essa, about what was still between them. What could be, now Veau lived here? But she knew he wouldn't tell her. Even before he'd renounced his title and come to live with the Fae'ch, Veau's relationship with Essa had been off limits.

They finished breakfast, and Axus came to collect them. 'The dragon egg awaits, Your Majesty,' said Axus.

Fyia sent him a flat look, trying to determine if he used her title out of respect, or if he was mocking her. Axus returned it with a smile that had Adigos stepping protectively to her side. Veau cocked an eyebrow, and Fyia avoided his gaze, following Axus through a small door into a dimly lit tunnel.

'What was that about?' Veau asked, holding Fyia's arm to slow her, so they fell a few paces behind the others.

'It's none of your business.'

'Are you and Adigos … after everything?'

'No.'

'Then why did he do that?'

'Because he's an idiot.'

'Fyia …'

She rounded on him. 'Don't lecture me, unless you want to talk about Essa … What, in all the Seven Hells, is going on between you two?'

Veau shut down. He shook his head, then followed the others. She would never understand her brother, or the special kind of torture he and Essa put themselves through.

Axus led them along a labyrinth of passages, winding this way and that through the mountain. They descended and descended, the air becoming colder, damper, and Fyia shivered as a thick layer of magic coated the air.

'Can you feel that?' Fyia asked Veau.

He nodded, flicking wary eyes to Axus, and Fyia said no more, wondering about the dynamic between the two.

They eventually reached a stone door, which Axus unlocked using his magic, placing a hand on the stone. He heaved it open, putting all his weight into pulling it towards him, and as soon as it cracked, ancient air rushed out, ruffling their hair.

'What was that?' asked Edu, stepping towards Fyia.

'That magic has been trapped inside for a long time,' said Axus. 'It wanted to escape.'

'Where will it go?' asked Adigos.

'Wherever it wants,' said Axus, stepping through the doorway.

They followed, and it surprised Fyia to find a maze of metal runners adorned the walls. A metal ball—presumably from the dragon clock above—slid down a section of runner, then disappeared into a trough of water against the wall. A raised circular pool full of shimmering amethyst-colored liquid stood in the middle of the room.

'What's that?' Fyia asked. She turned toward Axus, who was playing with dials and levers set into the wall next to the door.

He ignored her, and a deep rumbling filled the air. Edu and Adigos closed ranks around Fyia, looking for the threat. Veau walked towards the purple liquid. 'I wouldn't get too close,' said Axus, and Veau stopped in his tracks.

The rumbling became louder, rising through the ground beneath their feet. The noise was almost unbearable, and then three metal runners slid out of the pool, up into the air. They kept rising, lifting a copper platform through the liquid. It stopped just above the surface, then everything went silent.

Axus walked urgently to the platform, running a hand over the metal.

'What's wrong?' said Fyia, stepping up beside him. 'Where's the dragon egg?'

'The egg should be here,' he mumbled, 'on top of the platform. It's … gone.'

Roaring filled Fyia's ears. 'Has it hatched?' she asked, but Axus didn't seem to hear her. He was casting about wildly, as though the egg might have fallen to the floor.

'Could it still be down there?' asked Adigos. 'Maybe it came off the platform on the way up?'

Axus shook his head, then closed his eyes. A woman appeared, as though stepping through his body, wisps of white smoke obscuring her as she walked towards the platform.

Veau and Axus dropped to one knee, their heads bowed, eyes on the floor. Only one person could elicit that response.

'Isa,' said Fyia, unable to hide the awe in her voice. She was ancient … as old as the hills, if the legends could be believed, and powerful.

Isa ran her hand over the platform, standing still for several moments before turning to face the others. 'The magic is still intact,' she said. Her tone was wraithlike, seeming to be in the room, but also far away. 'I do not know how …'

'When was the egg last seen?' asked Fyia.

'No one has been in this room in more than a hundred years,' said Isa. The smoke cleared long enough for Fyia to make out her short stature, long auburn hair and pointed ears.

'Was the egg here then?' asked Fyia. Frustration crept into her tone; she was in no mood for Fae'ch word games.

'I do not know,' said Isa.

'When was it last *seen*?' Fyia asked again.

'No eggs have been seen for hundreds of years,' said Isa. 'It is time for you to leave.'

'Why?' said Fyia. 'We need to work out what happened to the egg … where it could be … if it's hatched …'

'Leave,' said Isa. She waved her hands slowly in front of her, palms up, fingers splayed.

Everything went dark, and when the world righted itself, Fyia, Adigos, Edu, and Rouel stood by the strange, closed portcullis, outside the mountain, surrounded by the belongings they'd taken inside. Fyia's guards gathered around them, giving them strange looks.

'They kicked us out,' said Edu, eyeing the height of the sun in the sky. 'Prepare the horses; it's time to go.'

The group was ready to leave in less than a quarter turn of the clock. The Fae'ch had healed Adigos' horse, and they rode as hard as they dared down the steep mountain path. They hoped to be out of Fae'ch lands by nightfall, and it was already past midday.

Fyia regretted not saying goodbye to her brother, and wished they'd had more time together. She dearly wanted to know about his new life: what he'd learned, if he'd made friends, all the wondrous things he'd surely seen during his time in the mountain. It was rumored many of the legendary sorcerers and fairies of old— those blessed with long life, anyway—called the mountain home.

They made it to the bottom of the mountain before nightfall, choosing a spot set back from the road as their camp for the night. Fyia's wolves slinked out of the woods, rubbing their heads against her legs, looking up at her with begging eyes. She scratched each of them behind the ear, and a missing part of her slotted back into place.

'The guards heard whispers of evil in the west,' said Edu quietly, coming up beside Fyia. 'There are rumors of a fight between the Emperor, and a group who have taken possession of his northern lands.'

'Do you think it's the Black Hoods?' said Fyia.

'I can't imagine why they would pick a fight with the Emperor, but it's possible,' said Edu.

'Maybe that's why they were at the mountain,' said Fyia, 'trying to secure an alliance with the Fae'ch …?'

'It doesn't seem likely. The Black Hoods have never tried to expand their territory before …'

'There's a first time for everything,' said Fyia. 'Maybe the Spider will know more.'

They ate, then sat around the campfire, Adigos fighting the wolves for space by Fyia's side. She eventually told them to move, and leaned into Adigos' warmth as he wrapped an arm around her shoulders, her Cruaxee lying at her feet. Fyia ignored Edu's stern

features, letting herself enjoy the comfort of Adigos'
firm muscles, and the way his whole being focused on
her. If Edu preferred to abstain, that was his choice, but
she saw no good reason to punish herself.

Rouel, who'd been subdued since Isa had expelled
them from the mountain, played a mournful song.
Somehow the sad tune seemed appropriate to Fyia too.

The King gave his blood,
Every drop he could spare.
It wasn't enough,
The clocks needed more.
The King couldn't do it,
But no one could help.
He drowned in a bottle,
The dragons, they fled.

Oh, dragons of Asred,
No longer fly through the air.
Oh, dragons of Asred,
Fled in the depths of despair.

They cast out the magic,
Every last trace.
They killed off the mages
And fairies and Fae'ch.
They outlawed the magic
And people with power.
Then sent dragon treasure
To five separate towers.

Oh, dragons of Asred,
No longer fly through the air.
Oh, dragons of Asred,
Fled in the depths of despair.

Adigos stroked Fyia's arm as Rouel sang, and she leaned further into his embrace. She closed her eyes, and Adigos, the music, and the crackling fire lulled her to sleep. As she approached the delicious cusp of oblivion, the image of a bear entered her mind, running through a frozen forest. Fyia instinctively uncoiled her Cruaxee bond, reaching for the bear, and it crashed to a halt, turned to face her, then roared at her mind. Fyia dropped the bond and lurched awake, a blinding pain shooting through her skull.

'What is it?' said Adigos, shifting so he could see her face.

Fyia sat up straight, desperately pressing at her temples. It was the same sound she'd heard when the Black Hood had touched his forehead to hers. Why had she reached out to the animal? Bears weren't a part of her Cruaxee … she'd tested them before … but it had felt right, normal, natural to do so.

The bear had rejected her, exactly as it should have. Had the Black Hood's magic warped her senses?

'Everything okay?' asked Edu.

'I'm fine,' said Fyia, then told them what had happened.

'You think the Black Hood did something to your magic?' said Edu.

'Maybe,' said Fyia. She reached for the bonds with her wolves, then searched for a nearby eagle. They responded as normal, much to her relief. 'My Cruaxee bonds seem fine. Maybe I'm just tired …' She got to her feet.

'Don't even think it,' said Edu, as Adigos made to follow. 'You're on watch.'

Adigos gave him an incredulous look. 'I need to stay with her.'

'I can stay with her,' said Rouel. 'I don't have watch duties until later.'

'*Warrior's balls!*' Adigos rounded on Edu. 'Why are you so determined to keep me away from her?'

'She only wants you for your body, and she doesn't look in any state to do much with that tonight,' said Edu.

Fyia considered intervening, but it would be better for them to blow off the steam, and she was interested to see how it would pan out.

Adigos grabbed the front of Edu's tunic.

'Bad idea,' Rouel whispered to Fyia.

'Oh, Brother,' said Fyia, on an exhale.

Anyone watching would assume Adigos had the upper hand. He was an inch taller, and carried far more muscle than Edu, but Edu was in charge of Fyia's personal protection for a reason.

Edu batted Adigos' hands away with barely a blink, then connected his palm with the center of Adigos' chest. It looked like nothing, but Adigos staggered back a pace.

'I don't want to fight you,' said Edu, watching Adigos intently.

'Then take it back.'

'My words were true; I cannot take them back,' said Edu, with a shrug.

Adigos growled, and Edu's eyebrow shot up. 'She doesn't trust you,' Edu continued. 'You need to come to terms with your position in her court.'

'You don't speak for her.'

'I'm repeating the words of my Queen, nothing more.'

Adigos balled his fists and took a step forward. Rouel sucked in a breath. Edu moved with lightning speed, punching Adigos in the chest hard enough to floor him.

'Usually, you would have seen that coming,' said Edu, as Adigos gasped for breath. 'You're letting your emotions get the better of you.'

'You're wrong!' Adigos spluttered, rolling to his side, still struggling to breathe. He swung his head towards Fyia. 'You can trust me, Fyia …'

'Edu, no!' Fyia and Rouel shouted together, and Edu's fist halted a hair's breadth from Adigos' face.

Instead, he gripped the front of Adigos' tunic and hauled his torso half a foot into the air. 'What is wrong with you?' said Edu, his voice dripping with disdain. 'You're a warrior; start acting like one.' Edu dropped Adigos back to the ground, then stalked away.

Part of Fyia wanted to go to Adigos and comfort him, the part of her that was the girl who'd loved him. But now she was his Queen, and Edu was right, it served no one for Adigos to forget his place.

Chapter Six

ADIGOS DIDN'T TRY TO join Fyia in her tent, so her wolves kept her warm while Rouel stood guard outside. She woke at sunrise, and found the camp already a hive of activity, preparing for another grueling day's travel back towards Selise.

Adigos was quiet, his ego bruised and battered from Edu's convincing victory. Fyia brushed a hand across his shoulder, squeezing gently before accepting a plate of eggs from a guard. She dropped down next to Adigos, but left a deliberate space between them.

'Anything to report from last night?' Fyia asked.

'No,' he said, looking away.

Fyia's wolves started to whine, sending an uneasy feeling through the bond. Fyia threw her eggs to the ground and jumped to her feet. 'Edu! We're under attack!' she screamed. She used her wolves' superior senses to pick up the strange humming sound that had alarmed them. 'It sounds like ... like it's coming from the sky ...'

The wolves snarled and circled, angry, but not understanding the threat. Fyia felt the same way ...

Archers. Projectiles. They needed things to fend off an assault from the sky.

'Get the bows!' she called, then reached out with her magic, scanning for eagles, praying some were in range. The Fae'ch mountains were teaming with eagles, and she prayed to the Mother some had roamed this way. She kept scanning as they got their first glimpse of the enemy, and Fyia struggled to make sense of what she saw.

She'd never seen anything like it … a flying boat? But the sails had been stitched together to form an enormous pocket that floated above the main structure. The hull and sail were attached together with ropes, the deck full of people scanning the ground, presumably looking for her. Essa had said the Emperor had flying machines, but Fyia hadn't imagined anything so big.

Fyia finally found an eagle, then two more, and instructed them to fly for the airboat. She told the eagles to attack the occupants, but leave the machine intact. They reacted immediately, but it would be several long spins of the hand before they arrived.

Edu sent archers forward, towards the threat, so they could both attack sooner, and not give away the main group's position. Edu gave the signal, and the archers fired. Their opening volley was lethal, every arrow finding its mark, their targets either falling from the boat or slumping back onto its deck.

The archers got three volleys off before retaliation came. Holes appeared in the boat's side, and then cannons poked through. *By the Warrior* … The attackers fired, and a terrible boom filled the air, Fyia's wolves howling at the sound.

There was no way of knowing if any of her guards had been hit, but her archers still fired, now from every angle, including behind. A pang of pride swelled in

94

Fyia's chest. Her soldiers were well trained; no one could argue with that.

Fyia urged the eagles to fly faster, and she felt them closing in, moving at breakneck speed. The boat fired another round from their cannons, the boom different this time, followed by a series of *thunks* as projectiles peppered the ground. From what Fyia could see, they looked like stones …

'Run!' shouted Edu. 'You should already be moving. Adigos …' But before he could complete his order, shadow wings appeared on the ground.

Fyia's face split into a smile as the eagles swooped down and clasped Edu and Adigos in their giant talons. The third eagle distracted the attackers, giving the others a fighting chance of making it to the boat unscathed.

Fyia knew she should run, but she couldn't tear her eyes from the fight. The eagles flew high and wide, making it to the boat. The cannons couldn't point upwards … evidently the vessel's designer hadn't anticipated an attack from above.

Adigos and Edu dropped to the deck, their weapons drawn and ready. The eagles grabbed two enemy soldiers and threw them to the ground, as Adigos and Edu slashed their way through their opponents.

The third eagle wheeled away, diving towards the ground. It picked up one of Fyia's guards and flew her to the boat, the other eagles following suit, adding two more to the fray.

Fyia's archers slowed their volleys, not wanting to hit one of their own, but it didn't take long for the fighting to die down.

Fyia breathed a sigh of relief when Adigos waved over the side to confirm their victory, and the boat began a slow descent. Fyia released the eagles, sending them thanks through the bond. She pushed aside the emptiness that filled her as she watched them go.

Fyia tracked the boat as it descended, Rouel by her side. Adigos had shouted they were looking for an open spot to land. They'd taken the crew hostage, including the pilot.

'Urgh,' said Rouel, shaking his hands as though to rid them of something nasty.

'What is it?' said Fyia, although, given his expression, she wasn't overly concerned. 'The attack?'

He shook his head. 'I know Edu's the best we have, but every time, my heart stops beating.'

Fyia smiled at his blatant admission of what she'd long suspected. 'The sideline's always the worst place to be,' she said. They walked in silence for a few moments, watching the boat float down. 'Why haven't you ever written a song about him?'

Rouel's face split into a grin. 'I've written plenty, but Edu says they're inappropriate for public performance.'

Fyia laughed, and then melancholy filled her. 'Has anything ever happened between the two of you?' Fyia knew it would be better to ask Edu; he was Rouel's superior, and her friend, but now seemed like a good time. And aside from her general intrigue, she needed to know if she had a conflict of interest in her personal guard. She probably should have asked sooner.

A wistful look crossed Rouel's face, and he shook his head.

'Do you love him?'

Rouel gave her a strange look. 'Of course … but not in the way you mean.'

Fyia cocked her head, not understanding.

'I've accepted nothing can happen between us. Edu doesn't see me that way … or, if he does, he would never admit it. You're his only true love, and he's devoted to you.'

Fyia screwed up her features. 'Edu has no romantic interest in me …' The very idea was jarring.

Rouel laughed. 'I don't mean like that. I mean, he believes in you. He loves your cause and your determination to see your mission through. He respects you, and values you more than the notion of a romantic relationship … with me, or anyone else.'

Fyia pondered that. It was sad in a way, but Edu was free to make his own choices.

'Do you love Adigos?' Rouel blurted, then looked sheepish. The question was impertinent, and Fyia should rebuke him, but she struggled to get her thoughts straight unless she spoke them aloud, and she trusted Rouel with her life.

'Do I want to write inappropriate songs about him?' she joked. Rouel gave her a look, and she smiled. Maybe she should promote him, so they could be true friends … he was so easy to talk to. She considered his real question. 'I want to rip his clothes off—I can't tell you how much I want to do that …'

Rouel chuckled. 'If you'd asked me that about Edu, my answer would have been a resounding *yes*!'

Fyia laughed wickedly. She'd never had an interest in Edu that way, but could easily understand Rouel's attraction. Edu was—objectively speaking—a very attractive man.

Fyia sighed. 'I'd be lying if I said I didn't have feelings for Adigos … I might even still love him. But my heart didn't stop when he landed on that boat; it didn't even falter. All I cared about was winning, and keeping us all alive.'

'He thinks he can bring you around,' said Rouel. He pulled back a branch and held it out of her way.

'I know, despite what I've told him … despite what Edu tried to drum into him last night.'

'Will you make a political marriage?' Fyia's wolves growled. 'Sorry … I'll stop.'

The wind whipped at Fyia's disheveled hair, and she pushed the stray wisps back off her face. 'No one knows what the future will bring,' she said. 'If I have to, I'll make a political match, but it certainly won't be with the Emperor, and marriage isn't what I want.'

'What do you want?'

Fyia stopped and looked at him. 'I want to make my kingdoms prosperous and peaceful, and to do that, I have to bring back the dragons.'

And I want someone who makes my heart stop. She batted the surprising thought away. No such man existed for her now, and even if they did, she'd sworn to never be so foolish as to give her heart away again.

The boat eventually landed in a clearing by a lake. Edu jumped to the ground as soon as they touched down, striding over to give a full report. Adigos oversaw the tethering of the flying machine, making their captives show him how.

'We killed most of them,' said Edu. 'None of them were warriors. The pilot seems willing to cooperate, along with the three crew members we left alive.'

'Commander!' a guard shouted from the boat.

'What is it?' said Edu. The urgency in her tone had him running for the flying machine.

'We found a stowaway.'

A second guard wrestled a writhing, middle-aged woman into view, forcing her over the side, so she landed at Edu's feet.

The first guard threw Edu a length of rope, and he tied the woman's hands behind her back, then maneuvered her into a kneeling position, holding her in place.

The woman started laughing, a crazed, frenzied sound that sent a shiver of unease down Fyia's spine.

'You're the Queen of the Five Kingdoms!' the woman said, between laughs. 'Look at you! You're *nothing* … and you'll never get the dragons, for *we* have them.'

Fyia's pulse raced. She fought to keep her expression neutral. 'Who exactly is *we*, and why should I believe a word from your lips?' The woman seemed deranged …

'The Emperor has the dragons,' she said in a singsong voice.

Fyia shuddered. The woman watched Fyia closely with her mismatched eyes, one light green, the other golden, her wild, short grey hair flailing about in the wind.

'You're lying,' said Fyia.

She cackled. 'He sent me to tell you.'

'Why would he do that?'

'He knows you want them … that you search for them … and he has them.' She gave a slow one-shouldered shrug, tipping her head so her chin met her raised shoulder. Her features contorted into an obscure expression that Fyia took to mean, *obviously*.

'What do you mean, *them*?' said Fyia.

'Why, all five, of course.'

'Impossible,' said Fyia. 'If you'd told me he had one, I might have been tempted, but all five? There's no way.'

'One hatched just recently,' said the woman, barking out a laugh as soon as the words left her lips.

'Show me proof.'

'The Emperor will be happy to, when you visit him.'

Now Fyia laughed. 'Gag her, lock her up, and watch her closely.'

The two guards jumped down from the boat, gagged the woman, then manhandled her back onboard.

Fyia exhaled a breath she hadn't realized she'd been holding as soon as the woman was out of sight. She was unnatural, her presence … wrong.

'They can't have all five,' said Edu, as though trying to convince himself. 'How could they?'

'But they might have one,' said Adigos. 'They could be bluffing about the other four, so you stop looking for the eggs and go to the Emperor.'

'Or maybe they have nothing,' said Edu, 'and the Emperor is luring you so he can kill you and claim all five of your kingdoms for himself.'

'Well, then the Emperor shall be disappointed,' said Fyia, 'because there's no way in all the Seven Hells I'm going to visit him. But I am going to explore my new flying boat.'

They loaded the flying machine, taking everything save for the food and equipment the guards tasked with riding the horses back would need. The rest of them— including two badly injured guards, and Fyia's wolves— would travel in the sky.

They buried the dead, interrogated the captured crew, meticulously searched the boat for anything nefarious, then took off with a rush of excitement. Fyia had flown plenty with her eagles, but this was new and exhilarating. She laughed as they cleared the forest canopy, then looked out across the horizon at her kingdoms. Her *five* kingdoms. She still couldn't quite believe it was true.

The boat was luxurious. No expense had been spared in its making, which, the pilot told them, was because his sister had built it as a gift for the Emperor. She had apparently convinced him to commission an entire fleet to be used as machines of war. If the pilot spoke the truth, Fyia would need many flying machines of her own.

Fyia looked behind them as they floated south, searching for glimpses of the Kingdom of the Black Hoods beyond the Fae'ch Mountains. Her blood hummed when she caught sight of the frozen lands between two peaks, something in her urging her north.

She'd always felt a pull in that direction, but it was stronger now than ever. Was it because she was so close? Or because the Black Hood at the party had done something to her magic? His chocolate eyes flashed in her mind, but she dismissed them. She couldn't go north. Her kingdoms needed her … needed flying machines. She had no choice but to deliver this one to Essa.

The others could do that, some part of her whispered, causing her wolves to look up in concern. She dropped down next to them on the deck, her back against the railing. They practically sat on her, neither of them thrilled at being in the air. *Don't worry,* she thought, petting them. *I'm not going anywhere.*

Fyia invited the pilot, Opie Baralli, to dine with them. The boat had food to spare, given most of the original passengers were now dead, and they had their own rations also.

The boat had a decent sized galley and lavish dining room that occupied the whole middle section of the first floor below deck. Two of Fyia's guards cooked, while Fyia instructed the others to rearrange the furniture into one long banquet table, which basked in the light of the setting sun streaming through the portholes.

'How did you come to be a pilot?' asked Fyia, tucking into the roasted venison from a deer her wolves had hunted.

'The inventor of this machine is my sister,' said Opie, with a shrug. 'She needs someone stupid enough to test out her creations, and that task usually falls to me.'

'There are more? Creations, I mean?'

Opie laughed, deep lines creasing the skin around his eyes. 'She has more creations than I can count.'

'Like what?'

Opie raised his eyebrows. 'War machines commissioned by the Emperor, but also other types of flying machines, boats, contraptions to measure the wind and rain, and … I don't know … many other things.'

Fyia peppered him with questions, warning him that Essa would be at least twice as bad once she got her hands on him. He laughed. 'Sounds just like my sister,' he said, sorrow in his eyes.

'Is she loyal to the Emperor?' asked Fyia.

'She's loyal, in the way of any normal citizen,' he hedged.

'Are you?' She looked him in the eye as he took a moment to consider. He was plain to look at, of medium height and build, with weathered skin and dark hair, but he had a friendly magnetism that pulled Fyia to him.

'I have no reason to be loyal to the Emperor, other than because he rules my homeland, which I hold dear.'

'Is he a good leader? A fair one?' asked Fyia, watching him intently.

'He's much like the Kings were here, I should imagine. He demands his taxes, lines his pockets, and whores extensively, if rumors can be believed. He has a close circle, whom he rewards handsomely. He's certainly clever, from what my sister's told me. He's shrewd and relentless, and resolute when he wants something.'

'Do the people love him?'

'They don't hate him,' said Opie.

Fyia took a sip of her wine. 'Who's the woman he sent?'

'I know not. I was told to fly her here to deliver her message, and nothing more.'

Fyia frowned. 'Then why did you shoot at us?'

Opie gave her an incredulous look. 'You shot at us first.'

She had to admit, that was true. 'How did you know where to find me?'

Opie shrugged. 'The Emperor told me you'd be in the Fae'ch Mountains … that's all I know.'

It's not like they'd kept their journey a complete secret, but it was still surprising the Emperor had found out so fast … unless … had Venir reached his court and sold her out? Had he betrayed her so openly … so soon?

'What will you do with me?' asked Opie, the tick of his jaw betraying his otherwise well-hidden unease.

'I'd like you to speak with Essa, my inventor.'

Opie's features pinched. 'The Emperor may kill me for no other reason than because I allowed you to steal his airship. If I tell your inventor anything, I'd be writing my own death sentence.'

'Then join my court. I can make it worth your while, and your sister is welcome too. I'm building a new kind of kingdom, where anyone can be prosperous, whoever they are.'

'Forgive me, but I've heard rumors not everyone in your kingdom is happy with your methods. Peace seems a long way off, let alone prosperity for all …'

'That's true enough,' said Fyia. 'Change is hard … even harder for those who stand to lose the unfair advantage they hold dear. It's impossible to please every one of my people, but it is possible to make the game fairer for all who play. I have that power, and I intend to use it.'

'Even if it turns your kingdoms against themselves?'

'It won't.'

'It might, without the dragons …' Opie looked shocked at his words, then fearful. 'I'm sorry, Your Majesty, I've overstepped. I am too used to arguing freely with my sister.'

Fyia waved a hand. 'If I punish everyone who speaks their truth, my rule would be no better than that of the Kings before me. You're right, my plan isn't without risk, but nothing worth doing ever is. Uniting the Five Kingdoms wasn't without risk either, but now I must make it mean something.

'I won't sit back and allow women to be oppressed, or turn a blind eye when market stall holders are taxed out of business. I won't tolerate corruption and fraudsters, just because it would make my life easier. Of course I'd rather there were dragons, but I'll damn well rule as I please, regardless.'

'Even if that means years of unrest for your people?' he said tentatively, obviously not quite believing her words.

'There's already unrest. Just because people aren't fighting in the streets doesn't mean a silent war isn't underway. Only those on the side of justice have no army and much to lose. But now they have an army; my army.'

'And you have much to lose.'

'You think I should hoard my titles and wealth? Build a palace and sit on my throne until I die? What's the point of everything I've achieved if I squander it? How would that make me any different from the tyrants I overthrew?'

'Many would be content to live a peaceful life, surrounded by those who love them,' said Opie, the entire room raptly focused on their back and forth.

'Many would. Many are alcoholics, gamblers, liars, and cheats. Should I follow their example too? If peace and quiet were all I craved, I would not be Queen of the Five Kingdoms today.'

Opie regarded her with open astonishment. 'You are certainly ambitious.'

'You sound surprised to meet such a woman, yet your sister can't be lacking in determination of her own?'

Opie laughed. 'It has nothing to do with your being a woman. The Empire does not discriminate quite like the Five Eastern Kingdoms. I suppose I'm surprised to meet any ruler with ideas like yours, but then, I've never known a conqueror, only rulers born to their thrones.'

Fyia waved a hand in the air and hissed. 'They care more about their bloodlines than their people; it's drummed into them from birth. They're like horses.'

'The same wasn't drummed into you?'

'I was no warrior, and because of that—and other factors—my parents would have happily let the reign pass to a distant cousin rather than to me. Happily, in this case at least, they neglected my education.'

Opie shook his head, a look of disgust morphing his features.

Silence fell, and Rouel filled it. 'A song, Your Majesty?' he said, with a mischievous smile. 'For I believe there is one you wanted to hear ...?' Rouel glanced at Edu, grinning broadly.

Edu's eyes flicked from Fyia to Rouel, a look of horror freezing his face as realization dawned.

Fyia went very still. She pursed her lips and frowned, then firmly shook her head. They had a command structure for a reason, and she would not undermine it.

Rouel shrank back, embarrassment staining his cheeks as he realized he'd overstepped. Perhaps she wouldn't promote him after all. 'Something upbeat,' she said tersely, 'and never do that again.'

Fyia left the dining room and headed up on deck. She couldn't get enough of flying, her soul drinking in the stars, the reflection of the moon on the river below, the peace that came with gliding through the air.

The only sounds were the whispering of the wind and the soft whir of the airship's rotors, turned down low, given the breeze at their backs.

She stood at the chest-height railing in the stern and took deep, nourishing lungsful of air. Her inner eagle urged her to throw herself over, to truly fly, to feel the rush of freefall before pulling up inches from the ground. If only she could.

A door opened on the starboard side of the cabin that sat atop the deck, letting the light and sounds of inside spill out into the night. Down in the dining hall, Rouel was playing a slow, gentle, end of night song.

Adigos appeared through the door. 'Leave it open a crack,' she said. 'I like the music.'

He did as she asked, then came to stand behind her, stopping so close she could feel the warmth of his body, even though they weren't touching. Her pulse picked up, anticipation coursing through her as she waited to see what he would do next.

He slipped his hand inside her cloak, then ran his fingers up her spine, from the base all the way to the nape of her neck. Her heart skipped a beat as he used his other hand to push her hair to one side, the slide of his fingers causing an eruption of gooseflesh across her skin. The wind on her neck sent a shiver down her spine, then his lips brushed against the exposed skin, and heat replaced the biting cold. He kissed her over and over, up and down her neck, behind her ear, on the corner of her jaw. His hands found her waist, and he caressed her there too.

Desire pooled in her core, and she leaned into him, tipping her head back against his shoulder. He turned her, wrapping her in his cloak, and she pressed herself against him, pushing her hands under his shirt, sliding them to the hard ridges of his back. He swayed them gently in time with the music, and the movement lit a fire in her blood.

'Adi,' she breathed, looking up at him. He dipped his head, his lips finding hers, and she sighed at the relief. They hadn't so much as kissed since the journey to the Fae'ch—Edu had seen to that—and her skin greedily absorbed the contact, demanding more.

The kiss deepened, and their lips parted, his tongue caressing hers. His hands slid over the curve of her behind, and his lips moved to her neck. She dug her fingers into his muscular shoulders, her eyes rolling back in her head at the rush of sensation.

She shivered, his cloak having fallen away, so she took his hand and tugged him inside. He followed without hesitation, and she led him to her luxurious bedchamber that occupied most of the bottom deck, where an enormous sunken bed awaited.

She closed the door behind them and leaned back against its frame, placing a hand on his arm when he tried to kiss her. She looked into his eyes, her free hand on his neck, caressing his skin, drinking in the intimacy. She didn't want him to go, but she had to tell him … remind him. 'This is just sex. You know that's all I can give you,' she said, quietly. 'I need to know you accept that. Truly.'

He leaned forward, pressing his forehead to hers. 'I love you, Fyia, but I know that's not what you want … what you need from me. Even if this is all I ever get, I want it more than you know.'

Fyia's chest split with warring emotions. She knew deep in her soul she would never give Adigos what he really wanted. A part of her still loved him, but she could never go back. Maybe that meant she should walk away … spare his feelings … but she wanted things too. She wanted his body to cover hers, to feel the hard contours of his war-trained muscles pressing her down, to relinquish control … if only for a night.

She knew Adigos could be commanding; she'd seen him that way countless times. Most feared and revered him as a warrior, a leader, and he was a grown man, capable of making his own decisions. Who was she to patronize him, and deny them both pleasure? Who was she to second guess his words? To presume she knew his feelings better than he?

He must have sensed the shift in her, or become tired of waiting, because he spun her around, so her chest pressed against the door, and urged her legs apart.

'I know you want this too,' he said, sliding a hand around her waist. He pulled up her tunic, then tugged at the laces tying her pants.

Fyia's heart thundered in her ears. She did want this. In this moment, she wanted nothing more. She wanted him just like this ... teasing ... demanding ... in control.

'Tell me you want me,' he said. His fingers played with the sensitive skin below her hip, and he pressed his arousal against the base of her spine.

'I want you,' she said, his words fanning the flames of her desire.

He slid his fingers to her core, and she sucked in a breath, his deft movements chasing away any lingering doubts. He growled into her ear, and she bucked against him. He chuckled, then nipped her neck before licking where his teeth had been. She moaned as his fingers made tantalizing circles, then he pulled down her pants and undergarments.

She unfastened her cloak, then spun, lifting her tunic over her head, so she stood before him in only a worn silk brassier.

He reached for her, tugging at the only scrap of clothing she had left, but instead of ridding her of it, he pulled the laces tighter, forcing her breasts higher, plumping them until they threatened to spill free.

He re-tied the laces, then traced the seam of the brassier, where it pressed into her trussed up flesh. She watched him intently as he lowered his lips, sucking her through the fabric, licking a circle around her peaked and sensitive nipple. She gasped and arched her back, offering herself up to him.

He pulled back, watching her with hooded eyes as he yanked down the fabric on one side, so her breast popped out of its binding. He palmed it, rolling the nipple between his thumb and forefinger.

She reached for his hips, but he grasped her arms and pushed them behind her back, holding them with one hand, sliding a finger through her sex with the other. She moaned and tried to rub against him, but he held her in place, then moved his hand back to her breast, kneading it, then sucking her nipple.

'Adigos,' she gasped. He moved his mouth to the breast still covered in fabric, worrying it through the silk, still squeezing the other with his free hand.

He released her hands and grabbed her backside, pulling her against him, then lifted her, carrying her to the bed. He lay her on her front, undressed himself, then knelt over her, running a finger down her spine.

He halted when he reached the small, golden scale nestled just above her tailbone. He skirted his thumb back and forth across it, and Fyia growled with impatience, turning her shoulders so she could see his face. This was not where she wanted his fingers.

His expression was one of wonder as he raptly examined the evidence of her fire-touch. 'Adigos,' she purred. His eyes met hers, then dipped to where her fingers pulled at the strings fastening her brassier, her breasts still half-contained.

His eyes went dark, and he lunged forward, batting her hand away. 'No,' he said, rolling her onto her back. He sat across her thighs, pinning her to the bed, leaning over her. She gave a breathy laugh as he captured her lips, his hand cupping her breast once more.

He covered her with his body, and she spread her legs in welcome, exhaling as he settled his weight and nudged against her core. Fyia thanked the Gods the women of her lands had retained enough magic to

110

make contraceptive spells, showing defiance in the face of the ridiculous rules of the Kings. Not that the Kings had minded. The hypocrites had been happy to whore with no consequence, turning a blind eye to the presence of magic when it suited them …

Adigos' skin was hot and soft, his muscles hard, sculpted ridges. Fyia explored him with greedy hands as he continued to tease her with his cock, and torment her with his lips.

'Adigos,' she moaned, tipping her hips. He chuckled, then pushed inside her. She gasped at the delicious shock of it, hooking her hands around his shoulders and wrapping her legs around his waist.

He moved with a lazy, infuriating rhythm, and she clawed at his skin. 'Adigos … I need …'

'I know what you need,' he breathed into her ear. He moved faster, thrusting harder, and she moaned, pressing her head back and grabbing handfuls of the bedding.

'*Warrior*,' she whispered.

'You're right, I am a warrior,' he said cockily, finally removing her brassier, laying her round breasts bare. He went up on his knees and lifted her hips, a hand wrapped under her back as he pounded into her. She moaned, her hands above her head as his movements pushed her back and forth. He spun her, pulling her up so they were both on their knees, her back to his chest, and he entered her once more.

His hands covered her breasts, kneading them as he moved his hips. She arched, and he growled, dropping a hand to her core. He sucked on her neck, and she lifted a hand to grab his hair, crying out his name as his fingers circled. She bucked, but he held her in place, working her harder. And then it hit, a cry escaping her lips as she convulsed around him.

Adigos huffed out a laugh and pinched her nipple, still pulsing his hips. She gasped as her body clenched harder. His movements became jerky, and he dug his fingers into her hips. '*Goddess*,' he groaned, then stiffened.

When the pleasure had passed, he lowered her onto the bed. She tucked into his side, and Adigos stroked her back, lulling her to sleep. This was exactly what she'd needed … release at the hands of someone who knew precisely what they were doing. She was glad she'd finally gained some benefit from his extensive practice with the maids.

Chapter Seven

THEY ARRIVED BACK IN Selise the following day. Fyia had summoned an eagle and sent it ahead with a message for the Spider, so the guards wouldn't shoot the airship down as soon as it came into view. The city walls were packed as they approached, cheers going up when Fyia waved.

They landed on the piazza in front of the council building, Edu and Adigos flanking Fyia as she walked up the steps, making sure the crowd didn't get too close. They needn't have worried; the onlookers shied away from her wolves, who snarled in warning.

A ball released from the clock as Fyia approached the top. She watched its journey before stepping through the entrance.

The Spider, Starfall, and Essa awaited in the council chamber. They stood and bowed, saying, 'Your Majesty,' as one.

Fyia nodded. 'Sit,' she said, taking her own seat. 'Anything I should know?'

'Venir confirmed the flying machines are real,' said Starfall, with a smirk.

'*No*,' said Fyia.

'Essa's found a location for your new palace,' said the Spider.

Fyia looked to Essa, who nodded in confirmation. 'And I have a layout for your review.'

Fyia smiled. She could always rely on Essa.

Fyia told them of their trip to the Fae'ch, including the attack on the journey there, and the one on the way back.

'We've heard grumblings from a few corners about your changes to the markets and guilds,' said Starfall. 'There could be more attacks.'

'Any word from Sensis?' said Fyia. She had, after all, insisted on the most radical changes in the Kingdom of Moon, where she'd sent her closest friend ...

'Last we heard, all was going well,' said the Spider, 'and Sensis took several squadrons with her. The university and guilds are reluctant to admit women, but they're not resisting ... not overtly, that is.'

'Good,' said Fyia.

Silence fell for a moment before Starfall said, 'What will you do about the dragon eggs?'

Fyia paused, looking her aunt in the eye as she considered her response. 'Do you believe the Emperor?' she asked.

Starfall laughed. 'Not for a tick. He's a lying ball of slime; there's no way he has five dragons.'

'Do you think he has any?' said Fyia.

'No,' said Starfall, resolutely.

Fyia looked to the Spider, who shrugged. 'The Emperor has seeded rumors he has dragons, but nobody has actually seen them, if they exist.'

'But do *you* think he has them?'

The Spider inhaled deeply. 'If he has—especially if he has five—it's strange he hasn't shown them off. He's an exhibitionist, yet he hides his most prized possessions? And there are no accounts from his staff; no singed curtains or scratched floors, no new area constructed to house them. And the Emperor hardly ever leaves the palace, so if he's keeping them elsewhere, he never visits.'

'If he had even a single dragon, he'd have it draped over his arm, present at every dinner and court function,' Starfall said with complete conviction.

'So he's lying,' said Fyia, sitting back in her chair.

'Even if he's not,' said the Spider, 'you can't enter his territory as he's requested; you'd never make it out alive.'

'At least not unmarried,' said Starfall, with a taunting smile.

'Then I have to go north,' said Fyia, 'to the Black Hoods.'

'Why?' said Starfall.

'Because they have a dragon egg,' said Fyia, sending Starfall a questioning look.

'Spider,' Fyia continued, 'we heard of attacks in the north of the Kraken Empire. Do you think it's the Black Hoods?'

'No,' she said. 'Venir is convinced the Emperor's being attacked by his own people. The Emperor wants to dig up the north, and the people there don't want him to. Venir says the north is rich in mineral deposits, and the Emperor wants to mine them. The people believe the minerals contain magic that protects the world. They keep destroying his mines.'

Fyia laughed. 'Nice to hear I'm not the only ruler being attacked by my own people.'

Starfall chuckled. 'Maybe you *should* marry him; you've got things in common.'

Fyia sent Starfall a warning look, which only made her laugh harder.

'But what about the egg in the south?' said Starfall. 'Why not go there?'

Fyia rounded on her aunt. 'The egg in the south?'

'Queen Scorpia's egg,' said Starfall.

'What?' said Fyia.

Starfall turned to the Spider. '*You* didn't know?'

The Spider pursed her lips and shook her head. Fyia would have smiled if she wasn't so frustrated. 'Where exactly is Scorpia's egg rumored to be?'

'In the Temple of the Whore,' said Starfall.

'The what?'

'One of the seven temples?' said Starfall, looking around at the sea of blank faces.

Fyia gritted her teeth. She waved her hand irritably, motioning for Starfall to continue.

'My Gods, your parents really did teach you nothing. The seven temples of the seven deities?'

Fyia shook her head, suppressing her rage. Did her brother know this stuff? 'Tell me,' said Fyia, taking comfort that everyone else in the room seemed as clueless as she.

'Back when the Five Kingdoms were united under the Dragon King, the people worshiped seven deities: the Gods of the Dragon, Brother, and Whore, and the Goddesses of the Night, Sea, Warrior, and Seven Hells. They built one magnificent temple for each deity, spread across the world. When the dragons disappeared, and the kingdom split into five, those deities fell out of favor for some, while others added more.'

'Wait, the Warrior's a woman?' said Adigos, his forehead furrowed.

'I've often wondered why no one cares about the anatomical inaccuracy of the expression *Warrior's balls*,' said Starfall.

116

'But Queen Scorpia's lands aren't part of the Five Kingdoms,' said Fyia. 'Why is there a temple there?'

Starfall shrugged. 'Maybe our ancestors had a sense of adventure ...'

'Do you know the location of the other eggs?' Fyia snapped.

'No,' said Starfall.

'And you didn't think to mention this before I went to the Fae'ch?'

'I really thought you knew ...'

'You didn't think it strange I chose the Fae'ch as my first port of call?'

'Not really; they're closest, and your brother's there. I thought you secretly wanted to see him.'

'I did want to see him, but ...'

'How is he?' said Starfall.

Fyia's eyes darted to Essa, whose back had snapped straight, before returning to Starfall. 'He's fine; don't change the subject.'

'Well, anyway,' said Starfall, as if her words were of no consequence ... as if they hadn't spun Fyia off her axis, 'now you have a lead.'

The way she said it, like it was all trivial ... Fyia stood abruptly. 'We'll take the airship to the Scorpion Lands,' she said.

Fyia was halfway to the exit before she remembered her captives. 'Oh, we came bearing gifts,' she said, opening the door.

Members of her bodyguard stood waiting outside, guarding Opie, and the deranged woman the Emperor had sent.

Fyia ushered them in. 'Essa, this is Opie. He's a pilot. His sister invented the airship. Spider, the woman is for you.'

Fyia took the airship to the Scorpion Lands. She made her wolves stay behind, much to their disgust, but they weren't suited to the climate, or the airship.

The island housing the Temple of the Whore was a long way south, the weather hot and humid, tropical forest bursting from every speck of free land. Fyia had sent an eagle, so the island would know to expect them, and Queen Scorpia had sent a message back, saying that, in a piece of good fortune, she was currently in residence on the island, and would look forward to meeting The Conqueror Queen.

The Conqueror Queen. Fyia wasn't sure how she felt about that. She was less conqueror and more liberator in her own mind, but it was better than other names she'd been called …

They flew in, and landed on a crystal-clear lagoon, because apparently the airship could also float on water. Fyia really needed a fleet of these things.

A welcoming party awaited them, most staring open-mouthed at the flying machine. Fyia disembarked, prowling down the gangplank, those waiting on the sand casting nervous looks between her and Edu, who strode menacingly behind. She made the others stay on the boat, Adigos grumbling under his breath as she left.

Fyia wore a long flowing blue dress, her hair braided, pinned up on her head. Starfall had warned her about the weather, so she'd dressed appropriately, but still had her dagger strapped to her leg, just in case.

Fyia approached an ornate, open-sided tent on the sand, rugs and a chair set out underneath the canopy, the chair occupied by a withered old woman.

The woman stood as Fyia entered. She also wore a long, floaty dress, her grey hair also pinned back, but, unlike Fyia, gemstones adorned every inch of her. Gold chains inset with stones clanked around her wrists, neck, and ankles. Her ears and nose were studded with bright gems, and her hair housed a riot of color.

'Queen Scorpia,' said Fyia, giving a small bow.

'Queen Fyia,' said Scorpia, doing the same. 'Welcome to the Island of the Whore. Come …' Scorpia held out her hand, motioning towards a path into the jungle, then took off with surprising agility, considering her advanced years.

They entered the jungle, and after only twenty paces, came to a large clearing covered by a canopy of leaves. Mottled light filtered through the greenery, and in the middle of the space stood a single elephant.

'I do not have a Cruaxee,' said Scorpia, 'but if I did, I am sure it would be the elephant. Sanya and I have been together since we were young. We may be old, but we still function quite well. Will you ride with me to the temple?'

The elephant's back was bare. 'I'd be delighted,' said Fyia, fascinated and excited. She could see Edu tense out of the corner of her eye, but Fyia was sure it was safe.

They approached the great grey beast, and the elephant stroked Scorpia's back with her trunk. 'This is my friend, Fyia,' said Scorpia, as though the animal could understand her words. The elephant—Sanya—reached out with her trunk, and Fyia laughed as she ruffled her hair.

'Pleased to meet you too,' said Fyia.

The elephant dropped onto one knee, and Scorpia scaled her leg, climbing lithely up onto Sanya's back. 'Coming?'

Fyia didn't have to be asked twice, and followed Scorpia with lithe movements of her own. The elephant stood, lurching them forward and back, but Fyia balanced easily, used to riding with no saddle. She heard a laugh, a delighted, child-like sound, then realized it had come from her own lips.

'She's quite something, eh?' said Scorpia, somehow directing the elephant towards a path deeper into the jungle.

'She certainly is,' said Fyia, staring in wonder.

'Just watch out for snakes,' said Scorpia, 'and pretty much anything else that moves; it'll all kill you.'

'How reassuring,' said Fyia, although she couldn't find the will to care, entranced by both the elephant and her surroundings.

They passed trees with incredible, blooming flowers, brightly colored birds making all manner of strange noises, and then a tiger strode across the path in front of them, pausing, staring with eyes of liquid gold.

'Beautiful, isn't she?' said Scorpia, the elephant not seeming to notice the cat.

'She is,' said Fyia. She'd only ever seen tigers in paintings, and they'd failed absolutely to capture this majestic animal's brutal beauty.

Fyia reached out with her Cruaxee bond. The tiger snarled, but Fyia felt intrigue alongside the cat's wariness, even if there was no synchronicity between them … tigers, alas, were not a part of her Cruaxee. It wasn't surprising. That she had a Cruaxee at all was remarkable. Having two animals was virtually unheard of, even throughout history. Three would have been downright greedy. The tiger moved on, melting into the jungle.

The land tilted upwards as they continued, and they climbed beside a tall waterfall, the water misting the air as it hit the plunge pool at the bottom.

They kept ascending until a stone building suddenly popped out of the trees, and they came to a halt by a pair of stone pillars that marked the entrance.

The jungle had claimed the temple, vines running up the pillars, branches reaching over, casting it in shade, plants poking out from cracks in the steps and walls. The temple had a tranquil beauty that took Fyia's breath away, despite the ruin—or maybe because of it—and the feel of the place was overwhelmingly calm.

'I can see why you like it here,' said Fyia, as she and Scorpia dismounted.

'You ain't seen nothing yet, girl,' said Scorpia, with a wicked smile.

Scorpia took off up the steps, once again leaving Fyia with no choice but to follow. They entered an atrium with a large bathing pool in the center, people sitting in the water, chatting, playing board games, lying back and floating. Dappled light illuminated everything, from the day beds to one side, to the pool, to the walkway that led deeper into the temple.

Unlike the temple where Starfall had lived, nothing about this place was sexual. Men and women both shared the water, some even giving each other massages, but it wasn't charged, it was … platonic, companionable.

'I thought this was the Temple of the Whore?' said Fyia, quietly.

'It is,' said Scorpia. 'It's full to the brim with recovering sex workers. You thought it would be like the Temple of the Night?'

'The Temple of the … The Temple of the Goddess, you mean?'

'Is that what your people call it these days?' she said with a scoff. 'It's the Temple of the Night Goddess, and always has been, as surely as this place is the Temple of the Whoring God.'

Fyia was going to have words with her aunt. Starfall had failed to divulge the temple she'd called home was one of the original seven. 'You're right, it's not what I expected.'

'Come,' said Scorpia, leading her past the pool, into the temple's depths.

Scorpia led Fyia into the very center of the temple, to where an enormous tree grew from the middle of a circular space. It punched through a perfectly round hole in the roof, its large canopy shading the room below. Vines had crept in, wrapping the pillars that circled the tree, each pillar itself encircled by a small channel of water.

'You have a clock?' said Fyia. She approached the small, almost hidden mechanism set into a pillar. She watched as a ball zigzagged down the tiny runners, then plopped into the water.

'Of course,' said Scorpia, giving Fyia an odd look.

'Only one?'

'We're at the end of the world. One was all we needed.'

Fyia raised an eyebrow, not sure what she meant. She walked the perimeter, running her hand across the pillars, their carvings mostly hidden by vines. 'What is this place?' said Fyia.

'It's a place of healing and protection,' said Scorpia. 'Healing for those who need it, and protection for …'

'… the dragon egg?' said Fyia.

'No,' said Scorpia. 'The clock.'

Fyia stopped in her tracks. 'Why would the clock need protecting?'

'My dear girl, this is a kingdom built on clockwork. If the clocks fall, we're all doomed. What could be more important?'

Fyia shook her head in confusion. 'I don't understand …'

Scorpia frowned. 'What do they teach you in those lands of yours?'

'That trade is important and magic is bad, if I had to summarize.'

Scorpia barked out a laugh. 'What of history?'

'What of it? The Five Kingdoms were once united under the Dragon King. He went mad, or became an alcoholic, depending upon which reports you believe, and the dragons died out. The kingdoms were split between five greedy Kings, but the dragons left five eggs. The eggs will hatch when a worthy ruler reunites the kingdoms.

'The descendants of the Kings, who'd always been wary of those with magic, took advantage of their diminishing power, and ousted the magical from their lands. As time went on, magic waned further, and our lands began to cool. The end.'

'What of the clocks?'

'What of them? They're an amazing feat of engineering, demonstrating our prowess to the world … I have to say, I'm surprised you have one here.'

'Why?'

'I thought they were only in the lands of the Dragon King. It surprised me to see one at the Fae'ch Mountains too, but I assumed it was because the Fae'ch helped set up the magic when the clocks were built.'

Scorpia's face morphed into something between incredulity and humor.

'What?' said Fyia, feeling as though a stone dropped through her stomach.

'I thought it was strange you didn't bring gifts.'

Fyia gave her a blank look. 'I brought gifts …'

'Not big ones.'

'Scorpia, what are you talking about?'

'I assumed you were here to ask for an alliance, to unite our kingdoms.'

'Why would I do that?'

'Because the Dragon King's kingdom was significantly bigger than the five kingdoms you have conquered so far.'

Everything inside Fyia dropped towards the floor. 'What do you mean?'

'My lands, your lands, the Fae'ch Mountains, the Kingdom of the Black Hoods, and the Great Glacier … they were all the domain of the Dragon King.'

Scorpia's words landed like a hammer blow, and rushing filled Fyia's ears. 'If what you say is true, how is it possible my people think otherwise?'

'Five selfish, greedy, egotistical Kings divided up your kingdoms between them. All they cared about was trade, riches, and proclaiming their excellence to the world. They wanted their own people to believe their five kingdoms were all that mattered, that *they* were all that mattered. Their descendants were no different.

'And the Emperor's ancestors were a tribal people, too busy killing each other to care about much else. They knew little of the Dragon King, other than to fear him. The Black Hoods and the Fae'ch shut themselves off, and I doubt anyone still lives on the Great Glacier. My own ancestors couldn't see much point in falling out with our neighbors, so stayed out of their domestic affairs. I must admit, until now, I didn't realize how bad the lies were.'

Fyia felt sick. Everything she'd ever known was a lie, and there could be no hope of the dragons hatching now. She hadn't, in fact, united the Five Kingdoms. She hadn't even come close. She sat heavily on a stone bench and covered her face with her hands, staring at the insides of her eyelids for several long moments. Endless thoughts rushed through her mind, endless emotions: anger, intrigue, embarrassment, dread.

Fyia looked up. 'So you thought I'd come to unite our kingdoms, because unless I do, the dragons will not return …?'

Scorpia shrugged, a hint of compassion breaking through her regal exterior.

'And you weren't against the idea?' Fyia asked. Despite everything, she could smell opportunity.

'Ha!' said Scorpia, clapping her hands. 'I wasn't against it, but I'm not for it either, especially given how little you know.'

Fyia supposed that was fair. 'Why are we all doomed if the clocks fall?

'When the clocks doth strike thirteen, the dragons shall return. But if the clocks do fall before, then fire will reign supreme.'

'Do you believe that?' said Fyia. 'That if the clocks fall, our world will burn?'

'Yes, I do believe it,' said Scorpia.

Fyia stood and approached the tree, trying to process the barrage of thoughts hammering her brain. Had her parents known about the five true kingdoms? Had her brother? That thought made her nauseous. She trusted him. They'd worked together when he'd given up the throne …

Her people would hound her to marry if they found out the truth, even more than they already did. They'd think her weak, naïve, and certainly they'd consider the dragons lost to time, never to return. For if she proclaimed she could reunite the five true kingdoms, they'd think her mad. Even so, she knew she could. Maybe that meant Scorpia's revelation had already tipped her into insanity …

But the Fae'ch egg was missing … that couldn't mean nothing. She turned towards Scorpia, surprised to see the old woman rushing towards her. It looked as though Scorpia were calling her name, telling her something, but Fyia couldn't hear her words.

Fyia's fingers brushed against the tree's bark … for some reason, she needed to feel the rough surface before stepping away …

The moment her fingers made contact, she was jolted backwards, upwards, hurtling into the sky. She came to an abrupt halt when she reached the tree's canopy. She didn't dare look down—or move at all—lest she fall. There was nothing below but stone, and falling would mean death.

Whatever force held her in place—magic, presumably—moved her upwards once more, tilting her so she faced the ground. But she couldn't see the ground. She could see tree, and, as the magic lifted her higher and higher still, the top of the temple, which, to her amazement, was entirely clear of vegetation. And … Gods … was that a map?

Fyia forgot she floated a hundred paces in the air. Forgot that if the magic let her fall, she would die, and greedily drank in the details painted in astonishing detail on the temple's roof. The tree occupied the space where the Kraken Sea should be, the Dragon King's Five Kingdoms outlined around it. The details were sparse, the map showing only seven circles, and a mass of lines—perhaps the waterways—connecting everything together.

Five circular gems the color of fire were set into the roof, each of them inside a circle, except for one, which sat atop the Fae'ch mountains. The circles, Fyia assumed, depicted temples, the gems dragon eggs … they had to be.

One was here, at the Temple of the Whore, one in the Fae'ch Mountains, one in the Black Hoods' lands, one on the Great Glacier, and one … what in the Seven

Hells …? One at the Temple of the Sea Serpent in her own lands. That couldn't be …

Something lurched in Fyia's chest, and whatever had supported her disappeared. She hurtled towards the ground, narrowly missing branches and the temple's roof as she dropped through the hole. She grabbed at the tree, trying desperately to slow her descent, but when she touched the bark, the world went black. Only the sensation of falling remained, down, down, down.

It got hotter as she fell, an orange glow reaching up towards her. It became unbearably hot, Fyia's nerves screaming at her to run. But she couldn't run, she could only fall.

Just when she thought the heat would set her on fire, something yanked her backwards, her head and limbs snapping forwards with such force her joints hurt and her brain smashed against the inside of her skull. It pulled her back to the circular room, and she fell to the floor of the temple, landing beside Scorpia's unconscious body.

'Scorpia!' said Fyia, forcing herself to move, despite the protests of her scorched flesh and battered limbs. 'Scorpia, are you okay?' Fyia took hold of her shoulders and gently shook, then lowered her ear to the old woman's lips. She took Scorpia's wrist, feeling for the pump of her blood. She was alive—thank the Gods—and suddenly came around, shoving Fyia back with strength she shouldn't possess.

'What were you thinking?' said Scorpia, rolling to her feet.

'I … what do you mean?'

'I told you not to touch the tree!'

'I didn't hear you …'

'You didn't hear me screaming from across the room?'

'I … no.'

'*Whoring magic*,' said Scorpia.

'What happened when I fell?'

'You grabbed the tree—like an idiot—and it pulled you inside.'

'It got hot …'

'*Fire will reign supreme*, remember?'

'You mean there's fire under our feet? Like, right now?'

Scorpia muttered an impressive string of expletives.

'Is the dragon egg down there too?'

'What does it matter? You haven't yet united the Five Kingdoms, and you never will with this reckless stupidity.'

'The Fae'ch egg is missing.'

'Ours is warded.'

'So was theirs.'

'*Damned Seven Hells.* This is my retreat from the stressful realities of running a kingdom …'

Fyia let Scorpia rant, waiting for silence before she met her gaze. Scorpia had had hopes for this meeting that Fyia had obviously not met, but the fact she'd had hopes at all gave Fyia strength. 'Are you going to show me the egg?'

'How could I not, after that revelation?'

Scorpia's façade of annoyance was a thin one. She wanted to see the egg as much as Fyia did, but … why? Was it merely because she was old and wanted to satisfy her curiosity? Or did she believe in Fyia … that she was the one of legend?

'Stand behind me, and whatever you do, do *not* touch the tree.'

Scorpia led Fyia from pillar to pillar, rummaging in the vines, twisting a hidden cog here, pressing a piece of carving there. Once they'd made a full circuit of the room, Scorpia stamped on the ground, and a deep humming filled the air.

'What is that?' said Fyia.

'Sush, and don't move.'

Fyia watched in amazement as the ring of ground directly in front of the pillars began to spin, the floor twisting open to reveal a gaping hole that extended at least a hundred paces down, to where an orange glow emanated from the blackness. A stone walkway was all that remained of the floor, stretching from where Fyia and Scorpia stood, across the void to the tree.

Fyia looked down, feeling the heat from below. 'How is a hole like this possible? We're at sea level ...'

'Magic,' said Scorpia, before setting off across the walkway. She didn't bother to look down, as though there weren't a death drop on either side. 'Come along.'

Fyia followed, her steps filled with caution, her heart thundering as she tried not to consider the imminent threat of death.

Scorpia reached the tree and held up her hands. 'If you touch the tree again, I won't be able to save you.'

'*You* pulled me back before?'

'Why else do you think I passed out?' Scorpia gave Fyia a scathing look, then turned her attention to the tree. She hovered her hands over the bark and closed her eyes, muttering words Fyia couldn't quite make out.

A creaking noise filled the air, and Fyia shuddered, hoping the walkway would hold. A whoosh of energy pushed her back a step as the creaking turned to a thunderous cracking sound, and fear careened around Fyia's insides. She hoped whatever came next wouldn't push her over the edge, but before she had time to consider a tactical retreat, the sounds ceased, and the room became eerily quiet, unnaturally still.

Fyia started in surprise at the great fissure in the tree's trunk. She could see daylight through the middle, and, hovering, suspended in the space inside, was a small, round metal ball.

'*Warrior's tits*,' said Scorpia, snatching up the ball. 'What the Gods-damned hell is this?'

Fyia gaped. It was an exact match for the ball Essa had given her. The one she'd given to her brother. Her mouth went dry and her brain went blank. They'd lied to her … tricked her … betrayed her.

'Well?' snapped Scorpia, as though Fyia should know something of note.

'That's where the dragon egg is supposed to be?' said Fyia.

Scorpia scowled, and waved a hand across the space in front of the tree. The cracking noise filled the air once more. 'I'd get a move on, if I were you,' said Scorpia. 'The walkway is about to collapse.'

Adrenaline shot into Fyia's blood, wrenching her back from her thoughts. She spun and sprinted back to the safety of the pillars. Scorpia was right behind her, although it took another spin of the hand for the tree to close fully, and only then did the section of stone nearest the tree fall away. The rest of the walkway followed, falling into the depths.

Fyia peered over, trying to see how far it fell, but the floor made a scraping noise and abruptly snapped shut.

'Damn,' said Scorpia. 'How could this have happened?'

'Who else knows how to access the egg?' asked Fyia.

'It's hard to say. My parents sent me here to learn when I was young. Back then, an order of sorts existed to protect it. To my knowledge, no one has opened the floor in my lifetime, but I suppose anyone could have … we don't guard the place.'

'Did they show you how to reset the wards?' asked Fyia, her voice full of wonder.

Scorpia laughed. 'My dear, I have only the barest lick of magic, same as most people. They taught me how to open the wards, no more. They reset themselves after each opening. Those with the skill and knowledge to wield such impressive magic are scarce indeed.'

'Did your ancestors banish those with magic too?'

'No. We would never have done anything so stupid, but few of the magical folk ever wanted to live in our lands. I don't know why ... maybe it's too hot for them here.

'When the Five Eastern Kingdoms outlawed magic, those remaining couldn't risk being so far from the rest of their kind, especially given your kingdoms sit between the Scorpian lands and the Fae'ch Mountains. A handful of them stayed, a few here in the temple, a couple in the capital. They're all dead now.'

'Can I see the ball?' asked Fyia. Scorpia didn't hesitate. She put it in Fyia's hand, and Fyia studied it from every angle, rolling it around her palm. 'Have you seen one of these before?'

Scorpia shook her head. 'It's reminiscent of the balls from the clock, of course, but never this size, and ... it's a strange color.'

It was a strange color: gold, but not yellow-ish, maybe with a hint of pink, and with shimmering streaks of metallic blue and green as it caught the light. It was perfectly smooth, and round, and weighty. In other words, identical to the one Essa had given her.

'You've seen one before?' asked Scorpia, watching Fyia closely.

Fyia considered lying, but the tension in the air told her Scorpia already suspected, and she needed Scorpia onside if she were to reunite the real Five Kingdoms. The thought depressed her ... she'd momentarily

131

forgotten about that little fly in her ointment … 'Yes, I have. My friend gave me one, and asked that I take it to my brother. She's an inventor—always coming up with strange new objects—so I thought little of it, and her relationship with my brother is … complicated. I thought it best not to dig too deeply.'

'Where could she have got it from?'

'I don't …' But she did know. The map on the temple's roof had shown the locations of all five eggs. There was no way Essa had been to the north, but she could have visited the Kingdom of Sea Serpents while Fyia was at war.

'What is it?' said Scorpia, impatiently.

'Did you know there's a map on the roof?'

Scorpia went still, raptly interested in Fyia's revelation. 'Of what?'

'Of the known world. I think it depicts the seven original temples, and five gemstones are set into the roof too.'

'You think they represent the dragon eggs?'

'It would make sense, don't you think? There was a gem set into the Fae'ch mountains, and one here, and one in the Kingdom of the Black Hoods.'

'Where were the other two?'

'One was on the Great Glacier, the other in the Kingdom of Sea Serpents.'

'In your own kingdom?' Scorpia said distrustfully.

Fyia nodded. 'I had no idea.'

'Ha! You expect me to believe that?'

'You can believe what you want, but it's the truth.' Fyia already felt stupid enough, and had little desire to be lectured by a foreign Queen.

'And you think your friend—Essa—took the ball from the temple there?'

'It's only a theory.'

'Did you find a ball in place of the egg at the Fae'ch Mountains?'

'No,' said Fyia. She shook her head, then added, 'But I wasn't close. It's possible Axus made it disappear before I could see, but that's tenuous at best. I must return to my lands and speak with Essa.'

Fyia left the temple and found Edu waiting outside, pacing back and forth.

'Thank the Gods,' he said. 'I had a bad feeling … what's wrong? Are those burns?' His eyes settled on the bare, red skin of her arms.

'We're leaving. I'll explain on the way.'

'Are we in danger?' he asked, having to stride out to keep up with Fyia's brisk pace.

'No.'

Try as he might, Fyia refused to give him further details as they hurried the short distance back to the airship. They boarded, and Fyia barked orders, instructing Opie to get them in the air as quickly as possible … to set a course for the Temple of the Sea Serpent.

'What the Gods happened?' Adigos asked when they were underway, surprised they had returned so soon.

Fyia led Adigos and Edu to the dining hall, where she made herself a sweet cup of tea. She told them all that had happened, including why they were heading for Sea Serpent.

'Is Scorpia not angry your visit was so brief?' asked Edu. He rummaged around in a drawer, then pulled out a glass jar filled with ointment.

Fyia smirked. 'Scorpia practically ran me out of the temple. She said I was welcome to stay for the usual pomp and ceremony, but if she were me, she'd already be in the air.'

'She sounds like a riot,' said Adigos.

'That she is,' said Fyia.

'She has a pet elephant ...' said Edu. He handed Fyia the healing balm, and she began smearing the foul-smelling stuff on her blistering flesh.

'I knew I should have snuck ashore,' said Rouel, carrying a tray of clay mugs out of the galley. 'A song about Queen Scorpia and her elephant ... now that would be a hit.'

'You can still write it,' said Fyia.

'Not with the same authority,' said Rouel, with a flounce.

'You'll see her when we return,' said Fyia.

'When we return?' said Edu.

'To unite our kingdoms,' said Fyia with a grin, her chest swelling with the possibility of it all.

'When we what?' said Adigos. 'You can't seriously ...'

'I can seriously, and Scorpia isn't against the idea, or so she said as she pushed me out of the temple. Although obviously there are a great number of things to agree.'

'That's an understatement,' said Adigos.

'What will you do about Essa?' said Edu.

'Go to the temple, find out if it's true, and then speak with her. Maybe there's an explanation besides treachery ...' Her insides roiled as she said the word. If she couldn't trust Essa, or her brother, then was there anyone at all she could?

Adigos stroked Fyia's arm as they lay in bed. She barely noticed, endless questions racing through her mind.

His hand paused. 'What is it?' he said. 'What preoccupies you most?'

She lifted her head from his chest, turning to look up at him, hair falling about her shoulders. 'All of it: Essa, my brother, the balls, the missing eggs. Who took them? What do they want to achieve? And now I must unite another five kingdoms … just … all of it.'

'You can't be serious …'

'About which …'

'… you haven't had enough of war?'

Fyia didn't appreciate his tone. She gave him a warning look, but he pressed on regardless.

'Can't you be content with what you have? You already have five kingdoms, people who love you, enough work to keep you busy for ten lifetimes …'

'Essa and Veau betrayed me.'

'They didn't.'

She sat up straighter, wincing as she pressed too hard on her healing flesh. 'How can you know that?'

'I know your brother, and he would never do that to anyone, let alone you.'

That's what Fyia had thought too, but … 'What if the Fae'ch have changed him? What if they've turned him against me?'

'This is what I mean,' said Adigos, running his fingers into her hair, cupping her nape. 'You're driving yourself mad … becoming paranoid. You could choose to be happy, to live contentedly for the rest of your days with what you already have. Start a family …'

She pulled his hand from her neck. 'With you, you mean?'

He turned away. 'Don't do that.' He rolled out of bed and paced to the window, looking out at the black sky. 'The legend could be nothing more than a dream … something made up by a bard, embellished over the years. Maybe there never were any dragon eggs, only some useless metal balls … a wild goose chase … a joke.'

'It's real.'

He rounded to face her. 'How can you know that?'

'I just do.'

'How?' He paused, waiting for her reply, but she said nothing. 'If you want us to come with you on another conquest, then at least tell us why?'

'Us?'

He closed his eyes. 'Me. Tell me why … please …'

'Just sex, Adigos; that's all this is. You should go.'

He shook his head, but headed for the door without protest.

She would unite the Five Kingdoms, and she'd be damned if she explained herself to anyone.

Chapter Eight

FYIA STRODE INTO THE Temple of the Sea Serpent, the fabric of her flimsy tunic billowing out behind her, buffeted by the crisp sea breeze. The others waited outside, only women allowed inside these walls.

Priestesses rushed to her side, half bowing as they hurried to keep up. 'Your Majesty,' said a priestess, 'this is a most welcome surprise. May we show you to the High Priestess? She'd be delighted to offer refreshments in her rooms.'

'No, thank you. Have her meet me in there.' Fyia pointed to one of several tunnels on the other side of the open expanse of temple floor. The opening was carved in the shape of a sea serpent's mouth, stone teeth jutting menacingly into the tunnel.

'Your Majesty, we mean no disrespect, but only the High Priestess may go into the mouth of the sea serpent.'

Fyia was undeterred, keeping up her brisk pace. She took a deep breath, steeling herself before stepping carefully between the serpent's teeth into the blackness beyond.

She let her eyes adjust, and gooseflesh fired across her skin. Making an enemy of the priestesses wasn't a smart move, but it was too late to think about that now.

She started moving again, inching her way along the dark corridor towards the barest chink of light at the far end. The floor was so uneven, she almost fell twice, but she eventually reached the light.

Her relief turned to dread at what she beheld. The tunnel spilled out onto a circular platform, open to the elements, a sheer drop to the sea on the far side. The platform had a hole in the middle of the floor, and steam poured through, the ferocious wind sucking it out to sea.

Fyia took a step back, scared the wind might knock her off, sending her to her death on the rocks below.

'Terrifying, isn't it?' said a soft female voice from behind her.

Fyia whirled around to find a tall, dark woman with mismatched eyes—one brown, one green—watching her.

'It is,' said Fyia, honestly. 'You're the High Priestess?'

'I am, Your Majesty,' the woman said with a bow.

'You know why I'm here?'

'Because of the ball?'

'There was no egg?'

The High Priestess gave a short laugh. 'There was never an egg. A dragon clock used to sit in that hole in the ground. It was damaged by storm after storm, until eventually it fell into the heat below. That happened years ago, before my time. The High Priestess found a small metal ball lying next to the hole. She hid it, and passed it to me before she died.'

'Why did she hide it from the King?'

The priestess scoffed. 'The Kings have never been friends of ours.'

'Did she know what it was?'

'No.'

'Did she try to find out?'

'If she did, she never told me.'

'Did you?'

The priestess laughed, the sound a light tinkle that seemed to blend with the wind. 'Where would I look? And anyway, we're more concerned with replacing the clock and closing the hole. It took years just to find a female engineer qualified to survey the damage.'

'Essa.'

The priestess nodded. 'I showed her the hole and the ball. She took the ball, then left. I haven't seen or heard from her since, and every day the smoke worsens. Will you help us close it, Your Majesty?'

'You can't use your magic?'

The priestess laughed. 'Much as we appreciate your making magic legal once more, ours has withered and all-but died. I'm scared even to try. Small healing magics and the like are all we can manage.' The priestess took Fyia's hand, then muttered a few words Fyia couldn't make out. The burns on her skin disappeared, her aches vanishing.

'Thank you,' said Fyia. She flexed her fingers, examining the healed skin, barely able to believe it.

The priestess staggered back against the wall. 'You see?' she said, breathing hard. 'Even that small working has left me frail and feeble.'

'I'm sorry,' said Fyia. 'I wish there was more I could do. I'll speak with Essa, certainly, but … what's down there?'

The priestess held Fyia's gaze for a beat. 'Fire of the Seven Hells, Your Majesty.'

Fyia sat back in her chair, glad to be reunited with her wolves, whose familiar weight pressed against her legs. Her Small Council stretched out along the table before her—all except Lord Eratus Venir, who was still across the Kraken Sea.

'Starfall,' said Fyia, 'if you'd be so kind.'

Starfall raised an eyebrow. 'Everything's going about as well as can be expected,' she said, with her characteristic nonchalance. 'The market owners delayed until the last tick, but they complied with your new laws. They're enforcing fair pay ... for now, at least.'

Fyia looked to Lady Nara for confirmation. Nara inclined her head.

'What of accessibility?' said Fyia.

'Lord Fredrik and I have implemented a new system to allocate market stalls,' said Nara. 'It's still not perfect, but it's better than before.'

'Good,' said Fyia. She was pleased to see they'd made progress, despite the reluctance of many influential loud mouths.

'The Spider and Essa have appointed a new university chancellor, as well as new leaders of the guilds,' said Starfall.

'Any backlash?' asked Fyia.

'Of course,' said the Spider, 'and we'll see more.'

'Such as?'

'Protests, barricades to prevent women from entering buildings, there's even been an assassination attempt on the new chancellor.'

'Who's behind it?' said Fyia.

'Too many to name, although I'm keeping a close watch on Lord Antice, and Sensis has deployed troops on the ground.'

'It's true,' said Sensis, 'which has slowed progress on training at the military academy.'

'Are they resisting too?' said Fyia.

'Some did,' said Sensis, 'but most of the ringleaders left of their own accord. Unfortunately, they've joined the troublemakers. We're making progress; those who stayed want to learn. Our tactics bested theirs, after all. We've also recruited three new intakes, many of whom are women.'

'Good,' said Fyia. 'What do you suggest we do about the troublemakers?'

'Stay the course,' said Sensis. 'The protests will run out of steam eventually … assuming they don't get a big win before that happens.'

'You've put security on all the new leaders?' said Fyia.

'Of course,' said Sensis.

'What about the woman we captured from the airship?' asked Fyia. 'Has she revealed anything?'

'No,' said the Spider and Starfall together.

'We've tried everything we can think of,' said the Spider, 'but she's refusing to answer a single question.'

'She cackles and babbles and tears out chunks of her hair,' said Starfall. 'We tried hypnosis, light and art therapy, aromatic scents, coercion … we tried it all, and none of it worked.'

The doors at the back of the chamber clunked and whirled as they swung inwards, and Lord Venir—uncharacteristically disheveled—stood in the doorway. Fyia covered her surprise as he strode to the table, then bowed low, no sign of his previous pretense of being hampered by age.

'Your Majesty,' he said, without his usual sneer. 'I came as fast as I could, bearing bad news. The Emperor has taken your silence as a snub. He believes you question his word …'

'You've seen the dragons?' said Fyia.

'No. No one has. The Emperor is on the warpath. He's sending troops.'

'When?'

'A few days at most. I came as soon as I heard. They have a fleet of airships … it won't be long.'

'Where will they attack?'

'I didn't have time to find out.'

'Get Essa,' said Fyia.

'She's outside,' said the Spider, already halfway to the doors.

'Essa,' said Fyia, as she appeared with the Spider, 'the Emperor is sending airships to attack; we must prepare our defenses. Sensis, where should we focus our efforts?'

'Depends what he wants,' said Sensis. 'Venir, any ideas?'

'He wants the Queen; he's obsessed with her.'

'Then he'll come here,' said Sensis, 'assuming he knows that's where you are.'

'Why?' said Fyia, looking at Venir. 'Why does he want me?'

'Because you're the most powerful woman in all the world, and he can't have you.'

'My parents aren't behind this?' said Fyia.

'Doubtful,' said Venir. 'The Emperor's court does not hold your parents in high regard, despite what they tell people.'

A deafening boom filled the room, coming from outside, shaking the glass in the windows, and then the air went still. They hesitated for barely a tick of the clock before springing into action. Fyia jumped to her feet, Edu and Adigos flanking her as she ran for the door, nearing it by the time the second boom sounded.

'Impossible,' said Venir, 'they can't be here already.'

'Protect the Queen!' shouted Sensis, as they ran into the corridor.

'Sensis!' Essa shouted over another great boom. 'Protect the clock!'

'What?' said Sensis, rounding on Essa. Sensis looked to Fyia, who'd also stopped in her tracks.

'There's no time to explain now, but we have to protect the clock,' said Essa.

She had no time to think, only to act. 'Do it,' said Fyia.

Essa disappeared as a guard sprinted down the corridor towards them. 'Report,' said Sensis.

'Bombs going off all over the city,' he said.

'Any airships?' asked Sensis.

'No.'

'Soldiers?'

'None so far.'

'We have to get you out of here,' Edu said to Fyia, his tone brooking no argument.

'We'll search the rest of the building,' said Sensis.

'Use my wolves,' said Fyia, the larger of the two running after Essa. 'If there's a bomb, they'll find it.'

Edu took Fyia by the arm and dragged her down the corridor. The Spider, Starfall, and other members of the council hurried behind them, escorted by Fyia's guards.

Edu reached the end of a seemingly dead-end corridor and twisted a wall sconce. A section of wall slid aside, revealing a dark corridor beyond. Edu quickly lit the waiting torches, then led them inside.

They all but ran through the tunnels, Adigos scouting ahead, while Edu stayed glued to Fyia's side. They made four or five turns, Fyia losing track of how many and which way, then hurried down two long flights of stairs. The air became damp and cold as they descended, sludge adorning the walls.

They reached a barred gate, and Fyia worried they were trapped, but Edu pulled out a flat circular disk with grooves and divots carved into its surface. He pushed it against the wall and twisted, and a clunking filled the air, the gate rising to allow them through. Edu pressed the disk against the wall on the other side, and the gate rattled closed behind them.

The tunnel here was dank and musty, a canal taking up most of the space. Fyia knew underground waterways ran across the city, but she'd never been down to see them. Rats scurried out of their way as they headed towards the light at the end of the tunnel, but, much to Fyia's disappointment, they didn't go out into the sunlight. Instead, Edu pressed another disk into the wall fifty paces from the tunnel's end.

The wall pivoted inwards, another dark and uninviting tunnel appearing beyond. Adigos led them, hurrying through the twists and turns until they reached a split.

'You,' Edu said to Fyia's bodyguards and council members, 'that way.' He pointed to the righthand path.

Fyia didn't hear the rest of his words, as the Spider was already ushering her, Starfall, and Adigos down the left fork. The smaller group moved even faster than before, and Fyia marveled at the speed the Spider's aged legs could travel.

After more twists and turns, the tunnel ended abruptly at a dead end. The Spider motioned for silence, then slid a panel in the wall aside, looking through the spy hole she'd revealed. 'Clear,' she said, pulling out a metal disk and twisting it against a stone. The wall slid silently open, and they all stepped through into a large and well-appointed kitchen.

'Where are we?' said Fyia.

'Safehouse,' said the Spider. 'One of many linked from the council building.'

'I sent the others to a different one,' said Edu, who'd caught up with them. The wall—wood paneled this side—slid closed behind him.

'How did you know about the tunnels?' Fyia asked Edu.

'The Spider briefed Adigos and I when we were here last,' said Edu. 'They extend all across the city, using the waterways as well as tunnels in the buildings themselves. There are spy holes everywhere.'

'Who else knows about them?' said Fyia.

'Hard to say,' said the Spider. 'Safer to assume they're not a secret, but Essa's been replacing the lock mechanisms to make them more secure.'

A boom shook the air, and Fyia rushed to the front of the house. She flew up two flights of stairs, searching for a window that would give her a view of the city. She found one, and almost wished she hadn't. Her view was limited—the safe house surrounded by other buildings—but smoke billowed across the sky.

Fire bells rang out, and scared men, women, and children ran through the streets, some dragging the injured behind them. Fyia couldn't tear her eyes from the desolation.

'The Emperor couldn't have pulled off something of this scale … not so quickly,' said Starfall.

Another boom caused the windowpanes to rattle, and Edu pulled Fyia back. 'Away from the windows,' he said.

She went willingly, turning to discover the window was in a library, the walls lined with books. She moved back into the room, and the others took seats on the stiff, upright furniture.

'You think it's my own people?' said Fyia.

'They might be your people now,' said Starfall, 'but they haven't been for long.'

'And you've hardly pulled your punches,' said the Spider. 'Your changes have been met with much disagreement …'

'My changes are needed,' said Fyia, hotly.

'Nobody's disputing that,' said the Spider, 'but you've made one or two people angry …'

'We need Sensis,' said Fyia.

'I sent Rouel back to get her and Essa,' said Edu. 'Once they've secured the council building, they'll come here.'

'*If* they secure the council building,' said Starfall.

Fyia gave her a disapproving look, then turned her attention to the scene through the window. 'Whoever's behind this, they'll be looking for me.'

'They won't find you,' said Edu.

'Unless they know about the tunnels,' said the Spider.

'When the bombs stop, we'll move to a safe house outside the city,' said Edu.

'They're destroying their own city,' said Fyia, shaking her head. 'Why would they do that? It hurts me, yes, but it hurts them more.'

Adigos was uncharacteristically quiet. He leaned against the window's shutter, staring outside.

Fyia brought her fists down on the back of a couch and shrieked. Being caged in here was making it worse. They needed to *do* something. They had to find whoever was responsible, and stop them from causing more destruction. They had to help the wounded, deal with the dead, give aid to those who needed it … and yet, the smart move was to wait.

She closed her eyes and took two long breaths, forcing calm into her veins, banishing the fury that longed to burst free. 'We need to get word out that I've fled the city, and make sure the Emperor's airships hear that news. Otherwise, as soon as this is over, the city's going to be hit again.'

'Where's the pilot?' asked Starfall. 'What's he called again? He should know how to find the Emperor's forces.'

'Opie,' said Edu. 'He's with the airship in a warehouse on the outskirts of the city. He's doing maintenance ...'

Starfall's face scrunched in disbelief.

'Guards supervise his every move,' said Edu, with a scowl of his own.

'I'll get him,' said the Spider. 'I'll go through the tunnels.'

'Adigos would be quicker,' said Fyia.

'You're not young anymore,' said Starfall, with a wicked smile. 'That's what she's really saying.'

The Spider ignored Starfall. 'Adigos will get lost in three ticks' flat. I'm the only one who knows the way, and am perfectly capable of making the journey, despite my *great* age.'

Fyia held her breath, then exhaled loudly. 'Okay,' she said. 'Let's just hope it's not already too late.'

The bombs stopped, and they waited. And waited. Staying put was sensible, but Fyia longed to be out there, helping. To do *something*. 'Rouel will be fine,' Fyia said to Edu, who paced by the door.

Edu scowled. 'Of course he will. Like all your guards, he's an accomplished soldier, and well trained. Don't worry about him.'

Wasn't that why Edu was worried? She could sense the emotion rolling off him in waves, but she couldn't comfort him ... didn't know how. Her parents had subscribed to the tough love school of raising children, which mostly involved ignoring them, or telling them to do better, their best never quite good enough. The closest thing she'd had to love was from a puppy, and her brother …

Finally, as the sun was dipping behind the spires and towers of the city, Fyia heard a clatter from below. She flew towards the stairs, but Adigos grabbed her around the waist, and Edu stepped in front of her, blocking her way.

'I'll check it out,' said Edu.

But before he'd reached the first step, Starfall called up from the kitchen, 'Sensis and Essa just arrived, and they brought a … guest.'

Fyia rushed to the kitchen, along with Adigos and Edu. 'Thank the Gods,' said Fyia, relieved to see Sensis and Essa in one piece. 'Did my wolves make it out?'

'They ran,' said Sensis. 'They helped bring down our friend here, and then pursued his accomplices.'

Fyia nodded. Her wolves could take care of themselves.

'Who is he?' said Fyia. She looked down at the big man kneeling before her, his dark hair speckled with grey. Blood splattered his face and clothes, and his nose was bent at an odd angle. His hands were tied behind his back, Sensis' hand on his shoulder, a not-so-gentle reminder he was at their mercy.

'We caught him helping plant a bomb in the council building,' said Sensis. 'There were three of them. The others escaped.'

'Has he told you anything?' said Fyia.

'Please,' said the man. 'They made me do it. They said they'd hurt my family if I didn't help them.'

'Who?' said Fyia.

'I don't know, Your Majesty. One had stars tattooed below her eye. They talked about support for their cause … but … that was all I heard.'

'When did they approach you?' said Fyia.

'A span ago—five days. They threatened my son. Please, Your Majesty, he's only four.'

'What did you think they ask of you?'

'I was to help them get into the council building. I've worked there for years as a caretaker. I was to show them a way in through the tunnels. I didn't know they intended to bomb the city …'

'No?' said Starfall, scornfully. 'What did you think they intended? Merely to kill the Queen?'

The man went white. 'No. No, of course not. I swear. I didn't know … I just … I had to protect my family!'

'Where is your family now?' asked Fyia.

'They fled the city. I had to get them away from those people … in case they went back on their word.'

'Convenient,' said Starfall.

'Please … you have to believe me!'

'Where are the others?' said Fyia.

'I … if I tell you, they'll kill me.'

'And what do you think will happen if you don't tell us?' said Starfall.

The man cast his eyes around wildly.

'Nobody needs to get hurt,' said Fyia. 'Tell us where these people are—and anything else that might help us. If you do, I'll reunite you with your family. I might even give you a reward.'

The man looked from Starfall to Fyia and back again. 'I … I need protection; they'll kill me if they find out.'

'That can be arranged,' said Fyia, 'but only if you tell me everything you know. Right now.'

'They planned to return to Moon,' said the man.

'They told you that?' said Fyia.

'No. I overheard …'

'Really …' said Starfall.

The man started spluttering … about how he was loyal to his Queen, would never really betray her … how he'd had no choice.

'Where were they staying in the city?' said Fyia.

'I don't know, Your Majesty,' he said. 'They came to my house. They never said … Please, that's all I know.'

'We need to move,' said Edu. 'Now. If they know about the tunnels, we've been here too long already.'

Fyia nodded, and Sensis pulled a hood over the man's face.

'I need to go back to my workshop,' said Essa. 'My assistants, and the things I have there … I need to make sure it's all safe.'

'You're coming with us,' said Fyia. 'Sensis will stay here and see to the rest.'

Sensis nodded.

'And keep this man in a cell until the Spider returns.'

Sensis nodded again, then hauled the man to his feet. If what he'd said was true … if those responsible for the bombs were truly from Moon, then her problems were worse than she'd wanted to admit.

She'd always known it would be difficult to unite five disparate kingdoms. Each one of her lands was fiercely independent, with an identity that was unique and firmly rooted. Each kingdom was proud … trusted their neighbors only so far as they had to, for trade and mutual benefit. What she was asking, for them to come together as one, would take time to accomplish. It seemed the dissenters had taken the lead in that regard, for members of Moon planting so many bombs could not have gone undetected by the people of Selise.

And Fyia was not a man. She was not a warrior. Her people did not respect her, and they wouldn't ... not until she gave them a reason so compelling they had no choice. Not until she had dragons.

Chapter Nine

FYIA BATHED IN A large pool in their new safe house. It was heated by hot springs, and Fyia mused that hers seemed more like a kingdom of water, rather than a kingdom of dragons, with the heated springs, aqueducts, and canals that carried the stuff everywhere. Maybe dragons liked water …

Starfall sat opposite in the ornate stone bath, and Fyia voiced her thoughts.

'Yours is a kingdom of ash,' said Starfall, 'and yet, you do nothing about it.'

'I know there's work to do,' Fyia said hotly. 'I'm making changes, which, I might add, is what got me into this mess …'

'You're off chasing shadows, rather than leading your people. You leave me to do the hard work while you dart around the world, obsessing over myths and legends.'

There weren't many whom Fyia would let speak to her this way, but she needed Starfall. And what Starfall needed was to blow off steam; she'd been antsy since they'd arrived at the safe house. 'It's too much for you?' Fyia said, splashing water over her shoulder.

'Don't goad me, child.'

The corners of Fyia's lips twitched in irritation. A good argument was exactly what Fyia needed too, to banish the cyclone stirring her blood, and prepare her for Essa.

Essa's betrayal still cut like a knife ... her brother's betrayal, and arguments with her aunt were like a storm in a teacup, brutal, destroying everything they touched, but short-lived and carefully contained. There was no harm in it.

'How dare you accuse me of chasing shadows? You deny the existence of dragons?'

'They existed once, long ago. They exist no longer.'

'They do exist,' said Fyia. Echoes of her dragon dreams rubbed across her skin.

'You hope they do,' said Starfall. 'But that is all you have; wishful delusions.'

'I know they are real, and you know I must find them, or I will forever have to look over my shoulder ... will always have enemies within my lands.'

'Stay and fight,' said Starfall, leaning forward. 'Give them a reason to believe in you.'

'I am giving them reasons ... have killed five kings. But there are those for whom only dragons will ever be enough.'

'Those like you, you mean?'

Fyia slapped the water. 'Yes, Gods damn it, those like me. Those who dare to step outside the boundaries others have laid down. I thought you, of all people, would understand that.'

'We're not talking about me,' said Starfall, her voice soft, but with a razor edge.

Fyia cast her eyes up to the ornate ceiling. A scene of water nymphs playing in a pond was painted there, and Fyia wondered if nymphs would ever return to her lands.

'You know my options are limited,' said Fyia, still looking at the ceiling. 'If I stay, they will undermine me every step of the way. I will be forced to defer to convention … to the rules of others.'

'You *should* marry,' said Starfall, her words purposefully inflammatory.

Fyia laughed cruelly as she met her aunt's gaze once more. 'And hand over everything I've accomplished? To become a trophy, good for nothing but bearing heirs?'

'So instead, you chase dragons in the hopes of greatness, letting everything you've fought for slip through your fingers …'

'I have already accomplished greatness,' said Fyia. Her aunt looked away. 'I will find the dragons, but I do not seek them for my reputation. Our lands will never be whole until they return.'

Silence settled, the only sounds the trickling of water as it flowed in and out of the pool.

'You know there are those who believe dragons bear the souls of all the fire-touched who came before?' said Fyia.

Starfall sent her a disbelieving look. 'You want to find them, so when you die you can live on? As a dragon?'

'No. I want to find them because they are part of who we are.'

'You're chasing a myth.'

'I am chasing the future my kingdoms deserve.'

Footsteps halted at the doorway, and Fyia looked up to see Adigos, his features hesitant. 'You called for me?' he asked. 'I can come back …'

Fyia had called for him. He'd been unusually sullen since she'd reminded him their relationship was sex and nothing more. Starfall stood, water streaming from her naked body, and Adigos shifted uncomfortably, averting his gaze.

Fyia stood also, wrapping herself in a robe as Starfall stalked from the room, with the barest nod of deference.

'Come,' said Fyia, leading Adigos to the couches where refreshments awaited. Her argument with Starfall had been disappointing, not giving her the release she'd sought, and her chest coiled tight with frustration.

She stopped abruptly beside a couch, and felt Adigos halt behind her. She reached for his hands, pulling him forward until his back was flush against her, then placed his hands on her breasts. He hesitated, so she reached back and stroked him through his breeches. He huffed into her shoulder.

'Fyia … I,' he said, his lips brushing the delicate skin of her neck. His words were reticent, but his hands began kneading her breasts.

She spun and looked up into his burning eyes. It was all she needed to see—he still wanted her—and she pounced, her feral mouth crashing into his, the knot of tight angst in her chest spurring her on. They devoured each other, their kisses deep, the rough scrape of his tongue over hers sending bolts of electricity to the base of her belly.

He pulled the flimsy material of her robe apart, and she released him from his breeches. He grabbed handfuls of her backside, hoisting her against him. She lifted her leg, and he wrapped it around his waist, supporting her as she guided him inside.

He moved, but it wasn't enough, so she urged him faster, clawing at his back. He lifted her, and she wrapped both legs around him, crying out as he pressed her back against a pillar.

He thrust into her with frantic movements, and she dug her hands into his hair, moaning and gasping.

'Gods,' he choked, 'Fyia …'

She convulsed around him as his thrusts became erratic. He groaned, making small pumping movements, and then stilled, panting, holding her to him.

He dropped her back to the floor, and the air went taut; something between them had changed. She pulled her robe closed, and he avoided her gaze as he re-buttoned his breeches.

'Adigos …'

'I love you, Fyia,' he said.

'Adi …'

'I want us to be together.'

'No.'

Fyia's mood took a turn for the worse. She should never have let him into her bed …

'Fyia …'

She let out a growl of frustration. 'This is over,' she said, forcing herself to meet his gaze, so he knew she meant it. 'You could have your pick of any woman … any but me. They swoon and bat their eyes as you walk by. And not only vacuous women, but intelligent, formidable ones too. Pick one of them to make you happy, for I will not marry you. I will not marry anyone.'

'We don't have to marry,' said Adigos.

Fyia barked out a cruel laugh. 'You would be my concubine?'

He scowled. 'Your consort,' he said, biting out the word.

'I told you from the beginning, this was physical, nothing more. You said you understood.'

'I do understand, but that doesn't mean I accept it.'

Fyia threw up her hands. 'I am going north. You are not.'

'Fyia … please.'

'I recommend you use the time without me to find a woman who actually wants to be your wife.'

Adigos had made Fyia's mood worse, and by the time she'd dressed and was sitting in her temporary study, it was a deep dark shade of black.

Fyia studied Essa—her supposed friend … a dear friend, and her brother's former betrothed.

Essa stood on the other side of the large alterwood desk, her spine ramrod straight. Ordinarily, Essa wouldn't have waited for Fyia's invitation to sit, but today she did. Either she sensed the tension in the air— how could she not—or someone had tipped her off. Maybe both.

'I won't waste our time with pleasantries,' said Fyia, when she'd let the silence stretch to discomfort.

Essa said nothing, her eyes cast down towards her feet. *Coward.*

'You betrayed me.'

Essa's eyes finally flicked up from the floor. 'No, Your Majesty.'

'Yes, Essa.' Fyia held Essa's gaze, daring her to interrupt again. Essa's eyes returned to the floor.

Fyia stood, then moved to a bookshelf behind Essa with the sole intention of making her uncomfortable. 'You *used* me to take that ball to my brother, who I need not remind you resides with the Fae'ch—a group with whom my kingdoms are not on the best of terms.'

Essa remained silent, and Fyia returned to her seat, summoning her wolves to her side. They'd arrived at the safe house not long before, and she petted them, taking comfort from their presence, and reminding Essa she could easily lose a limb.

'Tell me everything,' said Fyia. 'Leave nothing out.'

Essa nodded, and briefly met Fyia's eyes. She looked away as she collected her thoughts, her formidable mind taking a moment to prepare her words. 'Your brother and I still write to one another. We were both devastated when he … chose a life with the Fae'ch. Neither one of us wanted to let go.

'His letters are sporadic, but he often sends hints about things I should try … how I could improve an invention, or infuse my ideas with magic one day. I was grateful, and he never asked for anything in return … even though, if the Fae'ch found out, they could exile him.'

'He never asked for anything in return, until he did …' said Fyia, prompting her to get back on track.

Essa sucked in a breath, shaking herself. 'A letter arrived, asking me to go to the Temple of the Sea Serpent and deliver what I found to your brother. I didn't hesitate, and the High Priestess handed over the metal ball without question. She assumed I was there to help fix the hole left by the fallen clock.'

'Were you planning to help them at least?' asked Fyia. 'Or were you content to steal from them, and damn their welfare?'

Essa's face blushed a dusky pink. 'I plan to help them,' she said, hotly, 'but don't know how to close the hole. I'm researching the clocks … I believe them to be important.'

'Why does my brother want the ball?' said Fyia, interrupting her. 'What is it for?'

'I don't know,' said Essa, 'but whatever it is, it's linked to the clocks.'

'Not the dragon eggs?' said Fyia, leaning forward.

Essa shrugged. 'I must conduct more research … the texts now available at the university, and in the guilds of Moon, are beyond anything I could access before. But I've had limited time to explore … I have other duties … appointing a new chancellor, designing your palace, and now replicating the flying boat …'

'I ask too much?' said Fyia, her tone derisive.

'Of course not, Your Majesty. I merely sought to explain …'

'Then explain why you betrayed me? Why you tricked me into smuggling something precious to those whose intentions we do not understand? Tell me …' Fyia broke off and looked out of the windows at the darkening skies. 'Tell me why my brother lied to me … took the metal ball and said nothing of its origin, then gave no hint of what had transpired?'

'I cannot speak for Veau, but I acted as I did because …' She hesitated, folding in on herself. 'Because I love him. I did what he asked and shut my mind to the omission, because I believe in my heart he would never act against you. I believe, with certainty, whatever he's doing, he's doing for you, to help you. He loves no one in this world more than you …'

Not even me. Essa's unsaid words echoed in the air between them.

Veau had chosen a life with the Fae'ch, clearing the path for Fyia to be Queen of their home kingdom, or so the world believed. The truth was more complex, but the best rumors were often simple things. Never mind he'd hated his life, and the expectation that he— because of the river of golden scales across his face— would be the one to bring back the dragons. Never mind he couldn't control his magic, and was becoming a danger to others and himself … to Essa. Never mind he craved a simple, solitary life away from the eyes of the world. He'd understood the burden of leadership,

159

and had not wanted it. He'd been relieved when he'd handed the mantle to Fyia.

Did Essa know all that? Fyia hadn't pried into Essa's relationship with her brother because she'd respected their friendship. Maybe she was a friend no longer …

'You believe me responsible for my brother's departure?' said Fyia.

Essa went very still, then shook her head. 'It was his decision.'

'And yet your loyalty is to him, rather than your Queen?'

'It's not like that,' said Essa, a flash of defiance in her eyes. 'Veau is trying to help you.'

'Then why not tell me the truth?' said Fyia, her voice spiraling upward.

'Because Veau asked me not to.'

Fyia slammed her hand on the desk. 'You think that is good enough? Should I accept that as an excuse from all who wrong me? *I'm sorry, Your Majesty, but Starfall asked me not to tell you? I'm sorry, Your Majesty, but Sensis asked me not to tell you?*'

Essa said nothing.

'Well?' Fyia demanded. 'Should I smile sweetly and pity you, because my brother chose his own path? The path that was right for him, and not what you—in your selfishness—desired he do?'

'That is not fair,' said Essa, her words hard despite the tears pooling in her eyes. The sight of them emptied the well of Fyia's temper, and guilt filled the hole where it had been. She'd never seen Essa cry, not in all the years she'd known her.

But what should Fyia do? Let Essa walk free? Let her go unpunished? If she did, and others discovered Fyia's weakness …

'Leave,' said Fyia. 'I will think of an appropriate punishment. And in the meantime, prepare a report on the clocks and metal balls. I want to know everything you've found.'

Essa bowed, then spun for the door. Fyia rubbed her face in her hands, then screamed in frustration. She couldn't lose all those she held dear, for if she did, what was the point of any of it?

Fyia kicked off her shoes, threw open the doors to the patio, and ran down the steps. Her wolves flanked her as her feet raced from the harsh stone to the green grass of the rolling lawn. She ran away from the formal gardens into the woods, needing the energy she could only get from the wild.

She shouldn't be out without guards, even on the grounds of the safe house, but she wanted to be alone.

Fyia's shoulders dropped as soon as she crossed the tree line. Her heart pumped loudly in her ears as she sprinted along a game path, skirting ancient oaks, walnut, and chestnut trees, scaring rabbits and squirrels and birds.

She ran so fast her body screamed for air, her legs burning, her chest aching, but she pushed herself further, faster, leaping a fallen tree that blocked her way in tandem with her wolves.

They reveled in the exercise as much as she did, Fyia feeling their spirits soar as they hurtled through the undergrowth. And Fyia's spirits soared too, finally feeling the release she'd sought … the release she needed.

Fyia slowed, but kept running, sucking in long breaths, giving her body the air it craved. How she wished she could stay in the woods and never return … she tried the lie on, but it gave her no comfort, so she batted it away. The only thing she wanted was to find her dragons … prove to the world she was worthy … improve things for all. Although she did wish finding them didn't require more war and heartache, and that those she relied on could have some small respite before sacrificing themselves again.

Fyia's wolves sensed movement to the left, and then to the right, and Fyia took off at a sprint once more. Couldn't she have a single moment of peace?

She raced through the woods, her lungs protesting, using the senses of her wolves to guide her, but not two spins later, a pond blocked her way. A beautiful, reed filled thing with water lilies and dragonflies. She stopped abruptly, bending, her hands on her knees as she caught her breath.

'Oh, don't be so smug,' Fyia said to the trees. 'You caught me. Now, tell me you brought refreshments, because I am parched.'

Sensis and Edu stepped out of the trees, one on either side of where she stood. 'As a matter of fact, I did,' said Sensis, ignoring Edu's scowl of disapproval.

'That's why you went inside before following her?' said Edu.

'I know my Queen,' said Sensis, shrugging and pulling the stopper from a leather flask. Sensis took a swig, then said cheerfully, 'Doesn't taste poisoned to me, Your Majesty.' She handed the flask to Fyia with a mock bow.

Fyia took the flask and sat on a rock. 'The others think I should stay put and fix my kingdoms,' said Fyia, throwing a stick into the water.

'Adigos, you mean?' said Sensis. She dropped to the ground, a smile on her lips. 'So you can get married and have babies?'

Fyia rolled her eyes. 'So he can be my consort …'

Sensis barked out a laugh.

'Starfall wants me to stay too … says she doesn't believe in the dragons.'

'Starfall needs to get laid,' said Sensis. 'Send her a courtesan—or better yet, two—and she'll be happy once more.'

Fyia raised her eyebrows; it wasn't a terrible idea. 'I sent Adigos away … told him to find a wife.'

Edu laughed, and Fyia could see relief in his eyes as he snatched the flask. 'Did he fall at your feet and beg like a puppy?'

'Harsh …' said Sensis.

Unusual for Edu. 'Why do you dislike him so?' said Fyia.

'I don't dislike him, and as a warrior, there are few I'd rather have at my back … at least when our interests align. But I can't trust him. Not after he killed King Milo, an act for which he seems to believe he has atoned.'

'You think I should've been harsher with my punishment?' said Fyia. 'I sent him away for the rest of the war … I made him travel to the Fae'ch around the perimeter of the Five Kingdoms!'

'Then took him to your bed the minute he returned,' said Edu, the look on his face daring Fyia to contradict him.

Fyia filled her lungs, then exhaled a long sigh. Edu rarely spoke up like this, but when he did, he didn't mince his words … and he was usually right.

'My bed has been empty for a long time,' said Fyia, 'and a courtesan isn't an option for me.'

'It's not *not* an option,' said Sensis. 'We could find you someone trustworthy.'

Fyia shuddered. 'The idea of you two vetting my next sex partner is creepy.'

'Oh, I don't know,' said Sensis. 'It would be fun ...'

'Only if I get to vet yours,' said Fyia. 'Actually, that would be fun. Would you like a man, or a woman? Or both?' She gave a salacious flick of her eyebrows.

'We were talking about you,' said Sensis.

'It's more fun discussing you,' said Fyia, 'and I need a distraction. And don't think I've missed the way people look at you, Edu ... I'm sure we could find you a few willing candidates.'

'Please,' said Edu, 'don't make me sell your location to the Emperor ...'

'From what I hear, the Emperor's had enough practice to give even the most dedicated of courtesans a run for their money,' said Sensis.

'*The largest harem in all the world* ... isn't that what he calls it?' said Edu.

'Selling me off might finally make my courtiers happy, although I doubt for the same reasons as you two,' said Fyia.

They laughed, then sat in companionable silence, sharing the flask of wine as a breeze rippled the water in the dying light of day.

'Well, anyway,' Fyia said after a time, 'I've sent Adigos away.'

Sensis frowned. 'He's still at the safe house.'

Of course he was. 'Well, when Edu and I leave for the north, he won't be able to follow.'

'You've decided then?' said Sensis. 'You're going north?'

'You think I should stay too?' said Fyia, alarm coursing through her. It was one thing for Starfall and Adigos to want her to stay, but something else entirely if Sensis and Edu thought she was making the wrong choice.

'No, of course not,' Sensis said with a firm shake of her head. 'You have always been clear about what you want. I won't lie, I had hoped for some brief respite, or that the dragons would puff into existence once you killed the last King. But when was life ever so easy?'

'What about you?' said Fyia, looking at Edu, who had reclined on the grass, leaning back on his arms.

'Dragons,' said Edu. 'That's the mission. I have no interest in guarding a palace all day and night. I'd much rather be out exploring the world with you.'

'Do you think it's selfish of us?' said Fyia. 'I mean, right now, the Emperor's airships could be preparing to lay waste to my lands, but honestly, I care more about going north.'

'And why is that?' said Sensis.

'Because I want to find the dragons.'

'Because?' Sensis pressed.

'To make our lands whole,' said Fyia, 'and to prove I'm the one from the legends,' she added, with a cocky smile.

'Then no,' said Sensis, 'I do not think we are selfish. And your people won't either, when the frozen north melts, and the growing season lengthens, and dragons bring ash to fertilize the fields ... when you reunite all five of the great kingdoms in a peaceful, prosperous alliance.'

'When you put it like that,' said Edu, 'how could anyone disagree? Going north is the only sane choice.'

'Then hope the legends are true,' said Fyia, 'and that we are the ones to find the dragons.'

'You doubt it?' said Sensis.

'No,' said Fyia, as the purple light of the setting sun streaked across the sky. The echo of a dragon dream scratched a talon across her skin. 'I do not.'

'Spider, it is good to see you,' said Fyia. She took a seat in the building's magnificent orangery. It was heated by the hot spring, and filled with exotic plants from the south and west that wouldn't have a hope of survival in the climate outside.

Fyia leaned back in her woven seat as Essa and Starfall joined them, Sensis and Edu already helping themselves to tea and sweet treats.

The Spider bowed her head. 'Likewise, Your Majesty. I come bearing news.'

'Please,' said Fyia, waving her hand to indicate the Spider should go on.

'Opie got word to the Emperor's flying fleet. He took the airship—packed with an entire company of your guards below deck—found the fleet, and told them you had fled north.'

'Did it work?' said Fyia.

'It is unknown. Opie's instruction was to return the airship as a matter of priority, so he slipped away shortly after he imparted the news.'

Fyia nodded. 'I plan to leave for the north in the morning. When I do, Essa will go to the airship, and draw up plans for ships of our own. Spider, find carpenters—the best we have—and send them to her. Adigos will accompany Essa, as her guard.'

The Spider bowed her head, as did Essa, but not fast enough to hide her look of surprise. Adigos would be her guard in more than one sense of the word, keeping Essa safe, but also watching for another betrayal, or even worse, a defection.

'Now,' said Fyia, moving them on, 'it has become clear that uniting the five kingdoms I have already conquered is not enough to bring back the dragons.'

The Spider's sharp eyes widened a fraction, but Fyia continued, keeping it matter of fact. 'It never was enough, as they will only return when the Five Great

Kingdoms reunite, not my Five Eastern Kingdoms. Thus, we still have work to do.'

Fyia paused a beat.

'You've decided then?' said Starfall, rolling a leaf in her fingers. 'You'll abandon your kingdoms when they need you most?'

'She's not abandoning anyone,' said Sensis. 'We all knew what this was about from the start. You expect Fyia to be content sitting on a throne?'

'So her people are to suffer?' said Starfall, ripping the leaf from the plant's stalk.

'They won't suffer when we return with dragons,' said Edu. 'Quite the opposite, in fact.'

'And I already have the southern lands on side. Scorpia is keen to reunite, if it means the return of the dragons.'

'Why?' said Starfall. 'How does that benefit her? More likely, she's happy for you to go off on a wild chase, so she can ramp up the taxes she charges us on exports.'

'She has her reasons,' said Fyia, although she didn't know what they were … 'and I trust her.'

Starfall ripped the leaf to pieces, then scattered the shreds to the floor, but Fyia knew her aunt would come around … she always did.

'The Fae'ch are not hostile,' said Fyia, 'nor are the Black Hoods, so I have hopes of uniting on friendly terms. Which leaves only those on the Great Glacier … unfortunately, an unknown entity.'

'None of them will give up their sovereignty,' said the Spider.

Fyia nodded in agreement. 'I'm not asking them to. I'm merely asking that they unite with me in my quest to find the dragons, as part of a peaceful alliance.'

'But is that enough?' said Essa. She looked shocked she'd voiced her thought.

'We shall see,' said Fyia. 'Unless you have information to share with us on that score?'

'No,' said Essa, wringing her hands, 'and I ... I suppose the legend says the Five Kingdoms must be *united*, not that one ruler must rule them all.'

'Even if it is enough, the ruler must still be *worthy*,' said Starfall.

'Helpful,' said Sensis, dryly. 'Thank you for your contribution.'

Starfall flicked her fingers at Sensis.

'I am worthy,' said Fyia, her tone brusque and businesslike, 'and I will unite the kingdoms. I will find the dragons, and I will ride one for the rest of my days, not sit upon some gilded throne.'

'Assuming the dragon eggs still exist,' said Essa.

Fyia's eyes flicked to Essa's round face. She wasn't being antagonistic, but scientific, and Fyia sensed there was more to follow. 'Go on,' she said.

'You've visited the location of three out of five of the eggs,' said Essa, 'and all three eggs were gone.'

'Missing, yes,' said Fyia. 'Your point?'

'What if all the eggs are missing?' said Essa.

'Or were never there to begin with,' said Starfall.

'Or were destroyed,' said Essa.

'You can't destroy dragon eggs,' said Fyia, with a dismissive wave of her hand.

'Why do you say that?' said Essa.

'Because, how could you?' said Fyia. The dragons in her waking dreams endured temperatures hot enough to melt stone. The eggs would be the same, impossible to harm.

'So they must be somewhere?' said Essa. 'That's your theory? Even if they've all been taken from their hiding places.'

'Exactly,' said Fyia. 'It's just a case of finding where. But first, I must discover if the other two eggs are where they're supposed to be.'

'And while you're at it, you can sound out the Black Hoods, and the people of the Great Glacier,' said Edu, 'to see what it would take for them to join us.'

'Assuming anything will work,' said Starfall.

'Exactly, Edu,' said Fyia, ignoring her aunt. 'Two birds with one stone.'

'What do you require of us in your absence?' said the Spider.

'Selise is once more secure,' said Fyia. 'I'd like you and Starfall to keep it that way, and assess the damage, so we can rebuild.'

'The rebels quickly disappeared when my soldiers entered the city,' said Sensis. 'I will leave soldiers to help you, but I must return to Moon, to ensure training at the military academy proceeds as planned, and to weed out those leading the rebellion—with your help, if you are willing, Spider?'

The Spider nodded. 'As my Queen desires.'

'Of course,' said Fyia, 'although, if the Emperor's fleet attacks, that plan will have to change. I would like to know more of the Emperor's plans …'

Sensis nodded. 'I have checkpoints along the coast, watching for any sign of attack. Hopefully, they will turn north to look for you, or return to their home across the sea. We have plenty to deal with without the Emperor adding to our troubles.'

Fyia watched Starfall pluck another leaf from the hanging plant beside her. 'Starfall, there are few with the skill to keep my council in line, especially with the likes of Venir undermining me at every turn, and with rebels in the streets …'

Starfall nodded as she wrapped the leaf around her finger. 'Supporters of the status quo.'

'Supporters of the way things have been for too long,' said Fyia. 'I *will* bring about changes within my kingdoms, and there will continue to be those who do not like it.'

A sharp rap sounded from the door, and a guard entered, carrying a wax-sealed letter. 'This just arrived from the city, General.' The guard bowed low to Fyia, then held out the parchment to Sensis.

'News from a checkpoint,' said Sensis, ripping open the message.

The blood drained from Fyia's face as she waited for Sensis to read the words, dread shredding her guts.

'An envoy from the Emperor is approaching Selise in an airship,' said Sensis. 'They're demanding an audience with the Queen.'

Fyia exhaled the breath she'd been holding. 'No,' she said. 'Edu, we will leave immediately.' Fyia paused, her thoughts spiraling as she considered their predicament. 'I will bond some eagles for your use. Starfall, please return the woman we took hostage from the Emperor's airship. Tell them it's a sign of our good faith … that we have no interest in war …'

'And that you have no interest in marrying the Emperor?' said Starfall, a wicked look on her face.

'Yes,' said Fyia, 'that too, but find a way to soften the blow …'

'Pretty words aren't my strongest suit …'

'I'm sure you'll manage. And Essa,' said Fyia, halting on her way to the door, 'don't think I've forgotten about your report. I will expect it upon my return.'

'Of course, Your Majesty,' said Essa, with a dip of her head, 'I will continue my research.'

Chapter Ten

FYIA NEEDED SPEED ON her journey north, and stealth, so they took the airship, much to Essa's chagrin.

The journey was strained, even though it lasted only two days. They'd brought horses, and the quarters were close, with Fyia's full bodyguard on board. Fyia's stallion did not like flying. He stamped and snorted and bit out at anyone—horse or human—who got too close, and the guards grumbled that they had not joined Fyia's guard to become stable hands.

Opie landed the far side of the Fae'ch mountains, where they unloaded, continuing on horseback. Opie had warned against taking their only airship further into unknown territory. It was, after all, the only model they had to copy, and risking it would be foolish.

It was with a heavy heart that Fyia waved Opie goodbye. Even though his true motives and desires were uncertain, she liked the pilot and enjoyed his company. He was deferential, but not scared or sycophantic, his mind and wit sharp, his dry remarks often making her laugh.

Fyia turned away from the departing airship and breathed in the frigid northern air. She pulled her furs closer as she urged her horse along the narrow track north.

They knew not where the Black Hoods lived, nor did they understand the rules of this foreign land, but they headed for the temple, where Fyia hoped she would finally set eyes on a dragon egg.

Fyia surveyed the frozen land as they travelled, moving at a steady pace that afforded time to take in the snow-covered trees, white rabbits, and bold chipmunks. There was little else to distract, aside from a clearing every now and again. The path they travelled was well worn, tufts of grass poking through the blanket of snow.

'They must know of our presence by now,' said Edu, spurring his mount up beside Fyia's.

'And yet they let us continue,' said Fyia.

'If I were them, I would lay a trap, and have us walk straight into it.'

'It would be the wise thing to do,' agreed Fyia. 'Get us to do the hard work for them, while they sit back and watch … but what choice do we have?'

A bird called in the distance, and Fyia and Edu shared a dark look. 'Apparently we're getting close,' said Edu.

'Tell the guards not to fight,' said Fyia. 'We must demonstrate our peaceful intentions, even if they attack us.'

'It is already done,' said Edu, although he looked uncomfortable. It was no small thing, asking her guards to stand down in the face of an attack on their Queen.

Fyia had made her wolves trail them for the same reason. It was a shame, as her wolves could have provided valuable information about the whereabouts of the northern people. The terrifying, fear-inducing

Black Hoods, who might kill their party without even stepping from the trees. Fyia pushed the thought away. They wouldn't.

The Black Hoods she'd met inside the Fae'ch mountain had seemed reasonable, not to mention curious ... surely they would be intrigued to know why the Queen of the Five Kingdoms had ventured into their lands, uninvited and unannounced.

Although, of course, they already knew. Fyia hadn't been shy about declaring her intention to find the dragons. If they didn't want her to do that ... well ... then there could be trouble.

If the Black Hoods locked her up, half of her own people would probably rejoice. Sensis would come looking, to be sure, but invading the north to retrieve her would be a fool's game ... her army wouldn't stand a chance. The Black Hoods would probably attempt to ransom Fyia, but would her kingdoms pay?

It was dangerous, coming like this ... but it wasn't the most dangerous thing Fyia had done, and risks were sometimes necessary. If she wouldn't put her own neck on the line, then why should she expect anyone else to?

A figure in a black cloak, their hood up, stepped onto the path ahead. 'Halt,' said a bored male voice.

Edu and Fyia gave each other a look that conveyed so much, and then they smiled, because now the fun would begin.

They reined in their mounts, Fyia and Edu at the front. 'We mean no harm,' said Edu, his calm voice carrying far. 'My Queen requests an audience with your leader, that is all.'

'And yet you sent no word of your visit,' said the man, 'nor request to enter our lands. You merely ... invaded.'

Fyia laughed. 'Sir,' she said, 'I hardly think a party of twenty counts as an invasion. Or if it does, it is a foolhardy one.'

'It is foolhardy to ride into the lands of another with no warning, and without permission,' said the man. His words weren't hostile. He seemed to be testing them.

'And yet here we are, and I am no fool,' said Fyia. 'As my guard said, I merely request an audience with your leader.'

'Come to ask for his hand in marriage?' said the man.

'Ha!' said Fyia. 'Marrying the King of the Black Hoods is the very last thing I intend.'

'You insult my King?' said the man. His body morphed from a relaxed stance into something altogether more deadly.

'Of course not,' said Fyia. 'I have not met your King. I know him not, even by reputation … the Black Hoods conceal themselves so admirably. But I do not plan to marry anyone, despite the many proposals I have received since uniting the Five Kingdoms. Marriage is the furthest thing from my mind.'

'This way,' said the Black Hood. A horse stepped out of the trees, and the man swung up into the saddle, then spurred his mount into a canter.

Fyia was glad to increase their pace. A run was exactly what she and her horse needed, and if they were headed for a trap, at least she'd die with exhilaration in her veins.

They rode for no more than a turn of the clock, but the ground became more treacherous with every passing pace, the trees sparser, the air cooler, the freeze harder.

The Black Hood slowed his mount to a walk as they approached a small town. It was a strange mix of wooden huts and stone buildings, but whereas the huts sat atop the snow, the stone buildings were half submerged, some so deeply that upstairs windows were now at ground level and being used as doors.

Fyia gaped.

'Close your mouth,' Edu said quietly in her ear.

She snapped out of it and pulled herself up, so she looked regal on her impressive steed.

The Black Hood led them to a building in the center of the town. Fyia assumed they were in the town square, although it would've been more obvious before the dragons had disappeared and the north had frozen.

She'd never given much thought to what it would be like up here. Her own homeland, which had once enjoyed a temperate climate, now had long and arduous winters, but nothing like this.

'Leave your horses and guards here,' said the man. 'They will be looked after.' He nodded to a stone building to the left—a tavern. 'They will have rooms there.'

Fyia inclined her head. 'Most generous,' she said, 'thank you.' The tavern looked nice enough, at least the part she could see above the snow ...

Fyia dismounted, and handed her horse to a guard. She slid a reassuring hand over the beast's sweaty flank before following the Black Hood inside. Edu trailed behind her, and she could feel her wolves in the woods, wary, but not alarmed—a good sign.

'Wait here,' the man said to Edu. Fyia nodded as the man climbed deftly through a window, then she followed, trying to make it look as easy as he had—

trying to maintain her dignity—unsure who watched from within.

The window led to a hall, her feet landing on a stage of sorts, and the Black Hood headed for a set of steps off to one side.

Fyia paused, casting her eyes over the large open space, with its flagstone floor, beautiful vaulted ceiling, and stained glass windows—at least the ones above the snow line, the ones below were covered with boards.

At the far end of the room, a fire raged in a hearth big enough to stand in, a circle of comfortable-looking chairs beside it. Two of the chairs were occupied, the occupants teasing a litter of four fluffy puppies with tidbits. The Black Hoods laughed at the puppies' adorable exuberance, and Fyia couldn't help but smile.

'Your Majesties,' said the Black Hood escorting Fyia, 'may I introduce Queen Fyia Orlightus, the fire-touched ruler of the Five Kingdoms.'

The two in the chairs looked up—one man and one woman, both around thirty years of age. Fyia didn't have time to dwell on the use of fire-touched in her title. Did that engender respect in these parts? Maybe it had once in her own kingdoms too, but those days had long since passed.

The man got to his feet slowly, his eyes raking over Fyia's travel-ravaged form. She hadn't stopped to wonder what she must look like—or smell like. She was disheveled, and no doubt reeked of horse. Edu had suggested she wear courtly clothes, so as to be prepared for any eventuality, but she hadn't listened.

She watched the man as he took her in, his form pleasing, with short dark hair, stubble-covered jaw, and curious countenance. He was tall and muscular, although not overly so, and had a weathered look about him that implied he pulled his weight, not relying on others to do all the hard work.

Their eyes met as they finished their respective appraisals, and her chest fluttered, then went tight. They stood like that for a beat, two, something about him niggling at her consciousness.

'It is a pleasure to make your acquaintance, Your Majesty,' said the royal woman, interrupting their joint reverie.

Fyia hadn't even realized the woman had stood, but she didn't miss the provoking look the woman sent to the man—the King, presumably. Was she his sister? His wife?

'It is a pleasure to meet you too,' said Fyia, inclining her head. 'Forgive me, but I do not know your names.'

Fyia's escort cleared his throat. 'This is King Atlas …'

'Yes, yes,' said the King. 'And this is my cousin, Princess Zhura.'

'Distant cousin,' said the slight woman, sending him a testy look. She had long, dark hair and a way of moving that hinted at power. 'Like … so removed I'm sure everyone else out there in the snow is also a princess by the same measure.'

The King rolled his eyes. 'She does not appreciate her title.'

'If you're such a distant relation, then why do you have a title at all?' said Fyia.

'A good question,' said Zhura, with a half-smile.

A puppy rushed to Fyia's feet, and she scooped it up with a laugh. 'Oh my word, these are the most adorable …' The puppy licked her face, and she held it away. 'Urgh, no licking.' She set it back on the floor and crouched to pet it there instead.

She looked up to find the King watching her, something indeterminate about his lips, and she straightened.

'Why are you here?' said the King. His directness took her by surprise, although she wasn't sure why.

'You do not know?'

'I have my suspicions, although I prefer not to jump to conclusions.' His tone was hostile. Had she offended him? Was he angry she'd waltzed into his territory without an invitation? Or had her picking up the puppy been some kind of transgression ... people could be touchy about their animals ...

'I am here, Your Majesty, because I believe there is a way to restore prosperity to your kingdom and mine.'

'We are prosperous enough,' he said hotly. Although, a shadow of something less certain crossed his cousin's features.

'I don't doubt it. The Black Hoods are revered throughout the known world as a formidable force, but what if we could do more? What if we could melt the ice? What if we could make it easier on your people and mine?'

'You truly believe returning the dragons will do that?' he said, his tone scathing.

Fyia stood still for a moment, holding her ground. 'Yes.'

'The dragons are gone,' he said, dismissively, 'and even if they were not, you will never unite the Five Great Kingdoms.'

Fyia took a moment to collect herself ... of course he knew the true legend. She supposed it had been arrogant to assume it applied only to the Five Eastern Kingdoms ... although, in her defense, that was what she'd always been told. 'And why is that?' said Fyia.

'You will never unite the Five Kingdoms, because I will never unite the Five Kingdoms. You and your people cannot be trusted. You are a force of destruction, and oppression, and discrimination. That is why the Fae'ch—all magic users—were run out of your lands. That is why ... well, that is why your lands are like they are. I would never align my people with yours; it would be a grave injustice against them.'

Fyia's temper flared. 'How can you say that, when I am a magic user? Fire-touched, magic-touched, and with a Cruaxee? The very purpose of conquering my kingdoms was to bring about change ... to put an end to the things that so offend you ... that so offend me! Do you believe a land cannot change? Will you judge me by the actions of those I have overthrown?'

'Have you though?' said the King.

'What do you imply?' Fyia said quietly. His words stole the wind from her sails. 'Speak plainly, so we may not misunderstand one another.'

The King gave a short, derisive laugh. 'I imply nothing. You have held the reins of power for not even three cycles of the moon, and yet already your people— the people you seem to believe you can change—rebel in your streets. If you cannot control your own lands— your own people—how do you expect to form a union with mine?'

'A union can be many things,' said Fyia.

The King raised a suggestive eyebrow. 'Indeed, it can.'

Fyia's heart thudded in her chest. 'And my people rebel against the very changes you deem desirable. They rebel because I have invited magic-wielders back to my lands, because I have allowed women into the university and guilds, and outlawed the stranglehold a small, privileged minority have on trade. They rebel because I am a woman, and they can't comprehend that I have bested five Kings—five men!'

'Not single-handedly, from what I hear,' said the King.

Fyia went still. 'You seek to diminish my achievements?' she said. 'You think that the most

179

productive use of our time? To be in the best interests of your people?'

'I am sure you must be tired after your journey,' said the King. 'Aaran, please see our guests to their quarters in the tavern.'

Her escort bowed his head to his King, then held out an arm, directing her back towards the window.

The tavern? He was putting her in the tavern? Was he slighting her, or was that the best his kingdom could offer?

'You seem to have made quite an impression on the King,' said Edu, looking around her sparse room. It was below ground and lit by candles, the tavern's bar upstairs. It was cozy, with furs on the bed, and rustic wooden furniture. Edu's room adjoined hers, and looked much the same from what she could see through the open door.

'I'll admit we're not off to the best start,' said Fyia, sinking into an armchair. 'Do you think they were the Black Hoods at the Fae'ch party?'

'I couldn't say,' said Edu, 'seeing as you're the only one who met them.'

Fyia thought back to the man with deep brown eyes and shaved head, to Cal. The King had something of that man about him, but his eyes had appeared green in the dim light of the hall. Not that she'd been close enough to see for sure, but his hair and name were different.

She supposed the woman at the Fae'ch party could have been Zhura. Fyia hadn't got a good look at her that night …

Fyia shrugged. 'The Fae'ch magic changed all of us … maybe the man at the party wasn't really a Black Hood at all—just a Fae'ch trick—and I've felt no hint of the magic Cal used on me.' She reached for her wolves, their presence reassuring. 'And my wolves seem happy, rabbiting in the woods.'

Edu nodded. 'Good, because we're not equipped to deal with a magical attack.'

'No,' agreed Fyia. She longed for the day she would find someone who could help her understand her abilities … to teach her to use them properly.

Music started above, and a familiar voice drifted down. Edu and Fyia passed a look of understanding between them, then hurried up the stairs.

Rouel was on stage, lute in hand, singing of Fyia's might and prowess. Fyia inwardly cringed as all eyes in the room swiveled to her. They seemed amused, rather than angry at her guard's presumptively taking over their stage, so she gave a non-committal smile and headed to the bar.

The tavern was typical, with a large fire, rowdy men and women guzzling amber colored liquid from thick glass tankards, the warring smells of stale ale and stewed meat filling the air.

Rouel's song came to a close, and as he started up again—this time playing a fast, well-known tune—a man at a nearby table began banging on the wooden floorboards in time with Rouel's beat. Fyia tensed ever so slightly, but relaxed when a couple jumped up from a table near the stage. They took to the open area in the middle and began an energetic jig.

A smile took hold of Fyia's face as she watched them, and then, to her surprise, a hand drum joined Rouel's lute, and a soprano voice joined his baritone. Fyia could barely believe her eyes when she realized it was Zhura who'd joined him on stage. Not the usual pastime of a princess …

'Zhura won't be outdone,' said the King, coming up beside her.

'She does this a lot?' said Fyia, a little wary given their earlier interaction.

'She's our most celebrated entertainer … although, she's handy with a sword too, so don't make the mistake of underestimating her.'

'I rarely underestimate women,' said Fyia. 'I leave that to the men, and Rouel is one of my guards. I trust his skills with a sword as much as I enjoy his music.'

The King downed his beer and signaled to the bartender for two more. He held one out to Fyia, and she looked at it for a beat before accepting. She cared little for beer, but the King would surely mock her if she said so.

'Do you live in this tavern too?' she asked. She had to raise her voice to be heard, the floor now heaving with bodies. It was a wonder the floorboards held.

'No,' he said simply. 'The accommodation is not to your liking?'

His words were light, but Fyia sensed something beneath them. 'I care little for plush surroundings,' she said. 'My home has been a war tent for as long as I can remember. I am merely intrigued … would like to understand you and your people. That is why I'm here, after all.'

'Oh, is that the reason? I thought you'd come for my hand in marriage …' He laughed at her shocked features. 'That is one way to unite our kingdoms, is it not?'

Fyia shook her head; brutal honesty was one way to communicate … 'I can assure you, that is the last thing on my mind, Your Majesty. And if I must eventually marry, it will not be to you.'

His face contorted in mock outrage. 'You wound me, *Your Majesty*. I had all but planned our nuptials.'

She rolled her eyes. 'I'm sure.'

The music changed again, and the King's face split into a broad smile. It was alarming how quickly he morphed from very-pleasant-to-look-at into a thing of shocking beauty. Something in her own features must have betrayed that she'd noticed, because he leaned in close. 'Care to dance?' His words were a dangerous purr, little more than a whisper.

'No,' she said firmly. He had no qualms about using his looks as a weapon then … good to know. Did he think he was the first man who'd tried to sway her with a pretty face and easy flirtation? Or was he goading her? Or simply trying to cause her discomfort?

'Shame,' said the King. He stood and pushed away from the bar, his smile turning mischievous. He snagged the hand of a passing woman, and pulled her to the dancefloor. 'I suppose I should count myself lucky,' he said, loud enough for those around him to hear. 'They say east-kingdomers struggle to hold a beat …'

Fyia scoffed. 'An untruth my guards are amiably disproving,' she said. Four or five of her guards were merrily swinging each other around the floor, not to mention Rouel and his efforts on stage.

'Yes, you're right,' said the King. 'Maybe it's only the highborn of your lands who can't dance …'

Several of her bodyguard were highborn, but Fyia didn't give him the satisfaction of an answer. Instead she shrugged, as though he could be right, then turned back to her drink, not wishing to watch his no-doubt flawless movements.

Edu sat beside her. 'What a strange place this is,' he said.

'They have no regard for refinement, that's for sure,' said Fyia. 'Imagine if I hosted a royal guest in a tavern … my courtiers would have a fit!'

Edu chuckled. 'Starfall would approve.'

Fyia laughed. 'You're right, but I can't see Lord Venir warming to the idea.'

'Lord Venir will warm to no idea not of his own making, unless it is advantageous to him,' said Edu, darkly.

'Yes,' said Fyia, 'he will need to be replaced, but for now, I'm keeping my enemies close.' She took a sip of beer, having to force it down, fighting the urge to gag. 'By the Goddess, this stuff is truly foul,' she hissed.

Edu laughed again, but then faltered, a look of concern contorting his features. He quickly tasted her beer, and Fyia held her breath. 'It tastes like beer to me …' he said, some of the tension leaving his face.

'Well, I cannot drink it.'

'The King will be delighted,' said Edu. 'Another slight to use against you.'

Fyia scowled.

'But if you were to dance,' said Edu, 'and leave your beer unattended, I could not allow you to drink it upon your return.'

Fyia gave him a long look. 'The King wins either way.'

'What's worse? Dancing, or drinking beer?'

That was easy, for Fyia loved to dance. She did not love to drink beer. 'Come on then,' she said, grabbing Edu's hand.

'No, not with me!' said Edu. 'I'm your guard. I need to keep watch …'

'You can keep watch from the dancefloor. And don't argue, it's an order.'

Edu rolled his eyes. 'Of course, Your Majesty,' he said dryly, offering her his hand.

They took to the floor, and Edu punished her with spins so fast she almost lost her footing. Fyia laughed, her heart pumping wildly as they careered around the floor at a furious pace.

'Your Majesty,' said the King. He cut in so smoothly, Edu had little choice but to relinquish her.

'Your Majesty,' Fyia reluctantly replied.

'It would appear the rumors are untrue ...'

'A great shock, I'm sure,' she said, her words dripping with sarcasm.

'Indeed,' he said, then spun her under his arm.

She tried not to give him the satisfaction of a smile, so she smirked instead. 'You're not too bad yourself,' she heard herself say.

He inclined his head. 'Most kind,' he said, then pulled her into a tight hold, and set off around the floor.

Edu was happy to retreat to the edge of the room. From the shadows, he could watch openly, and listen to the revelers' unguarded drunken words.

'I was sure he was gay!' said the woman the King had pulled to the dance floor. 'He only ever dances with his cousin.'

'Trying to impress the Queen,' said an old man, knowingly.

'Why?' said a second woman. 'Not like we need the likes of her ...'

'Probably taken a liking to her ...' said the old man.

'How will Mama Bear like that?' said the second woman.

'Spells trouble,' said the first woman.

'He has to marry sometime,' said the old man, then, seeing her sullen face, added, 'What? You thought he'd marry you?'

The second woman laughed.

Edu moved on, nearing the stage. Zhura put down her drum, accepting a drink from the man the King had called Aaran.

'What is he doing?' said Zhura. Her voice was too low to hear, but Edu could read her lips well enough.

'Flirting, I believe,' said Aaron.

'Flirting ...' said Zhura, incredulously.

'Trust him,' said Aaron.

'I do ... but ...' Zhura shook her head, then surveyed the dancing. She watched Fyia and her cousin, their bodies pressed together in a way courtiers considered most inappropriate in Fyia's own kingdoms. 'We're being watched,' said Zhura, as her eyes flicked to Edu's.

Edu held her gaze, unembarrassed at having been caught. They'd let their guards down ... *they* should be embarrassed. Although, it was surprising Zhura had spotted him at all. Edu was well versed in stealth and concealment.

Zhura brought her hand up to her mouth and continued her conversation, shielding her lips from view. Edu inclined his head and moved on.

Fyia's second dance with the King came to an end, and she was about to take a seat, to turn away and remove his arm from her back, when the door to the tavern's window-sized entrance banged open. She wondered why they'd gone so far as to replace the window with a door, but hadn't made the opening itself bigger, so they could just walk through. But before she could ask, the room went quiet, and a big, broad man with a shaggy beard swung his legs through the window.

'Cal!' the man boomed, looking directly at the King. 'Nephew!'

The King hesitated, his eyes seeking Fyia's as the word echoed around her mind. *Cal*. The Cal from the Fae'ch party?

The King's hand brushed her bare arm, and Fyia's Cruaxee magic jolted to life in her mind. Eagles screamed, and her wolves snarled, racing towards her. What in the Seven Hells? Had he done something to her magic again? Was she in danger?

Edu stepped between Fyia and the King, and a dangerous stillness descended, all eyes watching as Fyia's guards formed up around her.

Her wolves sprang through the window, snarling and snapping their teeth, and the room erupted in fright, stools clattering, glasses smashing, the drunken crowd scrambling to get away.

'Call them off,' said the King, his voice low and urgent.

'I …' said Fyia. Pain lanced through her mind, her vision becoming a tunnel rimed with black. She looked wildly around, seeking some kind of clarity.

'You don't want to do this,' said Cal. 'Call. Them. Off.'

She didn't know how. Her wolves had come to her … she hadn't summoned them.

'Fyia,' said Edu. She swung her gaze to him, her mind swimming. 'We have to get out of here.'

She nodded. Edu was right, they had to leave … regroup …

'Call them off,' the King hissed, trying to step towards her. His countenance was cold and commanding, no hint of the flirtatious rogue from moments before. 'Before this gets out of hand ...'

Edu held the King back. 'Don't ...' he said.

'I ...' said Fyia, as the pain in her head intensified. Her wolves feigned attacks, keeping the northerners away.

'Fyia,' Cal said, his voice icy but imploring, 'stop.' The King's green eyes were all she could see now, blackness having stolen most of her vision.

She closed her eyes, shaking her head back and forth, trying to escape the pain. And then a bear roared through her mind, and everything went black.

Chapter Eleven

STARFALL ENTERED THE great glasshouse attached to Lord Eratus Venir's sprawling country mansion in Moon, right on the border of Moon, Plenty, and Sky. She had travelled with Sensis to Moon, and was passing on her return, so it would have been churlish to decline his invitation to visit the Venir estate.

The King of Moon had gifted the land to Venir's family many generations before, as thanks for their help in weeding out the Kingdom's magic-touched. The Venirs had been extremely good at it, the family renowned for their intelligence, along with their ability to sniff out opportunities to apply their sharp minds for personal gain.

'Ah, Lady Starfall,' said Venir, striding across the humid expanse, his shoes clicking on the stone floor. 'It is magnificent, is it not?' He held his arms aloft, encouraging her to cast her eyes over the glass and wooden structure around them.

'It is very impressive,' said Starfall, with a reluctant smile.

'Come … let us walk,' he said, stepping back and holding out his arm. She set off along a path through the middle of the lush greenery. The smell reminded her of the jungles of the south, as did the colorful birds that flitted from branch to branch.

'Flowers have always been a source of fascination for me,' said Venir. He nodded to a display of shocking pink blooms, where a host of butterflies sucked at the nectar.

'Why is that?' said Starfall, hating the circuitous nature of political conversation.

'Their purpose … attracting pollinators. They developed precisely for that purpose—for their own survival—and if they had not, our food—that which sustains us—would be much different. The system exists in perfect, fragile balance. It is remarkable, is it not? The ways of nature.'

A bead of sweat ran down Starfall's spine, her dress made for the crisp outside air, not the heat of the glasshouse. A planned side effect of Venir's preference to meet in here, no doubt. 'Did you have a point, my lord?' she said impatiently.

'In our carefully balanced system, Fyia is the flower. She exists to look pretty … to attract a pollinator.'

Starfall almost choked. She looked sidelong at Venir, shocked both by his casual use of the Queen's name, and his brazen sentiment. She wouldn't give him the satisfaction of showing her outrage, nor let fly the many choice words that strained the clamped seam of her lips.

'If she were successful,' Venir continued, 'and attracted an acceptable pollinator, then the balance of our system—the way we produce goods, trade, and all the rest—will surely fall seamlessly back into place.'

Starfall stopped walking and looked Venir directly in the eye. 'And just so there can be no confusion as to your meaning,' she said, 'the rebellion within the Queen's own kingdoms …'

'Would surely cease,' said Venir, as though he'd said something truly wondrous.

'And if she refuses to find an acceptable *pollinator*?' said Starfall.

'The system is already out of balance,' said Venir. 'I fear it would spiral into ever greater disarray … rebel activities would increase, interruptions to our food supplies would intensify …'

'But our supplies largely originate from your own glasshouses, do they not?' said Starfall, in mock surprise. 'Well, yours, and those belonging to Lord Antice, who is your nephew.'

When the Venirs had finished persecuting the magical, they'd turned to a different kind of weeding. They'd erected great glasshouses, enough to become the biggest suppliers of fruits and vegetables in the eastern kingdoms.

Venir coughed. 'We will do our best, but I cannot work miracles, my lady.'

'What makes you so sure the rebels will stand down if our Queen marries?' said Starfall, tired of the political dance.

'The Spider is not the only one with spies …'

Given Fyia could strip him of all he held dear with a click of her fingers, it was worrying Venir felt secure enough to issue thinly veiled threats, and to admit his involvement with the rebels. 'Did you have candidates in mind?' she asked lightly.

'The Emperor across the Kraken Sea,' said Venir, his voice firm. 'He is the obvious choice for trade, wealth, and if his flying machines are any indication, then I dare say technology also. Although, if the Queen would prefer, we have many eligible men within our own lands ... Lord Antice, to name but one.'

Lord Antice indeed ... Venir's nephew. Venir had balls, she would give him that much. 'Then you should put your case to the Queen upon her return,' said Starfall.

Venir smiled harshly. 'I trust *you* to make the Queen see sense.'

'The Queen does not take orders from me, my lord.'

Venir sniffed. 'She's not even here. The people know you're the one in charge ... the one capable of understanding our delicate predicament, of swaying the Queen to our cause.'

Our cause. Of course, Venir was not merely a messenger. He was power hungry, and Fyia had snubbed him, making changes that would hit him in his overflowing pockets, changes that, ideologically, he could not accept.

Starfall nodded her head. 'I make no promises, my lord, but I see how a marriage could be advantageous to our kingdoms. I will think on it.'

Venir bowed his head. 'Of course, my lady. A wise choice.'

Fyia opened her eyes, blinking against the bright glare of the sun through the window. She groaned at the pain thudding against her skull, and footsteps came immediately to her side. 'Your Majesty,' said Edu, taking her hand, 'are you okay?'

'I think so,' she said groggily, her throat dry and scratchy. 'What ... happened? Where am I?' Her words were sleep slurred, her brain sluggish, her eyes taking an age to adjust to the light. She remembered the tavern, her wolves, *Cal.*

'This is the Queen Mother's house,' Edu said quietly. 'The King decided this the best place for you, after … whatever it was that happened.'

'The Queen Mother?' said Fyia.

'The King's mother,' said Edu, 'and former Queen. Her son—Cal—became King upon his father's death … although, from what I hear, succession wasn't clear cut. He had to fight for it, and it was recent.'

Edu's words were interesting, but Fyia's mind was slow. At least her eyes had adjusted. 'Help me sit,' she said. He did, and she grunted against the pain in her head. She made small rocking motions with her eyes clamped shut, waiting and praying to the Goddess that the blows against her skull would soon pass.

Eventually they ebbed, and she opened her eyes, Edu's concerned face hovering in her line of sight. She waved to make him back up. 'How long have I been here?'

'Only a few turns,' he said, handing her a glass of water.

She gratefully accepted, and drank deeply, relishing the cool relief as it slid down her throat. 'What happened?'

'You blacked out, and I carried you outside. Your wolves followed, which calmed matters a bit. The King thought it safest to bring you here.'

'I heard the roaring in my head again, when the King touched me. He's the one from the Fae'ch mountain.'

'I know,' said Edu. 'He told me that much, although wouldn't say any more.'

'Do you think we're in danger?' she said. She cast her eyes through the window, although she couldn't see much but half-buried trees and snow.

'I don't think so,' said Edu, refilling her water glass. 'They don't fear magic here as they do in our lands. If anything, they seem more respectful after your Cruaxee display, or so the guards say; I haven't left your side.'

Fyia nodded. Her Cruaxee liked it here. She could feel her wolves' contentment through the bond.

Before Fyia could pepper Edu with more questions, a knock sounded from the door, and Zhura entered. She gave a small bow, then said, 'The Queen Mother would like to see you, if you're feeling up to it.'

'Why?' said Fyia.

'Because those with a Cruaxee are rare, and she would like to meet a kindred spirit.'

Fyia threw back her covers. 'The Queen Mother has a Cruaxee?'

Zhura gave Fyia a blank look, then turned and left. 'I will be outside when you are ready.'

Fyia was ready in moments, despite the great pain in her head. Edu followed a step behind as Zhura led them down a grand staircase, taking them below the snowline, into the kitchen of the large house.

The kitchen spanned most of the bottom floor, the windows boarded to keep out the snow, the space lit only by candles and the fire in the cookstove. A huge wooden table—the top well worn by time—stretched across one end of the space, and at the other, in front of the stove, sat a woman in a low wooden chair.

Zhura left them at the door with a look of ... was that ... commiseration? And then she was gone, almost before Fyia had time to blink. Fyia glanced at Edu, who shrugged.

She stepped further into the warm room, and Edu followed, but waited by the door as Fyia approached the woman by the stove.

Fyia didn't know how to address the Queen Mother, so she said nothing, giving a shallow bow, conferring respect, but not deference.

The Queen Mother looked up from the reeds she was braiding, and nodded in return. 'Sit,' she said.

Fyia disliked the woman's tone, but did as she was told. The Queen Mother looked younger than Fyia had expected, the lines on her face not so deep, her hair— pulled back in a tight bun—still mostly black, her hands deft as she braided.

'Why did you not call off your wolves?' said the woman.

Fyia faltered, both from the directness of her question, and because she didn't know the answer. But then she remembered what had thrown her. 'The King lied to me. When his lie was revealed, my Cruaxee sensed my distress and came to my aid.'

'You did not call them?'

'No,' said Fyia.

'But why not call them off?'

'I thought I was in danger,' said Fyia.

'Why did you pass out?' said the Queen Mother, her eyes not leaving her work.

'Maybe you can tell me?' said Fyia, her voice firm. Fyia got the sense the Queen Mother was used to being obeyed, but Fyia wouldn't be pushed around.

The Queen Mother raised her head. In the firelight, the woman's eyes were little more than two black orbs, but she held Fyia's gaze for several beats. 'Maybe I can,' she said, then went back to her braid.

Fyia waited for more, but none came. The silence stretched, then yawned, then gaped, but Fyia would not be the one to break first. Unfortunately, the Queen Mother showed no signs of doing so either.

Fyia reached for the reeds in the basket to the Queen Mother's side, and plucked three strands from the bushel. She looked closely at the Queen Mother's technique, tied the reeds together, and then copied the woman's movements. If she were to sit here all day, she might as well keep herself occupied.

They sat like that for a turn of the clock, maybe two, and then footsteps approached from the door.

'You called?' said the King, his voice cold like iron, betraying no hint of congeniality.

The Queen Mother didn't look up, but Cal met Fyia's gaze as he surveyed the scene, showing no concern for her health. When and how the woman had summoned him, Fyia did not know, but he seemed agitated.

'Why did you touch this woman with your Cruaxee?' said the Queen Mother.

Fyia baulked. What did that mean? He had a Cruaxee?

The King—Cal—came up short, as though his mother had slapped him. 'That is none of your business, you meddlesome old crone.'

Fyia frowned at his tone … his words, but the Queen Mother laughed. 'You are riled. I wondered if I would see that in you again. I am pleased to have born witness to this momentous occasion.'

Fyia didn't know what she meant, so she looked from one face to another, trying to glean some detail that would help her understand.

The King said nothing. He stalked to a shelf and selected a bottle of clear liquid, along with three small, sturdy glasses. He dragged a low table to the middle of the Queen Mother and Fyia's chairs, placed the bottle and glasses upon it, then poured himself—only himself—a glass, and knocked it back. He refilled, then took a seat, leaning back in the chair as though settling in for the long haul.

The Queen Mother gave him a scathing look.

'Help yourself,' he said to Fyia, with a wave of his hand. 'It's early, but I'm afraid this could take a while, and the alcohol numbs the discomfort.'

Fyia set down her braiding and leaned forward. 'Seeing as frank conversation seems to be your preferred method, I will speak plainly. I am here because I seek to unite the Five Kingdoms, and return the dragons to our lands. I am sure you will agree, it is in everyone's interests ... I was shocked to see the extent of the freeze here in the north, and I propose a treaty between our great nations.'

The Queen Mother coughed. 'You propose a marriage?'

Fyia stopped, unable to prevent the crease of her brow. Did the woman not understand the word *treaty*? 'I propose an economic arrangement that works for your kingdom and mine.'

'So you do *not* want a marriage?' said the Queen Mother.

'Marriage is the very last thing I want,' said Fyia.

A smile pulled at the corners of the King's lips, and Fyia couldn't help but wonder why. Was it the situation he found amusing, or her outright rejection of his hand?

'But you want the dragon egg, do you not?' said the Queen Mother.

'Of course,' said Fyia. 'In order to bring back the dragons, we will need eggs.'

'You know how to hatch them?' said the King, his words a smug challenge.

'No, but ...'

'Well,' he said, interrupting her, 'it is impossible anyway, because the egg may only be retrieved by a member of our royal line ...'

'A member through blood or *marriage*,' the Queen Mother added.

Fyia's face heated, and she was grateful for the dim light. 'Then either of you could assist me,' said Fyia, 'once we come to an arrangement that suits us all.'

The Queen Mother chuckled. 'That is not how it works,' she said. 'If you want the egg, you must be the one to retrieve it, and if you are not a Black Hood, you may not even enter the temple.'

'We all want the egg,' Fyia countered.

'There is no union between the Five Kingdoms,' said the King, 'and if you cannot do that, it matters not.'

'Two are united,' said Fyia. 'Three, if you join us, and you are on good terms with the Fae'ch … it is not an insurmountable challenge.'

'What makes you sure you're the ruler of legend?' said the Queen Mother. 'That you are worthy of dragons? You cannot even control your own kingdoms, or your Cruaxee, nor did you know Cal had touched you with his …'

'My kingdoms will fall into line,' said Fyia, sitting back in her seat, 'and they outlawed magic in my lands, it is true, but I am magic-touched, and fire-touched, and I am willing to learn. I want to learn. I am good at learning.

'We have seen no dragons for hundreds of years. None of us can foresee the challenges we will experience when they return, but there will surely be challenges. Whoever leads us then must be capable of learning, or all will have been for nothing. I know that. I am no conquering king who believes he knows all … I embrace that which I neither know nor understand.

'I may not have had teachers to impart the knowledge you value and possess, but I do not consider that a source of shame, Queen Mother. I seek those who can teach me, and my thirst for knowledge is my strength, not my weakness.'

The Queen Mother inclined her head. 'Very well, but you are not fit to lead until you understand your gifts. My advice is to find someone to teach you.'

Cal returned to his own apartment at the top of the tallest building in Anvarn. He closed the door and soaked in the blessed relief of silence. It had been nothing but people and words—or screams—since the Queen had arrived, and it was fraying his edges.

He kicked off his boots and reclined in a fur-covered chair, rested his feet on a fur-covered stool, and looked up through the dome of glass above at the stormy grey sky. *Bliss.* He closed his eyes and reached for his Cruaxee—his bear—and found her splashing in a river at the top of a small waterfall. She let him settle into her mind and watch through her eyes. She wouldn't tolerate him doing more ... not unless the reason was urgent.

Cal's body sank into the furs, his mind unclenching, his bear his only focus. He inhaled deeply, getting faint traces of the pine and snow surrounding her, the splash under her paws, the smell of berry juice that stained her muzzle. And then a salmon leapt from the water, and she pounced, catching it easily in her jaws.

The rich taste of fish oil trickled into his mouth as she bit into the flesh. She ripped its skin from its body, then ate its eggs and brain. *You could bring the rest for me, you know*, he said through their bond. She couldn't understand his words exactly, as he could not understand her thoughts, but she knew what he wanted, and she promptly tossed the rest back into the water. Cal chuckled. *Thanks.*

His door banged open, and Cal swiveled his head to see Aaron and his cousin striding into his space, bottles clinking inside their leather satchels.

'By all means, come in,' he said. He sat, and accepted the ale-filled bottle Zhura held out.

'What in the name of the Goddess' tits are you doing?' said Aaron, taking the seat opposite Cal.

Cal took a long swig from his bottle, the bitter liquid burning a trail down his throat. 'With regards to?'

'Fraternizing with the Queen of the Five Gods-cursed Kingdoms,' said Aaron, 'just in case you've lost your mind to the extent you actually don't know what I'm talking about.'

Cal took another drink. The truth was, he had no idea what he was doing. He was drawn to her, but she was a volcano set to explode, and she would take everyone with her when she did. He should get out of the path of her blast … send her away.

Aaron continued, 'She's got daddy issues … and mummy issues. She bumped her brother out of the line of succession, and from what I hear, her aunt is a strange beast.'

'She's interesting,' said Zhura, cracking open an ale for herself. 'I'll give you that much.'

'No one's saying otherwise,' said Aaron, his eyes going wide. 'She conquered five Gods-damned kingdoms—and my, but she's no warrior—only the Warrior herself knows how she managed it … but that doesn't mean you should *fraternize* with the woman.'

'She's magic- and fire-touched,' said Zhura, 'and has a Cruaxee … that probably has something to do with it.'

'Yeah, and she has good people,' said Aaron. 'That guard—Edu—he looks like a flake, but there's something about him that scares me …'

'He was spying last night,' agreed Zhura. 'He's not stupid.'

'Why did you take her to the Queen Mother?' said Aaron, finally addressing Cal, who had returned his gaze to the roof.

'Oh, sorry, did you need me for this conversation?'

Zhura rolled her eyes. 'Answer the question.'

'Things were … uncertain in the tavern last night. Putting the Queen of the Five Kingdoms under the Queen Mother's protection seemed prudent.'

'You think it's wise to let that witch spend time alone with a foreign Queen?' said Aaron.

Cal breathed deeply. 'She's loyal.'

Aaron scoffed. 'That woman is loyal only to herself.'

'She wants what's best for the Black Hoods,' said Cal. 'It's what she's always wanted … at the cost of all else.'

'What if she deems the Queen of the Five Kingdoms best for the Black Hoods?' said Zhura.

Cal stared his cousin down. 'Are you implying I don't know how to deal with the Queen Mother?' he said darkly

'No,' said Zhura. 'But she's crafty, and you have a lot on your plate, and Fyia seems crafty too …'

'Zhura … both of you … let it go. Fyia knows nothing we need fear. She can't use her magic … she doesn't even know how to control her Cruaxee.'

'Not yet,' said Aaron. 'But she's a looker … won't be long until she finds someone to teach her.'

'Better hope that teacher is friendly to the Black Hoods,' said Zhura.

'Her teacher is most definitely that,' said Cal.

They both went still, fixing him with intense eyes.

'I have agreed to teach the Queen about her Cruaxee …' His bear pulled angrily on their bond, but he couldn't bring himself to regret what he'd done. He'd touched Fyia with his Cruaxee without thought, because he'd … needed to, but he knew he couldn't trust her. She was here for her own ends, nothing more. She'd shown no respect for him or his people, turning up as she had, and she chased glory.

He would teach her, yes, because he'd touched her with his magic, but he would hold her at arm's length then send her on her way. No more flirting, or touching … he would not get caught in her net of dreams and destruction.

'You've … what?' said Zhura.

'Goddess' tits,' said Aaron.

'I'll teach her the basics—so she is no longer a danger to herself—then send her back to the south.'

'Uh huh,' said Zhura, watching him closely.

'And while I'm doing that,' said Cal, 'keep an eye on Edu, and the rest of her guards. I don't want them snooping around.'

Edu escorted Fyia to the library—another half-submerged building in the center of town. The day already felt long, yet it was barely midday, and the town was in the full swing of daily business, the streets filled with market stalls selling all manner of interesting things: leather clothes and satchels, honey, candles, antlers, furs, dried meat, hot food, nuts and berries, ink and parchment.

Boisterous voices—both male and female—rang through the air, and Fyia couldn't help but smile as a woman loudly scolded her husband. This was what she wanted for her own kingdom … for women to own enterprises and have autonomy, free to demand a fair price for their wares, for them not to have to bow and scrape to their men. It was possible. She'd always known it was, and here was proof, in the flesh.

'Snoop around while I'm with the King,' Fyia said to Edu. 'I'll be safe with him, and we need information if we are to persuade him to show me their egg.'

'You could seduce him,' said Edu. Fyia turned sharply to look at his features, unable to tell from his voice alone if he was joking. Edu laughed.

'It's not funny,' said Fyia, although a smile pulled at her lips. 'I want to know why the relationship between the King and the Queen Mother is so strained. If he hates her so, why is she afforded such respect?'

'I will see what I can find, but it may take a few days. The people have become tight-lipped since your wolves burst into the tavern last night. Let us hope the ale in the tavern today loosens their tongues.'

Fyia nodded as they reached the front of the imposing library building, its doors half a pace below the level of the surrounding snow. Presumably beneath the snow were stone steps that had once led up to the door, but now they'd dug a step down into the snow, allowing the original doors to be used.

Fyia entered and surveyed the large, open space. It was warm, oddly, although she saw no fire or other method of heating.

'He's upstairs,' said Zhura. She appeared seemingly out of nowhere, then strode past them with barely a check.

'Is everything okay?' Fyia said to her retreating form.

'Sure,' Zhura replied, but neither stopped nor turned.

'What's got into her?' said Fyia.

'I'll try to find out,' said Edu, but he didn't leave. He was still casting his eyes around for threats.

'Go now, before she disappears,' said Fyia. 'I'll be fine in here, and if I'm not, my wolves are close.'

Edu nodded, then reluctantly followed Fyia's order. 'Good luck,' he said, 'oh, and try not to cause a diplomatic incident … or get killed.'

'Funny,' said Fyia.

Edu strode away, and Fyia took a moment to drink in her surroundings. The place was beautiful … the middle of the space big and open, with stacks lining the edges of the enormous oval room. The stacks went up three—and in some places four—levels, each getting narrower as they towered on top of each other. Stairs that were little more than wooden ladders linked the levels, the pillars carved with ornate scenes featuring all manner of creatures: wolves and bears and dragons and pixies.

At the end of the room, a wide staircase led up to a landing, and then split, one half going left, the other right, each section allowing access to the third level of stacks. The wooden railings were also carved with intricate woodland scenes, and Fyia couldn't help but run her hands over them as she slowly climbed the steps.

A clattering caught Fyia's attention, so she took the lefthand path towards the sound, almost running into Cal when she reached the top. He seemed to be descending in a hurry.

'Ah,' he said dryly, taking a step back, 'good of you to finally make it.'

He seemed flustered, and Fyia wondered if that was because she was a few minute-spins late—the result of too much ogling at market stalls—or because he'd had an argument with his cousin.

'Apologies,' she said sweetly, although she made sure her expression told him he was being an ass.

'This way,' he said. He spun on his heel and led the way up a much smaller staircase.

This one too was beautifully carved, and she remarked on it.

'Yes, I suppose so,' Cal replied, then said no more.

Chatty. Fyia kept quiet as she followed him up the long, steep stairs, wondering where he could be taking her … the roof? Maybe he planned to throw her off …

They stepped into a room at the top, and Fyia gasped. It was breathtaking: octagonal, and much smaller than the vast expanse of the library below, with windows set into each of the eight sides, which made it light and airy, yet intimate.

A brightly colored mural adorned the ceiling, depicting a clearing with a host of animals on one side and people on the other. In the middle of the two groups, an enormous golden dragon scale lay on the ground, reflecting the light of the setting sun, basking the scene in rich, golden light.

'The triarchy,' said the King.

'The what?'

'The three types of magical being: magic-touched, fire-touched, and Cruaxee.'

'What about pixie and fairies and fae, and all the others?'

'The three *human* types,' he clarified. 'And you are all three.'

A shiver ran down Fyia's spine. She'd never considered how many types of magic there could be. Had never thought that the witches of the Fae'ch— magic touched humans—had magic that was somehow different to the magic of the fae, or that her Cruaxee was different to either of those things. Magic was magic … it just appeared in different ways. Or at least, that was what she'd thought. Although, that could still be true … there was just so much she didn't know.

'And you?' she asked. Apparently he had a Cruaxee, so maybe he was magic- and fire-touched too.

'No,' he said pointedly.

She wasn't sure if she'd insulted him, so turned back to the mural. 'Whoever painted it was very skilled.'

'Indeed,' he said. 'If you will take a seat.' He held out his arm towards the only furniture—a pair of chairs in the middle of the room, directly under the dragon scale above.

They faced each other, and as they sat, their knees became uncomfortably close ... so close, she had to take care not to brush against him.

'What will you teach me?' she asked.

'Yes, we didn't specify, did we,' he said, his tone clipped.

After the Queen Mother had suggested Fyia seek help, she'd left them alone in the kitchen. Cal had made to leave, but Fyia had said, 'Please,' and the word had stopped him dead. He'd turned to look at her, and she'd made her plea. 'Imagine you'd lived my life, knowing you were magical, but with no knowledge of what that meant. With no one to turn to. No books. Only mistrustful glances and deep suspicions.'

Cal had stayed silent for a moment, then turned his gaze to the ceiling, as though asking the Gods to give him strength. 'Meet me in the library at noon,' was all he'd said.

Fyia waited for the King to speak, studying his face as he avoided her gaze. Was that because he disliked her? Or maybe he was indifferent, other matters occupying his mind. His nose was straight, his cheekbones high, his jaw strong and still covered with stubble. His hair was dark, and getting a little too long—he'd run his hand through it more than once since she'd arrived in the library—and whatever thoughts held his mind also creased his forehead.

He wore dark clothes—as befitted the King of the Black Hoods—made from soft, stained leather, with small golden clasps securing his long doublet. Clasps that, if she were not mistaken, had been fashioned in the shape of dragon claws. The fabric fit him snugly, so Fyia could make out the muscular lines of his arms, broad shoulders and torso.

She looked back to his face, and found him watching her. She hadn't registered the movement of his head, apparently too pre-occupied by the shape of him to notice …

She held his gaze, refusing to look away as it became uncomfortable, intense, intimidating. It was a purposeful move on his part, and she tipped her head to one side in silent question.

Cal snapped his eyes away and took a deep breath. 'We will start with the basics,' he said. 'Feeling your Cruaxee, calling them, bonding with them, sending them away …'

'I know how to do all of those things,' said Fyia. Or at least, she thought she did. She'd never had instruction, so perhaps her way and his were not the same.

'Then why did you not call off your wolves in the tavern last night?' he said hotly.

'Because you lied to me …'

'I did no such thing.'

'You withheld your name, and changed your eye color, with the express purpose of hiding your identity!'

'Even when it became clear I meant you no harm,' he said, 'you still refused to stand them down.' He ran his hand through his hair once more, looking as though he might rip whole chunks from his scalp.

'Because I didn't feel safe, and then a bear roared in my head, and then I blacked out. Was that … the

Queen Mother said you touched me with your Cruaxee? Is that why I heard her? Is the bear yours?'

Cal stood abruptly and turned towards a window. 'Yes,' he said quietly. 'She is mine.'

'She doesn't seem to like me,' said Fyia, attempting to lighten the mood, but her words fell flat.

'She barely tolerates me most of the time. She did not appreciate my using her to touch you.'

'What does that even mean?'

'It's … complicated,' said Cal, his eyes still looking out of the window.

'Is it dangerous?' said Fyia. She stood and moved to the opposite window, filling with frustration. 'Could your bear hurt me? When I blacked out, is that because she attacked me?'

'My bear is chafing against the touch, that is all.'

'But what is the touch?' Fyia snapped. 'Are we bonded?'

'No!' he said, whirling to face her. 'Of course not. You said you knew how to bond …'

'I am bonded to my wolves … that does not mean I know everything.'

'The very reason I suggested starting with the basics …' He fixed Fyia with his deep green eyes, letting his irritation shine through.

'Fine,' she said, storming back to her chair, 'then let us start with the basics.'

'Indeed,' he said through gritted teeth. He too returned to his chair.

'Cruaxee magic has always been rare,' he began, speaking quickly, as though it pained him, 'even before magic was outlawed in your lands. It is unknown how it comes about, but is to some extent hereditary.'

'Your mother has a Cruaxee too?' said Fyia.

The King looked displeased at her interruption, but nodded. 'Do either of your parents?'

'No,' she said, shaking her head. 'Much as my mother would have secretly liked magic, she had none of her own.'

'And yet both you and your brother are fire- and magic-touched?' said Cal, leaning forward a little.

'My mother's ancestors were fire-touched. I don't know if they had magic … or if my father's ancestors did. My parents and I are not close, and I never had a way to find out more.'

Cal nodded, processing her words. 'Does your brother have a Cruaxee?'

'Will the answer to that question help me understand what you've done to me? Or are you merely satisfying your curiosity?'

Cal frowned. 'Well, anyway, Cruaxee have always been rare. There is little written about our kind, so you must understand my knowledge is also limited.'

'Less limited than mine,' said Fyia, trying to chivvy him along and get to the good stuff. 'What do you know about bonding?'

'There are several kinds of … connections we can make with Cruaxee. Life bonds, as you have with your two wolves, and I have with my bear.'

Fyia pondered that. The bond with her two wolves did feel different to the other bonds she'd had, but she hadn't realized she'd done anything differently with them.

Cal saw her confusion. 'You didn't know?'

Fyia shook her head. 'I've bonded with many—the same way each time—but my wolves chose to remain when I released them.'

'They chose to bond,' said Cal, with a shrug. 'We don't get to make all the decisions.'

'Can any animal I bond with choose a life bond?' said Fyia.

'I don't know,' said Cal. 'We can short bond with many, but only a very few want to bond in return. And it's not like we can speak with the animals … we get only a sense of them.'

'But there's a way to touch others with your Cruaxee …?' Fyia prompted. 'Like you did to me?'

Cal nodded. 'The touch imprints a kind of … echo of our bond onto another.'

'Why do it?' said Fyia. 'What's it for?'

'It allows us to use our bonded animal's senses, even if our animal is not present, and feel our bonded animal's sense of the person too.'

Fyia shook her head in disbelief. 'How is that possible?'

'Magic,' he said sardonically.

'What of the animal?' said Fyia.

'They experience the same things you do … you're using the animal's senses, after all.'

'That's why your bear roared?' said Fyia, everything becoming clear. 'Because she was suddenly assaulted by … me?' And Fyia had tried to push back along the imprint … had offered the bear membership of her own Cruaxee … Cal's bear. 'No wonder she doesn't like me.'

'It surprised her,' he said. 'I gave her no warning.'

'Why did you do it?'

Cal shook his head. 'Maybe the Fae'ch magic affected my rational mind.'

Fyia scowled. 'Your mind is not so easy for them to alter as your eye color. Can you remove the touch?'

'No. Or at least, I don't know how.'

'So every time we're in the same room …'

'No. It's not constant. I must choose to use the connection, and my bear will only tolerate my borrowing her senses for so long. She needs them to survive.'

'Good,' said Fyia. 'Don't use it again.'

Fyia descended the steps to the main part of the library, preoccupied with thoughts of why Cal had done it … created her magical bond with his bear. Had the magic of the Fae'ch truly scrambled his senses, or was he hiding some other motivation he didn't want her to know? She had no reason to trust the Black Hoods, just as they had no reason to trust her.

At least she'd learned something—that she too, if she so wished, could use her life-bonded Cruaxee in this way. The ability to use her wolves' senses without their presence was intriguing. The only reason she hadn't tried it out on Cal was that it was permanent, and he didn't truly understand the magic. Magic was tricksy, and mischievous. Only a fool would trust that a Cruaxee echo … imprint … touch … whatever it was … could be so simple. How could it be? He'd linked his bear to her forever …

Maybe she could use the echo to her own advantage … could she tap into the bear's senses also? The bear would surely fight her, but she could try. Or maybe that was what Cal wanted, so he could exile her from his lands for attacking his bear …

She couldn't let the King distract her. She was here for the egg, and to unite their nations. The knowledge he'd offered was a bonus—penance for the bond Cal had touched her with—but she couldn't take her eyes off the prize.

She reached the library's entrance, and found Rouel awaiting her. 'The King has requested your presence in the town hall,' he said, his voice low and unusually serious.

Fyia nodded, a prickle of unease travelling down her spine. 'Do you know more?'

'Something to do with Edu ... that's all I know.'

Fyia took off towards the town hall at a brisk pace, this time ignoring the stalls filled with wonders. It was a short walk, and as she climbed through the window, she assessed the scene—Edu sat on a sturdy wooden chair, Zhura, Aaron, and Cal standing over him. How had Cal got here before her? Was this the reason he'd ended their session so abruptly? If so, how had he known?

'You sent for me?' said Fyia, her voice light, and an easy smile on her lips.

'I caught your commander snooping,' said Zhura.

'How do you mean?' said Fyia, noting Zhura's irritated expression.

'I think my words are clear enough.'

'What does Edu have to say?' asked Cal, apparently not yet up to speed either.

'Zhura was spying on me,' said Edu. 'She's been trailing me all morning, so I asked a couple of questions to flush her out.'

Zhura made a warning noise deep in her throat. 'I may go wherever I please, seeing as I am a Black Hood. You may stay in our lands only so long as our King sees fit ... which depends on your ability to observe respectful boundaries.'

'Do respectful boundaries include searching our rooms?' said Edu. 'Because I believe they have been combed from top to bottom.'

It wasn't surprising ... par for the course when visiting foreign lands.

Zhura clenched her teeth.

'If there are things you wish to know, why not just ask me?' said the King.

'Cal ...' said Zhura.

'We have nothing to hide,' said Cal. He dropped into one of the comfortable seats by the fire. 'Come … sit.'

Fyia sat, and the puppies appeared through the door at the back of the hall. She scooped one up into her lap, where it promptly curled up and went to sleep. Cal watched her, something lurching in her chest when she met his predatory gaze.

'What do you want to know?' he said, his voice hard like iron.

'Why is your relationship with the Queen Mother so strained?' she asked, not breaking eye contact.

'Because she did not support my bid for the throne when my father died.'

'Why?'

Cal raised an eyebrow. 'There was another she considered more suited for the role.'

'Who?'

'Seriously?' said Zhura. She gave Fyia an incredulous look, then turned her ire on Cal. 'You're going to let her pepper you with questions, and expect nothing in return?'

Fyia smiled. If she were to unite their kingdoms, open dialogue was essential. This was good. 'I will happily reciprocate,' she said. 'Ask me whatever you wish.'

'Why did you overthrow your brother?' said Zhura, sitting on the arm of Cal's chair.

Cal frowned, although Fyia wasn't sure why.

Fyia went still; rumors about her brother were the ones she hated most. She stroked the puppy's fluffy fur, the motion calming. 'I didn't. My brother had a … difficult relationship with his magic. He had no desire to lead our kingdom … had no desire to even *be* in our kingdom. He wanted to abdicate. He asked me if I would mind taking on the role.'

Zhura raised her eyebrows. Apparently she found the truth farfetched. 'Why did he go to the Fae'ch?' she asked, leaning forward. 'Why did they accept him?'

'He wanted to be among the magical,' said Fyia. 'As to why they accepted him, you'll have to ask him, for although I could guess, I do not know.'

'How did you do it?' said Cal, scooping up a puppy of his own. 'Take all five kingdoms?'

Fyia shook her head and donned a censoring expression. 'Your turn first.' Cal shrugged, so she continued. 'What would it take to unite our nations?'

'Other than marriage?' Zhura said lightly.

Fyia ignored Zhura, her eyes fixed on Cal, who was watching her once more. Fyia assessed him with fresh eyes, and as far as marriage prospects went, he was certainly the best she'd had. Handsome, in his prime, magical, a king clearly respected by his people. And the Black Hoods were reclusive, but they were a wealthy nation, feared and esteemed by all the lands. Not to mention, they could help form a union with the Fae'ch … no small benefit.

'Many things,' Cal said at last, 'but mostly, I would need proof you care less about conquering nations than doing what is right for your people.'

'Everything I've done is for my people,' said Fyia.

'Then why are you here with us, trying to expand the reach of your empire, when your homelands are in turmoil?' said Zhura.

'Because I wish to bring back the dragons,' said Fyia, 'for their good—even if they can't see that yet— for the good of all. That has been my aim from the beginning … my calling. I have no desire to sit on a throne and live out my days in boredom, playing politics. There are others far more skilled at that than I.'

'Like your aunt?' said Zhura.

'To name but one,' said Fyia, unsure exactly what Zhura was implying. 'That's it? To form an alliance with the Black Hoods, I must prove I care about my people?'

Cal held her gaze for a moment, absently stroking the puppy in his lap. 'How did you do it?'

Fyia glanced at Edu, who still sat on the uncomfortable wooden chair, Aaron leaning against the wall not far behind him.

'I could never have done it alone,' she said. 'Overthrowing my parents was easy—they were not good to their people—but after that, things became more complex. I won't bore you with a detailed account, but I relied heavily on my general—Sensis—and on my Cruaxee, but that has come with a cost.

'My people are wary of magic. As you know, until recently, it was outlawed in our lands. There are also those who do not appreciate being ruled by a woman.'

Zhura's expression softened a little.

'Believe me when I say it was not easy,' Fyia continued, 'but I knew, with unwavering certainty, I was doing what was right. I know I can give my people a better life, even without the dragons, but I also know I can find the dragons, and when I do, I can do so much more.'

'How do you know?' said Cal, shifting in his chair, hanging on her words.

She leaned back. 'Show me your egg, and I will tell you.' Question time was over.

Cal sat bolt upright in his bed, the memory of Fyia's scent in his lungs. When she'd risen from her chair to leave the hall, he'd stood also, the movement putting them closer together than was comfortable.

He hadn't used the Cruaxee-touch on purpose, but he'd smelled her scent of wild roses and cut grass, and it was like his bear had been curious … wanted to find out more about the woman he'd bonded her to.

Cal had inhaled deeply, the smell enhanced a thousand-fold by his bear's superior sense of smell. It had been all he could do to hold himself together … he'd had to leave, and now the smell invaded his dreams, robbing him of sleep for the third night in a row.

Images of Fyia kept flashing across his mind. The stubborn set of her jaw, the regal way she held herself, despite her middling stature, the sun shimmering off her dark hair, the light of curiosity in her azure eyes. He'd believed her when she said she wanted the best for her people, but Cal wanted the best for his people too, and he wasn't convinced that meant allying with the foreign Queen.

Fyia wanted to tear the world down, and he didn't doubt she could do it, but was she capable of building it back up again? She seemed convinced the dragons would return, but … why? Cal had once dreamed of being the one to find the dragons, but when he'd won the battle for his kingdom, more important matters had possessed his every waking thought, chasing the childish notion from his mind.

He worried about how to feed his people when their lands were growing colder by the season. How to hold his people together in the face of such a threat … Eventually, they would have no choice but to migrate or starve. If they allied with Fyia, perhaps the Black Hoods could go to her lands, but her people would not like it … there would be bloodshed and hardship.

Cal threw back the furs covering his naked body, dressed quickly, then headed for the library. He had always buried himself in books when he couldn't sleep, combing for inspiration, or answers, or any kind of diversion from whatever unwelcome thoughts invaded his mind.

Chapter Twelve

FYIA PATTED HER WOLVES as she returned to Anvarn, pulling on the boots she'd stashed in a hollow. She'd needed to run, to reconnect with the wild after three frustrating days of learning from the King. Or in fact, not learning, for it seemed he knew little more than she.

She wanted to avoid discovery, either by the Black Hoods, or by her own guards, who by now had probably realized she was missing. She watched, ensuring the place was devoid of life before sneaking back to the tavern.

She was about to make a dash for it across the town square, when her wolves alerted her to a movement in the shadows. She watched as the cloaked figure moved towards the library, then as they quickly climbed the steps and ducked inside.

Fyia moved without conscious thought. Whatever they were doing, they didn't want to be spotted, which meant whatever they were doing, it was certainly worth investigating.

She paused when she reached the building's threshold and listened for movement. She heard the dull thud of footsteps off to the right, near the wall.

Fyia snuck around the edge of the room, keeping to the shadows of the stacks until she came across a wrought-iron railing that disappeared into the floor. She hadn't seen it earlier, set back against the wall as it was, and she hadn't had time to explore.

She barely hesitated before descending the steep, circular steps, trying not to make a sound. Her wolves had to stay at the top, the stairs too steep, and their claws too loud, and they whined at her through the bond. *Oh, hush*, she thought, trying to concentrate, and they quieted down, straining their ears for any sound.

Fyia reached the bottom, glad to find it warm, for she hadn't bothered to take a cloak on her run. She waited for her eyes to adjust, then spotted a blueish light up ahead, although she had no idea what it could be.

She moved cautiously forward, careful where she placed each footstep. She noted the shelves of books stopped as she got closer to the light, which seemed to come from the floor.

'What are you doing here?' said a familiar voice from behind her. She jumped and spun around, Cal's face mostly hidden in shadow.

'I was out for a run. I saw someone come in here … I didn't know it was you …'

'Well, now you've satisfied your curiosity, you can leave,' he said, striding towards the light.

Fyia followed. 'I haven't actually,' she said. 'Oh …' Cal stopped by a small pool of water, the light a reflection of the moon, which shone through a hole in the ceiling. The pool was a raised structure made of stone, with copper pipes attached to two sides.

'There's a hot spring here,' said Fyia. It explained why the library was so warm.

'Yes,' said Cal. 'Are you done now?'

'Do you use it to heat other buildings?'

'No.'

'Why?'

'I came here for peace and quiet.'

'Couldn't sleep?' she asked, not wanting to leave this place, or his company. There was something about his intense demeanor, the way he switched so easily from carefree cad to brooding King, the austere way he looked at her …

He didn't answer, so she circled the pool, taking in every detail she could make out, which wasn't much in the gloom.

She looked back to find Cal gone, and something lurched in her chest … something that felt a lot like disappointment. He'd been cold and aloof since they'd danced in the tavern, but she was drawn to him in a way she'd never been drawn to another. She couldn't understand why … maybe it was the Cruaxee-touch …

Fyia reached for her bond with his bear, feeling her way through the faint, strange connection.

'What are you doing?' said Cal, suddenly in front of her, a hint of concern tinging his confident tone.

'Exploring the bond you placed on me,' she said. His scent of gorse, pine, and freshly fallen snow was enhanced, far stronger than usual. It made her heart race … made her lightheaded, and she shut her eyes, trying to shake away the sensation, trying to pull back, willing her mind to focus on more important things. His bear didn't want to let go, and chased her.

Fyia's heart thudded loudly in her ears as she reached for her wolves, who whined in her mind. She concentrated on them, letting their senses fill her as she raced away from the bear.

Her wolves still sat by the books above, and the smell of musty, leather-bound volumes mingled with the King's scent, diluting him until the bear lost interest, and Fyia had control once more.

'Don't do that again,' said Cal, as though in pain, his voice stern and distant.

'If you didn't want me to use the bond, you shouldn't have touched me with it,' she countered.

He was so close his scent invaded her once again, this time without the help of his bear's senses. She needed to put distance between them, but as she tried to move away, he grabbed her arms, his fingers firm.

'If my bear attacks you through the bond, there is little I can do to stop her. She is strong and wild and willful. She possesses a stubborn streak not unlike your own that is impossible to control.'

Fyia's head swam. 'Release me,' she breathed. His scent was overwhelming, and the feel of his strong hands through the thin cotton of her shirt made her breathless. Fyia was glad Edu wasn't here … he wouldn't have let anyone get away with touching her this way, regardless of their importance. He would have caused a diplomatic incident and been proud of it.

Fyia knew she should push him away … make him take a step back. She knew well enough how to, because Sensis and Edu had both insisted on training her in self-defense. Neither of them had fully trusted the approach of the other, so they'd trained her twice over, not to mention the constant refreshers they both liked to deliver. But she didn't push him away, because part of her didn't want to—a dominant part.

Cal dropped his hands and took a step back. 'I just … need you to understand the danger,' he said. 'To take it seriously. I don't want my bear to hurt you.'

'Then why did you touch me with your Cruaxee bond?' said Fyia, her voice rising in frustration. She took a few steps away, washing her face with her hands.

'Be careful over there,' he said, his tone urgent. He moved towards her, and she backed up a pace. He stopped. 'Fyia, there's a hole … I don't want you to fall.'

She looked at the ground, searching for the hazard, and found it without difficulty. 'Why is there a hole in the floor?' she said, inching closer.

'Don't,' he said. 'It leads to the mechanisms that control the hot water pumps. It's a long way down.'

Fyia wasn't sure what possessed her, but she decided she would like to see the mechanisms, maybe because of the note of panic in the King's voice. What was down there he didn't want her to see?

Fyia sat, dangling her legs over the edge of the hole, which was easily big enough for her to fit through.

'Fyia, don't,' said Cal.

'Why not?'

'It's dangerous.'

'Why?'

'If you fall …'

'I won't,' said Fyia, shuffling over a little.

'You …'

'I've found a ladder.' She tested the rungs with her feet to make sure they were sturdy.

'There's no light down there.'

'Then I'll come back up.'

'Why go down in the first place?' he ground out.

'Because, as you only just pointed out, I have a stubborn streak, and I want to.' She swung herself fully onto the ladder, and deftly descended into the blackness below. It seemed important to the King that she did not go down there, but he'd given her no choice with the Cruaxee-touch, so she would give him no choice in this, and see how he liked it.

The thought sounded petulant as it passed through her head, and the part of her that was a responsible, level-headed leader almost made her climb back up. But then her feet touched solid rock … it wasn't so far down.

'Fyia,' said a voice from above. She heard the tapping of Cal's feet searching for the wooden ladder.

'You're coming down?'

'What in the Whore's name do you think?' He was angry, and making no attempt to hide it. 'Stay where you are.'

'There's a sliver of moonlight,' she said. It was some distance away … impossible to tell how far, exactly.

'Fyia, stop!' Cal shouted, his voice so commanding, her feet rooted to the spot. Her breath hitched, and she turned back towards the ladder, where she could make out the barest of shadows nearing the bottom. No one ever spoke to her that way, and it was … invigorating.

'Why?' she said, longing to see the furious expression that was surely on his face.

He fumbled with something to the side of the ladder, and then a torch flared to life. He turned towards her, his face lit by flickering flame, and he was glorious in his fury. His eyebrows had pinched together, forming a crease at the top of his nose, his eyes—dark in the low light—bored into hers, his jaw clenched.

Fyia's lips parted in surprise. She couldn't look away, her eyes drinking him in. He moved menacingly towards her, and her skin rippled with sensation, the hairs on her arms coming to life. When he reached her, he leaned down into her space, stealing her air, close enough that she could see the dark open pupils of his eyes.

'That is why,' he said. He stepped past her, drawing her attention to the drop only two paces away.

'Oh, Goddess,' she murmured, shaking her head. She was unsure if the recent proximity of his burning eyes, or that she'd nearly fallen to her death had affected her more.

They stood on a ledge that jutted out into a cave, a drop on two sides. Fyia surveyed as much of the space as she was able in the insufficient light, but could see little aside from rock walls lined with pipes.

Fyia inched closer to the edge, to where the sliver of moonlight shone into the cave, and looked down. The drop wasn't as big as she'd originally thought, and another ladder connected the ledge to the ground below, to where ... no, that couldn't be right. 'Bring the torch over here,' she said to Cal. 'Is that ... do you have aqueducts this far north?'

Cal came up behind her and held the torch aloft, his features now resigned. 'Evidently,' he said.

Fyia traced the edges of the waterway with her eyes, from where it appeared through the cave wall, to where it left the circle of torchlight.

'Is your curiosity satisfied?' said Cal.

'No,' said Fyia. 'I'm going down there.'

'Fyia,' he said, grabbing hold of her arm.

This time, she used her training and spun out of his grip. 'Do not try to hold me against my will,' she said slowly, her face a portrait of fury.

'Then stop trespassing.'

'That is hardly what I'm doing ... I'm ... researching, for when our kingdoms unite. The aqueduct is a promising sign; it means there was probably a trade route between our kingdoms at one time. When we thaw the north, we'll be able to use them for trade once more.'

The King seemed to falter at that. 'Well, now you know,' he said, 'and we can both return to our business.'

'This is my business,' she said, grasping the top of the ladder, 'and it should be yours too.'

'Don't lecture me,' he snapped.

She paused, looking up at him. 'I'm not. I am trying to find ways for us to work together, for the prosperity of both our kingdoms.

'And what are you doing in the face of such an opportunity? Dragging your heels? Why? Because I am foreign? Because I'm a woman? Or maybe because you're too proud to admit when someone else has a good idea.'

Fyia continued her descent, and to her relief, Cal didn't try to stop her. In fact, he followed. He could have walked away and taken the torch, leaving her to fumble about in the dark.

'Your words are far from the truth,' he said. 'They show how little you know of me, and how naïve you are of the north.'

She plucked the torch from his hand, and he frowned.

'Why would I partner with someone like you?' he said. 'Why commit my people to your impulsive, reckless obstinance?

'Just look at you now … this is not your land, and yet you treat it as your own. You ignore my wishes— even though you are my guest—not to mention that you are a danger to yourself. You could have broken your neck.'

Fyia couldn't deny his words, for they were true. But if she were a man, would he consider her reckless and obstinate, or would he think her confident, determined, and worthy of adoration? She was committed to succeeding by any means necessary, and she would not apologize.

Not to mention, her gut was sure he didn't want her down here for some reason she had not yet discovered. Or at least, part of him didn't want her to discover it. He was still here, after all.

Fyia followed the raised edge of the aqueduct to where it disappeared through the far cave wall. She stepped onto the lip and leapt across to the other side. It was an easy jump, but Cal called out in alarm. 'Fyia, what are you doing?'

Getting hotter then. 'Exploring,' she said, following the cave's jagged perimeter.

Cal jumped the water too and came up behind her. 'Enough is enough,' he said, trying to make a grab for the torch. She ducked his hands and flitted away, stopping when her boots splashed in water. Warm water.

'This is the hot spring that heats the library?' she said, looking back at Cal.

'Of course,' he said tersely.

Fyia held up the torch, studying as much of the pool as she could, but it stretched past the circle of torchlight. She was about to continue her walk of the perimeter—at least the bits she could reach—when a glint on the far side of the pool caught her eye.

'What is that?' she said, stepping into the water a pace.

'What is what?' said Cal, looking about ready to shove her into the pool.

'That,' she said, the torch illuminating the edge of a metal object.

'It's nothing,' he said. 'Now, can we please go back? People will be starting to wake; they'll wonder where we are.'

Fyia stepped back onto dry land, and Cal's features filled with relief. 'Thank you,' he said, turning away. But Fyia didn't follow. She propped the torch against a rock and quickly pulled off her boots.

Cal spun and made for the torch, but she was too fast for him, snatching it up and dancing into the water. 'If you want it, you'll have to come and get it,' she said in a singsong voice fueled by her exhilaration.

Whatever he didn't want her to see was on the other side of this pool, so she hitched up her pants and moved swiftly through the water. It was shallow to start, but the gradient became steeper as she progressed, so she halted and held up the torch. She'd only made it a few paces, but that was all she needed, because the whole of the metal object was now illuminated, and Fyia gasped as she took it in.

'A clock?' she said. 'You have a dragon clock?'

'It would appear so,' said the King. 'And now you've had your fun, if I were you, I would get out of that water as a matter of urgency.'

'Why?' said Fyia. She cast nervous glances at her feet, worried some terrible creature might be about to pull her under.

'Because in three minute-spins, that water is going to boil.'

Cal watched the infuriating women with grim resignation. It didn't really matter she'd discovered their clock. It wasn't a great secret, even though the Queen Mother liked to make out it was, but short of man-handling the Queen back up the ladders—a task for which he had no stomach, and, if Fyia's reputation were accurate, might leave him with a knife in his back—there was little he could do but watch. The more he protested, the more curious she became.

Fyia scrambled out of the water and pulled on her boots. It had been a risk, letting her wade into the pool, but she hadn't gone far ... he probably could have hauled her out in time, and he'd used the Cruaxee-touch to monitor the temperature of the water on her skin. She'd told him never to use it again, but this was for her own safety, and she'd refused to listen to his protests, so he had little trouble justifying his actions to himself.

Unfortunately, his bear had taken an interest in his use of the bond, and was now pushing against his mind, trying to glean as much about the Queen as she could. That meant he could smell Fyia, and see her, and hear her every move in startling detail. He was having trouble breathing, because her scent had hijacked his mind, so he closed his eyes to center himself, pushing his bear away.

'What is it?' said Fyia. She moved to his side, placing a hand on his arm.

He jerked away. 'Don't,' he snapped, his heightened senses sending shots of electricity out from her touch.

Fyia backed up, faltering. 'Sorry ...' she said, studying him, 'but what ...' Fyia frowned, then closed her own eyes. 'Did you ...' She trailed off, seeming to fight something within herself too.

No. He reached for his bear, and tried to force her away from Fyia, but there was little he could do. Fyia was already using the bond, which meant she could sense the same things he could. He spun, striding back towards the aqueduct, but Fyia followed him, refusing to give him the respite he craved.

'Send her away,' he said.

'I don't know how to.'

'You do,' he said, hoping it was true. 'Whatever you do to dismiss your wolves ... do that.'

'I ... what is that?' she said, looking at something over his shoulder, next to where the aqueduct went through the wall.

228

He followed the direction of her gaze, everything much easier to see than it had been before. The Cruaxee-touch was allowing them both to use the bear's senses, even though she was many leagues away. He'd only ever achieved something similar when the bear was by his side, and never like this ... so clear.

He found what Fyia had—a faint door-shaped outline in the wall next to the aqueduct. He'd never seen it before, and they rushed to the door together, eagerly feeling for a handle, or some way to lever the door open.

'Wait,' said Cal, 'stop touching it. We can use my bear's senses to smell for clues.'

Fyia didn't hesitate. She moved her head close to the wall and sniffed around the crease, while Cal did the same on the other side. It felt ridiculous, and more of Fyia's sweet, distracting smell filled his lungs, but there was also ... something ...'

'Here,' said Fyia. She reached for his arm, but stopped herself before her fingers made contact.

Cal didn't have time to dwell on the deluge of feeling that flooded him, because Fyia was holding the torch low, pressing and prodding at the wall near the floor.

'What is it?' he said, crouching close beside her, trying to see.

'It's a small circular indent with a pattern of circles. I've seen something similar before. We need ...' Fyia broke off. 'Can you smell metal?'

Cal inhaled another deep breath. 'I can smell metal everywhere,' he said, pointing to the pipes and clock.

'No, something different.' She moved, following the scent.

And then he picked it up too. A metallic tang slightly different to the rest, like copper mixed with some other metal.

'Here,' said Fyia. She lifted a rock halfway between the hidden door and the water, revealing a small round disk.

'What is that?' said Cal. He should probably be worried about uncovering his kingdom's secrets alongside a foreign Queen, but he was so intrigued, he couldn't find it within himself to stop. And for some reason, he didn't want to send her away. Nor did his bear, apparently, who still lent Fyia her senses. Did his bear have a choice? But if she really didn't like it, she would attack as she had before … He had so many questions, but Fyia was on her feet, moving back towards him.

'It's a key,' she said, pressing the disk into the indent in the wall, then turning.

A slight scraping noise filled the air, and the door opened inward a crack. Fyia pushed it, and it swung with little protest. A whoosh of cold air sucked at the room just as a bubbling noise began behind them.

'You were telling the truth then,' said Fyia, looking back at the pool of boiling water, steam rising from its frothing surface.

'I am not in the habit of telling lies,' he said sternly.

Fyia held his gaze for a moment, seeming to assess him anew, and he suddenly noticed how close she was. He could reach out and stroke the hair off her face … trace the line of her jaw, but before he could decide whether he would, she stepped into the tunnel.

'Fyia,' he called after her. 'We should tell the others where we are. It is selfish of us not to, and if anything happens ...'

Fyia laughed. 'Someone will find us, for although you apparently have no knowledge of this place, another has visited quite recently. The scent is fresh.'

Fyia pocketed the circular key and swung the door closed behind them, although not all the way, then set off at a brisk pace.

Cal sniffed again, and found she was right. Someone had been here, and he knew exactly who it was.

Chapter Thirteen

FYIA'S ANGER AT CAL'S using the Cruaxee-touch had abated as soon as she'd realized how useful it was. Then she'd welcomed the bear in. The bear had come willingly, for she'd been equally intrigued about Fyia. But as Fyia and Cal marched along the seemingly endless tunnel, the aqueduct the only feature of interest, the bear grew bored and left them, taking her superior senses with her.

It was probably for the best, because the enhanced smell of Cal was making Fyia restless, especially as he began to sweat. It was all she could do to put one foot in front of the other.

'Where do you think it leads?' she asked, when the bear's senses had abated enough for her to concentrate.

He seemed conflicted, so she continued. 'I'm going to find out either way. We have plenty of water, and we can go for days without food, so unless you're planning to force me to turn around, you might as well just tell me.'

Cal exhaled loudly. 'You are exasperating,' he said. 'Thank you.'

'It wasn't a compliment.'

She turned back and shot him a sly look. 'I know.' She meant to look away, but her eyes lingered on his face. His frown lines had become fixed, and tension gripped his shoulders.

Fyia stopped walking, and pulled him to a stop too. He looked down at her hand on his arm, and she hastily dropped it. Why did he hate her touching him? Did he really dislike her so much?

'What is it?' she said, concern lacing her tone.

'This tunnel almost certainly leads to the Temple of the Dragon.'

'What?' she said excitedly. 'The home of your dragon egg?'

'The sacred home of our most ancient beliefs, and a place *you* may not visit.'

'Because only Black Hoods are allowed?' said Fyia, the Queen Mother's words coming back to her.

'You make it sound trivial, but you don't understand what the temple means to my people … what they will think when they discover I have taken you there.'

Guilt punched a hole through Fyia's gut. 'What will they think?' she said gently. Infuriating as the King was, she didn't want to get between him and his people … not when they obviously loved him.

'That I have betrayed them … allowed an outsider into our sacred space … desecrated it. When the dragons disappeared, the Black Hoods closed their borders, because the rulers of the other kingdoms fought petty, meaningless battles, while my people suffered the consequences.'

'You mean the freezing of the north?' she said.

'None of it was our fault, and yet southerners cannot understand what life has become for us …' He trailed off. He looked as though he wished he could

233

take back his words, then surprised her by ploughing on. 'And now I am accompanying one of those selfish southern rulers to our most hallowed ground. Placing the needs of a foreign Queen above harmony in my own lands. For when my people discover what I have done, there will be those who call for my abdication … maybe even my head.'

His eyes bored into hers, his expression resigned. He knew she would not turn back unless forced, and she knew he would not force her. She'd been clear since her arrival she sought the egg.

Fyia nodded her understanding. They would continue, but there would be consequences when they returned. They walked on in silence, Fyia wishing she had an answer to his problem. She didn't want to hurt him, but she didn't owe him anything either, and finding the dragons was for the good of everyone, even if it cost him his throne.

Cal was silent for most of the walk, and Fyia wondered what plagued him. Only his concerns about her being here? Or was something else on his mind? The Black Hoods had done a good job of presenting a mysterious, united front to the world, but behind their well-constructed appearance, maybe they had the same problems everyone else did.

After many turns of the seemingly endless trek, when Fyia and Cal were both tired and grumpy, they found their way blocked by a man-made wall, and Fyia's heart gave an excited squeeze. The aqueduct ran through a hole in the construction, and the water wasn't quite to the top, so Fyia stuck the torch as far through as she could, craning her neck, hoping for a clue as to what lay beyond. It was futile, for the wall was thick, and she could see little.

They searched the wall from top to bottom, looking for any sign of an indent, or the telltale crevice of a door's outline. They found nothing.

'What about over there?' said Cal. He jumped the aqueduct to examine the wall on the far side, and Fyia followed. She immediately wished she hadn't, as the area was small, her arm rubbing against Cal's as they searched. She crouched to the floor, trying to give him space, but given the proximity of her face to his groin, and the way his body went suddenly rigid, that was a bad idea too.

Just as she was about to stand and jump back over the aqueduct, giving him space to search alone, her fingers found a round groove in the stone. 'Here!' she said, the word coming out as an excitable squeal.

Cal looked down as she pulled the circular key from her pocket, then tried it in the lock. Nothing happened.

'Goddess,' she cursed. She twisted it to try another angle, but to no avail.

'Let me try,' said Cal, crouching to take the key from her hand. The action put their faces close, their breath mingling. Fyia didn't miss the dip of his gaze to her lips, her breath hitching as he slid his hand over hers.

The touch took her by surprise, as did the trickle of sensation low in her belly, but then he snagged the key from her fingers and dropped her hand, and she felt foolish. He just wanted the key … and an opportunity to toy with her, and she'd walked straight into it.

She stood, then jumped back to the other side of the water, sucking in the cool air as he fumbled with the key, uttering his own curses under his breath.

'It doesn't work,' he said.

'No, really?'

Cal shoved the key into his pocket, then began taking off his clothes.

'What are you doing?' she said, forcing her eyes to remain on his face.

'Undressing,' he replied, his shirt following his cloak and padded leather doublet to the ground.

'Thank you, I can see that,' she said. 'But why?'

'I don't want my clothes to get wet.'

'You're going to swim through?'

'Do you have a better option?'

She didn't, and she couldn't let him go by himself.

'Feel free to leave your clothes on,' he said, 'but we have no way to dry them, and I needn't remind you we're in the frozen north. If you wear wet clothes, you will most likely die.'

Fyia huffed. 'You're not worried about booby traps?'

'Not particularly,' he said. 'Why would anyone booby trap the water supply?'

'Because it comes through a secret passage.'

'That leads to a library owned by my people.'

Fyia picked up a rock and threw it into the water. Nothing happened, and Cal kept undressing, removing his boots and socks.

She picked up a second rock and threw it as far through the hole as she could. Again, nothing.

'Happy now?' said Cal, as he pulled down his breeches, not bothering to turn away. She didn't give into the temptation of letting her eyes roam south.

'You go first,' she said with a sigh, pulling off her own boots.

'Yes, that was my plan.'

Fyia slipped her shirt over her head as he bundled his clothes and weapons in his cloak. He didn't wait for her to finish undressing before lowering himself into the water. It wasn't particularly deep, only up to his waist, and if it was cold, he didn't flinch. Fyia wrapped up her clothes, watching carefully as he reached the hole and ducked down, so only his face and hands were out of the water, keeping the torch and his clothes dry.

He turned to face her just as Fyia dipped in a toe. '*Mother*!' she said, pulling her foot back.

Cal laughed, and Fyia couldn't even bring herself to care that his eyes studied her naked form in the shadowy light.

'You have special northern blood that keeps you warm, don't you?'

'Not that I know of,' he said, chuckling. 'You just have to do it.'

'Great pep-talk, thanks.' She sat on the edge of the aqueduct, took a few deep inhales, and then pushed herself into the water.

She gasped, but refused to whimper, concentrating on breathing through the cold. She picked up her clothes with shaking hands, then followed Cal.

He cocked an eyebrow as she came up behind him, her tightly balled clothes only partially covering her naked breasts, her nipples peaked against the cold. She cared more about preserving body heat than Cal seeing her naked form.

'See you on the other side,' he said, 'and try to avoid the water snakes.'

Fyia flinched. 'Ha ha,' she said, but her pulse spiked, because she wasn't completely sure he was joking.

She didn't have time to dwell, as Cal was already through the hole and moving away on the other side. She had no desire to be left in darkness, so quickly ducked her shoulders, her breaths becoming staccato, her whole body trembling at the shocking cold.

Fyia stood as soon as she emerged on the other side, a sea of gooseflesh covering her skin as the air hit. She shivered, unable to concentrate on anything but making it to where Cal was now dressing. Somehow, he'd already replaced his breeches, socks, and boots. He offered her his hand as she reached him.

Fyia didn't hesitate, passing him her clothes, then taking his hand, her body shivering so violently she could barely make her limbs work.

'Here,' he said, wrapping her in his cloak and pulling her into an embrace. 'My body heat will help.'

She nodded, or at least tried to through the shaking.

He'd trapped her arms between them, and she slid them to either side, pressing her naked torso against his. She sucked as much warmth from him as she could, marveling at the heat radiating from Cal's sculpted muscles.

He pulled away a little, and a protest sounded in the back of her throat before she could stop herself. 'I'm just getting my shirt and doublet,' he said with a laugh. 'It'll help.'

She released him, and he slung the clothing over his arms and shoulders, but didn't fasten them, leaving his chest exposed, then pulled her in once more.

Eventually, she stopped shaking enough to realize his hands were rubbing soothing circles across her back. Her naked back. Inside the cloak he'd fastened around her neck. Apparently he'd done away with the no touching rule.

'You should get dressed,' he said into her hair.

He was right, she should get dressed, but not one single part of her wanted to leave the circle of his arms. For so long, Fyia had held all the power, and even when others stepped up—Sensis and Edu and Starfall—Fyia was still the one they looked to. Even when Adigos had taken charge in bed, it had been an act—a fun pretense she'd happily indulged in. But here, with Cal, it didn't feel that way. He wouldn't defer to her because she was a queen. He was a king, after all, and she was in his lands.

Which meant … if he didn't want to be here, he wouldn't be. Despite the threat to his position—the supposed betrayal of his people—he was here, she realized, because he wanted something. But what? Adventure? To piss off the Queen Mother? Because he wanted the dragons too?

The uncertainty of it delighted her. Here she was, alone with a man who was outside her control, who had motives of his own. When had she last had such a thrill? Was he an adversary, or an ally? Had he Cruaxee-touched her as part of some bigger strategy, or because he was as impulsive as she?

'Fyia?' he said gently. He slid one hand to her nape, the other moving to push back the cloak's hood. He hooked a finger under her chin and peeled her face from his chest, forcing her to look up at him. 'Are you okay?'

A ripple of concern crossed his features, so she smiled reassuringly. 'I think so,' she said, 'but I don't want to leave your delicious warmth.'

He huffed out a laugh, then turned her in the circle of his arms. He shifted the cloak too, so it covered her front, her bare back now against his chest. He slipped a hand around her waist, and Fyia's body melted, her pulse racing at the barely there caress of his fingers.

'We're going to sit,' he said, then lowered them onto a chair. The shock of that fact finally jolted Fyia into noticing her surroundings.

'Where are we?' she said, taking the clothes Cal offered her. She fumbled with her garments under the cloak, Cal holding her steady, and, Fyia noticed, not letting her backside come into contact with his groin. It was a shame, for it was both hot there and intriguing, but his strong, callused hands in the dip of her waist were a good consolation, scorching against her cool flesh.

She slipped on her socks and boots, but lingered before pulling up her pants, savoring the last moments of Cal's touch. He surprised her by holding her brassier under the cloak, sliding it up her arms so she could fasten in at the front. Her icy fingers fumbled over the hooks, and she fought the urge to ask him to help, wondering what his big, assured hands would feel like on her breasts. A shiver ran through her at the thought, and she finally stood, not allowing herself to turn thoughts into action.

Cal stood too, his torso shielding her from the air, and he slipped her shirt over her head, then unfastened the cloak, so she could pull the shirt down and tuck it firmly into her pants.

'You should have brought warmer clothes,' he said, his lips still close to her ear.

'If only I'd known this was how my day would unravel …'

To her surprise, Cal refastened the cloak around her neck and pulled up the hood. 'You need it more than I do,' he said, and she wasn't going to argue.

She wrapped the soft, plush, heavy fabric around her, inhaling the snowy, musky scent of him. 'Thank you.'

He nodded, then picked up the torch. 'Welcome to the Temple of the Dragon.'

Cal took a step away. Now the heat had returned to his body, he couldn't stand so close to Fyia without signs of his arousal becoming obvious. And anyway, they were here for more important reasons.

The aqueduct had deposited them in a small antechamber off the main expanse of the temple, and he watched her as she explored the cavernous space. She followed the aqueduct—which was sunken into the floor—all the way to where two thrones sat atop a set of wide, shallow steps. The aqueduct bisected the thrones, making them seem oddly separate, at least if one ignored the enormous stone dragon with one claw on the back of each throne, its snarling head hanging down between them.

Fyia paused at the base of the steps, then forged ahead before Cal could summon the words to stop her.

'I thought these were a myth,' she said, turning so she stood before the throne on the right. They were made of dragon glass, the arms and backs decorated with gold, and dragon ivory. The decoration seemed to float in thin air, as the glass was almost impossible to see.

'No,' said Cal, swallowing hard. Would she go through with it? Sit atop a dragon throne? She was fire-touched, and had self-belief strong enough to tell her she was worthy, but she hadn't yet found the dragons, if indeed she ever would.

Cal had come close to placing his own rear on those thrones more times than he could count. At first, sharp words from the Queen Mother, or a member of the Dragon Order, had stopped him in his tracks, and later, the respect they'd instilled in him had kept him away. But they weren't here now. Nobody would discover them. And it was only a chair, for Gods' sake.

Fyia's face split into a beaming smile as he joined her. He looked out over the expansive throne room, imagining a time when it had been packed with humanity, full of members of a single great nation, united under the Dragon Kings and Queens.

He imagined that the enormous circle of stained glass opposite the thrones didn't hold views of the tips of snow-covered conifers. That outside the colossal double doors made of dragon steel, it was sunny and warm, and that the ground bore the fruits of summer.

And then bitterness filled him, for he had never known a summer. Sure, the days got longer in the north, the same as they did in the south. If one travelled far enough into the northern territories, the summer offered no dark hours at all, but that was not the kind of summer he craved. He wanted his people to sustain themselves once more, to rely on no one. For if the world were to discover the formidable Black Hoods were not as self-reliant as they seemed …

'Well?' said Fyia.

'Well?' he replied, pulling his mind back from his imaginings.

'Are we going to do it?'

'You don't believe the legends?'

'I don't know the legends.'

'Do you want to?'

Fyia held out her hand, offering it to him. 'I know better than to believe songs and superstitions,' she said. 'If I had listened to the words of others, I would not be where I am now.'

'In a temple covered in ice?' he said. 'Inappropriately dressed, and entirely at the mercy of a foreign King?'

She smiled a slow smile, then said, 'Exactly.'

He laughed and took her hand. *To hell with it.* They sat on the thrones, their arms stretched inelegantly between them, hands joined under the foreboding mouth of the stone dragon. Fyia bit her lip through her grin. Her eyes darted about as though half expecting the ancient temple to come crashing down around them.

When it didn't, Cal let go of Fyia's hand and sat back on his throne, unable to find the will to chastise himself for calling it *his*. Because it was. And the other was hers. It felt right ... natural ... foretold. And now he was here, his hands resting atop the dragon ivory inlaid in the arms of the dragon glass throne, he wondered that no Black Hood had claimed it before. That they'd been scared to even climb the steps. That no one else had wanted to bring back the dragons.

Cal had only ever voiced his desire to find the dragons to Aaron and Zhura, usually when drunk, when he could pass off his words as intoxicated dreams. But now, sitting here with Fyia, on the thrones his ancestors had sat atop, he knew with absolute certainty this was his path.

Unlike Fyia, he'd listened to those who'd told him he couldn't, or shouldn't, or that he was dreaming, that he should put all his energy and more into solving the immediate problems his people faced. But Fyia was right. If they always focused on the smoke in front of them, they would never douse the flames of the underlying blaze.

'It suits you,' said Fyia. Her head rested against the back of her throne, the dragon's claws hovering protectively above her.

'You too,' he said, reaching out his hand once more.

She eyed it, hesitated for a tick, then took it. Cal couldn't stop the excitable smile that stole control of his face.

'What?' she laughed, biting her lip.

'I'm going to help you find the dragons.'

'You are?' She tugged on his hand.

'You're right. It's the only way to solve our problems. The only hope we have of peace and security … of unfreezing the north.'

'And in return, you want to keep that throne you sit atop?' she said, her tone still light, but her eyes telling him she was only half-joking.

Cal squeezed her fingers, then dropped her hand and stood. 'Want to see the dragon egg?'

'You've been here before?' Fyia asked, as she followed Cal through an almost hidden door behind the stone dragon.

'My people have an annual celebration here, on Dragon Day,' he said. 'The Dragon Order used to live and worship here, but it became too difficult to survive, so now they live close to Anvarn, and come here only once a year with the rest of us. I've never been able to explore freely.'

'You didn't pull the King card?' she said, raising an eyebrow.

'I've been King for only a few cycles of the moon, and I'm careful about picking my battles.'

'You never snuck around in the middle of the night?'

'Oh, believe me, I tried. The place was always teeming with people, and the devouts were well versed in heading off young Black Hoods in search of adventure. I suppose, after so many years of being caught, I stopped trying. There were always more important things to do.'

'But you've been down here before?' He certainly seemed to know his way around, navigating the narrow, winding corridors with barely a check in his long strides.

'When I became King, the devouts showed me the egg.'

'You've seen it?' asked Fyia. A jolt of surprise hit her so hard she nearly fell over her own feet.

'No. No one has seen it in hundreds of years, but they showed me where it is, and explained theoretically how to retrieve it.'

Fyia rolled her eyes at the now familiar pattern. Whoever had decided no one should ever set eyes on the eggs was a total idiot.

They passed door after door, and Fyia's fingers itched to reach for the handles. 'Don't you want to see what's inside?' she asked, for he strode past with barely a glance.

'They're bedrooms for the devouts,' he said. 'I've explored almost every room on this level. That was easy. It's the lower levels where things got tricky.'

'But you're planning to poke around now?'

'What do you think?'

Fyia's chest constricted at his conspiratorial smile. 'So that's the real reason you came? A man after my own heart.'

He checked his pace, his eyes meeting hers for a heartbeat. Then he was off again, and she had little choice but to go after him, unless she wanted to be stranded in the dark. She wondered when she'd last been the assistant to another's desires. Had he planned this whole thing? Had he known about the tunnel? Was that the real reason he'd been in the library?

He turned a corner, then led her down a flight of steep stairs, the air around them becoming warm and humid. 'There are hot springs here too?' she asked, concentrating hard on where to put her feet.

'I don't know,' he replied. 'I asked the devouts, but they wouldn't tell me.'

'Something for us to explore after we retrieve the egg,' she said, excited at the prospect. But a sinking feeling filled her stomach, because although she held a single thread of hope, it seemed likely the dragon egg would be missing, that they'd find one of the strange metal balls instead. And then she'd have to explain to Cal what it was … or lie to him …

'Here,' he finally said. He stopped in front of a bland wooden door at the bottom of another flight of stairs.

'Inconspicuous,' she said, trying the handle, but finding it locked.

Cal pressed three stones in quick succession, and a low click reverberated through the air. An enormous slab of stone in the wall next to the door moved towards them. Fyia's mouth fell open. 'Sneaky,' she said, curling her fingers around the edge, and helping Cal pull it towards them.

'Clever,' he countered, then stepped into the corridor on the other side. The corridor was short, and after a few paces, they emerged into a nondescript stone-walled room. They were on a raised platform, next to steps that led down to the sand below.

Cal paused, looking at something across the room, and Fyia stepped past him, heading down the stairs.

She had one foot on the first step when Cal realized what she was doing. 'No!' he screamed, then yanked her back. He spun her, so his body pressed her flat against the wall, his hands covering hers, pressing those hard against the stone too.

'What?' she stuttered, but he said nothing, only pressing her more thoroughly against the rock.

Apparently they were in danger, but she couldn't discern the threat, so her mind noticed the feel of him against her. His muscular arms that wouldn't let her move an inch, his chin resting against her temple, his … and then she heard it, a great yawning sound like a dam breaking, or a building collapsing.

'Cal …?' she said, hearing the tremble in her voice, but not finding the will to care.

'Stay perfectly still, and we'll be alright,' he said, although he didn't sound certain.

'Booby traps?' she whispered.

'Booby traps,' he agreed.

'I should have known …'

'Yes, you should,' he said, his voice not angry exactly, but it wasn't friendly either.

A swooshing noise filled the room, accompanied by a surge of warm air strong enough to make the loose strands of Fyia's hair whip around her face. And then everything went still, and silence fell.

'What in the Seven Hells was that?' said Fyia. She tried to see, but he refused to budge, using his hips to pin her against the wall.

'Wait,' he hissed, then the sound of something dropping filled her ears. Not just one something, but lots of somethings, hitting the sandy ground in a series of impacts. 'Close your eyes, and cover your mouth and nose.'

She did as she was told, clamping her eyes shut, and pressing her face into the hood of his cloak. A screeching noise filled the air. It started close, then moved away to the other side of the room, until silence fell once more.

'Okay,' he said, releasing her. 'Are you alright?'

Fyia nodded, although he probably couldn't see her in the dusty gloom.

'This time, don't move,' he growled. He stepped back into the tunnel and retrieved the torch he'd thrown there. She wanted to ask what had happened …

why he hadn't pushed her back into the tunnel too, but didn't. There was probably a reason, and she wasn't sure she wanted to know how close she'd brought them both to death.

Cal turned his attention to the far side of the room once more. 'There,' he said under his breath, so Fyia only just caught the word. He shuffled a few paces to his right, then handed the torch to Fyia. 'Put it in the ring,' he said, then stepped out into the void. But instead of falling to the ground, his foot landed on something, and he stood suspended in mid-air.

'Goddess,' she said, inching forward.

'Don't you dare.' Cal held out a hand. 'Stay there. I will be back in a few moments with the egg.'

'But …'

'It's dragon glass,' he said. 'Extremely difficult to see, especially in this light.'

Fyia nodded. Now she knew what she was looking for, she could see it under his feet.

'Do not move, or we're both dead,' he said. He looked her in the eye with such force, she knew he wasn't exaggerating.

Fyia nodded and backed up against the wall. 'I won't,' she said, her heart in her mouth as he took step after careful step across the glass.

Fyia couldn't see what Cal did when he reached the far side, even when he lit another torch. She thought he might have reached into an alcove, then a metallic clicking filled the air, followed by a whirring, and finally a protesting squeak.

His silence spoke volumes, and she called, 'What is it? Have you got it? Tell me what you've found!'

'It's not here,' he called back, his words laced with disappointment and confusion.

'There's nothing at all? Are you sure?'

He turned, and she could sense his suspicious look more than see it.

'You knew?'

'Knew what? What's there?'

Cal pocketed whatever he held in his hand, then turned back across the walkway. Fyia held her breath, worried his anger would make him careless, his footsteps less precise than before.

Cal stepped onto the ledge and headed back into the tunnel. 'Cal! What did you find?' she asked, snatching up the torch.

He ignored her, striding out, so she had to jog to keep up with him.

'Cal!' she said again, irritation running hot in her veins.

He pushed the wall closed behind them, then headed deeper into the corridor. She grabbed his arm, spinning him to face her. 'What did you find?' she asked again, ignoring his murderous eyes.

'Did you know?'

'Know what?'

'That the egg wouldn't be there?'

'How could I have? Tell me what you found!' Her eyes dropped to his breeches, where she could see the bulge of an object in his pocket. She was tempted to reach for it, but knew he wouldn't react well if she did.

Cal made a furious growling sound, then pulled out a strange metal ball she wasn't surprised to see. He held it in the palm of his hand, but wouldn't hand it over.

Her expression must have confirmed his suspicions, because he exploded forward. She backed away, but hit the side of the tunnel, nowhere to run. 'Tell me why you don't seem surprised to see this.'

His face hovered inches away, his features set in a cold, ferocious snarl. She found she liked him like this, and half toyed with the idea of provoking him further, just to see what he would do. But that would be childish, and she needed him, so instead she huffed out a breath and tore her eyes from his.

'I found a ball like that in the Temple of the Whore.'

Cal moved back so he could more easily see her face. 'In the south?'

Fyia nodded. 'And another was found at the Temple of the Sea Serpent in my own Kingdom.'

'What are they?'

Fyia shrugged. 'I wish I knew.'

'What about the Fae'ch egg?'

'Axus said there was nothing on the platform where the egg should have been, but if he found one of those balls, he could have easily hidden it … he is fae, after all.'

'Why didn't you tell me?'

Fyia shrugged again. 'You've been my ally for less than a turn of the clock, assuming you haven't changed your mind about what you said upstairs.'

Cal scowled. 'I'm not changeable by nature.'

'But we are yet to hammer out the terms of our arrangement, whatever it will be …'

Cal took a long breath. 'You've checked four eggs. Where is the fifth?'

Fyia fought the urge to withhold the information, but if they were truly to be allies, he had to believe she trusted him … whether or not that was the case. 'On the Great Glacier,' she said, 'but I don't know exactly …'

'The Temple of the Warrior,' he said immediately, cutting her off. 'My people have long believed a dragon egg to be kept there.'

'Then we know where we must go next. Do you have a relationship with the people there? For trade?'

Cal laughed. 'The people there? There are no people. Only the Emperor's mining operations perched atop the endless ice.'

'You've been?'

'Not personally, but we regularly send scouts to ensure they don't set their sights on our lands. The Emperor is a conquering sort.' He gave her a meaningful look. *Just like you.*

They searched the depths of the temple for several turns of the clock, finding little of note. Cal was all but ready to call it a day when he stumbled across a small staircase hidden behind a tiny lip in the wall. 'Over here!' he called to Fyia, who was examining a large stone in a section of wall at the edge of the torchlight.

Her inquisitive eyes were alight as she came near, the torchlight reflecting off the streak of pure white in her hair. She fascinated him ... a constant surprise, with the energy of a furnace, even if her body didn't produce heat like one. She still had his cloak firmly wrapped around her, skirting the floor as she walked. He liked seeing it there, although he shouldn't, nor could he reconcile the confusing stir of emotions she elicited in his gut—deep, furious hatred that it occurred to him might not in fact be hatred at all ...

She cared for nothing but her goals—not even the troubles of her own people trumped them. Cal was yet to decide if that made her noble or selfish, and in turn, what his own choices said about him.

'Are we to stand here all night?' she asked.

Her words jolted him back from his thoughts, and he realized she was probably right—it would be nighttime already, and they'd been missing for an entire day. Guilt sucked at him, but he pushed it away. His people could survive without him for a single turn of the sun, and this—helping Fyia bring back the dragons—was for their good as much as his own.

'I found a staircase,' he said, leading her down into the bowels of the temple. The stone walls changed to rock, and the humidity increased.

'Oh good, I could do with a bath,' said Fyia.

'So long as it doesn't boil you alive.'

'I'm willing to take my chances.'

'I think you might be insane,' he said, turning back to look up at her, two steps behind.

She scowled. 'It's merely my dazzling sense of adventure … and a desire to be warm to my core. Your cloak is appreciated, but this place is freezing.'

She wasn't wrong. 'I knew you were a soft southerner …'

'Wow,' she said, drawing his attention back to the stairs. 'Is that … gold?'

'What?' A golden glow illuminated the last few steps. They hurried to the bottom, bursting out into a cavern filled with a series of bubbling pools, and … Gods … no …

'Are those dragon scales?' Fyia breathed. 'Now I understand.'

Cal's attention snapped to Fyia. 'What do you understand?'

'Everything,' she said. She reached out a hand to touch the nearest scale. It was enormous—bigger than Cal.

He would have pressed her further, but the spectacle was too distracting, elation thrumming through his blood. This changed everything …

'Your mother's been keeping this place from you,' said Fyia. Cal could practically see the cogs turning in her mind. 'That's why you're forced to have her around.

It's why you defer to her, despite her lack of support. For this is the source of your wealth—how you feed your people when you have no way of growing crops, and animals are scarce. This is why you really came.'

Cal ran a hand through his hair, wishing she'd stop … willing her to continue, impressed by the sharpness of her mind.

'And it's why you're on good terms with the Fae'ch, when they are friends to no one … rarely even deign to be civil.'

'Aside from to your brother,' he said, the words out of his mouth without thought.

Fyia gave a half laugh. 'Aside from to my brother,' she agreed. 'But then, his face is a spectacle of its own, and if rumors are to be believed, they desired a fire-touched to reside among them.'

'But not you? Even though you have more to offer? A Cruaxee?'

'Did they want you for your Cruaxee?'

Cal hesitated. 'The Fae'ch couldn't care less about me, but they want these scales more than anything else. They're a powerful negotiating tool.'

'What do they do with them?'

'Magic,' he said cryptically, for he didn't know more than that.

'And now you hold all the cards,' she said, spinning around, taking in the thousands—tens of thousands—of scales.

'Yes.' Now he held all the cards.

'I knew not to trust your little speech this morning about how your people might overthrow you.'

'I spoke the truth,' he said, 'but now I have the scales …'

'You're in control.'

'We should return,' said Cal, his mind awash with tasks: dealing with the Queen Mother, keeping the location of the scales secret … Did the devouts know the scales were here? Were they the ones who retrieved them? No. Cal thought back to the scent he'd smelled at the tunnel entrance. Not the devouts …

'No,' said Fyia. She unclasped his cloak from around her neck and let it fall onto a scale.

'Fyia …'

'I'm going to get warm,' she said, stripping off her boots and pants.

'That is a terrible idea, and we have no food. You must be starving … I know I am. And there is much to do, not to mention they've probably sent search parties after us.'

'Don't you want one night off? Where no one needs you? We can hunt for breakfast in the morning, and return after that. And anyway, the dried meat and berries in your cloak are quite delicious.' She gave him a cocky smile that had him stepping towards her.

'You stole my food?'

She invaded his space, wearing nothing but a shirt, a tempting smile on her lips. 'I did.'

He cupped her cheek. He'd found her intriguing since he'd first heard the songs sung in her honor, but he knew she wasn't for him. She cared only for herself … and achieving the impossible. But something about this place—their discovery—made him want to throw caution to the wind … to celebrate.

She went up on her tiptoes as Cal lowered his lips, and their mouths met in a sensual caress. She tasted of the dried reindeer meat he always carried in his cloak, mixed with her sweet summer scent of roses and freshly cut fields. He longed for those scents to return to his own lands. He'd only ever smelled them when he'd sneaked into her kingdoms, and now here they were, buffeting his senses like a tantalizing promise.

She pulled back, looking up at him with a question in her eyes. He thought for a moment she might walk away, but then she leaned towards him, and this time, when their lips met, no other thoughts filled his mind.

The kiss deepened, and Cal's tongue caressed Fyia's. His lips were soft but commanding, and she happily relinquished control, letting her body melt against his, letting him lead the way.

She groaned into his mouth as his tongue played with hers. He pulled her against him, his hands on her behind, fingers massaging through the flimsy fabric of her shirt.

He went slowly, the kisses demanding yet exploratory, unhurried and assured. He felt so right, every part of him a delight under her fingers ... the solid cords of muscle, stubble covered jaw, silky hair. And his lips had been made by the Gods, for a kiss had never felt so good, stealing her breath, wiping her brain clean of anything but the feel of them.

Cal turned her, then pulled her back by her hips, one hand sliding to her breasts, the other brushing her hair to one side. He ran his nose down her neck, then nipped her nape before kissing his way back to her ear.

Fyia shivered at the intensity, sensation firing from her toes to the top of her head. She barely knew where he touched her, for he seemed to be everywhere at once, lips and hands working together in perfect harmony.

He pinched her nipple, and she tipped her head against him, then reached back, sliding a hand between them, cupping his arousal through his breeches. He exhaled loudly in her ear, and a trickle of desire collected in her core. She tugged at his doublet, and Cal's hands flew to help, yanking it open. He lifted her shirt, then pressed her naked skin to his, grunting when their flesh collided.

They stilled a moment, then Cal dropped to his knees behind her, holding her hips with his hands—scalding against her skin—and kissed her backside. 'Fyia,' he said, as his fingers traced down her spine, 'it's beautiful.'

She was going to argue that a scale could hardly be considered a thing of beauty, but then he kissed her there, and she felt a pleasure so intense she crumpled forwards, moaning. 'Is it sensitive?' he asked, doing it again to test his theory.

'Gods,' she said, pulling away, the sensation too much. She turned to look down at him, running her hands through his hair. 'It never has been before, but … yes.'

He pressed his face to her stomach and kissed her, his hands cupping her backside. She ran her fingers down the shells of his ears, and he choked, squeezing her buttocks and pressing his face more forcefully into her.

'What …?' she asked, then realized the texture behind his ears was … strange. She pulled one ear lobe forward and examined the back, shocked to find a tiny row of scales stretching from the top to the bottom. She ran a finger down it once more.

'Fyia,' he groaned. 'Warrior … help me.'

'That bad?'

'That … something,' he said, running a finger over her own scale in revenge.

'Okay,' she said, grabbing hold of his arm, 'truce. We need to talk about your fire-touch.'

'Do we?' he said, pressing his lips to the inside of her thigh.

She caressed his ear. He moaned, but didn't stop. Instead, he moved his lips to her sex, licking and sucking, one hand sliding over her scale, which made her buck against him. 'Cal,' she breathed, 'I'm going to …' He sucked, and she cried out, convulsing, holding his head as waves of pleasure hit. But as the waves turned to ripples, and then disappeared, the scale on her back warmed. 'Cal … look …'

'Something's happening to mine too,' he said, and she pulled at his ear until she could see.

'Oh my Gods … they're glowing!' She spun and pulled up her shirt.

'Yours is too,' he said. 'Has this ever …?'

'No. You?'

'Never.' He brushed his lips across her glowing golden mark.

'But you've had sex … right?' The words escaped without thought. He raised an eyebrow, and he was right to … that mouth had had practice, and she wasn't complaining. 'Maybe it's because we're surrounded by dragon scales?' she said. 'Like calling to like, or … something?'

Cal shrugged. 'Or maybe it's because we're both fire-touched.'

'Maybe,' she agreed. She turned and sat on his legs. 'Whatever it is, I want to make it happen again.' She kissed him, playing with his earlobe with one hand while reaching for the fastening of his breeches with the other. She freed his impressive erection, but he caught her hands.

'Fyia … we … I think we should stop.'

She went still. 'Why?' He'd flinched earlier when she'd touched him … that was probably why. But he'd changed his mind somewhere along the way … when they'd sat atop the thrones. She'd learned long ago not to second guess the thoughts of others, for guesses were usually wrong, or at least, not the whole truth. But … was he regretting this already?

Fyia shivered, cold hitting her both inside and out. Cal wrapped his arms around her and kissed her gently before resting his forehead against hers. 'Do you want to?' he said.

She was suddenly unsure. Moments before, she'd been determined, had wanted nothing more in the world. She rarely thought too much about these things. Sex was pleasure, nothing more. But maybe he was right, because this did feel dangerously close to more. She needed Cal politically, for the good of her kingdoms, and he was going to help her find the dragons. He clearly had resources that would help—not least a room full of invaluable dragon scales—and she didn't have jurisdiction over him … couldn't send him away if it got messy, like she'd done with Adigos.

She kissed him again, drawing strength and heat and comfort from his lips, but she didn't press for more … didn't deepen the kiss, or tip her hips against him. She pulled back with resignation in her eyes, then stood, tearing herself away, almost every part of her wanting to remain in his embrace. 'You're right,' but most of her didn't believe those words, because the phantom feel of his lips still lingered, and she longed to feel them on every part of her.

Fyia crouched next to a hot spring, hovering her hand over the top. The heat was such that it would burn if she touched it. No bath in that one. She continued around the cavern, from pool to pool, but they were all the same—scorching.

She sighed as she turned back to Cal, then redressed. 'They're all too hot.' Her cruel mind played pictures of sinking into deliciously warm, bubbling water, and then she shuddered, the cave not freezing like upstairs, but not overly warm either, despite the hot pools.

'We can sleep here and return in the morning,' said Cal. He chewed on a slice of dried reindeer he'd retrieved from his cloak. She nodded, having no desire to return to the real world a tick before they had to.

Cal lay down, his back pressed against a large dragon scale that had tipped onto its side, and patted the ground beside him. 'We can share the cloak, and our body heat,' he said, no hint of innuendo in his tone. It must happen all the time in the north … needing to share body heat and no more.

Fyia's stomach flipped as she lay next to him, her back against his chest. He wrapped the cloak around them, cocooning her in his arms, and Fyia nearly purred from happiness. He was a furnace, and he smelled like winter celebrations. She wondered what he'd do if she tasted his skin. Flinch most likely, and maybe even move away. She couldn't bear the thought, so instead, she wrapped her arms over his. She listened to the sound of his breaths, felt the beats of his heart, and let the steady rise and fall of his chest lull her to sleep.

Chapter Fourteen

SENSIS SWIPED HER SWORD left, then right, the streets of Medris—Moon's capital—no longer safe to walk at night … or during the day, if she was honest. Tonight, the rebels were particularly active … they were up to something, but Sensis didn't know what, and the Spider had sent no word.

She ran the hundred paces to the military academy, calling for the guards to open the pedestrian gate. The archers on the battlements rained a volley of arrows into the road behind her. Sensis heard bodies thudding to the ground, but couldn't afford a glance back to look at them.

She reached the safety of the academy's walls, glad to leave behind the stench and filth and danger of the streets. Until recently, every inch of Medris had sparkled in the midday sun, scores employed to make it so. Since Fyia had decreed women could become guild members, join the military, and attend the university, things had gone south. Not only had the street cleaners disappeared—presumably to join the rebels, or maybe because they feared them—but much of the food produced by the high houses of Moon was mysteriously going missing.

Officially, the houses blamed the rebels, but none seemed to be suffering financially from the so-called losses, and the Spider's spies reported increased export shipments to the Kraken Empire and the Scorpion Lands. Those who did suffer were the city's poor, who had little choice but to turn to the rebels for aid … rebels who didn't seem to be going short themselves.

'Any update on the supplies?' Sensis asked her commander. She'd been trying to get aid into the city— aid from their Queen, so Fyia didn't lose all support here—but the glasshouses of Moon produced most of their surplus food.

Sensis had asked Starfall to either ban exports and seize supplies, or import more from their trading partners, but so far, she'd received no answer.

'This came for you.' He handed her a piece of parchment bearing Starfall's wax seal.

Sensis scanned the letter, and her stomach sank. So much for importing from the Empire.

'What is it?' asked the commander.

'The Emperor's attacked the Kingdom of Sea Serpents. Lady Starfall has put a ban on all trade with the Kraken Empire, and ordered troops to the front.' The bulk of Fyia's army camped near Selise, as Fyia's new capital city had been their best guess as to where the Emperor would attack. Every day the attack hadn't come, a kernel of hope had grown in her chest that the intelligence had been wrong, or that the Emperor had chased Fyia north instead.

Sensis had been wrong to hope. It would take many days for the army to get to the coast of Sea Serpent, by which time it would be too late. They would have to fight a long, protracted war to retake their lands, all while giving the rebels more ammunition against Fyia's rule.

On the upside, at least the high houses could no longer sell their "stolen" food shipments to the Empire. Maybe it would even hurt their pockets enough for some to consider lending Fyia support. Not to mention, Sea Serpent were the financiers and suppliers of wines, perfumes, and fine liquors to the world. The high houses of Moon wouldn't like it if they had to go without those things.

'I must go to the capital,' said Sensis. 'You're in charge while I'm gone. Intelligence continues to be our top priority, along with protecting the women joining the guilds and university, and winning hearts and minds. But most importantly, we must find the head of the rebel snake, so we can cut it clean from its body.'

'Yes, General,' said the commander. Unfortunately, Sensis had a good idea who sat at the head of the snake, and he rarely came out of his hole.

'The Emperor has set up shop in the Temple of the Sea Serpent, and has seized much of the surrounding land,' said the Spider. 'He's insisting on meeting with Fyia, and has agreed to hold off on further military advances until after that meeting.'

'At least that gives the army time to move closer,' said Starfall, looking at her hands.

Lord Venir scoffed, as did Lady Nara, the only other members of the small council currently in Selise. Starfall was apprehensive about pulling Sensis out of Moon, given the unrest there, but she had little choice; the Emperor was the greater threat.

'War in my home kingdom is not desirable,' said Lady Nara, barely containing her fury.

'War is not desirable anywhere, child,' said Starfall.

'We cannot afford fighting in the streets as we have seen here in our capital, and in Moon,' Nara continued. 'The costs are simply too great.'

'You'd prefer our Queen to hand the Kingdom of Sea Serpents to the Emperor without a fight?' said Starfall, her lips curling into a snarl. This woman had no right to be here, on Fyia's Small Council. She was a coward.

'There is a very simple solution to all this,' said Venir, looking bored as he lounged back in his chair.

It took great effort for Starfall to keep her expression neutral … he was like a dog with a bone. 'I couldn't begin to guess your meaning,' she said sarcastically.

'If the Queen were to marry the Emperor, we would have a neat and tidy resolution,' said Venir.

'You'd hand over not just Sea Serpent, but all of the Five Kingdoms to a man we know so little about?' said the Spider.

'We know plenty about him,' said Venir, 'and he was perfectly reasonable when I visited his Empire.'

'You met him for no more than a score and a span,' said the Spider, 'and my spies do not agree with your analysis.'

'Your spies are overly dramatic …'

'Stop,' said Starfall. 'There is little point in our discussing this. The Queen will do as she pleases, regardless of the voices at this table.'

'Then she condemns us not only to war with the Empire, but continued unrest among her own people,' said Nara. 'Marriage is the only solution that avoids bloodshed.'

'Sometimes bloodshed is necessary,' said Starfall, pointedly.

'Maybe if the unrest was in *your* home kingdom, you would think differently,' said Venir.

Starfall snorted. 'I doubt that. Has Essa made progress with the airships?'

'She has,' said the Spider. 'We have sent many carpenters, and I believe they have begun production.'

'Good,' said Starfall. 'Then send an airship to retrieve the Queen from the north, so we may discover her opinions firsthand.'

Cal woke the following morning—what he assumed was the morning, given they had no way of telling the time—to find he'd rolled onto his back in the night. Fyia was on top of him, her cheek resting against the muscles of his chest, his cock hard and pressing into her stomach.

He had to get away before he did something he would regret … something that could jeopardize the future of his people. For no matter how much he wanted her, his people would always come first, and Fyia didn't seem keen on marrying any time soon.

Why was he even thinking about marriage? *He* wasn't keen on marrying any time soon. Although, if he were to take a wife, she was the most suitable candidate in all the known world … aside from the Emperor's daughter. But there was no way in the Seven Hells he would give the Emperor access to the Black Hoods' lands. He probably shouldn't entertain letting the Queen of the Five Kingdoms get her hands on them either …

Cal began to ease himself out from underneath her, but she gripped his side, stopping him in an instant. She slid a hand to his groin and grasped him through the fabric of his breeches. He exhaled in surprise, but didn't move, waiting to see what ill-advised thing she would do next.

She freed him, then took him in her hand, and he groaned, pressing his head back against the ground. He should stop her, but he hadn't shared a bed with anyone in … since before he'd become King. His people wouldn't take kindly to him whoring, and he had no intention of marrying any of the women from his town. Which meant, aside from a tryst here or there with a travelling actor, musician, or stall holder …

'Fyia,' he breathed, as she squeezed, then pumped up and down. '*Warrior* …'

'She won't help you,' she laughed, then lowered her head and licked the length of his shaft.

He bucked. 'Gods, Fyia, I …' He could barely think straight.

She did it again, then covered the tip with her mouth, sucking gently. 'Goddess,' he groaned. The feel of her around him nearly undid him, and then she took him deeper, bobbing her head so he hit the back of her throat.

He growled and slid a hand into her hair, and she hummed, the sensation sending vibrations through him that had him lifting his hips off the floor. She lifted her eyes to meet his, licking him again, flicking the underside of his cock with her tongue.

'You want me to stop?' she said, trailing her fingers up and down.

He couldn't form words, so he shook his head, his eyes never leaving hers.

She pumped her hand, cupping his balls with the other, and he was done, choking her name as he spent himself over her fingers, which stroked him until the last spasm.

His head dropped back to the ground, and even though he knew he should have stopped her, he couldn't bring himself to regret it. He wanted her more than he'd ever wanted another. Some part of her called to him. Maybe it was because they were the same—fire-touched, with a Cruaxee, the King and Queen of their lands—or maybe it was simpler, that they just … fit.

'Fyia …' he said, as he tried to still his racing heart.

She smiled, then laid her head on his chest. 'Seemed unfair for me to have all the pleasure. I wouldn't want you to think I'm the kind of Queen who takes but never gives, and once we're back in the real world …'

'Believe me, I enjoyed last night,' he said, stroking her hair.

They lay in silence for a moment, Cal drawing circles on her back. 'How did you do it?' he asked.

She rested her chin on his chest as she looked up into his eyes. 'Bring you such pleasure? Well …'

He poked her side, making her squirm. 'You united five kingdoms …'

She played with the ridges of muscle on his stomach, a mischievous look on her face. 'Of course, I started by usurping my poor, defenseless big brother … everyone knows that.'

He poked her again. 'Seriously …'

'I told you … my brother gave me his crown, and without my aunt—Starfall—I never could have taken the throne from my parents. Without my general, and Edu, and my spymaster, and my Cruaxee, it would have been impossible.'

'But you led them.'

'I did,' she agreed. 'People think great leaders are the warriors out front, swinging their swords, beating their chests, proving their power to the world. My parents mocked me for years because I was no warrior, and nor did I care for the usual pursuits of a lady. That's when they started calling me Fyia. To ridicule me. Because they said I had no fire inside me, and only a single dragon scale—nothing compared to my great and powerful brother. They were jealous, because they had no magic of their own, and thought I squandered mine.

'But I am skilled at watching and learning— especially from the mistakes of others. I'd seen mighty warriors overthrown in the training ring because they got cocky ... let their guard down. And I watched children as they played, and saw it was not always the biggest, or strongest, who led the gang. It was the one who could make the others *believe* in them. That's what a true leader does. Sure, some of them stand out front, beating their war drum, and people can believe in that, but that's not the only way. It's certainly not the most effective way.'

'So you gave them something to believe in? That's all it took?'

She laughed and gently pinched his skin. 'No, that is not *all* it took. But it was the start, and it carried us through our darkest times. I believe in the dragons. I believe in myself. I believe we can and will return our lands to their former glory, if we fight hard enough. And I am yet to hear an argument to convince me otherwise. I remind myself at my most difficult moments that I am no warrior—I don't need to be—I need to be smart, to lead, to keep a level head when everything is going to hell, to have people around me I can trust, who have the skills I don't possess ...

'Sensis is my warrior, Edu my council and my protection, Starfall my ... I don't know what she is, but she has backbone enough for all of us.'

'And your brother?'

Something painful took hold of Fyia's face, and he wished he hadn't asked. 'I thought he was my most trusted friend, but … he tricked me. I gave him the metal ball found in the Temple of the Sea Serpent. He didn't tell me what it was, or why he wanted it.'

'I'm … sorry.' Cal couldn't think of anything else to say.

'What about you?' she said, meeting his gaze. 'Why didn't your mother support your bid to become King?'

He inhaled a long breath. 'She's not my mother,' he said, his voice full of pain.

'She's not?'

He shook his head. 'I was the illegitimate child of the late King. He and the Queen Mother had two children, but they were both killed in the same avalanche that took the King. They were spoiled, brattish children whom she doted on, despite her intelligence. And my father loved her wily ways, which, to be fair, usually served the Black Hoods well.'

'Who did she support instead of you?' Fyia asked, stroking his chest.

'My distant cousin.'

'Zhura?' said Fyia, meeting his eyes again.

He laughed. 'No. The Queen Mother has little respect for Zhura. It was Zhura's brother. He was in the Queen Mother's pocket, and she wanted to rule through him. He even had a Cruaxee—snow cats—but he was no match for me and my bears.'

'You killed him?'

'I had no choice,' said Cal. He tried to send away the images of the dying man's blood spilling out across the snow, the eyes of his nation watching on, cheering his victory.

'Did the people support you?'

268

'Most did, especially because I'm fire-touched, and because of my Cruaxee—Zhura saw to it there wasn't a single person who didn't know—and I look like my father, and have worked with my people since I was a child … that helped.'

'Zhura seems a loyal type.'

Cal nodded. 'Her and Aaron both.'

'What of your real mother? Did you know her? Is she still alive?'

Cal clenched his teeth. 'She lived in the far north—a Priestess of the Dragon—that's all I know, and that she had a Cruaxee. The order sent me to the King when I was born, and my father never saw her again.'

'I'm sorry,' she said.

He laughed. 'Don't be. I never knew her, but I hope she brought my father joy for the short time they knew each other.'

'Did the King treat you well?'

'Yes. That's what made the Queen Mother despise me most. He wanted me to take the throne after his death. He saw the truth of my half-siblings, and it sickened him to think they would one day lead his lands.'

Fyia blew out a breath. 'It's the perfect tale for a bard.'

Cal laughed and kissed the top of her head. 'They'd probably twist it into a sickly love story.'

'Part of me hopes so,' said Fyia. 'I'm a sucker for a sickly love story.'

'No,' said Cal, unable to believe it. 'Tell me you're joking …'

She laughed. 'I am not. Myths and legends and epic love … and don't pretend you're not tempted by mysteries from the past, or you wouldn't be here. That, and you want to ride a dragon.' She raised an eyebrow, and he didn't miss her double meaning.

'I would love to ride a dragon,' he said, squeezing her backside, 'but we shouldn't linger; there is much to do.'

Fyia groaned and buried her face in his neck. It made his chest constrict, and when they sat, he pulled her lips to his, their kiss long and lingering. He could happily spend the day lying here with her … maybe even a span of days, or a cycle of the moon … the thought was disturbing. There were few he could tolerate for more than a few turns of the clock before feeling suffocated under the weight of their presence.

He dropped a final, chaste kiss on her lips, then stood, for if he didn't do it now, he never would.

Cal and Fyia climbed the wide, magnificent steps that led from the throne room to the outside world. The enormous temple doors had been frozen open, and once, the whole length of the steps had allowed access to the temple, but as they climbed, they entered a narrow tunnel through the ice, emerging through a hole barely big enough for a single person. They blinked against the bright sunshine as they stepped out into the clear, blue-skied morning.

They'd filled their pockets with small dragon scales—Cal apparently trusting that Fyia would give most of them back—and he'd hooked his cloak around Fyia's shoulders. He'd looked like he might kiss her again, but had pulled away. It was probably for the best, or so she told herself.

'I'll find us breakfast,' said Cal, as they stepped onto the snow, heading for the tree line. Fyia luxuriated in the feel of the sun on her face, almost missing the flash of movement in the trees, but Cal didn't. He pushed her behind him and drew his sword as four tanned men stepped out of the trees.

The men wore brightly colored woolen coats, tassels hanging from their round hats that immediately identified them as belonging to the Kraken Empire. But what in the Seven Hells were they doing here?

'You have it?' one said, moving towards them.

'Have what?' said Cal, tracking them with his sword. Fyia had no weapon, but she felt for her Cruaxee, searching frantically for wolves or eagles nearby. She found an eagle, bonded, and summoned it to her. He would probably arrive too late, but she had to do something.

'The ball,' said the same man, his accent lilting.

'Ball?' said Cal, doing a good job of feigning ignorance.

'We know you set off the traps,' the man said, as the others fanned out around them.

Warrior's balls. This was bad.

'What are you talking about?' said Cal, putting on a frustrated tone so good it almost convinced Fyia.

But the man was done talking. He lunged for Cal, swinging a braided rope at Cal's sword while swiping with a short sword of his own. Cal dodged, and Fyia caught the rope a fraction of a tick before the man whipped it back. She grabbed the weight at the end and pulled with all her might.

She caught the man off guard, and he stumbled forward, right onto Cal's waiting blade.

'I thought you weren't a warrior,' Cal said, through a disbelieving laugh.

'I'm not. But I am plucky.'

Cal laughed again and handed her a dagger. 'Back to back,' he said, as the remaining three men circled.

Fyia knew the odds weren't good, and the men seemed not to know who either of them were, which was both a blessing and a curse. If they'd known, at least the men would be less likely to kill them.

One attacked, then the other two in unison, two going for Cal while the first lunged for Fyia. Fyia spun away, running for the tree line, ducking behind a tree before her attacker could catch her. He circled the tree, lunging this way and that, laughing at her strangled cries every time she had to switch direction.

Fyia's heart nearly burst with terror. And then something hard caught her in the chest—his rope—winding her so thoroughly she bent double, gasping for breath. The man yanked her back by her hair, Fyia working desperately to get air into her lungs.

He laughed in her face. 'Not so fearsome now,' he said, his breath stinking of stale beer and dead things. She fought the urge to wretch as he pulled her arms behind her, turning her to face where Cal still fought near the entrance to the temple.

Cal whirled this way and that, his movements fluid and precise. He was terrifying, more so even than Edu, and Fyia's mouth fell open as she watched. 'Watch him die,' the man said into her ear, then transferred her wrists into one large hand and grabbed her breast with the other.

Fyia didn't move, her body rigid, giving him none of the fight he so clearly wanted. She willed Cal on, inwardly breathing a sigh of relief as he felled one with a deft, lightning-fast stab of his sword. But it took him a moment to retrieve his weapon, and the other man was behind him, attacking with terrible ferocity.

Fyia summoned her magic—all she possessed. She knew not how to wield it properly, and most times she'd tried, it had ended in disaster. But now disaster would most likely ensue if she didn't use it, and she couldn't lose Cal. So she sent a torrent of power at the man, charging him, willing it to stab the attacker over and over, seeking any organ vital for life.

The man fondling her gasped and let go of her breast, gaping at the remains of his three comrades. He took out his knife and turned his eyes to Fyia, a fury there so primal she dove to the ground without thought, screaming Cal's name.

But before Cal could do so much as turn in her direction, a deafening roar filled the air, and Fyia's attacker hit a tree with such force, the cracking sound must have been the breaking of his bones.

An enormous, ferocious bear stood over the man, then tore the man's head from his body as though he were a rag doll. Fyia shivered at the raw display of power, then scrambled to her feet and rushed for Cal. Part of her knew this was his bear … could feel her own connection to it … but it was unlike any Cruaxee bond she'd had before. If she told the bear to stop, it would not heed her, and if it attacked Fyia, there would be nothing she could do.

Cal pulled her into an embrace. 'Are you hurt?'

'I'm fine,' she said, wishing she could shake off the feel of the disgusting man's hand. 'Are you … you're bleeding!'

'It's nothing,' he said. He showed her a shallow slash across his forearm, and she was glad to see he was telling the truth.

His bear strode out of the trees, and Cal put his hand on the animal's head, scratching behind her ear. Fyia smiled, but was tentative. The bear was colossal, taller than Fyia, and able to swipe her aside in a blink.

The bear lowered her muzzle to Fyia, snuffled her, then butted her, forcing her back a pace. Fyia knew better than to show fear, so she recovered her footing and stepped forward, reaching out a hand, holding it to the side of the bear's face. The bear waited for a beat, then rubbed her face against Fyia's palm. Fyia scratched, and the bear eagerly pressed into her touch.

'Careful,' said Cal, 'or she'll follow you around, expecting you to do that for turns on end.'

'Seeing as she just saved my life, I am in her debt …'

'As I am in yours,' he said, questioning eyes fixed on Fyia. 'It's no secret you're magic-touched, but I must admit, I wondered if the rumors were true …'

'Because I don't display it every chance I get?' said Fyia, bitterness lacing her words.

He waited a beat, watching her closely. 'Because using magic in your kingdoms will likely get you killed … or at least, that's how it used to be, but the same is not true in my lands. If I were you, I would have used magic from the moment I crossed the border. I wouldn't want to hide my talent.'

Fyia exhaled a laugh. She hadn't even thought of using magic, nor had she known she was allowed. Her magic was unwieldy and willful … dangerous. She'd had accidents almost every time she'd reached for it—not that she'd had a teacher—so she'd tramped it down and kept it locked away for years, never even thinking of letting it out. The idea of doing so now scared her. She couldn't bear the thought of hurting someone, and if she hurt someone like Cal … It would cause a diplomatic incident. That wouldn't be fair to her people.

'What's funny?' said Cal.

'I used my magic because it was the only way to save you. If I hadn't, you would probably have died. So if my magic had accidentally killed you, no matter. That's the level of *talent* I'm working with.'

Cal nodded slowly, his bear demanding scratches from him now. 'You never had lessons?'

'Who would have taught me?'

Cal shrugged. 'I thought maybe you had access to the Fae'ch … your brother …'

'My brother's magic is even more unpredictable than mine,' she said hotly. 'He struggled to keep it on a leash and left because of it. He hoped the Fae'ch could help him.'

'You never asked them to help you?'

Fyia fixed Cal with a scathing look. 'I don't know what your relationship is like with the Fae'ch, but in my experience, they help no one unless it's in their own interests.'

'They showed you the egg … or at least, tried to …' He trailed off, presumably asking himself what Fyia had been pondering since the moment the Fae'ch had agreed to show her. Why? Staying up all night at the party had been too easy a test, which meant they'd wanted to see the egg too. But, why?

'They lost a bet,' she said with a shrug.

He gave her a disbelieving look, and she rolled her eyes.

'I can't work it out,' she said.

'Hmmm,' said Cal. He refused to pet his bear, regardless that she was nudging him hard enough to push him backwards.

The bear gave up on Cal and turned back to Fyia, nudging her instead. Fyia scratched her, but the bear kept pushing, becoming agitated.

'Leave her,' said Cal's sharp voice. He stepped between Fyia and the bear, facing his Cruaxee down. Fyia shuddered. She knew the strength of her own Cruaxee bonds, but she didn't know if Cal's worked the same way, or if his magic was as strong …

Fyia felt for her own bond with the animal, and the bear snarled. Fyia immediately let go, but the bear pushed Cal aside and growled in Fyia's face, then shoved her hard, sending Fyia sprawling to the ground.

Cal was up and on his feet in a moment, standing once more between Fyia and the terrifying animal. She felt a searing heat through her bond with the bear, and the animal shied back. She lowered her head, then turned, slinking back into the trees.

'I told you she's dangerous,' said Cal, offering Fyia a hand. Cal's face had drained of color, and he ran a hand through his hair.

'She's ... something,' said Fyia, watching the bear's retreating form.

'She likes to remind me she has a mind of her own every now and again,' he said, then looked Fyia over, guilt gripping his features. 'Did she hurt you?'

'I'm fine. A little shaken, I'm not too proud to admit, but unharmed. Although, if I stand out here much longer, I might lose a few toes to frostbite ... aren't you cold?' She wrapped his cloak more firmly around herself, not wanting to give it back.

He smiled and shook his head. 'We should get back inside. We'll just eat whatever's left in my cloak.'

'No need,' said Fyia, her gaze turning to the sky. An enormous eagle appeared above the trees—easily the biggest Fyia had ever bonded—and Cal's eyes went wide as the bird landed. 'He'll fly us back to Anvarn.'

Fyia leaned into Cal's warmth. He'd wrapped his cloak around both of them as they sat atop the great albatross eagle. Between his body heat and the eagle's, she could almost block out the freezing cold, made so much worse by the chill of the wind as they drove through the air above the trees.

'You're sure he can make it with both of us?' said Cal, eyeing the ground below.

'I wouldn't be up here if I wasn't,' said Fyia, her tone sharper than she'd intended. They could already see the outline of Anvarn in the distance, and Fyia's stomach plummeted. She'd enjoyed her day of freedom. She couldn't remember the last time she'd spent a whole day with only one other person, and as it turned out, Cal was a person she was happy to spend time alone with. Even though she knew it was madness, she wanted more.

She breathed him in, inhaling a long breath, forcing his scent into the depths of her lungs. Then she concentrated on committing to memory every tiny nuance of his touch. The way his thumb traced the line of her lowest rib, the flex of his muscular thighs against her as he balanced, the occasional brush of his stubble-covered jaw against her nape.

Was she imagining it, or had Cal's arms just tightened around her? Had he too just sucked in a lungful of air, his nose pressed to her neck? Was he doing the same? Committing her to memory?

She turned her head to see his face, and his lips captured hers before she had a chance to take him in. She moaned into his mouth, because this was exactly what she wanted, but knew she shouldn't have. Her whole body reacted to his touch, melting into him.

He sucked her bottom lip, and she tipped her head back, giving him access to her neck, but he pulled away. Fyia tried to tug him back, but his words froze her in place.

'There is a way to seal our kingdoms together. One that could work for both of us,' he said, his lips pressed to her ear.

Fyia twisted as far as she could, watching him for several flaps of the eagle's wings, letting his words sink in. 'Marriage?' she said, making sure she understood.

He nodded, and a trickle of excitement filled her stomach. She smiled, and he kissed her again, a long, lingering kiss, showing her what could be hers.

'Think about it,' he said. 'We both have worse marriage prospects, and you're tolerable, I suppose.'

She swiped him, but he sat up straighter, his posture becoming regal, and Fyia turned her gaze forward. The town was close enough now to make out people moving this way and that, setting up market stalls for the day.

A hunter emerged from the woods, carrying a carcass around her neck, and Fyia felt an affinity to these people and their way of life. It was a harder existence than in her lands, to be sure, but something about it called to the animal within her.

The eagle set them down a league from the town, so as not to startle the townsfolk. Cal and Fyia watched him take off into the sky, flying back the way they'd come. Fyia sent her gratitude through the Cruaxee-bond before releasing the eagle, marveling at its sheer power and size.

By the time they made it to the town hall, a small crowd had gathered, watching them with interest. No doubt word had spread that the foreign Queen and their King had disappeared. Speculation was surely rife.

Fyia's wolves slipped out of the crowd, flanking her as she walked, forcing Cal a step further away. They harbored some hostility towards him, similar to what she'd felt from Cal's bear, and Fyia wondered why. It hadn't been there before the trip to the temple … maybe it was because they could smell him all over her.

Edu and Zhura appeared from inside the town hall, harboring glowers so similar Fyia had to stifle a laugh. Zhura pulled Cal aside, saying something in low tones, and Edu did the same to Fyia.

'There's trouble in the south,' said Edu. 'They sent an eagle. The Emperor attacked the coast of Sea Serpent ... attacked the *Temple* of the Sea Serpent ...'

'What?' said Fyia. Zhura seemed to be telling Cal something important, and Fyia had to force her full attention back to Edu. 'You think he's looking for the dragons too?'

'I don't know, but he's taken land and prisoners. If you want to keep your kingdoms, we have to go. Starfall is sending the airship; it should be here by noon.'

'Okay,' said Fyia, too many thoughts racing through her mind for her to process everything at once. Cal rushed away, and Fyia almost followed, but her kingdoms were more important. Edu nodded over Fyia's shoulder, and one of her guards followed the King.

'We went to the Temple of the Dragon,' Fyia whispered. 'The Black Hoods' egg is missing too.'

'I assumed that's where you'd gone,' said Edu, everything about him chastising her.

'I didn't have time to tell you.'

'My Queen may do as she pleases.'

Fyia sent him a dirty look. 'I'll tell you everything later, but the dynamics here are going to shift.'

Edu leaned forward, all jokiness gone. 'Something's going on with the Queen Mother. Zhura and Aaron found her trying to leave with the King's uncle, and detained them both.'

Fyia nodded. It made sense. 'The Queen Mother isn't Cal's real mother. She's been blackmailing him. The Black Hoods are sitting on an incredible cache of dragon scales. They use them to buy favor with the Fae'ch, and to trade, but Cal didn't know where they were.'

'You found them?'

Fyia nodded. 'The Queen Mother must have known he would find them eventually. She must have had an escape plan ready, and bolted as soon as we found her secret passage beneath the library.'

'There's a tunnel all the way to the temple?'

'An aqueduct.'

'Did you know they ran this far north?'

Fyia shrugged. 'The map at the Temple of the Whore showed lines running up here, and to the Great Glacier, but I didn't know if they were aqueducts or something else. I guess the one here would suggest that's exactly what they are.'

'Cal,' said the Queen Mother, as he entered a dingy room under the snow line.

'You can call me *Your Majesty*,' Cal snapped. His hand curled around a small dragon scale in his pocket.

The Queen Mother raised an eyebrow. 'You found them, then?'

'You knew I would ... it's why you tried to run, is it not?'

She shrugged.

'Because you knew I would have no choice but to kill you when I returned,' said Cal. His guts churned at the thought of killing in cold blood, but he would do what he had to for the good of his people.

'You could let me live,' said the Queen Mother, affecting an air of innocence.

He couldn't let her live. She would always be a thorn in his side. She would partner with anyone who wanted to overthrow Cal, and in return, she would promise dragon scales ... the only wealth the Black Hoods could lay claim to. Or she would tell everyone the location of the scales and use the resulting chaos as a ladder.

The one thing she would not do was slink off into the wilds and quietly live out her days. And even if she wanted to, there was nowhere north of the Fae'ch mountains where she could reasonably hope to survive on her own. Not to mention, she'd tried to make off with a fortune in scales.

'So you can stick a dagger in my back the first chance you get?' he replied.

'Why would I do that?'

'Because you're spiteful and angry. You hate that my father had an affair, and that he was happier with my mother than he was with you. You can't stand that I'm a good leader, and that my people love me. You're consumed with grief over the loss of both my father and your children, and for that I pity you, but it's twisted you … made you vengeful, so now you have nothing else in your life to live for.'

'You hold yourself in high regard,' she said, picking hay off her cloak.

'There could have been a place for you here,' said Cal. 'You would have been valued and respected, but you snubbed those who tried to help you, and now you must pay the price.'

'And what of your uncle?'

The traitorous brother of the deceased King. He would align with whomever offered him personal advantage, and could not be trusted. 'Seeing as he also tried to steal from my kingdom, and knows the whereabouts of the dragon scales …'

'He does not,' snapped the Queen Mother.

'You expect me to believe you personally travelled to the temple to retrieve the scales?' She wouldn't put herself to so much trouble, not to mention, he'd smelled his uncle's scent in the tunnel.

'I have entrusted the knowledge of the scales to no one.'

'You're lying.'

She cocked her head to one side as she looked at him. 'Why would I lie?'

'Because, as I've already mentioned, you're angry and spiteful.'

'Who could I trust with such knowledge?'

'I know not, but the scales we took to the Fae'ch were heavy. How could you have retrieved them by yourself?'

The Queen Mother laughed. 'I may be old by your standards, but I am not yet frail. I am one of our best hunters, and am no stranger to carrying great weights over long distances.'

Cal didn't believe her, but it mattered little. Both she and his uncle would die by his hand; he couldn't take any chances.

'Meanwhile,' said the Queen Mother, 'you've been fraternizing with the southern Queen ... have shown her our most sacred space. *She* knows the location of the Black Hoods' only remaining wealth, and could wipe us out in a blink. Your people will challenge you for this insult.'

'Are those your last words, or is there anything else you'd like to say?'

She went still, and Cal saw fear in her eyes; she knew she couldn't escape her fate. It sickened him, but he would do what he must, and it had been a long time coming.

Aaron and Zhura led the Queen Mother and Cal's uncle to where two wooden blocks waited in the snow.

Fyia pulled her cloak tightly around herself, grateful for the layers of clothing and gloves she now wore. But her insides went cold, dreading what was to come.

The prisoners had hoods over their heads and made no sound. They were dressed only in white tunics, their feet bare. She wondered who would deliver the killing blow ... Aaron or Zhura, or some other executioner? Or would Cal draw his own blade?

She didn't have to wait long for an answer, for Cal—black hood up so it covered his face—stepped out onto the snow. A morbid silence descended as he took his position behind the prisoners, a ripple of anticipation running through the gathered crowd as he drew his sword and lowered his hood.

He addressed his people, but Fyia didn't hear what he said, for his Cruaxee-touch suddenly stole half of her senses. She noticed only the lines across his brow, the regretful set of his jaw, the feel of his racing pulse.

He'd shaved his head, his lush dark hair gone, so he looked like he had when she'd first met him inside the Fae'ch mountains. Had he killed someone before that meeting too? Was that why he'd shaved his head then? Was this a regular chore?

Not a soul made a sound as Cal's words ended. He looked imperial as he pushed back his cloak, his muscles flexing as he raised his sword. Zhura pulled the hood from the Queen Mother's head, so Fyia could see the gag in her mouth, presumably to stop her from revealing the location of the dragon scales to all. The Queen Mother had nothing left to lose, after all.

Barely a tick passed before Cal swung his blade. It went through cleanly, separating her head from her body, red arterial blood pumping out onto the pristine snow. A crow screamed overhead, then dove at Cal. Zhura pulled a slingshot from her pocket, felling the Queen Mother's bonded animal with lethal accuracy.

Cal blinked, his eyes remaining closed a beat too long, his only reaction.

Cal's uncle tried to shy back, making terrified noises through his gag. He still had a hood over his head, but his senses had told him enough to send him into a frenzy. Zhura and Aaron wrestled him down onto his own block, then pulled off his hood.

Cal was as quick as before, but his uncle tried to avoid the blow, and Cal caught the man across his shoulder instead of his neck.

Fyia winced as the man screamed, collapsing sideways onto the block. Cal didn't hesitate, finishing the execution instead of leaving him to die a slow and painful death in front of the whole town.

'Bury them,' said Cal, breathing hard as he cleaned his sword, 'and then we drink.'

Chapter Fifteen

FYIA JOINED CAL IN the tavern, along with what seemed to be the entire town. The mood was strange, both somber and buoyant … maybe because Cal was buying for everyone.

'My people are sending an airship to collect me,' said Fyia, perching on the stool next to his at the bar. 'The Emperor has attacked my lands, and is demanding an audience.'

Cal nodded, then knocked back a large measure of clear liquid.

'We don't have much time … they'll be here soon.'

Cal turned his head away, facing the packed room behind. 'Another!' He shouted, and the room cheered in reply.

'We should agree how our lands will work together …'

Cal nodded, but still he didn't look at her, and a prickle of annoyance ran down her spine. The events of the morning must be taking a heavy toll, but they had responsibilities … there was no time to wallow.

'I think the Emperor's looking for the dragons too,' she said sharply.

'Makes sense.'

'Can we speak privately?' said Fyia. She was uncomfortable with the number of eyes watching them, the number of ears straining to hear their words.

Cal pushed back his seat, the wooden legs scraping across the floor. He grabbed a bottle of something amber colored and carried it with him as they descended to Fyia's room below the snow line. Edu, Aaron, and Zhura followed behind.

The room seemed small by the time the five of them were inside, and Fyia felt the loss of the windows, the space claustrophobic. 'We should hash out the bones of the agreement between our kingdoms,' said Fyia, sitting on the wide windowsill.

'There's to be an agreement between our kingdoms?' said Zhura, sending Cal a questioning look.

Cal held her gaze for a beat and then nodded.

'We need time to discuss this,' Zhura protested. 'You can't expect us to agree to terms set out over the course of a single turn of the clock.'

'Of course,' said Fyia. 'I would never expect that, but it would be helpful to find a starting point … something we can take to our people as a sign our alliance is real … beneficial to both sides.'

'What do you propose?' said Cal, turning his weary gaze to Fyia.

Fyia faltered. His vibrance was gone, even if strength still shone in his eyes. She wished they could speak alone, to discuss his proposal, but there was no time … and she hadn't had time to think about it. She barely knew anything about the Black Hoods, or Cal, for that matter.

Maybe he'd used her as a convenient way to find the dragon scales, and the rest was nothing but a game

… Usually, she refused to trust anyone until they'd been thoroughly tested, and Cal's motives were unclear. She believed he wanted what was best for his people, and he wanted the dragons to return to unfreeze his kingdom, but would he turn on her if it suited him? How could she tell for sure? A marriage might suit them both now, but what if their interests diverged …?

'I propose trade,' said Fyia, 'and technology. We will keep your secrets, and will open a formal trade corridor between my lands and the lands of the Black Hoods. We will help you keep animals and grow crops indoors, in heated buildings and glasshouses.'

'We tried that already,' said Aaron, 'but seeds are crafty buggers … they know it's frozen solid outside.'

'Our lands have cooled also,' said Fyia. 'We have learned a great deal, and will be happy to share that knowledge.' Although Fyia could well imagine Venir's outrage when she instructed him to share his hard-won secrets with the infamous Black Hoods.

'And in return?' said Zhura, full of suspicion.

'You will help us build a strong relationship with the Fae'ch. Help me discover what they know of the dragons—if they also found a metal ball in place of their egg—and help convince them to unite with us, so we may return the dragons for the benefit of us all.'

'Why would we help you?' said Zhura. Her gaze flitted from Cal to Fyia and back again.

'Because you wish to restore your lands to their former glory,' said Fyia, 'and without the dragons, you have no hope of doing so.'

'As soon as you have the dragons, you could betray us,' said Zhura. 'How do we know we can trust you?'

'The same way I know I can trust you,' said Fyia. 'Because it is in my interests. If we are successful in uniting the Five Kingdoms, and return the dragons to our lands, but then the union were to crumble, we must assume the dragons would leave once more.'

A knock sounded from the door, and Rouel stepped through when Aaron swung it open. 'Your Majesty,' said Rouel, 'the airship is in sight.'

Fyia nodded. 'Thank you.'

Rouel left, and Fyia turned her gaze to Cal. He was studying her with the intensity of a hawk stalking prey.

'Do you agree with the general terms?' said Fyia, moving around and gathering her possessions.

'We will need to discuss details about trade ...' said Cal, his tone flat, 'how many glasshouses and so forth you will help us build. And the Fae'ch barely tolerate us ... I have no confidence we can help there, over and above our ability to ransom our dragon scales, which will not engender fond relations. However, in principle, I agree to an alliance with your kingdom ...' He paused. 'With you.'

Fyia held his gaze and inhaled a long breath. There was so much she wished she could say. She gave a curt nod, then held out her hand. Cal took it, and she held on for a moment too long, but when she tried to pull away, Cal refused to release her. 'I have one additional term,' he said, finally dropping her hand.

Fyia cleared her throat, not trusting her voice ... not trusting herself right now at all. 'What is it?'

'I will accompany you on your journey south, so I can see your lands, as I have shown you mine, and so I may attend your meeting with the Emperor.'

Fyia's head swam.

'And when the meeting with the Emperor is done,' said Cal, a hint of a smile in his eyes, 'we shall travel to the Great Glacier, and find the egg at the Temple of the Warrior.'

Fyia found herself nodding before she'd considered any of the pros and cons.

Zhura growled her disbelief. 'Need I remind you, you just executed the Queen Mother and the former King's brother? There will be unrest … some will call for your head. We are yet to send word to the other towns and villages … what should we tell the representatives they will surely send when they ask where you are?'

Cal swung his head to face his cousin. 'Tell them whatever you must in order to keep the peace. Tell them of our new alliance. Tell them my actions are in the interests of our people. Tell them the Queen Mother was a spiteful old bag who never recognized my authority, so she had it coming, for all I care. I am sure, when the engineers arrive from the south, there will be much to keep our people busy … much excitement and promise.'

A dark look took hold of Zhura's features. 'You're running away?'

'No,' said Cal, forcefully. 'I am securing a better future for our people. I can do nothing here that you cannot, but the Emperor's men attacked me in the heart of Black Hood territory only this morning. We have stayed out of the world's politics, and that has served us well, but the Emperor has invaded … he has brought a fight to our doorstep, and I will not roll over and let him take that which is mine.

'I wish to meet our enemy and take the measure of the man. Is that a task you desire, Zhura? Is it a task I should give to another?'

Zhura said nothing, although Fyia wasn't sure if that was because she knew her King was right, or because anger had clamped her mouth shut.

'I will address our people,' said Cal, 'and then, I will go south.'

Cal and Fyia boarded the airship. The eager faces of Adigos, Opie, and Essa greeted them, none of them hiding their questioning looks in Cal's direction.

'Your Majesty,' they said together, as they bowed.

'Good to see you all,' said Fyia, with a smile. 'This is Lord Calemir Talos, of the Black Hoods. He will be joining us.'

They'd agreed to keep Cal's identity a secret, so he could enjoy the freedom and security associated with being a mere ambassador.

'It is good to see you too,' said Adigos. His eyes lingered on Fyia, then turned to appraise Cal. Adigos frowned, as though Cal presented a tricky mental problem he couldn't quite work out.

'Come,' said Fyia, motioning to Edu and her guards to board, 'we leave at once.'

The airship became a tangle of activity, guards and crew running this way and that, loading the horses. Essa and Opie disappeared to the helm in the middle of the airship that housed the instruments needed for flight. Adigos fell in at Fyia's side, seeming to believe this his rightful place.

'You may assist Essa,' said Fyia. 'I will show our guest around, and we will reconvene in the dining room in a quarter turn.'

Adigos hesitated, but held his tongue in front of Cal. Fyia wondered if he would have had the two of them been alone … she doubted it, which meant he still hadn't learned his lesson.

Fyia led Cal into the hull of the ship, down the two flights of stairs to her lavish private quarters. 'I'm not sure what we have available in terms of cabins,' she said, as he put down his bag, 'but I'm sure we can find you something suitable.'

Cal's eyes scanned the room, taking in the plush rugs, the large chairs nailed to the floor, the inviting bed. He walked to the curtained window and looked out, perhaps saying goodbye to his lands, perhaps regretting his impulsive decision to fly south ...

'Your cabin looks perfectly suitable to me,' he said, interrupting her thoughts, his eyes still trained on the land beyond the window.

She couldn't tell if he was joking, mocking, provoking, or being serious, so she changed the subject; he was still in a strange mood. 'How did your people take it?'

'Predictably.'

'Some well, some badly?' she said with a smile.

Cal nodded. 'As is always the way.'

'The burden of leadership ... you can never please everyone.'

'If we find a way to thaw the north, I may achieve just that.'

'*When* we find a way to thaw the north, many will complain about the way we went about it ... about the return of dragons, the use of magic we don't understand, alliances that will surely never hold ...'

'That may come later,' Cal conceded, 'but first, they will be universally pleased. Believe me when I say times for the Black Hoods have not always been easy.'

Fyia longed to know more about what his people had been through, but the view changed, the window climbing the lengths of the trees until open sky filled the glass, and a knock sounded at the door.

'Your Majesty,' said Adigos' voice through the wood, 'we are ready for you.'

Fyia didn't believe for a second that Essa and Opie were already at the long banquet table in the dining room. 'I will be there in a moment,' she said. She waited for the sounds of Adigos' retreating footsteps before addressing Cal once more. 'Would you care to join us?'

He nodded. 'I would.'

He made for the door, passing so close that Fyia put out a hand to stop him before considering if it was wise. She knew she should drop her hand from his arm, but her fingers itched to do so much more, so leaving it on his bicep felt like a compromise. Cal looked at her hand, then into her eyes, and Fyia found it suddenly hard to breathe. 'I like your hair,' she said eventually.

'Thank you,' he said, leaning in a little, as though to kiss her. Her pulse spiked, and her eyes flicked to his approaching lips, but the kiss never came. Instead, he said, 'How did you get that streak of white in your hair?'

She turned her head away, shrugging off her disappointment. 'I was born like this. Some say it's because of my magic, but if it is, I know not what it signifies.'

A knock sounded from the door once more. 'Your Majesty?' said Adigos, his tone urgent.

Fyia dropped her hand with a huff and threw open the door. 'What?'

Adigos moved back a little, and his eyes flicked to Cal, probably to see if he was still fully clothed. 'It's Essa,' he said. 'She's gone.'

Cal took a seat halfway along the table in the airship's plush dining room. The dining room—like every other inch of the ship—was lavish, intricately decorated, and luxurious. No detail had been overlooked, from the crushed velvet upholstery, to the carvings around the windows, to the rugs that half swallowed up his boots.

He tore his attention away from the finery to assess Fyia's entourage—minus her inventor, who'd apparently made a getaway just before take-off.

'She told me she was coming to see you,' said Opie—the ship's pilot, and a man of the Kraken Empire, from what Cal could tell.

'And nobody saw her jump the rail?' said Fyia, her tone full of disbelief.

'She's crafty,' said Adigos. He kept throwing curious, possibly hostile glances in Cal's direction. Had Adigos and Fyia had a tryst? Did the noble harbor feelings for his Queen? For although Fyia had not formally introduced the man, he could be nothing but a noble, given the set of his shoulders, his fine attire, and the entitled way he moved.

He was good-looking to be sure, and had the air of someone who knew his way around a sword, but there was something about the man that made Cal nervous … like he acted too often on impulse … like he subscribed to some unknown code of honor that only those from his privileged circle were privy too, clinging to it regardless of circumstance.

'No one saw her,' said Edu.

Cal didn't dislike Adigos, per se. He seemed loyal, but the way he was looking at Fyia now she'd turned her attention to Edu … *Mother spare him*. He was pining like a lost puppy.

Cal moved his gaze to Edu, who seemed a little on edge … unusual for him, given what Cal had witnessed in Anvarn. Was it just the loss of Essa—Fyia's most prized engineer—or did something else trouble him?

'Shall I send guards after her?' said Edu.

'No need,' said Fyia. 'We know where she's going … I just hope they don't kill her.'

'Or take her hostage,' said Edu.

Fyia laughed cruelly. 'They can try, but I won't pay a copper to save her, regardless how brilliant her mind might be. She's betrayed me one too many times.'

Despite Fyia's harsh words, Cal could feel her disappointment. 'Where has she gone?' Cal said into the heavy silence.

'To the Fae'ch,' said Fyia. 'Or, more accurately, to my brother, whom she loves. I had hoped she would help us, but she's made her choice … my brother, not our cause.'

'*Our* cause?' said Adigos, his forehead furrowed.

'The Black Hoods have become our allies,' said Fyia.

Adigos half nodded. 'Something was agitating Essa,' he said. 'Something about the clocks … I don't know what, but it seemed serious.'

'You think she's gone to tell my brother all she knows?'

Adigos shrugged. 'Love makes people do stupid things.'

The weighty silence returned. So Adigos loved Fyia, or once had …

Fyia stood. 'We head for Selise, so I may meet with my council. Cal, I would like to discuss details of the treaty between our kingdoms, if you would be amenable?'

'As Your Majesty wishes,' said Cal.

'Please find Cal a cabin,' Fyia said to no one in particular, as she made to leave.

'Your Majesty …' said Adigos, who had sprung to his feet the moment Fyia got to hers.

She rounded on him. 'Yes?'

'I would offer my assistance. I hail from Plenty—as you know—and can provide valuable insights that may help in the construction of a successful treaty ... could make it more palatable to our people.'

'Thank you, Adigos. I will summon you if I require an opinion on the views of the *common-folk* of Plenty.'

Fyia didn't bother to hide her jibe. Cal knew not if the term had some special meaning between them, but it was clear Adigos was anything but a man of the people, with his fine clothes and clipped accent.

By the time Cal and Fyia entered Fyia's cabin, a potent mix of emotion poured off her. He clicked the door closed, and Fyia paced to the desk, placed her hands upon it, then paced back, not stopping until she was so close he could see the specks of topaz in her blue eyes.

Since boarding the airship, Cal hadn't thought once about the heads he'd hacked from their bodies, or the attack they'd survived that very morning by the Temple of the Dragon, but seeing her like this ... frustrated, disappointed, angry, caged by the actions and expectations of others ... it dredged up the same feelings in him. It hit him like a battering ram, perhaps because of the Cruaxee-touch that bonded them, perhaps her magic was acting on him, or maybe it was all his own doing. Whatever the cause, it made him move, and she responded in a heartbeat.

They came together in a frenzy of hands and limbs and mouths, her fingers exploring his newly shaved hair, his arms wrapping her up, pressing her to his chest.

He slid a hand to her backside, as she slid a finger around the shell of his ear. He jerked, once again surprised at how sensitive his scales were to her touch. He groaned into her mouth as she did it again, and pulled her against his hardening cock, his fingers seeking the scale at the base of her spine.

She moaned, then bit his neck, the sharp sting bringing Cal to his senses. Nothing had changed … they were not betrothed … this was still a bad idea.

'Fyia,' he breathed. He placed his hands on her hips, holding her in place.

She moved her mouth back to his lips and kissed him, cupping his face in her hand. 'I know we shouldn't,' she said, pressing her cheek to his, 'but I want to.'

'Marry me,' he said, 'and then we can.' She stilled, and he kissed her gently. She sucked his bottom lip into her mouth, and for a moment, the sensation made him lose all sense of time and space.

'Cal, I …' She pulled back to look him in the eye. 'If we were to marry, I would require an arrangement that would not be … standard.'

Cal frowned in confusion. 'You would wish to take other lovers?'

She smiled. 'That's not what I meant …'

'Then, what?' He couldn't think of a single explanation for her words.

'I won't hand control of my kingdoms to you,' she said. 'I've fought hard for everything I have, and …'

'A husband has that power in your lands?'

Fyia nodded.

'It is not that way in my kingdom. I would have no control over that which is yours, and you would not control that which is mine. In my lands, marriage is a partnership of equals … couples make choices together.' Fyia smiled, and the delight in her eyes made Cal's heart thud faster. 'But what if two men, or two women marry in your lands?'

Fyia's expression became shuttered. 'They can't. One of the many rules I intend to change.'

Cal's father had always said the Five Kingdoms were as backward as they were advanced, and now he understood what he'd meant.

Fyia stepped away. 'You are the most tolerable prospect so far, I will admit. Not only are you handsome ...' Cal smirked, 'but an alliance with your nation makes sense for both of us. But ...' she paused, taking care over her words, 'I've been against the idea of marriage for so long ... have only seen what it means in my kingdoms ... I need time to digest the idea.'

Cal resisted the urge to pull her back to him, to reassure and claim her. He would respect her wish, even if doing so hurt his heart.

Fyia moved away from Cal, not trusting herself to be near him. She sat on the bed and studied him ... his relaxed demeanor, his new hair, his deep green eyes. She could never hope for a better match, so why was she hesitant? What was she so afraid of? *Venir and his cronies*, said a voice in her mind. For she had not yet changed the marriage laws in her kingdoms, and didn't know if it would be wise, on top of all the other changes she'd forced through.

Maybe the Spider had been right. Maybe she should have taken things more slowly ... should have played the damned political game. For in her kingdoms, cities burned, food was scarce, and the Emperor had seized a quarter of the Kingdom of Sea Serpents.

If she'd been less rash, perhaps she would have avoided two of those three problems. But then, how many women were now in the guilds, or attending the university who could not before? How many honest traders could sell their goods in the markets who'd been kept out or extorted? Were those gains not worth the sacrifice?

Cal sat in a plush armchair, drawing her attention back to him, her insides clenching as he openly appraised her. 'You told me your lands have suffered,' said Fyia. 'What did you mean?'

Cal held perfectly still for a beat, then exhaled. 'We haven't always known about the dragon scales … in fact, they are a fairly recent find. The devouts of the Order of the Dragon hid them, considering them sacred relics that no one could touch, let alone trade. Only the most senior members of the Order knew of their existence, and they believed the temple would collapse if the scales were removed.'

'Wow,' said Fyia.

Cal half laughed. 'They believed the spirit of the last dragon would return and melt the whole place to the ground.'

Fyia shook her head. 'Crazy.' It was amazing what people could be convinced of, especially when higher powers were involved.

'You don't believe in the Gods?' said Cal.

Fyia frowned. 'I believe in magic. Maybe there were those in the past who had powers to eclipse anything we have today … but the Temple of the Dragon is still standing, despite your trading scales with the Fae'ch.'

Cal nodded. 'It is.'

'Who discovered them?'

'The Queen Mother,' Cal said darkly.

'How?'

Cal chuckled. 'She was a member of the Order of the Dragon. They may not have romantic partners, but my father caught her eye—and she his—during the annual pilgrimage. She was beautiful and mysterious, and she told my father she would show him a secret that would change the fortunes of our people, if he agreed to marry her.'

Fyia raised her eyebrows. 'You can't fault her ambition.'

Cal looked at the carpet. 'She had many attributes that made her an asset to my kingdom, but she had an ego to match. It was like she always had something to prove, despite her position. She was responsible for a great deal of good, but …'

'People are never wholly one thing or another,' Fyia said gently.

Cal nodded. 'Before she showed my father the scales, our people lived hand to mouth. They raided other lands, and only ate what they could hunt, steal, or grow. Until recently, we could grow crops along our southern border, but now we can't even do that; it's too cold all year round. When the scales run out, we will have little choice but to abandon our lands, or turn to raiding once more.'

'I know a Queen who wouldn't like that very much,' said Fyia, with a look of mock affront.

Cal smiled. 'When that Queen marries me, my people will be her people also.'

When. Fyia's chest went tight. 'If only the King of the Black Hoods had the same certainty about finding the dragons, for then his people could grow crops of their own once more.'

'Would you chase me if I raided your lands?' Cal asked.

Fyia couldn't help but laugh. 'I couldn't let a foreign King take such liberties.'

'You'd never catch me … I've had a lot of practice, you know.'

'But your father had the scales before you were born …?'

299

'The Queen Mother insisted on keeping up the skills of raiding,' said Cal. 'My father disagreed, but he rarely went against her wishes … maybe some devout part of her still worried about an attack from the dragon spirit. My father eventually put a stop to it, much to the Queen Mother's disgust.'

'So if I were to marry you,' said Fyia, with a coy smile, 'I'd be marrying a common thief?'

Cal shook his head, his features fierce. '*When* you marry me, it will be to a warrior who knows how to take care of those he loves.'

Chapter Sixteen

FYIA STRODE INTO HER magnificent council chamber in Selise, Cal a pace behind. Cal's eyes roamed the cavernous space, from the carved stone pillars, to the stained-glass window, to the inner workings of the dragon clock exposed above. His own kingdom had many wonders, but everything here was bigger ... grander ... more imposing.

The councilors stood and bowed low, but Fyia quickly waved them to their seats, and they sat at a large table that looked odd in this great hall. It was more a throne room than a council chamber, but no throne sat atop the dais, only a long, granite table, worn and aged.

Four women and one man looked enquiringly at Cal as he took a seat to Fyia's right.

'I have brought with me a representative from the Black Hoods,' said Fyia, indicating to Cal with her hand. 'They have agreed to ally with us in our quest to bring back the dragons. Lord Calemir, this is my Small Council: the Spider, Lady Starfall, Lady Nara, Lord Venir, and High-Commander Sensis Deimos.'

'A pleasure to meet you all,' said Cal, with a bow of his head. 'I look forward to working with you, for the benefit of both our kingdoms.'

Lord Venir was an aging man, but his eyes were sharp as he studied Cal. He clearly wished to say something, presumably hungry for the details of their agreement, but he held his tongue as Starfall—Fyia's aunt—took charge.

'As you know, we have faced many problems in your absence, Your Majesty,' said Starfall. 'After the army cleared Selise of rebels, the troublemakers retreated to the Kingdom of Moon, where they have become a dagger in our side.'

Fyia nodded, listening intently, Cal sucking up every detail of their interaction. The way Starfall almost chastised her niece, but stopped a hair short ... the respect in Fyia's eyes, acknowledging and appreciating the role her aunt played ... the way the others watched them closely too.

'The streets of Moon's capital are not safe,' said Sensis. 'There have been many attacks on women, and the high houses claim the rebels have stolen food shipments. This has led to food shortages both in Moon, and more widely across the kingdoms.'

'*Claim*?' said Venir, his features pinched. 'You question the word of the most noble houses of Moon?'

There was something about the way Venir looked at Starfall ... some expectation of support, but Starfall barely blinked.

The Spider—an old, wiry woman—coughed lightly. 'My web is wide, Lord Venir. The high houses have increased their exports. They are not clamoring at our door, complaining of losses, demanding we do something about the rebels. In fact, they have been remarkably quiet on the matter.'

Venir's face turned ruddy. 'I represent the high houses in this chamber,' said Venir. 'I have not been quiet on the matter. My nephew …'

'Yes?' said Fyia. 'How is Lord Antice? I believe he has not returned to Selise, to attend the meetings of the Extended Council?'

The Spider had greeted Fyia as soon as the airship touched down, whispering in her ear for most of the short walk to the council building. Cal wondered what other news the spymaster had imparted.

'He is a busy man, Your Majesty,' said Venir.

'Too busy to do the bidding of his Queen?' said Fyia. 'I let him keep his lands and his title—despite his lineage—because he swore fealty to me. If I cannot trust him to follow simple orders, I will take those privileges away.'

'Antice has the utmost respect for …' said Venir.

'Actions are what I require,' said Fyia, 'not words. He will attend the next meeting, or he will lose all he holds so dear.'

'Very good, Your Majesty,' said Venir, through visibly gritted teeth.

Cal tried to remember the details Fyia had told him on the airship. Venir was the Warden of the Sky Kingdom in the south—the smallest of Fyia's five kingdoms, which bordered the Kingdoms of Moon and Plenty. However, Moon—the second smallest, but powerful kingdom—was the kingdom of Venir's ancestors. He held large estates and sway there, along with his nephew, Lord Antice, who'd been the next in line to the throne of Moon before Fyia had killed his father.

Cal despised the snake-like men and women attracted to the quagmire of such politics, and distrusted the motives of Venir and Antice. Their kingdoms were small, but powerful, especially if they formed an alliance.

Moon controlled much of Fyia's food supply, and Sky held the only metal mines found in Fyia's lands. From what Fyia had said, she could trust none of the wardens from any of her kingdoms. If it were up to Cal, he'd be tempted to cull them all and start anew … although, whoever replaced them probably wouldn't be any better. Damned politics.

'I have troops policing the streets of Moon, and protecting the women seeking an education,' said Sensis. 'Perhaps if we hold out long enough, the rebels will realize life is much the same, even if women have access to education, but it's possible we'll need a more radical solution …'

'Such as?' said Venir.

Sensis gave Venir an almost condescending look. 'As you know, I'm not in the habit of sharing sensitive strategic details more widely than is strictly necessary.'

'But there is an *obvious* solution,' said Venir, as though the others were missing something a child could see.

Fyia stared the man down. He lost some of his gusto, but kept going regardless. 'Marriage, Your Majesty.'

The words hollowed out Cal's insides. He glanced at Fyia, who's attention was still on Venir.

'The rebels have made it clear, if you were to marry a suitable man, they would work with you, rather than against you,' said Venir. 'There is no shortage of suitable men; I have compiled a list … Lord Antice, Lord …'

Cal was gripped by the insane urge to claim Fyia as his. To tell this pitiful man if he thought he could control her through marriage, he was sorely mistaken.

Fyia gave Venir a disapproving look, the kind a teacher would give an unruly student, then turned to Starfall. 'Let us move on. Tell me of our other problems.'

'The Emperor has invaded,' said Starfall, humor tugging at the corners of her lips, 'and is demanding an audience with you.'

'And if I decline?' said Fyia.

'I doubt he'll stop until he owns all of the Kingdom of Sea Serpents, along with its banks, vineyards, and perfumeries,' said the Spider.

'Ah, well, at least in that case my home kingdom will finally have something to rejoice over,' said Fyia, flippantly. 'The distilleries of the Starlight Kingdom would do a roaring trade.'

'Your Majesty, I must protest …' said Lady Nara.

'No need, Nara, that was a joke,' said Fyia. 'I have no intention of letting anyone take what is mine, including your homeland. I will meet with the Emperor and hear his demands, but first, tell me all we know.'

'Why must council meetings be such a bore?' said Fyia. She leaned her head back against the arm of a couch, her body strewn along its length.

'The meetings are fine,' said Sensis, from an armchair across the room. 'The problem is you.'

'How dare you!' said Fyia, in mock outrage. 'I'm Queen … there can be nothing wrong with me.'

'There's nothing wrong with that King you brought back with you either,' said Sensis, with a smirk.

The Spider chuckled from her perch on a window seat overlooking the pretty, formal gardens. The townhouse was another of the Spider's safe houses;

Fyia wondered how many she had spread across the city … across the Five Kingdoms.

Of course the Spider had known … there was little Fyia could ever hope to keep from her, but Sensis? 'How did you know?' Fyia asked.

'With genes like those,' said Sensis, 'how could he be anything other than a king …?'

Fyia rolled her eyes. 'Edu told you.'

'For your protection,' Sensis confirmed.

They'd spent much time during the council meeting discussing the glasshouses and other technology they would send to the Black Hoods in exchange for assistance with finding the dragons. Venir had been spitting by the end. He'd insisted the search for dragons was futile, and that the people of Moon would not stand for giving away their secrets. Cal had cut off Venir's protests with the promise of dragon scales, and Venir had done little but splutter ineffectually after that, seeing as dragon scales were the most highly prized commodity in all the known lands.

'Not from the King,' Sensis clarified. 'I have no plans to protect you from him …'

Fyia hurled a cushion at her friend. 'It's not like that …'

'Have you seen the way he looks at you?'

'Please,' said Fyia.

'Sensis is right,' said the Spider. 'If he plans to attend the meeting with the Emperor, he will need to work on his face.'

'Nice as his face unquestionably is,' said Sensis. She barked out a laugh at Fyia's exasperated expression.

'Do you have plans for him?' asked the Spider, turning her all-seeing gaze on Fyia.

'I'm sure I don't know what you mean,' said Fyia.

'Oh, Gods …' said Sensis. 'You like him!'

'I do like him. He will be a strong ally.'

Sensis threw the pillow back with terrifying speed, and Fyia only just got her hands up in time.

'Tell me what you withheld earlier,' said Fyia, firmly changing the subject. Yes, she liked Cal … she liked him a lot, but that didn't mean she should act on it. Although he was right, their marriage would solve several of her problems …

The Spider nodded in a way that told Fyia this was not the end of the Cal conversation. 'The Emperor has some trump card, although I don't know what. He doesn't have dragons, that much has become plain; he's not even pretending any longer. In fact, he now claims he never said he had them at all …'

'That man cannot be trusted,' said Sensis.

'And yet, I must trust him enough to put myself at his mercy,' said Fyia. 'In my own lands.'

She hadn't let herself dwell, but it stung that the Emperor had invaded, that there had been nothing she could do about it. His force was superior, with scores of airships and fresh troops. Her troops were ready for a rest, and now they endured a long march before facing the Emperor's army … if it came to that.

'Whatever he has,' said the Spider, 'he'll want something big in return …'

Fyia didn't want to think about what that meant. Something big like land, money, resources … her? Venir had wanted her to marry all along, as had most of her nobles. It was reason enough for her to refuse the hand of any suitor … including Cal, but maybe she was being unnecessarily stubborn. Marrying Cal wouldn't be a capitulation if it was what she wanted …

'Something big like you,' said Sensis, 'just in case you missed the Spider's meaning.'

'What are the laws regarding marriage in the Empire?' Fyia asked, ignoring the jibe.

'The husband takes it all,' said the Spider, 'although women have far greater rights and freedoms than here. Before marriage, they are subject to few restrictions.'

'So something big like handing over all five of my kingdoms,' said Fyia. 'I don't think so. What of an alliance? What does he want?'

'He wants what most men want ... more,' said the Spider. 'More land, more influence, more treasure ... he wants the world to revere him, and right now, everyone's talking about you.'

'There is a prize better than me or my kingdoms,' said Fyia, 'and he already has land and wealth.'

'Oh?' said the Spider.

'Dragons,' said Fyia.

'You can't be serious,' said Sensis.

'He obviously wants them, or he wouldn't have spread the rumor he had them,' said Fyia.

'You would promise him a dragon?' said the Spider. 'For what?'

'He's not fire-touched; he won't be able to control a dragon,' said Fyia. 'But maybe he doesn't know that. Or maybe he's arrogant enough to believe it doesn't matter.'

Sensis considered the idea. 'I mean, it's got potential.'

'Or maybe he knows about the fire-touch, and seeks a way to bring you under his control,' said the Spider. 'To control the dragons for him.'

'He'll get a dagger in his back for his trouble if he tries,' said Fyia.

'Could you stick him in the front?' said Sensis. 'I'm sick of people complaining about your honor, so I'd appreciate a little variation ...'

'I'll let you take that up with Edu,' said Fyia.

Sensis laughed. 'Any news on Essa?' she asked the Spider.

The Spider shook her head. 'My spies have found no trace. It's not surprising, seeing as my network in the northern lands is sparse.'

'Cal will be glad to hear that,' said Fyia.

Sensis and the Spider exchanged a loaded look that Fyia chose to ignore.

'Why did she run?' said Fyia. 'Did something happen?'

'No,' said the Spider, 'not as far as I can tell. She came to me before she left and told me of her concerns about the clocks.'

'What was she concerned about?' said Fyia.

'Several have crumbled away, and steam rises from where they once sat. Essa worried the whole Temple of the Sea Serpent would melt into the sea, and the construction of your new palace has halted, because the ground gave way. Three workers fell into a pit of magma.'

'Many parts of my kingdoms rely on hot springs,' said Fyia. 'Why is this strange?'

'Essa has a theory that the clocks control the magma,' said the Spider. 'If the clocks are destroyed ...'

'Is that why she ran away?' said Fyia. 'Because she thinks my lands could go up in flame?'

'I'm not sure,' said the Spider, 'but she suggested creating an inventory of clocks, and making repairs where necessary. She was animated on the topic ...'

'Very well,' said Fyia, 'and order a search of our libraries ... maybe an inventory already exists.'

'On the upside,' said Sensis, 'I hear the markets are functioning much better than before ... outside of Moon at least.'

'In fact,' said the Spider, 'many of the markets are reporting increases in footfall and sales, and traders find it hard to grumble when there's more money in their pockets.'

'Wow,' said Fyia, sarcastically. 'Who would have thought change could be good?'

They waited two days in the safe house, just long enough for Fyia's eagle to take a message to the Emperor, and to receive his reply. Fyia spent the time buried in an endless list of queries, tasks, and requests Starfall had stored up while Fyia had been in the north.

Lord Antice had again requested she visit Moon, so they could *honor and celebrate her* ... that was laughable, given the rebellion he himself more than likely headed. Was his plan to kidnap her?

She wrote congratulatory letters to the new—female—Chancellor of the University, and to the first female guild members who'd been brave enough to join. She approved additional gold for repairs to the bombsites in Selise, then she wrote to Lady Nara and Lord Fredrik. Although she had mixed feelings about them both, it was important to recognize good work, and they'd done a fine job on market reform. Fyia just hoped they hadn't started a black market to bolster their own income on the side. The Spider assured her they had not, but Fyia didn't trust them.

By the end of the second day, Fyia was crawling up the walls. She needed to get out ... to run with her wolves ... escape the confines of the house and its occupants.

Cal had been conspicuous in his absence, and Fyia missed his steadfast presence. The Spider—who, of course, kept tabs on his every move—assured her he was safe and merely exploring the city, but after spending days together, it was strange not to have him by her side.

She was busy planning her escape, when her eagle returned with word from the Emperor. He would meet her at her earliest convenience, and would allow her and her entourage safe passage. That she needed his permission to travel through her own lands smarted, but a thrill raced down her spine. She'd been itching to move, and now she could.

Fyia stuck her head out of her office. 'Tell Opie to ready the airship,' she said to Edu, who stood guard by her door, 'and tell the Spider to retrieve Cal.'

They were up in the airship within a single turn of the clock, Cal jumping aboard moments before lift-off, his arms laden with goods he'd purchased from the markets. Fyia smiled at the sight of him and his hoard, wondering what had caught his eye.

Cal entered Fyia's cabin, joining Edu, Fyia, and Sensis, who were discussing logistics.

'Your Majesty,' said Cal, bowing.

'Your Majesty,' Fyia replied, smiling as she nodded her head.

Edu and Sensis exchanged a knowing glance, then made to leave. Before they'd taken two steps, the cabin door swung open, and the Spider entered, Adigos and Essa behind her.

'Essa!' said Fyia.

'Your Majesty,' said Essa, bowing low.

'How did you get here?'

'I suggest we start further back than that,' said the Spider, icily.

Fyia nodded. 'Please.' She scrutinized Essa's confident, no-nonsense features. She seemed as she always did, which was strange, as ostensibly, she was a traitor to the crown. Adigos had the sheepish look of a man not quite sure if he were in deep water.

The Spider took a long breath, and for a split tick, Fyia saw her great age. She wondered how many more

311

years the Spider could keep up the relentless pace of her work, and who would replace her. No doubt the Spider already had it planned …

'I went to your brother,' said Essa, jumping in before the Spider could get started. 'Not because I'm the love-sick kitten you think I am.' Her words were sharp, and guilt sank through Fyia's chest. She'd never thought of Essa in those derogatory terms, but they'd all assumed Essa still pined for Veau, which, now she'd been called out on it, wasn't very Essa …

'I went to retrieve this,' said Essa. She held out the metal ball Fyia had given Veau.

Fyia's breath hitched, then her chest swelled. Essa hadn't betrayed her.

'I asked you to give it to him because I wanted to know what it was. I've never seen a metal like it, but Veau is with the Fae'ch; they have information we do not, especially about the dragons.'

'And did he?' said Fyia. 'Know anything?'

'Not really. He found out what he could, but Axus grew suspicious, so Veau asked me to retrieve the ball. He wanted to ensure it made it safely back to you.'

Her brother hadn't betrayed her. Essa hadn't betrayed her … or, she had, but in the same misguided way that Adigos had when he'd killed King Milo in her name. Essa would have to be punished, but her intentions had been good.

'Essa told Opie of her plans,' said the Spider. 'He agreed to send the first of your new airships on a test flight to the Fae'ch mountains to retrieve her. Adigos went on that flight.'

Adigos' face drained of color. 'I didn't know of Essa's plan,' he blurted. 'Opie told me a few days ago, which is when I went to get her … I wanted to make sure she made it back safely, and there was no time to send word …'

'It's my fault, if you're looking for someone to blame,' said Essa. 'I wanted the Fae'ch to think I'd run away to see your brother, and that you sent Adigos after me.'

Fyia's head swam. 'What did Veau tell you about the ball?' She would deal with punishments later. Right now, she wanted details.

'Not much,' said Essa. 'I had only moments with him alone. He said it was to do with the dragons … that it was a metal only the dragons could produce.

'The Fae'ch were in a furor over their missing egg, but he'd heard not a single rumor about something else being found in its place.'

Fyia looked at Cal, who had furrowed his brow. Were the Fae'ch just better liars than everyone else, or had they really found nothing? And if that was the case, what did it mean?

'How will you punish her?' said Cal. The others had filed from the room, Fyia requesting only he stay. He'd seen the looks they'd all shared, the disappointment in Adigos' eyes, but Cal couldn't give a damn.

Fyia set down the metal ball Essa had given her. They now had three between them, and Cal wondered about their importance. Were they some joke? Or were the perfectly round, shiny objects needed to bring back the dragons? Did the eggs even exist? What if the balls were all that had been hidden from the start?

'I don't know,' Fyia said on an exhale. 'When Adigos betrayed me, I sent him away so he missed the fighting … wouldn't get the glory he sought, but it doesn't seem to have worked. If I deprive Essa of the thing she loves—her inventions—I suspect it will harm me more than her in the long run.'

Cal sat, watching as Fyia's brain whirred. It was almost painful to witness. 'Come here,' he said, his eyes never leaving her.

She met his gaze and a smile spread across her lips, but she didn't move. 'Cal …'

'Come here,' he said again. A broad grin spread across his features, and elation bubbled in his chest. 'I like your cloak, and want to inspect it, just in case I ever find myself in need of its warmth.'

Fyia looked down, as though surprised to find she still wore her cloak. She rolled her eyes indulgently, then approached him. She stopped a pace away and unfastened the clasp, letting the heavy fabric fall to the floor.

'Even better,' said Cal, then tugged her down onto his lap.

She sat across him, her lips on his in an instant, her kisses deep and full of need. 'I missed you,' he said.

She stroked her thumb across his lip. 'I missed you too.'

'Have you decided yet?' he said, his fingers caressing her thigh.

'Cal … I …'

'Because if you have, there's a very comfortable-looking bed just over there, and you could use some stress relief.'

She kissed him again, and he leaned his head back against the chair, savoring the feel of her hands against the stubble of his hair, and of her leg pressed against his growing erection.

'What did you buy at the market?' she asked.

'Almost everything I set my eyes on.' Images of the opulence—the likes of which they could only dream of in his lands—flashed before his eyes.

The Black Hoods could get their hands on spices, dried fruits, and nuts—although he'd never seen them laid out like in the markets of Selise—but the exotic fruits, pastries, and delicate vegetables didn't survive the arduous journey to the north. 'Have you tasted bananas? And those spikey fruits ... what are they called?'

'Pineapples?' she said with a laugh.

'No, the little ones.' He frowned, trying to remember.

'Lychees?'

'Yes! Aren't they delicious?'

'They have the texture of eyeballs.'

'You eat eyeballs here?'

'Some people do ... you don't in your lands?'

'Sometimes we have to. Or at least, we did, before we found the scales. We ate everything we could get our hands on.'

Fyia's expression turned sad, so he nipped her lip. 'Will we be able to grow fruits like those in the glasshouses a certain Queen has promised?'

Fyia smiled as she shrugged. 'I'm not a great horticulturist, although I'm sure Venir could tell you.'

Venir had joined them on the airship, much to Cal's bafflement. 'Why is he here? He seems to be the worst snake of them all ...'

'Because he spent time with the Emperor.'

It wasn't a straight answer, and Cal thought about pressing her on the matter, but she kissed him, and all thoughts but one flew from his mind. 'Have you decided yet?' he asked again.

Fyia pressed her forehead to his. 'I'm coming around to the idea,' she said, but refused to meet his gaze.

'Are you hiding from me?' He put a finger under her chin and forced her head up.

'No,' she said, petulantly. 'I think we should test the goods before committing. A lifetime of bad sex would be a travesty.'

'You could just build yourself a harem ...'

'Hmm, you're right, I could ...'

He dug his fingers into her ribs, making her giggle, the sound so delightful he did it again. He bent forward as she squirmed, dropping kisses on her neck, then jaw, then lips.

'Please,' she breathed.

Cal wasn't sure how he'd become the one to need convincing ... hadn't the decision been mutual? Now it seemed pointless, for they'd already crossed the line of no return. He couldn't pretend he didn't have feelings for her, and the last few days without her had been torture.

He lowered his face to the visible flesh at the top of her shirt, kissing the crease of her breasts. She arched her back, pressing herself into him, and he pulled the fabric down, exposing the swell of one round breast. He kissed and nipped at her skin, but her clothes hampered his efforts. He growled in frustration, pushing her away just long enough to rid her of her shirt and brassier.

She unbuttoned his shirt, mewling as their hot, naked skin came together. He caressed her dragon scale, and she moaned into his neck, the sound setting him on fire.

He picked her up and took her to the bed, placing her on her front. He removed their remaining clothes, so he had an uninterrupted view of her pert, full ass and toned back. He straddled her thighs, massaging her, and she moaned again, arching against the mattress.

He leaned forward and ran his nose across her scale, gleaming gold in the midday sun. She shivered, and he kissed it, then licked it with the tip of his tongue.

She arched harder, opening her legs as much as she was able, his cock pressing into the space between her thighs.

He lay forward, covering her with his torso, and moved his hips, the sensation of nudging against her opening overriding all logical thought. He slipped a hand beneath her pulsing hips, and she moaned as he caressed her sex.

'Cal,' she said into the bedding, her voice muffled.

'Fyia,' he replied. He kissed her spine as his fingers continued to circle.

'Do it,' she said, sounding half-crazed … sounding like he felt. He needed no further encouragement. He pushed inside her, exhaling loudly as he took what he'd denied himself for so long. He stilled, knowing if he moved, it would be over in a heartbeat. He used his fingers to torment her while he became accustomed to the heady feel of her around him.

He moved, slowly, savoring every minute sensation as he thrust in and out, cherishing her moans. He pulled out, and she protested, but he moved them so she sat atop him, so he could see her face, and breasts, and kiss her lush, plump lips.

She sank onto his length, her legs spread wide, and she gasped, her hands on his shoulders, her back arched, presenting her breasts like an offering. He took one in each hand, pinching her peaked nipples, and she bucked her hips harder as she rode him. He lifted one breast, sucking the nipple into his mouth, then bit her gently.

'Yes,' she breathed. She slid her hand to the base of his neck, using him for purchase as she slid up and down.

'*Warrior*,' he groaned, releasing her nipple as she tilted her hips. He moved his hands to her backside, and her moans became frantic, her movements desperate. She stiffened on a moan, convulsing around him, taking him over the edge with her. 'Fyia,' he breathed into her neck. 'Goddess … Fyia.' He bit her shoulder, his mouth needing something to sink into, and she cried out, convulsing again, rocking to eke out the pleasure.

He caressed her until she finally stilled, and then she kissed the shell of his ear, her breath against his sensitive scales making him shiver. He brushed his fingers against her lower back, across her own golden mark, and she moaned, rocking her hips once more, but this time, their scales didn't glow.

'I'm definitely thinking about agreeing to marry you,' she murmured, 'but we should do that a few more times, just to be sure.'

Chapter Seventeen

'SAY YOU'LL MARRY ME,' Cal ground out. Fyia's back was against the wall of her cabin, his mouth on hers, her hand down his breeches.

'I might ... but I need just one or two more ...' He removed her hand, then yanked down her pants and underclothes. Words failed her as he buried his face between her thighs, pushing his tongue inside. 'Cal,' she breathed. Her legs threatened to buckle as he added his fingers to the task, and she exploded, her insides convulsing.

Cal stood, freed himself, and pushed inside her. He lifted her off the floor, his rock-solid arms holding her seemingly without strain as he pounded into her. They were nearing the Temple of the Sea Serpent, their time running out, and it had made them both frantic. They'd slept little, eaten nothing, and ignored every attempted interruption, even the last one, where Sensis had not-so-politely asked them to keep it down, because her cabin was next door, and she wanted to sleep.

A knock sounded from the door next to Fyia's head, just as Cal came on a string of expletives, with a series of short thrusts. Fyia had to stifle a laugh.

'Your Majesty,' said Edu's voice. 'We land in ten spins of the hand. We respectfully request you join us, so we may discuss tactics.'

'I'll be with you in just a moment,' said Fyia, then kissed Cal until her head swam.

They'd been on their way to breakfast, but hadn't quite made it out of her cabin. Fyia re-dressed, and kissed Cal one last time before swinging open the door.

'You forgot this,' said Cal. He dropped her cloak around her shoulders and fastened the clasp. She threw a heated look back over her shoulder, and he kissed her cheek.

Fyia and Cal entered the dining hall with their heads held high, their shoulders back, and with no hint of abashment. And, except for Adigos, who couldn't tear his eyes from the two of them, the others carried on as though Fyia and Cal hadn't kept half the airship awake all night.

Fyia accepted a plate of bread and eggs from one of her soldiers, then sat beside Opie at the table. 'Tell me,' she said, 'how are women treated in the Kraken Empire?'

Opie set down the forkful halfway to his mouth, then thought for a moment. 'They are treated … well … it's complicated. They have more freedoms than in your kingdoms, there is no doubt of that. My sister invented this flying machine, and was free to do so. Women can own businesses, and gain an education, but when they marry, their assets transfer to their husband.'

Fyia frowned. 'Why may they look after their own affairs before, but not after?' she said, feeling the burn of injustice in her chest.

Opie shrugged. 'A quirk of the system, I suppose. Most husbands allow their wives to do as they please, at least until they have children, and then they are largely confined to the home.'

Fyia shook her head. How had it become like this in some kingdoms, but not others? The Black Hoods had no such senseless rules, nor Queen Scorpia's kingdom in the south. Her own kingdoms were even worse. Why?

'Your Majesty,' said Rouel from the doorway, 'we are descending.'

Fyia nodded and pushed back her chair. She was ready.

Fyia stood on deck, flanked by her wolves. She would not go cowed to the Emperor ... would make him look upon the strengths she possessed ... strengths he did not. But as they touched down, and Fyia's eyes scanned the awaiting group, she found no man matching the description the Spider had given her. Instead, a short, good-looking man, and a tall, good-looking woman appeared to be in charge.

Fyia descended the gangplank, and the woman stepped forward. Her hair was long, black, and shiny, and she was scantily clad under her heavy cloak, the fabric of her pants light and colorful, with long slits up the sides. 'Your Majesty,' said the woman, with a half-bow, 'it is a pleasure to welcome you.'

The words were sugary sweet, but laced with poison. They were in Fyia's lands, after all. It should have been her welcoming them, not the other way around. Fyia gave a small, stiff nod.

'I am Princess Re'lah, and this is my brother, the Crown Prince Panat.'

Fyia inclined her head in greeting, first to the Princess, and then the Crown Prince, who wore brightly colored but plain clothes.

'Please,' said Re'lah, 'you must need refreshment after your long journey.'

Of course she knew the airship was well appointed—Fyia had stolen it from her father, after all—but Fyia graciously accepted, and they filed inside the ancient Temple of the Sea Serpent.

Fyia could barely contain herself during the two turns of insufferable small talk that followed. The Prince and Princess plied them with tea and sweet treats in the open space just inside the temple's entrance, referring not once to their father, or his whereabouts.

'Where are the priestesses?' Fyia asked, her patience running thin. She could still feel Cal's mouth all over her, and it was infuriating she couldn't so much as look at him, lest she give away his importance to their enemy.

"They … left,' said the Princess, becoming uncomfortable.

'Where did they go?' asked Adigos. He seemed to have taken a liking to the woman. Fyia quite liked her too, given she seemed to be hiding razor sharp intelligence behind her beauty. She had the quiet ferocity of a woman frequently underestimated, and Fyia would not do her that disservice. Her brother, on the other hand, was a dunce. An entitled, opinionated, self-important one, which made him all the more dangerous, especially given he was next in line to the throne.

'I do not know,' said Re'lah.

Cal moved to a table laden with food, and Fyia joined him there as Adigos engaged the Princess further.

'I wish I knew how to use my magic,' Fyia said in a low voice, pretending to deliberate between two bite-sized pastries. 'Maybe then I could control the Emperor's mind, and make him do my bidding.'

Cal picked up a slice of pineapple, still apparently fascinated by the fruits of warmer climes. 'Much as I'd like to see what you'd do to the poor Emperor,' he said, 'it's probably for the best … the power would go to your head.'

'It would not,' she said, in mock outrage. 'But imagine if I could click my fingers and make him disappear.'

'Is that possible?' said Cal, glancing at her in surprise.

Fyia hid her chuckle. 'Probably not, but it would be fun. Maybe someone's already done so …'

Cal smirked.

'How much longer do you think he'll keep us waiting?'

Footsteps sounded from the direction of the inner sanctum, and they swung their heads to see who approached. Fyia's wolves sniffed the air, and she used their senses to enhance her own. 'It's the woman we found on the airship,' said Fyia. 'We believe her to be close to the Emperor. She's … eccentric.'

The short woman appeared at the tunnel entrance and grinned wildly, her hair in disarray around her face. Was she some strange court jester? The woman scanned the room, and when her eyes found Fyia, she laughed wildly.

Edu and Sensis moved closer, and Cal went very still, as did Fyia. Was this meeting nothing more than payback for stealing the airship, and imprisoning the Emperor's messenger? Who was this woman?

The woman came closer, her steps surprisingly neat, compact, precise, until she stood only six paces away. Edu and Sensis stood by Fyia's side, and her wolves snarled out a warning.

'Your Majesty,' said the woman. She bowed low, holding her arm out in a flourish. '*Such* a pleasure to see you again.' The woman's mismatched eyes flicked up to Fyia's while she was still in a bow. Something about the woman was dangerous, some sense of awareness prickling along Fyia's skin.

The woman's mouth snarled into a smile. 'I thought so,' she said, cryptically, then stood. She whirled away in a perfectly balanced pirouette, clapping her hands loudly. 'May I introduce … the Emperor.' She announced the words, clapping her hands again, and then a tall, fat, dark-haired man stepped into the room.

Fyia hadn't heard him approach, nor had her wolves sensed him, yet two columns of people filed into the room, fanning out along the walls. Did the Emperor have magic? Or have others around him who did?

Jewelry dripped from the Emperor, his clothes brightly colored and finely spun, a large, elaborately decorated fan in his chubby fist. The Emperor's children bowed low and stayed there. The Emperor sized up Fyia, who wore only her usual tunic and close-fitting pants—albeit one of her finest examples—her hair scraped back into a regal bun.

The Emperor waved his fan, and his children stood, their faces careful masks of calm serenity. Fyia couldn't help but wonder about their lineage. The Princess was tall, with dark skin and hair, but the Prince was short and fair. She knew the Emperor had multiple wives, so she presumed they had different mothers … were the children rivals, or friends?

'Your Majesty,' said the Emperor. His eyes roamed across Fyia's body.

'Your Excellency,' said Fyia, matching his tone.

'Let us sit,' said the Emperor. Members of his entourage jumped to do his bidding, clearing a huge round table of food, and bringing heavy wooden chairs.

Fyia's entourage took one side, some sitting, some standing, and the Emperor took the other, only he and his children taking seats. Venir and Cal sat on either end of Fyia's side, and she was glad for the round table, for it meant she could see their faces.

Fyia waited for the Emperor to start, but he took his time, looking at each person on her side for several moments, then studying Fyia for quite some time before opening his mouth. She sat, spine straight, shoulders back, and scrutinized him in return.

'I have something you want,' the Emperor said eventually.

'My land?' said Fyia. 'I am aware.'

The Emperor's face scrunched. 'Yes, that,' he said, waving for someone to bring him tea, 'but other things too.'

'Such as?' said Fyia, her tone businesslike.

'Such as this,' he said. He pulled a perfectly round metal ball from his brightly colored robes.

It took great effort for Fyia not to react. She kept her eyes trained on the metal ball, scrutinizing it for any discrepancy … any sign that it was not what she knew it to be. Where had he got it? The Great Glacier, or the Fae'ch mountains? Or were there more in the world, waiting to be found?

'And what is that?' said Fyia.

'Ha!' The Emperor laughed. 'Your poker face is not the worst I've seen, but neither is it the best, girl.'

Girl. His dropping any pretense of respect so soon was a bad sign.

'What is it?' Fyia repeated, for although she knew in one sense, in another, she had no clue …

'It is a ball made of a special metal that I … procured.'

'Where does one *procure* such things?' said Fyia.

The Emperor laughed again, as though this were sport. 'The Fae'ch are a tricksy people. Outsmarting their kind brings a special kind of pleasure.'

Then this was the ball from the Fae'ch mountain. The mad woman appeared at the Emperor's shoulder, and he held out his hand. She took it, then bit the meat at the base of his thumb. Fyia's stomach roiled as the Emperor grunted in what seemed to be a mix of pleasure and pain. What in all the Seven Hells? His children barely blinked, so presumably this was not an abnormal occurrence.

'You bought it from the Fae'ch?' asked Fyia, when the woman released him.

He smiled. 'No,' he said cryptically. 'And also, yes.'

'What does it do?' said Fyia, leaning forward in her chair.

'It is needed to bring back the dragons, of course,' he said. His features were those of a cat with all the cream.

'How so?' said Fyia.

He raised a single finger and waggled it back and forth. 'I have something you want,' he said, holding up the ball, 'and you have something I want.' He pocketed the ball.

Fyia fought to remain calm, telling herself not to hurl her dagger across the table. 'What do you want?' she said evenly.

He chuckled as he leaned back in his chair, then turned serious. 'I have much: a colossal empire, a mighty army, ships that fly in the air … but what I do not have, is the ancient blood of the Five Great Kingdoms beating in my children's veins.'

The Emperor had spent his life consolidating that which his father and grandfather had crafted. They'd wiped away the nomadic traditions that had existed in their lands for countless generations. They'd built great cities and made much wealth, but had always stayed on their side of the Kraken Sea.

The Emperor had been happy to trade and profit from relations with those outside his lands, but had never shown an interest in visiting, nor seriously pursued taking a foreign wife, with the exception of when he'd agreed with Fyia's parents that he would marry her … She'd chalked that up to her parents, more than the Emperor, because if rumors could be believed, he usually found the idea abhorrent, considering his own people superior to those from foreign lands. Maybe the rumors were wrong.

'And I do not have dragons,' the Emperor continued. He drew out the word *dragons,* relishing each syllable.

'Neither do I,' Fyia said, flippantly.

'But you want them, and you need this to get them,' he said. He held up the ball again, twisting it in his fingers so it caught the light.

'Is that so?' said Fyia. She wished she could afford a glance at Cal, to see his reaction.

'It is,' he said smugly. 'I will help you find them, and abstain from decimating your kingdoms with my superior forces.'

'How kind.'

'And in return, you will marry me, and give me an heir with magic … an heir of whom I can be proud.'

The words hit Fyia like a hammer. They were no surprise, but this was no cocky noble trying his luck, and now she had something to lose. The Emperor wasn't lying when he said his forces were superior, given his fleet of airships. Fyia's troops were seasoned warriors, but they'd never fought a foe in the air.

Fyia plastered an unconcerned smile on her face. 'Is that all?' she said. She met the eyes of each of her party in turn, starting with Venir, and ending with Cal. Cal, who made her heart race, who she knew now with absolute certainty she wanted to marry, not this patronizing ball of repulsion.

'Yes,' she said, nodding slowly, still looking at Cal. Every bone in her body itched to go to him … to get away from the Emperor.

'Yes?' said the Emperor. Her seemingly straightforward answer was so shocking, no one paid any attention to Cal as he rose from his seat. 'But you turned me down before …'

Fyia's eyes moved to the Emperor's children, to the heirs who apparently did not make him proud. If she were to marry the Emperor, any child she had would be immediately in their sights. Fyia had never pictured herself with children, nor as a brood mare.

Her focus snapped back to the man across the table.

'No,' she replied. He thought he'd won, but she would never marry him, not for anything, including something as precious as the dragons.

'You said …' the Emperor started, but Fyia cut him off.

'I cannot marry you.'

'Oh?' said the Emperor. He was confused, but still of the opinion the encounter would eventually go his way. He looked to Lord Venir, which, although not overly surprising, was more blatant than she'd expected; more evidence of the Emperor's confidence.

Venir's expression turned sour. Apparently he recognized the shark-infested waters, but then, his family had always had a knack for survival.

'You see,' said Fyia, 'I find the many rolls of fat around your midriff quite unattractive.' The Emperor's mouth pursed, as though he'd swallowed a wasp, and one of his entourage gasped. 'But that is not even the tip of all the reasons I will never marry you. You are arrogant, deceitful, harbor many fugitive nobles from my lands—most notably my traitor parents—and you seem to believe that you can *force* me to comply with your every whim and wish. That is not a trait I desire in a husband.'

The Emperor laughed, still so sure of success, even in the face of Fyia's fervent refusal. 'My my ... we shall have some fun, you and I, for I like it when my women put up a fight.'

The Emperor's daughter closed her eyes a beat too long, and Fyia wondered if it was just because of her father's sexual innuendo, or for some darker reason.

'You're forgetting you have no choice,' he said. 'You may think whatever you wish—that is one thing I cannot control—but without me, there will be no dragons for you or anyone else. And we all know how much you want the dragons to prove your worth.'

Fyia laughed. 'You're so confident. Yet have you not noticed everyone on my side is unconcerned?' Except Venir ...

The Emperor's eyes flicked across her people, still seeming not to notice Cal's empty chair.

Cal conversed with a member of the Emperor's entourage, standing almost directly behind the Emperor's seat. He'd chosen a lowly member, presumably so no one would pay much attention.

'Tell me then,' said the Emperor, now rankled, 'what trump card you mistakenly believe you hold.'

'I cannot marry you, because I am already betrothed,' said Fyia.

The Emperor cast an uncertain glance at Venir, but Venir's astounded features had turned to Fyia.

Fyia chuckled. 'You should choose your spies more wisely; Venir knows nothing of import.'

Venir's mouth opened and closed like a fish.

'Who?' said the Emperor, with war in his eyes.

'Me,' said Cal. He'd moved close to the Emperor while all had been focused on the storm Fyia was creating.

The Emperor whirled to face Cal's voice, his guards leaping to the Emperor's defense as they finally realized the threat. But they were too late, because before they could reach him, Cal ran a knife across the Emperor's throat. 'Atlas Calemir Talos,' he said, 'King of the Black Hoods.'

The place turned frenetic, but Cal cared only about getting to Fyia, who—Cal was pleased to see—was already in the middle of a formidable circle of protectors.

'Adigos, Sensis, protect the Princess,' said Fyia, as Cal replaced them.

Cal turned in time to see Princess Re'lah pull a knife from the Crown Prince's back. Already, the Emperor's guards had turned on her, closing in.

Fyia pulled out her own blade. She hid it in the folds of her cloak as she moved towards where Venir and the Spider sheltered behind a pillar. The others followed, casting about for threats.

The commotion died down quickly, Sensis and Edu making short work of the Emperor's private guard.

Only the Princess remained, amid a sea of dead bodies, kneeling in the blood of both her father and her brother.

The mad woman had disappeared, and although Fyia sent guards to search for her, Cal doubted they'd find her. Magic spilled off the woman in waves. He wondered who she was really, and how she'd come to serve the Emperor.

'Are you the new leader of the Kraken Empire?' Fyia asked the Princess. 'Or do you have other siblings you need to dispatch first?'

Adigos helped Re'lah to her feet, then offered her his cloak. She'd lost hers in the ruckus, and her flimsy clothes were soaked with blood. She accepted, although her features were full of thunder.

'I have always been the rightful heir,' said Re'lah. 'I am my father's oldest legitimate child, yet my father chose my idiot brother over me.'

'Well,' said Fyia, 'you saw to that well enough. Let me be the first to congratulate you, Your Excellency. And when you have secured your throne, I would be keen to discuss an alliance, for the good of both our nations.'

The Empress inclined her head. 'Thank you. I look forward to that day.'

'Ah … Your Majesty,' said Venir. He stepped forward, his movements uncharacteristically tentative. 'Might it be wise to send an envoy with the Empress, to … provide what support we can in this turbulent time? If that would please Your Excellency, of course,' he added quickly, bowing to them both.

'Excellent idea,' said Fyia. She looked to the Empress for agreement.

'I would appreciate that,' said the Empress.

'Wonderful,' said Venir, straightening his spine. 'I would be most pleased to accompany …'

'Not you,' said Fyia, her tone sharp. 'Adigos will be our envoy.'

Adigos faltered, then bowed. 'Thank you for the … honor, Your Majesty.'

'Adigos is a lord of the prominent Artek family, of the Kingdom of Plenty. His bloodline stretches back many centuries, in case such distinctions are as important to you as they seemed to be to your father. If we can help in any way, please do not hesitate to ask.'

'I will need my father's body,' said Re'lah.

Fyia paused, but Cal slid his hand into hers, pressing the Emperor's metal ball into her palm. 'Of course,' said Fyia.

'I congratulate you on your upcoming nuptials,' said the Empress, eyeing their joined hands, 'but I must take my leave … there is much to do.'

Fyia's royal delegation regrouped at Lady Nara's extensive coastal estate, where they saw to endless tasks. Sensis sent soldiers to ensure the Empress—and her troops—left as promised. The Spider found the priestesses of the Temple of the Sea Serpent, and informed them they could return to their home. And Fyia briefed Adigos on his duties as envoy, then sent him off across the Kraken Sea. Adigos had seemed excited for his mission, and Cal suspected it had something to do with the beautiful new Empress …

'We found him trying to escape, as you predicted,' said Edu. He hauled an indignant Venir into the beautiful reception room in the wing Nara had hastily had her servants prepare for Fyia's use.

The front of Nara's mansion faced the sea, the room's doors thrown open, revealing a white veranda, and a lawn that ended in steps down to the sand. The day was cool but fair, and the salty sea breeze played with the gauzy fabric at the open windows.

Cal wished it was only him and Fyia ... he had so much he needed to say, but the room had filled with Fyia's closest advisers. Edu deposited Venir on a linen-covered chair—the only one available—and Fyia wasted no time before beginning her interrogation.

'You have somewhere to be, Venir?' said Fyia. She looked up from her seat behind a desk by the open window.

'Yes, Your Majesty. The Emperor's death will have many consequences for your kingdoms. I was wasting no time in taking precautions, so you may avoid ... trading losses, and so forth. We must manage the message of the Emperor's death carefully, for the good of the Five Kingdoms.'

'Where by *the Five Kingdoms*, you mean you, Lord Antice, and the other despicable nobles of Moon and Sky? The same nobles who have been interrupting food supplies across my kingdoms?'

'Of course not, Your Majesty ... I would never dream of ...'

'Profiting from the misfortune of others?' said Fyia. 'Never!'

'*Always* more like,' said Sensis.

'Is that not why you've been angling for a match between myself and the former Emperor? Or with your *nephew*?' said Fyia, sitting back, a smile on her lips.

Venir floundered, then collected himself. 'No, but Lord Antice would make a fine king.'

'You think the man behind the rebellion would be an asset to my reign?' said Fyia, openly smiling now.

'He is an asset to the Five Kingdoms. He knows the people, has lived in Moon his whole life ... has the old blood running in his veins.'

Why these people cared so very much about bloodlines, Cal could not fathom. What difference did it make? And Venir had not denied Lord Antice was the man behind the rebellion …

'You could not find a better man to guide you,' Venir continued, 'to unite your kingdoms, so they become a power feared by all once more.'

"To *guide* me?' said Fyia. Her face had set into an expression of abject fury. Venir didn't seem to notice.

'How will the people of Starlight react if you marry some dirty Black Hood?' said Venir. 'There will be a second rebellion!'

Cal knew enough of Fyia's people not to be shocked by the insult, but Venir's failure to notice his Queen's reaction was astounding.

'You have done well,' said Venir. 'No one could say otherwise, but we need a steady hand on the tiller now. The seas ahead are rough … you need a vigorous man to lean on, not the gaggle of rash women around you, especially as you must concentrate on giving the kingdoms an heir.'

'Enough,' said Fyia, standing and drawing her dagger. 'You are an old, ineffectual, cockroach of a man.' She took several menacing steps towards him, and he finally had the sense to keep his mouth shut. 'You and your fellow *leaders* care only about lining your pockets, so you may laugh with each other about how clever and important you are.

'You think there is only one measure of a man: his ability to bloat himself on wealth, so he may secure the best filly to breed his children, and wield his wealth like a weapon. But what are those men when you strip away their lying and cheating and scheming? They are nothing, for they have nothing that money cannot buy. Their wives detest them, their children long for the day they will die, and their friends pray they will fall from their gilded perches, so another of them may display their ill-begotten feathers and preen at the world.

'You *dare* to think your nephew could *guide* me? Are you blind? Can you not see my achievements? Or are you so controlled by your base instincts to dominate and breed that it is impossible for you to comprehend the evidence before you? You, who thinks he is so clever and important … who thinks he is above the crown itself, because it does not sit on the head of a *man.*'

Fyia had become a raging ball of righteous anger, and Cal reveled in every moment. She was magnificent, powerful, demanding the respect she deserved. She would be an asset to his kingdom. He itched to hear the ideas she would bring, the knowledge she would share, just as he longed to ride a dragon beside her. For if anyone could return the dragons to their lands, it was her.

'I … I …' said Venir, his voice a scared stammer. Despite knowing Fyia had killed three Kings by her own hand, it had taken until now for Venir to realize the mortal threat before him.

'I should offer my betrothed the opportunity to stick a knife in your guts for calling him a *dirty Black Hood*, but you deserve to die at the hands of a woman.' Fyia took several more steps towards him. 'But worse than that, you should know that your chosen heir— your nephew—will get nothing after your death, for I am stripping you of your land, titles, and wealth. They now belong to Lady Sensis Deimos.'

'No,' breathed Venir. His eyes found Sensis, as did all other eyes in the room.

Cal looked at Sensis too, but her features were a mask. She bowed. 'I thank you, Your Majesty, although such a reward is unnecessary.'

'It is necessary,' said Fyia, 'for not only have you served me to the very best of your extensive and formidable abilities—and you would deserve this reward for that alone—but your home kingdom disregarded your talents, refused to train you, and told you your worth was for breeding alone. For that, you deserve reparations.'

Sensis bowed again, and when she looked up, Cal saw the raw emotion in her eyes. Fyia nodded at her friend and smiled.

'You cannot take away all my family has built!' said Venir. 'Antice will not stand for it.'

Fyia turned back to the weasel, Edu holding him down as Fyia moved closer still. 'Eratus Venir, you have schemed with the Kraken Emperor, plotted against your Queen, and incited rebellion. For your treachery and treason, I sentence you to death.'

Fyia closed the gap between them, and Venir's eyes went wide. 'No! Your Majesty!' He squirmed, but Edu held him in place, and Fyia stuck her dagger in his guts.

Fyia watched for a while as Venir howled and swore, and then she finished him. 'Apologies for the mess, Lady Nara,' she said.

Fyia ran on the beach, then swam in the ocean. There were reports the kraken were increasing in number, but they rarely came so close to shore, and this wasn't her day to die. She lay back on the sand, the chill wind eroding the trauma of the day, and Fyia felt herself relax for the first time in as long as she could remember.

Yes, she still faced rebellion, but the threat from the Kraken Empire was no longer, she had a fledgling fleet of airships, her brother and Essa had not betrayed her, and Venir's execution would send a strong message to the rebels … along with news of her engagement to the King of the Black Hoods.

Maybe that would lead to a new rebellion in her home kingdom, but Fyia couldn't find it within herself to care. All she could think of was leaving for the Great Glacier, where she prayed to all the Gods they would find answers. *They*. For she and Cal would go together, and the thought sent a thrill up her spine.

By the time Fyia returned to the house, the late autumn sun had almost dipped below the horizon. She headed straight for the open fire, holding out her hands to the warmth.

'Hey,' said Cal.

Fyia jumped. Cal lay on the sofa, stroking her wolves. She'd felt her Cruaxee, but hadn't realized he was there too. 'Even better,' she said, dropping onto the sofa next to him and snuggling into his heat.

He wrapped an arm around her, and her wolves head-butted him in protest. They'd suddenly decided they liked him …

'Sorry,' said Cal, 'the Queen takes priority.'

'And you're spoilt,' she added.

A comfortable silence settled over them, but Fyia's thoughts raced.

'Are we going to talk about it?' said Cal, his hand stroking her hair.

She looked up at him. 'Which bit?'

He laughed. 'I was thinking of our engagement.'

'Oh … which bit?'

'I won't hold you to it, if it's not truly what you want.'

'Cal …'

'You were under duress, and we have much learn about each other, and each other's people. There is much to agree, but … I wish to marry you,' he said, looking into her eyes.

Fyia kissed him. 'I wish to marry you too,' she said, 'which makes us more fortunate than most royals. I actually like you.'

Cal rolled his eyes affectionately. 'Your lands are so much bigger and more intricate than mine. I have but one kingdom to satisfy. You have five, with so many differences of opinion and selfish desires.'

'You have dealt with the same,' she said.

'Yes, but I mean, if we wed in my kingdom, it would be simple. We would go to the Temple of the Dragon, and all would be invited, but that won't work here.'

'No,' Fyia agreed, 'but I don't want to think about that now … or at all, in fact. That's why I have a Small Council … and an Extended Council. Maybe we'll have a celebration in each kingdom …'

He nodded. 'It's so different here. Political …'

Fyia squeezed his hand. 'Venir was the worst of them; I promise not everyone is so bad.'

He squeezed back. 'Why give Venir's lands to Sensis?' he said. 'Why not Starfall, or one of the others?'

Fyia inhaled deeply. 'Sensis grew up in Moon. She knows the land and its people. The leaders there saw her talent, but shunned her, were scared she might best the boys, so wouldn't even let her hold a sword. Her family was neither rich, nor influential, so there was little she could do. In the end, she ran away. I'm glad she did, for without her, I wouldn't have won … she is the most important member of my team.

'Starfall already has lands and property in the Kingdom of Starlight. She runs her affairs from afar, and has no interest in amassing more. The wardens have estates already, the Spider is happy on her web, and Essa and Edu are next in line, but neither of them are concerned with land and titles. Essa has all the research funds she desires, and Edu … well, I don't know exactly what he wants, but it isn't that.'

'Does Sensis want land and titles?'

Fyia shrugged. 'She came from a merchant family of middling means. She grew up around the likes of Lord Antice, and they always looked down on her for her lack of wealth and influence. She has nothing to prove to anyone, and she knows that, but I think a part of her has always wanted those things, if only to throw it in the faces of those who doubted her.'

A ruckus sounded from the corridor, and Fyia sat to see who invaded their quiet moment. Everyone. Cal pecked her on the lips, then whispered, 'Have fun,' before he stood and left the room.

Traitor.

They peppered her with a never-ending list of topics, from Venir's funeral arrangements, to announcements about her marriage, the titles Sensis now held, and what felt like hundreds more besides.

When they finally ran out of things to ask her, Fyia started on a list of her own. 'Cal and I intend to travel to the Great Glacier immediately. In our absence, please change the marriage laws, so men and women are equal partners.'

Starfall paled, and Lady Nara averted her gaze. Fyia knew it would not be easy—she may even face new rebellions—but she could not marry Cal until the changes were made, so she had little choice.

'When the nobles complain, focus on the positives,' said Fyia. 'Remind them they are getting what they wanted. I am marrying, and an alliance with the Black Hoods is advantageous to my kingdoms. Not to mention, we are now friendly with the Kraken Empire, and have a strong alliance with the Scorpion Lands. Trade will boom.'

Fyia reached into her pocket and pulled out a handful of dragon scales, each no bigger than a fingernail. She handed one to each of them. 'And if they persist with their complaints, show them these.'

By the time Fyia was finished, the night was almost over. She found Cal on the beach, looking every inch the Black Hood, with his coal-colored cloak, his hood raised.

Opie and the airship waited on the sand, and the sight raised the hairs on her arms. The dragons were close … she could feel it.

Cal threw her cloak around her and clasped it at her neck. 'Ready?' he said.

'Ready,' said Fyia. She pulled up her hood and took his hand. 'North, to the Great Glacier.'

I hope you enjoyed *Kingdoms of Shadow and Ash,* and if you did, I would really appreciate a rating or review wherever you buy books, on TikTok (especially here), or any other social media. Just a rating, a few words, or a line or two would be absolute perfection, and will help others find my stories. Thank you for your support.

READ NEXT: Book two in the *Shadow and Ash* series, *Dragons of Asred.* Buy it here: https://books2read.com/DragonsOfAsred

And if you want more from the *Shadow and Ash* world, check out *House of Storms and Secrets*: https://books2read.com/stormsandsecrets or join my newsletter for a free short story: *The Water Rider and the High-Born Fae,* a story set under the Fae'ch mountain: https://www.subscribepage.com/ShadowAndAsh

Also from HR Moore: *Nation of the Sun*

Their demon lives spun around each other, their souls, like magnets, pulled back together in every lifetime.

Amari has a perfect life. She's a successful food critic, and is marrying a high-flying human rights lawyer. But the day before her wedding, a stranger, Caspar, tries to solicit her help. She sends him away, but can't shake the feeling that she knows him.

When Amari's new husband has to leave the country before their honeymoon, Amari tells Caspar she'll help him. But Amari and Caspar are attacked by an assassin, forcing them into hiding at the London headquarters of the Pagan Nation. Here, she discovers she's an ancient and powerful demon, someone who reincarnates, and that Caspar is her soulmate.

As she's drawn into Caspar's world of standing stones and feuding nations, Amari can't deny the deep connection that pulses between them. But she can't remember her past, she has a husband, and finds herself torn between two irreconcilable lives. And not only that, but the Pagans have secrets they refuse to reveal: Why did Amari avoid Caspar for a hundred years? And what happened between Amari and the leader of a rival nation in the past? To determine if she can trust Caspar, if she should help him, she must wake her demon soul, and bring back her memories. For one thing is certain: when that happens, the tables will turn.

Nation of the Sun is perfect for anyone who loved A Discovery of Witches, and those who fantasize about stone circles containing magic.

Nation of the Sun *is book one in the complete* Ancient Souls *series, and is available now through all major retailers.*

CONNECT WITH HR MOORE

Check out HR Moore's website, where you can sign up to her newsletter:
http://www.hrmoore.com/

Find HR Moore on Instagram, TikTok, and Twitter: @HR_Moore

Follow HR Moore on BookBub:
https://www.bookbub.com/authors/hr-moore

See what the world of *Shadow and Ash* looks like on Pinterest:
https://www.pinterest.com/authorhrmoore/kingdoms-of-shadow-and-ash/

Like the HR Moore page on Facebook:
https://www.facebook.com/authorhrmoore

Follow HR Moore on Goodreads:
https://www.goodreads.com/author/show/7228761.H_R_Moore

TITLES BY HR MOORE

The Relic Trilogy:
Queen of Empire
Temple of Sand
Court of Crystal

In the Gleaming Light

The Ancient Souls Series:
Nation of the Sun
Nation of Sword
Nation of the Stars

Shadow and Ash:
Kingdoms of Shadow and Ash
Dragons of Asred

Stories set in the Shadow and Ash world:
The Water Rider and the High Born Fae
House of Storms and Secrets

http://www.hrmoore.com

Printed in Great Britain
by Amazon